OPERATION THOR

by

Frederick E. Smith

THUNDERCHILD PUBLISHING
Huntsville, Alabama

This is a work of fiction. All of the characters, organizations, and events portrayed in this novel are either products of the author's imagination or are used fictitiously.

OPERATION THOR

ISBN-13: 978-1986874526
ISBN-10: 1986874524

Published by Thunderchild Publishing. Find us at
https://ourworlds.net/thunderchild_cms/

Dedication

To
Our close and dear friends of many years
Margaret Wilkinson
And
Peter Skipworth

Acknowledgments

The author wishes to acknowledge his debt to the authors of the following works of reference:

Edward Bishop, *Mosquito: Wooden Wonder,* Pan/ Ballantine

M.S. Hardy, *The de Havilland Mosquito,* David and Charles

R.M. Clarke, *De Havilland Mosquito Portfolio,* A Brookland Book in conjunction with *Aeroplane*

Bekker, *The Luftwaffe War Diaries* (Macdonald)

Adolf Galland, *The First and the Last* (Methuen)

Richards and Saunders, *Royal Air Force 1939-1945* (H.M.S.O.)

Sir C. Webster and N. Frankland, *The Strategic Air Offensive Against Germany 1939-1945* (H.M.S.O.)

Alfred Price, *Instruments of Darkness* (Wm Kimber)

Chapter 1

The Junkers 86P was circling lazily in the stratosphere. In the rare clarity of a late autumn anticyclone, a vast panorama of the northern British Isles was visible below. Scottish mountains lay in shrunken folds and islands dotted the frozen sea. As the Junkers completed an orbit and began another, the condensed gases from her twin engines formed a huge white circle in the rarefied air.

An urgent voice in his intercom drew the pilot's attention. Picking up a pair of binoculars, he pushed up his smoked goggles and stared down. At first he could see nothing but the vast terrain of islands. Then he spotted an object no larger than a wasp climbing upwards. He answered his observer's question. *"Ja,* I think it is a Spitfire."

The observer sounded anxious. "Can it reach us?"

The pilot kept his glasses trained on the wasplike shape. "They haven't so far. So I don't see why this one should."

His observer sounded doubtful. "It's an adaptable aircraft, Jurgen. They might have squeezed a few more thousand feet from her."

"Hans, we're flying over 43,000 feet. There isn't a plane in the British Isles that can fly this high. Stop worrying."

Hans sounded aggrieved. "I wouldn't worry so much if we were armed. If the Tommi catches us we're a dead duck."

"He won't catch us, Hans. We've got at least three thousand feet on him."

Hans saw his pilot was right five minutes later. The Spitfire had almost reached its ceiling and was beginning to yaw in the rarefied air. Jurgen grinned at his observer. "What did I tell you? We're as safe as houses up here."

Although still four thousand feet below them, the Spitfire was clearly in trouble as its airfoils began losing support. As the two Germans stared down, one wing suddenly dipped and the slim fighter went sliding down out of control. With a laugh, Jurgen turned to Hans. "Satisfied now?"

Still watching the Spitfire, Hans saw its pilot had given up the fruitless chase and was making for his base. He gave Jurgen a relieved grin. "If Spitfires can't reach us, that means we can thumb our noses at the rest of Tommi's aircraft."

"That's what I've been telling you all along. Now get the rest of those photographs taken. We've got the other ports to photograph before we start back home."

Brigadier Simms was standing at the window of the library at High Elms when Davies entered. Courteous as always, he swung round and approached the Air Commodore with outstretched hand. "Hello, Davies. It's good of you to come at such short notice."

Davies, whose chilled figure looked small in his thick RAF greatcoat, was relieved to see there was a fire in the library. "Hello, sir. I'm sorry I couldn't make it this morning. But they're keeping me busy at Group HQ these days."

Simms led him round a long table towards the fire. "You look cold. Would you care for a cup of tea?"

Davies nodded. "Yes, I think I would. Winter's come early this year."

The elderly Brigadier pressed a bell push on his desk. A few seconds later a girl in army uniform appeared in the doorway. "You called, sir?"

"Yes, Mary. Bring tea for two, will you? And put a bottle of brandy on the tray, please."

The girl smiled. "Yes, sir."

As she disappeared, Simms turned towards Davies. "Take your coat off, Davies, and make yourself comfortable. Or would you prefer to keep it on for a while?"

With the elderly army officer wearing nothing but his standard uniform, Davies was almost driven by shame to obey. Then, feeling a draught from the large French windows, he took refuge in a fib. "Not for the moment, thanks. I got chilled coming here. My car's heater has broken down."

Simms gave a sympathetic tut-tut. "Then stand in front of the fire. The tea won't be long." As Davies obeyed, the Brigadier changed the subject. "I believe your squadron is attacking the V1 sites in Holland at the moment."

Davies tried to hide a scowl but failed. "Yes. That and army support work. They've been doing nothing else since Buchansee."

Simms could understand the small, peppery Air Commodore's irritation at his special service squadron being used on tasks that almost any fighter-bomber squadron could perform. "Have you had many losses?"

"Nothing to equal those at Buchansee. But as there's a great deal of low level work involved, there is a steady drain of crews."

"I take it you haven't had any reports of those Buchansee aircraft being sighted again?"

Davies held his hands out to the fire. "No, thank God. The Yanks haven't either. I think we wiped out that research centre in time. But only just."

"You've never had any repercussions from the Americans, General Staines in particular, about what happened?"

Davies shook his head. "No. Staines kept his word. Mind you, so he should. If my boys hadn't done the job they did, some of those new aircraft might be attacking his B-17s by this time."

Simms hid a smile at Davies's defence of the operation that had nearly given him apoplexy at the time. "What's the news of your wounded crews? Is Harvey out of hospital yet?"

Davies scowled at the name. "Yes. He came out two weeks ago. He'll be fit for operations any time now."

"What about Moore? I take it he won't be allowed to fly over Europe again?"

Davies turned back to the fire. "No, worse luck. I'll never get a better squadron commander."

"What will they do with him? Will he be sent to the Pacific theatre?"

"No. I'm keeping him on my staff for a while. He knows too much about Jerry and his tactics to be wasted out there."

At that moment the WRAC girl arrived with her tray. As she left the library Simms picked up the bottle of brandy. "You'll have a drop in your tea, Davies?"

Davies hesitated, then decided it was a very cold day. "Just a tiny tot. If you're having one, that is."

Simms poured a stiff tot into both cups. "So that means you need a new squadron commander. Have you decided on anyone yet?"

Davies's restlessness betrayed the problem he had wrestled with ever since the Buchansee affair. "As we've been operating in sections, we haven't really needed one since Buchansee. But when we have, Henderson has used Millburn."

"Has he been satisfactory?"

"So far, yes. But we can't keep him in that role."

"Why not?"

"Millburn doesn't like being a flight commander, never mind squadron commander. He doesn't like the discipline the job entails. Millburn's too much a free spirit."

"Then who will you choose?"

Davies took a sip of tea before replying and gave a slight grimace. Although he liked the feel of brandy warming his stomach, he did not like the taste. "I haven't decided yet."

"Whom does your CO favour?"

"Henderson? He'd like to give it to Harvey. So would ninety per cent of the crews. Harvey was always a popular flight commander."

Simms smiled. "Then what's your problem?"

In other circumstances the testy Air Commodore might have resented such questions from an army man. But although Simms was only ten years his senior, Davies had found him almost a father figure in the many operations they had carried out together, and it was something of a relief to discuss his problem with a service man outside the RAF.

"It's the damned promise I made to Anna, his wife, after she agreed to be our agent in Bavaria again. I said I'd give Harvey a long rest from combat flying, and, God knows, if anyone deserves it Anna does, the times she's risked her life for us. On top of that it's no secret that Harvey and I get on like a couple of cockerels squabbling over a farmyard full of hens. If he were squadron commander, God knows what feathers would fly."

Simms hid a smile. While Davies could justifiably be seen as a truculent cockerel, it was hard to envisage the tall, raw-boned Harvey as one. "I think you'd be able to handle him, Davies."

"I'd handle him all right," Davies grunted. "But whether I want the trouble is another matter."

As Simms poured out a second cup of tea, Davies wondered why he had been called to High Elms. A Yorkshire centre for the Special Operations Executive and only a twenty minute drive from Sutton Craddock, it was the place where many of the 633 Squadron's special operations had been planned, from their suicidal raid in the Swartfjord to their mission at Buchansee. As a consequence, since receiving Simms's message, Davies had been hoping that some task of importance was involved. Although it was Simms's gentlemanly way to exchange courtesies first, Davies was thinking it was high time he got down to business.

"Whoever you choose I'm sure it'll be the right man," the Brigadier said. "But now let me explain why I asked you here today. How high can your Mosquitoes fly?"

Believing it was coming at last, Davies felt his heartbeats quicken. "It depends on the type and the load. Our standard combat aircraft can operate at well over 30,000 feet. Our photo reconnaissance Mossie can fly higher but she's unarmed."

"If you armed her, could she reach 43,000 feet plus?"

Davies shook his head. "No. She couldn't reach it with or without weapons. Why do you ask, sir?"

Simms took a sip of tea before replying. "I take it you know all about the Germans' Junkers 86P aircraft?"

Davies's puzzlement grew. "Yes, of course. They've been flying on and off over this country since 1941. They've been seen over Russia and the Middle East too."

"Am I right in thinking that so far we've not been able to shoot them down?"

Davies disliked making the confession to an army man but had no option. "I'm afraid so. The early Spitfires couldn't get anywhere near that height. Even the FV1, which was pressurized and had extended wingtips, couldn't make it."

"Does that mean we haven't an aircraft in service that can reach them?"

"Not quite. De Havilland were asked by the Director of Technical Development if they could produce a special high-altitude fighter from their range of Mosquitoes."

"And did they?"

Davies's enthusiasm for his favourite aircraft showed in his reply. "Yes. They did a marvellous job. As I understand it, they used the high altitude W4050 version and made so many modifications that eventually it reached over 43,500 feet. Believe it or not, they did all that in less than two weeks. It was an incredible feat."

"But it didn't shoot down any JU86s?"

"No," Davies confessed. "But only because Jerry had stopped sending them over by that time."

"Is this modified aircraft still available?"

"I expect there are a few around. But I'd have to check on that."

"I wish you would, Davies. Because on the few clear days we've had recently, the JU86s have come back."

Davies showed surprise. "I've not heard that. Where are they operating?"

"Not as high level bombers. That's probably why your group hasn't been alerted. We only got notice of them from the Admiralty. They're concerned because the objects of their reconnaissance seem to be ports or naval fleet Bases. Not the southern ones. Only northern and eastern ports from Scapa Flow down to Norfolk."

Davies was trying to work out where his special service squadron was involved in all this. "If they're paying so much attention to the Fleet, it must mean they're up to some naval shilly-shallying themselves. What does the Admiralty think? Submarine activity?"

"No one knows at the moment. We've come into it because London wants us to contact our agents in Norway, Denmark and Holland to see if any unusual naval activity has been noticed there in recent weeks. It might even be they have a secret naval weapon they've developed. Even if our armies are back in Europe, we know

10

the Germans are still hoping their massive secret weapons programme will save the day for them. So this sudden surge of reconnaissance must be taken seriously."

"What exactly do you want us to do?" Davies asked. "See if we can take care of these JU86s?"

"I thought you might like to take on the job, Davies. We could ask the Banff Wing to take care of it but as we've worked together successfully before and as you're the Mosquito experts, you're obviously our first choice."

Hoping some large scale enemy activity had been discovered and earmarked for an attack, Davies was disappointed that the task seemed a relatively minor one. "Yes, we'll take it on, but we'll need to get one of these specialised Mossies. If we can, it shouldn't be too difficult a job."

"Good. Then can I tell London we've got things in hand?"

"Yes, I'll get on to it right away." Davies picked up his cap from the table, then continued more in hope than in anticipation. "Do you think it might lead to something bigger?"

Simms was fully aware of Davies's problems. Ever since the small Air Commodore had persuaded the Air Ministry to let him raise a special service squadron, he had been faced with jealousy from his peers, and only the squadron's row of successes had saved it from being reduced to a mere front line squadron. After a quiet spell, Buchansee had come as a godsend but no one knew better than Davies how short on memory his enemies were. "I can't say that, Davies. But if it does you'll be the first to know."

His need forced Davies into his confession. "I need a big job, sir. With our armies in Europe screaming for more aircraft, those sods up top will be snapping at my heels like a pack of wolves if something doesn't turn up soon."

Showing sympathy, Simms escorted Davies to the door. "Regretfully I can't promise anything. These flights might only have to do with our convoys and supplies. But we ought to know more after our agents have radioed in their reports. I'll let you know as soon as we receive them."

Davies found he was shivering as he descended the stone steps to the courtyard where his car was standing. With his earlier hope of a large operation dashed, his thoughts were irritable and peevish. Why didn't the Brigadier, an older man, feel the cold as much as he? For that matter, why didn't he think about others and insist on more warmth in that damned library? Seeing his WAAF chauffeur talking, as usual, to a young officer who was standing beside her car, Davies vented his feelings in a shout. "Come on, Hilary. Stop your flirting and get that car turned round. I want to be at Sutton Craddock before it gets dark."

Chapter 2

Adams peered from the window of his 'Confessional'. "Millburn's late, isn't he?"

Sue Spencer, his slim, attractive assistant, glanced up from the map she was studying. "Only a few minutes, Frank. I don't think there's anything to worry about yet."

Adams moved back to the long table where she was sitting. "I suppose not. But Millburn takes such chances you feel he must catch it one of these days." When the girl did not answer, he sat down somewhat heavily on the bench seat and picked up his pipe. Seeing it had gone cold, he put a hand to his tunic pocket for matches. Then, as if the effort were too much, he gave a small sigh and replaced the pipe on the table.

The girl was watching him with some concern. She had worked with Adams, the station Intelligence Officer, for over two years now and because much of their work involved the de-briefing of air crews after operations, she knew his ways and his emotions as well or better than any wife. Time and again, when crews failed to return, she had seen his pain and his loss. She had also witnessed his profound relief when they received news that some pilot or navigator, believed killed, was known to be alive and safe. Emotion of the kind Adams displayed tended to be scarce in wartime and Sue had often felt his humanity and sensitivity helped to make her work bearable.

At the same time she had learned that Adams' emotions were more complex than mere sentimentality. A man in his forties, slightly bulky of build and needing to wear glasses, Adams, who thought war was the ultimate obscenity, had a secret envy of the young aircrews he mingled with daily. To some it would seem a paradox, a confusion of sentiments, but Sue saw it as an extension of his humanity. Adams hated cruelty above all things and possessed the kind of mind that could imagine the fear and misery of life under the Nazi heel. Thus it followed that, in spite of loathing war, Adams envied the young fliers who for years had brought hope to the enslaved people of Europe.

Sue was watching him now. Unable to sit still, he had risen and was walking towards a wooden filing cabinet. "What is it, Frank? You've been on edge all day."

Adams paused by the cabinet and removed his glasses. As always she thought how vulnerable he looked without them. He tried to smile. "Does it show that much?"

"It does to me. What's happened? Or don't you want to talk about it?"

Adams pulled out a handkerchief and wiped his glasses. "No, it's not a secret. At least it won't be once she arrives. Valerie wants to get out of London and come up here again."

The girl showed surprise. From the confidences the two of them had shared, she knew all about Valerie, his wife. An elegant, good-looking and waspish woman whose penchant was for handsome young officers, Valerie had long lost patience with the intelligent and sensitive Adams who was fifteen years her senior. After a spell at the local inn, The Black Swan, where she had relieved her boredom by entertaining officers from the airfield, she had spent the last year in a London flat. With London full of American officers with money to burn, Sue knew Adams had no illusions about the life she was leading but a loyal streak in his nature refused to condemn her, arguing instead that war did strange things to people and when it was over she would find her equilibrium again. At the same time Sue had noticed that he had spent his leave that year with friends in the nearby town of Highgate.

Knowing all this, she found it surprising that Valerie should want to return to Sutton Craddock. "What are you going to do, Frank? Ask Joe Kearns if he can put her up in the pub again? Or try to get her a place in Highgate?"

Adams replaced his glasses. "I haven't made up my mind yet. I only got her letter this morning. I suppose Joe could put her up now that Anna's gone back with Harvey to their bungalow. But without transport she wouldn't have much to do here and Valerie soon gets bored. It might be better to look for a place in town."

Knowing he believed Valerie would soon be involved in another affair if she lived close to the airfield, Sue felt herself aching for him. "You're probably right. There's practically nothing to do around here in the winter and the bus service to Highgate is pretty awful."

He looked relieved, as if her opinion took away some of the guilt he had been feeling. "Perhaps when things quieten down I'll take a look round Highgate. It might be a bit easier to get rooms these days."

She knew what he meant. There had been a time when wives were allowed to live near to the airfields so that their aircrew husbands could billet out with them. It was believed home life would ease the terrible stress of aerial combat.

No belief was ever more mistaken. As in no other war in history, wives would see their husbands leave home in a morning as if going to the office and yet know each day might be his last. The effect was traumatic on both sexes. For a man, war is only endurable when home life is a distant and secure dream in his mind; for his wife, only when she is not witness to his perils. Put one beside the other and their nearness makes a hell for them both.

So the order had been promulgated that no wife must live close to the airfield from which her husband was operating. Although not many of the young aircrews of 633 Squadron were married, there were other airfields in the vicinity with their quota, and so vacant rooms had appeared in Highgate for the first time since the outbreak of war. With his role of Intelligence Officer putting him in the category of ground staff, Adams was not covered by this order and so could live out with Valerie if his CO gave him permission.

"What will you do if you find her a room, Frank? Will you apply to live out?"

The time it took Adams to reply did not suggest enthusiasm. "I don't know. I suppose it'll depend on the accommodation we get."

Feeling he did not want to talk about it any further, she changed the subject to one that was causing arguments and heated discussions throughout the entire squadron.

"Have you heard any more about what's going to happen to Harvey now he's out of hospital, Frank?"

Adams shook his head. "No. All I know is that he's back convalescing with Anna at their bungalow near the OTU centre and that he'll be fit for duty in a week or two. What'll happen to him then I don't know. For that matter I don't think Davies knows either."

"You don't think Davies is still going to punish him, do you?"

"No. He more or less confirmed that when we all visited Harvey in hospital. But he might decide to put him back on combat flying again."

"In spite of his promise to Anna?"

"Yes, but remember he made that before the Buchansee affair. If afterwards Harvey chose to fly himself, you can hardly blame Davies for feeling he's entitled to renege on his promise."

"But we all know Harvey did it to protect Moore."

"Of course we do. But Harvey did break every rule in the book in doing it. To be honest he's a lucky man not to be cashiered."

"I suppose he is. But it'll be a terrible disappointment for Anna if he is put back on combat flying again."

"Davies knows that. I think it's one reason why he hasn't made up his mind yet. But it's not the only thing he has to consider. It was always Harvey's ambition to be the squadron commander and he was shattered when Moore was brought in over his head to rebuild the squadron. Harvey's always believed it was another example of our class system at work."

"Do you think it was?"

"Oh, yes. There's no question about it. I was there when Davies admitted as much to General Staines after Buchansee. So Davies has a problem if he brings Harvey back. If he doesn't give him the promotion, not only will Harvey's old bitterness come back but he'll have most of the aircrews sharing it with him. Now that Moore can't fly over Europe again, nearly all of them want him as their leader."

16

"But surely after Buchansee Davies couldn't go over his head again?"

"This time I don't think Davies would want to. I think he's learned the lesson that he'd never get a better leader. But Davies is still only an Air Commodore: there are plenty of officers above him who still believe in the divine right of Eton and Oxford."

She had never heard Adams express criticism about the social structure of Britain before. "Does that mean you don't like our class system either?"

"I detest it," Adams said, with uncharacteristic venom. "Not only because it's unfair but because it's also so damned wasteful. Doesn't Harvey's case prove that?" Then, as if ashamed of his outburst, he gave an embarrassed laugh. "I sound like a red-hot Bolshie, don't I?"

Fascinated by this new facet of him, she wanted to continue their conversation but at that moment they both heard the sound of Merlin engines approaching the airfield. Hurrying to the door of the Nissen hut, Adams threw it open. As he peered at the low, threatening sky, Sue who had followed him, recognised the lone Mosquito that was beginning to orbit the airfield. "It's Millburn," she told him. "I can read his identification number."

They watched the Mosquito circle over Bishops Wood at the far side of the airfield and then squat down on the runway. As its tyres squealed and threw back spray, a transport appeared and began accelerating along the airfield perimeter. As the Mosquito finished its run and swung towards its hard standing, Adams gave a murmur of satisfaction. "They seem to be all right. I can't see any damage, can you?"

"I thought there was a little smoke coming out of one engine and some damage to the fuselage," she said. "But I could be wrong."

The bitter draught blowing through the open door was reminding both of them that winter was only a stone's throw away. Closing the door, Adams led the girl back to the table. "I wonder what moan Gabby will have this time."

She noticed how lighter his tone was since sighting the aircraft. Millburn, an American volunteer in the RAF, and his Welsh navigator, Gabriel or Gabby as he was known to one and all, although a thoroughly professional couple in the air, were notorious on the squadron for their banter and pranks and there were few personnel on the station who could resist them. She laughed at his comment. "We'll find out soon enough if I know Gabby."

"They're the oddest couple I've ever met," Adams said. "They play all kinds of rough tricks on one another, they wrangle about almost anything, and yet I'm quite sure they'd die for one another. Why can't we have relationships like that in peace time?"

Feeling his question might bring back his earlier mood if followed up, she was careful in her reply. "I think it needs danger to bring it out, Frank. The lives most of us live in peacetime develop jealousies rather than friendships."

Outside there was a squeal of brakes, the slam of a metal door, and the sound of the Bedford transport accelerating away. As footsteps approached the door, a querulous voice with a Welsh accent reached the couple inside. "You know there's a bloody big hole in the fuselage, don't you?"

"Of course I know." The American accent was western: Millburn came from El Paso. "I've got eyes, haven't I?

"That's what I keep asking myself. How does anyone with eyes attack a flak post? Don't you ever stop to think about me, Millburn? I don't want to be a bloody hero like you."

"There's no chance of that, kiddo. No chance at all. Gremlins like you just stay sneaky and mean. Front, back and sideways."

"Why did they land me with you, Millburn? I've never done anything to deserve it."

"Are you kidding? The biggest moaner in the West? I guess you're my punishment for volunteering for your goddamned RAF."

Sue, meeting Adams' twinkling eyes, burst out laughing. "They're on good form today, aren't they?"

Before Adams could reply the door burst open and the couple entered. Both were still wearing their bulky flying suits and carrying their parachutes but there the resemblance ended. Millburn was a tall good-looking man with an unruly shock of dark hair. Gabriel was a diminutive figure whose sharp features and somewhat large ears had earned him the nickname of Gabby the Gremlin. Although their argument had ended up with Millburn grinning, Gabby was showing indignation as the two of them made their way to the table.

Reaching it, Millburn clicked his heels mockingly. "Mission completed, sir. Another Kraut rocket site has bitten the dust."

"I know, Tommy," Adams said. "The rest of your section told me. Why didn't you come back with them?"

"Our starboard radiator got hit and as the engine started warming up I told my guys to come back home while I took it easy."

"Who hit you? The flak post?"

Millburn gave his infectious grin. "So you heard my little gremlin bellyaching outside, did you? Yeah, it caught us with a few rounds but nothing serious."

With the attack now out in the open, Gabby was able to vent his feelings. "Nothing serious? They damn nearly chopped us in two."

Adams felt he must act his part, at least for a moment. "You know the order about not attacking flak posts, Tommy?"

"Yeah, I know, Frank. But this post was back among the trees and it might have pranged my guys when they came down. I'd call it a justifiable attack, wouldn't you?"

Watching the two men, Sue was thinking Millburn couldn't be playing his hand better. At one time, in deference to Adams' rank and age, the American had always called him "sir". Although in those days it had been the correct address, Sue knew it had made Adams feel old and detached from the aircrews. But in recent months Millburn and one or two other senior aircrews had resorted to the familiar "Frank". Although some would argue it stemmed from Millburn's promotion to Flight Commander, Sue believed it derived from Adams' exploits in Norway during Operation Valkyrie when Adams had shown unexpected courage and resources. The secret pleasure this familiarity gave Adams made Sue certain he believed it too.

Adams was pushing an enlarged photograph towards the American. "Show me where it was sited, Tommy."

Millburn jabbed a finger at a clump of trees behind the V1 site. "In here. They'd chopped down enough trees to give their guns a full field of fire but covered the top with camouflaged netting. That's why your photo-recce people missed spotting it."

Studying the photograph again, Adams saw there was no tell-tale red circle round the site. Relieved, he sat back in his chair. "If our lot missed it, then you're in the clear. Mind you, you still shouldn't have attacked a flak post and mustn't do it again, but in these circumstances I can put in a favourable report."

Millburn grinned at the scowling Gabby. "What did I tell you, you little creep? It was done for John Bull and Merrie England." He turned back to Adams. "Is that all, Frank?"

Adams nodded. "Yes, I got all the rest from your section. Would you both like tea and sandwiches? I can get the WAAFs to bring something in."

Millburn shook his head. "Not for me. I'm off to the Mess once I'm back in uniform. But I'd like a word with our beautiful Sue before I go." Moving towards the girl, he sat on the table before her. "How's it going, honey? Have you seen the light yet?"

The girl laughed. "What light, Tommy?"

"The light of commonsense, honey. What else? Why don't you forget that pianist guy of yours and go out with me some evening? A girl can't live on memories. I'm here, all bright and shiny and eager, and that's what counts."

There was a sniff from Gabby. "Listen to him. He thinks he's God's gift to women. Why don't you get wise to yourself, Millburn? Every WAAF on the station has got you taped by this time."

Millburn grinned. "Listen to the Swansea Stallion talking. Who dropped a clanger in Bishops Wood just before Operation Crisis and thought he was going to be made into meatballs?"

About to answer back, Gabby realised the dreaded secret might come out and had to content himself with a glare. With his grin broadening, Millburn turned back to Sue. "You're not going to be foolish, are you, honey, and miss out on pleasures beyond your imagination?"

With her cheeks pink by this time, Sue glanced at Adams for help. "I'm afraid so, Tommy. But thanks for the offer just the same."

Millburn sighed. "And I thought all the girls on this station were house trained. You haven't been doing your job properly, Frank."

At that moment one of Adams' telephones rang. Answering it, he gave a start. "Yes, he's with me now, sir. Do you want him right away? Yes, I've finished the debriefing. Very well, I'll tell him."

Replacing the receiver, he turned to Millburn. "That was the CO, Tommy. Air Commodore Davies is here. He wants to see you right away in the CO's office."

Showing surprise, Millburn rose from the table. "Davies? When did he arrive?"

"I don't know. He certainly hasn't come in his aircraft or we'd have seen it."

"Does he want just me or both of us?"

"He only mentioned you."

Millburn shrugged. "OK, I'll get over." He glanced at Gabby. "You leaving or staying?"

Gabby picked up his parachute. He was grinning maliciously as he followed Millburn to the door. "You know what it's about, don't you? He's heard about that flak tower and he's going to bounce you all the way to Berlin."

"You've got it all wrong, you little fart. He's giving me a medal for putting up with the biggest moaner in the RAF. Maybe the VC, because I don't deserve any less."

The door closed behind them, leaving the faint smell of combat from their flying suits, the sweat, cigarette smoke, oil, and cordite fumes. Catching the smell of it, Adams sat motionless for a moment, then gave a laugh as he turned to Sue. "They never change, do they?"

Her cheeks were still pink from Millburn's banter. "I've never known characters like them. But what do you think Davies wants with Millburn?"

Adams, who secretly dreaded Davies's visits in case it meant another dangerous operation for the squadron, lifted his shoulders. "I've no idea. But it doesn't sound too bad if it's only Millburn he wants to see."

Chapter 3

"That's about it," Davies finished. "Can you do it?"

Henderson, 633 Squadron's big Scottish CO, who had a distinct ambivalence towards the tasks given him by the enthusiastic Davies, was looking relieved. "Is that all you want, sir? For us to try to shoot down this JU86?"

Davies, still disappointed by the minor task he had been given, fell back on sarcasm. "What did you expect, Jock? An operation to capture Hitler?"

Henderson took the acerbic comment with his usual fortitude. "You have to admit you usually bring us bigger jobs than this, sir."

Davies scowled at the reminder. "Don't look so pleased I haven't. Frankly, I don't see why Simms thought it worthwhile bringing me all the way from Group to talk about it. But I suppose it's important to the Navy if their shipping movements are being monitored."

Henderson glanced at his office window against which rain was now beating. "All the same , there can't be many days at this time of the year when the JUs can fly. I can see they might be a problem in summer or even in October but not now."

"It's been a cold autumn, Jock, but there have been quite a few clear days and there could be more yet."

Henderson was prevented from replying by a knock on the door. Millburn, still in his flying suit, appeared a moment later. "You want to see me, sir?"

"Yes, Tommy. Or at least Air Commodore Davies does. Come in."

Millburn entered and gave Davies a salute. Davies motioned him to a chair. "I believe you've just got back, Millburn. What was the problem?"

"We'd a bit of damage to our starboard engine that slowed us down. But nothing serious."

"What about your flight? Did they all get back safely?"

"Yes, sir. We're all OK."

"Good. Now I'll tell you why I've called you in."

Millburn listened to Davies's explanation, showing surprise only when Davies told him that JU86s had been flying over eastern seaports for the last six weeks. "I thought they'd quit back in '42/43."

"They did but at least one of them is back again and London wants us to get rid of it. As you and Gabriel fly the squadron's photo/recce plane, we think you're the men for the job." Davies turned to Henderson. "I know it'll disrupt your command structure, Jock, but while you're busy with these V1 sites, it shouldn't matter too much. It's up to you to do the juggling but I'd suggest Van Breedenkamp takes over Millburn's place until he gets back."

Henderson, who resented Davies interfering in his sphere of influence, bit back a comment and turned instead to Millburn. "How do you feel about the job, Tommy?"

Millburn shrugged. "If we had the right ship, it'd be no problem. But we can't do it in old Z-Zebra. She's got no armament and wouldn't get within five thousand feet of a JU86. They can make 43,000 feet, can't they?"

"43,000 and more," Davies said impatiently. "But we know all that and it's taken care of." He went on to tell Millburn about the modified Mosquitoes. "I've approached de Havilland and they've found one for me. It'll be ferried here tomorrow. I want you and Gabriel to crew her. All right?"

Millburn was not a man to dodge asking questions, however difficult to answer. "OK sir. We get a ship that'll take us up to the JU's ceiling. But how do we put it all together?"

"What do you mean, put it all together?"

"I'm talking about the problems, sir. How do we know which port the Krauts will choose on the next fine day?"

Davies scowled. "We don't know."

"Then there's the time factor. If the Krauts are flying at 43,000 feet plus, we need to be up there when they arrive. Otherwise they'll be halfway back across the North Sea before we make their altitude. Do you know how long it takes this pressurised Mossie to reach 43,000 feet?" Davies's irritation came from his own inability to solve the problems of interception. "Of course I know, De Havilland got one of them up to 43,500 in 35 minutes." Millburn's shrug said it all. "You said there were three or four of these Mossies, sir. Are they still around?"

"If they were, I'd have one flying over every eastern seaport in the country, Millburn. That goes without bloody saying. But so far we've only got this one and your job is to do the best you can with it."

"We'll have to choose one port or we'll be running around in circles. Have you any preference?"

Henderson, who had been listening carefully, decided it was wise to break in at this point. "As Scapa Flow is the Navy's main base, wouldn't that be the one to choose, sir?"

"God knows, Jock. Jerry's last reconnaissance was over there but he might choose some other port the next time. Or he might cover all the ports in every sortie. With the bloody weather adding to the problem, I wish we'd never been landed with it but, as we have, I'll have to make it your pigeon." As he was speaking Davies rose from his chair. "It's like a lunatic asylum back at Group with Montgomery and Patton screaming for more and more aircraft and I can't waste any more time on the bloody thing."

The big Scot rose with him. "We'll do our best, sir. I'll get Adams working on it right away."

Nodding, Davies opened the office door, only to pause and gaze suspiciously down the corridor. Coming to his side, Henderson smiled. "It's all right, sir. Laura's on leave at the moment."

"I'm glad to hear it," Davies grunted. "Another swipe from that Amazon and I wouldn't live to see in the New Year."

With that Davies hurried down the corridor, his wide trousers flapping round his legs. As Henderson closed the door, Millburn stared at him curiously. "What was all that about, sir?"

Henderson chuckled. "A few weeks ago when he came to see me my WAAF clerk didn't spot him coming down the corridor and

24

sent him tippling arse over elbow. As you know, Laura's a big lass. He got so many bruises that ever since he takes it easy when he passes her office."

Millburn grinned as he rose from his chair. "If the guys find that out, they'll stand her champagne to do it again."

Considering the missions Davies had given them in the past, Henderson thought it wasn't a bad idea at that. Returning to his desk, he picked up a phone. "Tell Squadron-Leader Adams to come to my office right away, will you?"

Gabby looked like a cat presented with a bowl of cream. "You took the job, didn't you?"

"I'd no goddamned choice," Millburn told him. "He thinks we're the right guys for the mission and that was it."

"Then why aren't you looking more cheerful? It's going to get us off those V1 sites. It'll be like a holiday."

Millburn stared at him. "A holiday? What are you talking about?"

"How often do we get clear days this time of the year? Hardly any. That means we'll be able to do as we like. We'll be near seaports, so if you take your car we can go into town every day. Think of the girls we'll meet. We're in luck, boyo."

The American dropped on his bed and gazed at him with scorn. "Don't you know anything about your own country? Don't you know what those seaports in Scotland are like in winter?"

Gabby paused. "Scotland. You never mentioned Scotland."

"That's where your main naval bases are. And those seaports are like the end of the world. Grey houses, grey churches, Scotch mist, and full of big hairy sailors."

Gabby looked shaken for a moment, then rallied. "So what? There'll be girls, won't there?"

"Yeah. Salvation Army girls. Dispensing Bibles and singing hymns. Right up your street, kiddo."

Gabby's scorn had a hollow ring that suggested a need for reassurance. "You're talking out of your trousers, Millburn. Scottish girls are like girls anywhere. I knew one before the war and she was gorgeous. I never heard her say no once."

25

"Sure, they're great outside Scotland. But you'll be right inside it. Right in Presbyterian country. That means all the good girls are kept indoors at night and the bad ones are down on the docks with the matelots. So where do you fit in?"

Gabby sniffed. "If a man's got what it takes, he can always get himself a girl, Millburn."

"Sure he can. He can also get himself a hammering, you little shortass. Have you forgotten how your Navy acts when the RAF try to steal their girls? What about that big matelot two months ago who would have torn your head from your shoulders if I hadn't gotten in his way. That was only in Scarborough when the bastards were outnumbered. Think what it'll be like when there are only a couple of us against a few shiploads of 'em."

Gabby's uneasiness broke surface at last. "It couldn't be that bad, could it? Hartlepool, Newcastle and Hull are big cities and the Navy can't be everywhere."

"Hartlepool, Newcastle and Hull aren't in Scotland, you moron. And Scotland is where we're most likely to go. How about Scapa Flow for starters? Just treeless islands, ships, and thousands of bloody-minded, sex-starved matelots. How'd you like to spend your Christmas there?"

Gabby was beginning to look faint. "They wouldn't do that to us, would they, Millburn?"

"Why not? That's where the JU's have been seen."

Unnerved, Gabby began searching for a straw. "Then they probably won't go there again. Can't you tell Henderson that? Don't we have any say where we go?"

Millburn was enjoying himself now. "Not a say in the world. It's the Admiralty who'll decide and they've got no love for the RAF. So you brace yourself, kiddo. You might have to become a celibate for Christmas and the New Year."

With the weather planes reporting heavy mist and rain over the Channel, the squadron's sorties over the V1 bases were cancelled the following morning but the crews were put on standby in their flight offices in case conditions improved. With their nerves unable to relax, most airmen hated being on standby and restless men tried different ways to pass the time until they were stood down for the day. Four of the hardened old timers, Larkin the stringy New Zealander, Machin, the Eire volunteer, "Stan Baldwin", the black lawyer from Barbados, and the estate agent, Joe Elgin, spent it playing their customary cut-throat game of poker. Jock Smith and Killingbeck played game after game of table tennis and McDonald tried to concentrate on a new Hank Jansen thriller he had borrowed from his navigator.

The rest were either gazing at magazines, chatting, trying to doze in their chairs, or listening to the crew rooms' radios. With almost every man drawing on cigarettes, the rooms were dense with smoke and one of the few non-smokers, a young newcomer named Liston, found it too much for him and he slipped outside to escape.

Although it was a grey, damp day, the air smelt fresh and Liston took in deep breaths of it. Reluctant to go back into the smoke-filled rooms, he was about to take a walk down the perimeter path when he heard the muffled drone of engines. A moment later the landing lights around the airfield switched on, shining brilliantly through the grey autumn mist and reflecting back from the lowering clouds. The sound of engines drew nearer and began to circle the airfield. Thirty seconds later a slim aircraft appeared in the lights and began preparing to land.

By this time men inside the crew rooms had heard the engines and a number of them had spilled outside to watch the newcomer with interest. More than one navigator was expressing respect for the crew's skill in finding the airfield on such a day. Larkin's voice with its New Zealand twang sounded above the general buzz of excitement. "Hey, Millburn. This must be the kite Davies has found for you."

The Mosquito was now taxiing towards the tarmac apron in front of No. 1 hangar. As it arrived and its propellers ceased spinning, officers from the Administration Block were seen approaching it. Millburn, now in the front of the curious aircrews, waved to Gabby who was pushing towards him. "Come on, boyo. Let's see what they've given us."

As Millburn ran towards the hangar, at least a dozen men followed him. Mosquitoes were loved by their crews and a new version was always examined and discussed with the keenest of interest. As he neared the high-altitude version, Millburn heard Gabby's aggrieved voice panting behind him. "Must you run so fast, Millburn? No one's going to steal the bloody thing."

Millburn grinned. "What's the matter, shortass? Aren't your legs long enough to keep up with real men?"

As he reached the Mosquito he saw its two-man crew talking to Henderson. Noticing Millburn, the Scot called him over. "Here she is, Millburn. Come and have a chat with the crew. They'll tell you all about her."

For a moment Millburn imagined Henderson looked amused but at that moment the landing lights switched off. With the American's eyes not yet accustomed to the gloom, his first thought was how effeminate the pilot looked beside his navigator who sported a large moustache. "Hiya", he said. "You did a great job getting here today."

The pilot smiled. "We often have to fly in poor weather. It comes with the job."

With the pilot's voice a full octave above his own, Millburn was nonplussed for a moment. Then he leaned forward and peered at the piquant face framed by a thick fur collar. "You're not a girl, are you? A real girl?"

The girl pilot smiled at him. "Yes, I'm real. At least my friends seem to think so."

The grinning Henderson came to Millburn's rescue. "Haven't you heard we're using women ferry pilots these days, Tommy? As you see, they do quite a job."

Millburn could not take his eyes off the girl's attractive face. "Yes, sir. A hell of a job. I'm very impressed."

The girl's eyes twinkled at him. By this time the panting Gabby had reached the aircraft and Henderson waved him forward. "This is the other member of the crew, Millburn's navigator. I'd like you to run over the plane with them both before you go back to Hatfield."

The girl nodded. "When would you like that done, sir? We are supposed to return first thing in the morning."

Henderson shrugged. "Do it now if you're not too tired. Then you can spend the evening with us in the Mess."

As the girl nodded and addressed her navigator, Gabby tugged at Millburn's sleeve. As the American turned to him, Gabby's voice was a disbelieving whisper. "What's going on, Millburn? That pilot isn't a girl, is she?"

Millburn grinned. "No, she's a ten foot tall Zulu warrior. And you keep your grubby little hands off her while we're looking over this ship or I'll serve you up for soup in the Mess tonight."

Chapter 4

The Mess was crowded that evening. Although the RAF had been using women ferry pilots for over two years, 633 Squadron had never seen one before and the girl, Carol Manning, was surrounded by admirers when dinner was over. Wearing uniform that enhanced her slim and attractive figure, she soon proved to have a delightful sense of humour. As a consequence it took all Millburn's expertise to ward off the competition. "Don't take any notice of these characters, Carol. They don't know how to treat a girl properly."

The girl smiled. "Don't they, Tommy?"

"No. The WAAFs say they've no finesse."

"The WAAFs tell you that, do they?"

"Yeah. I'm like a big brother to them."

The girl nodded at a table at the far end of the Mess. "That one doesn't look too friendly towards her big brother.

Millburn followed her eyes and saw a pretty blond WAAF officer sitting there with a glass in her hand. Seeing Millburn glance at her, she gave him a black look and then turned her head sharply away. Millburn had to think fast. "She's probably jealous because you're a pilot and she's not."

"You think that's what it is?"

"Sure it is. She's bored doing chores for the Adjutant."

The girl broke out laughing. "Tommy, you're a terrible flirt. Why don't you admit it?"

Millburn had never looked more innocent or hurt. "Where do you get that idea from? I've been ordered to stay with you because I gotta learn all about this ship you brought in. How does that make me a flirt?"

"But I've already shown you everything and run over the specifications with you."

Seeing a crowd of young officers, with Gabby prominent among them, gazing his way and knowing his time with the girl was under threat, Millburn hastily drew her away to an empty table. "I wasn't listening too well. We'd just got back from a mission and my ears hadn't adjusted. What exactly did de Havilland do to boost her altitude?"

Carol laughed again. "All right, I'll give you the benefit of the doubt. They pressurised the cabin, extended the wingspan, fitted smaller wheels, took out some of the fuel tanks, and reduced the pilot's armour. By the time they finished she was down to just over 16,000 lbs in weight." Then, seeing how his eyes had been moving over her face, she shook her head. "You haven't been listening to a word I've said, have you?"

Millburn had not. He had noticed again the dimples that came into her cheeks when she smiled and was wondering why his heart gave a double beat every time it happened. "Yes, I have," he lied. "Go on."

She laughed. "No. You took in everything the first time."

The decibels in the Mess were rising as drink took its effect. Millburn stole another look at the group of young officers. From Gabby's urgings and the flushed faces that were staring their way, Millburn knew it was only minutes before his tête-à-tête with the girl would be over. He leaned across the table. "Do me a favour. Take a walk round the airfield with me."

She hesitated. "I don't think that's a good idea. Everyone will see us leave."

"Couldn't we let them think we're going out to look at the ship?"

Her cheeks dimpled. "I don't think anyone would believe that, do you?"

On tenterhooks as he saw Gabby urging the other officers to follow him, Millburn made a great effort. "Please, Carol. You leave in the morning. If we don't get out of here soon, all those drunks will drop on us and we won't get a chance to talk again."

31

Glancing across the Mess she saw he was right. She hesitated again, then nodded. "All right. Just for a short while. But let me leave first. I'll meet you in front of the first hangar."

Relieved, he watched her walk towards the far door, thinking how gracefully she moved. A loud groan sounded across the Mess as her retirement was noticed and two officers ran forward to talk to her. Pausing, she smiled at them, said something, then disappeared through the door. As the disappointed men walked back, a malicious voice sounded in Millburn's ear. "What's happened, Millburn? Has she thrown you over?"

Millburn felt suddenly benevolent. "Hello, you little creep. I was wondering when you'd stick your sharp nose in."

"She's too good for you, boyo. She's got class written all over her."

Millburn grinned. "Yeah, that's true. She's engaged to the Duke of Westminster. So there's no point in wasting time on her, is there?"

Knowing his man, Gabby was immediately suspicious. "You're seeing her outside, aren't you? Where're you going? To one of the dispersal huts?"

Millburn rose. "Why don't you belt up and get back to the bar? You'd better make the best of things, boyo. You might be on short rations in Scapa Flow next week."

Certain now his suspicions were correct, Gabby saw no reason why he shouldn't benefit from them. "I'll tell you what I'll do, Millburn. For a couple of quid I'll doss up with Larkin tonight and you can use our billet. I can't say fairer than that, can I?"

Millburn was surprised by his sudden reaction. Grabbing the Welshman by the shoulders, he swung him round. "Get back to the bar, you little pisspot. And you make one more crack about her and I'll slice you into small pieces and salt you for Christmas." With that he gave the indignant Gabby a push and made for the door.

As he left the Mess he found to his relief that the rain had ceased. With only a few shaded lights visible round the hangar, he could see no sign of the girl as he approached it, nor was there any sign of her as he walked round to its huge sliding doors. Through a gap between them, he could see ground crews working on two

32

Mosquitoes. Not wanting to be seen by them, he drew back, walked round to the side of the hangar and waited.

Standing there he was glad he had donned his overcoat before leaving the Mess. A breeze had taken the place of the rain, light in itself but enough to bring a chill to the night. As a couple of mechanics passed him and eyed him curiously, he began to think the girl had made her promise merely to escape his attentions and he felt both embarrassed and disappointed. Then he saw a small figure walk round the rear of the hangar and his heart did its disturbing double beat again. "Hello, Tommy. I'm sorry if I kept you waiting but I needed to borrow an overcoat and it took me some time to find a WAAF my size. Most of the girls seem to be out or in the Mess."

"That's OK," Millburn told her. "Are you going to be warm enough?"

"Oh yes. I borrowed a pullover too. I'm buried in clothes." She glanced across the airfield. "Where are we going?"

"I figured we could walk round the perimeter track. Is that OK?"

"Yes." She smiled at him. "Lead the way."

He took her past the transport pool, past the corporals' Mess from which music was issuing, and through the rows of billets until they reached the ten foot track that ringed the airfield. Ahead of them storm lanterns were visible on hard standings where ground crews were still working on picketed Mosquitoes but they only served to darken the shadows that lay on the track. Above, the clouds were starting to break up in the stirring wind, and patches of starlight could be seen. The girl pointed at one. "The weather's clearing. You'll be able to test fly my Mosquito tomorrow."

"Can't you stay and go up with me?" he asked.

"No. I'm under orders to report back tomorrow. The Adjutant has already detailed a transport to take me to Highgate. I'm taking the train back to base."

Millburn was finding himself tongue-tied, something he had rarely experienced with a girl before. As he struggled to find words, one of the squadron's gun emplacements loomed out of the night, its twin barrelled Hispano cannon pointing skyward. Seeing its two gunners peering down at them, Millburn called a cheerful greeting. A few seconds later, when he and the girl were well past the emplacement, a low wolf whistle sounded. Grateful for the chance it gave him, Millburn turned to her. "As you hear, our ground gunners have good taste."

She laughed. "What, in this light? I think they're just lonely up there."

"No. Those guys have good eyesight. That's why we select them."

The first of the picketed Mosquitoes was now coming into sight. Untended by ground crews, it looked like a huge bird in the starlight. As she paused for a moment, Millburn turned to her. "What is it?"

She gave a low laugh. "I think I'm just envious. It must be marvellous to be a pilot in a squadron as famous as this."

Although Millburn was as secretly proud of his squadron's record as any other member, he contented himself with a guarded answer. "It's OK, I guess."

"You guess? Don't you realise the name this squadron has among the public? Before the invasion of Europe its operations and successes kept peoples' hopes alive when everything else seemed to be falling apart. The squadron's a byword out there. So is it any wonder I'm envious?"

Without knowing it, Millburn had lived long enough with the British to develop their habit of understatement. "The guys do their job, I guess. Yeah, they're OK."

"Is that why you stay here? Because of them? With your experience the Americans must have asked you many times to make a transfer."

Unused to having his emotions examined, Millburn frowned. "I haven't thought about it that much. It's true there are some good guys here." He nearly said, "and some good guys who've got the chop" but bit off the words in time.

"Tell me about them," she said. "Which ones are your closest friends?"

Millburn gave a half-laugh. "I don't know. It's something a guy doesn't think about."

"You must know the ones you like most of all."

Millburn shrugged. "Well, there's Frank Adams, the Intelligence Officer. Frank's a great guy."

"Is he the Squadron Leader in his forties?" she interrupted. "The one who wears glasses and sat near the CO at dinner tonight?"

"Yeah, that's Frank. He's a man you can talk to. Everyone likes Frank. And the poor guy's got a wife who focuses on every young guy who gets in her sights. She's coming up from London in a few days and I know Frank's dreading it."

She made an expression of sympathy. "Who else are your friends?"

"Ian Moore and Frank Harvey, I guess, but Harvey's gone on rest to an OTU and Moore's working with Davies these days. So we don't see much of either anymore."

"Wasn't Moore your squadron commander?" she asked.

"Yeah. He was shot down over the Loire on D-Day but we helped him escape from the Krauts a few weeks ago. Davies intended him to lead our last mission but none of the boys were happy about it. Particularly Harvey."

She glanced at him curiously. "But I thought escapee aircrews weren't allowed to fly over Europe again in case they were shot down and made to give away the names of their rescuers."

"They aren't. But Davies got Moore a special dispensation for that mission."

"It must have been a very important one," she said. "Can you tell me about it?"

With the object of the Operation Crisis a secret from the public and Davies having made it clear to all and sundry that no one was to talk about Harvey's extraordinary behaviour, Millburn knew he would have to tread warily here. "It was a big job but it worked out OK because in the end Harvey took Moore's place. And he did a great job."

"Did Harvey volunteer for it?"

Millburn was wondering why he found it so easy to talk to the girl about squadron affairs. "Yeah, you could say that. Harvey's a strange guy. After the Swartfjord job, he expected to get command of the squadron and when the Brass Hats went over his head and brought Moore in, all hell broke out for a while. But once the two guys got to know one another, they became the best of friends. So I guess Harvey felt Moore shouldn't take the risk of being captured again."

35

"You're very lucky, you know," she said quietly. "It must be wonderful to have friends like that who will risk their lives for you."

Millburn was fast realising this was a girl who reminded a man of things he took for granted. "It's part of the job, I guess. You help a guy and the next time he helps you."

"That's why I envy you." When the American didn't answer, Carol went on: "But we were talking about your friends. What about your navigator?"

Millburn grinned. "You mean the Swansea Stallion?"

"The what?"

"The Swansea Stallion. He's Welsh, you see. And he likes girls. But he has another nickname. We call him Gabby the Gremlin. That's because of his ears and his sneaky ways."

She laughed. "The WAAF who lent me this overcoat says you never stop teasing one another. Is it true?"

"You have to keep gremlins down, particularly when they're your navigators. Otherwise they'd set you down in Krautland or Russia. And gremlins don't come any worse than that little runt."

Having already learned from the WAAFs that the big American and his diminutive navigator were closer than brothers, she only smiled at his comments. "What about the other crews?"

"We've got the League of Nations here. There's a South African, Van Breedenkamp — he's the other flight commander — there's a Kiwi, Larkin, there's an Irish volunteer, Machin — the guys say he's from the IRA and used to throw bombs at the English before the war — and there's Stan Baldwin, the black guy from Barbados. Most of the other guys are British kids they send us from OTU. We used to get volunteers from other squadrons but they've dried up lately."

Millburn did not elaborate on his last statement. In spite of the squadron's fame, the hazardous missions it had been called on to perform had by this time spread the reputation it was a suicide unit, so eliminating all but the most dedicated crews.

She had smiled at his description of Machin. "You still haven't told me why you haven't transferred to the Americans."

He grinned. "Someone has to keep these Limeys in order. You saw how they were acting in the Mess tonight. If I hadn't been with you there's no telling what might have happened."

He liked her laugh. It reminded him of a joyful carillon of bells. "So that was why you stayed with me?"

He grinned. "What else?"

A pool of yellow light appeared as they neared another picketed Mosquito. Storm lanterns were set round a scaffold under its starboard wing where two men were working on the engine. As they came opposite the aircraft, Millburn paused. "Do you mind waiting a moment?"

"No. Go ahead."

She watched him walk over to the men and say something to them. The conversation lasted no more than a minute before he returned. "Sorry about that. Is it OK if we go on?"

Nodding, she waited for him to explain his behaviour. When he made no comment, she glanced back at the Mosquito. "Is that your aircraft?"

"Yeah. That's old T-Tommy."

"What's the problem with the engine?"

"She was overheating today. So they're doing a check on her."

"Why? Was it flak damage?"

"I told you. She was overheating."

"Yes, but that was because you were hit by flak. I heard someone mention it over dinner."

He frowned. "OK. A piece of shrapnel hit our radiator. So what?"

Seeing he didn't want to talk about it, she allowed him to ask questions about her work while they walked the rest of the way round the airfield. When they reached the cluster of WAAF billets at the other side of the hangars, she glanced at her watch. "I'll have to go now, Tommy, or I'll never be up at five in the morning."

"Is that when you're leaving?"

"I'm afraid so. I have to catch the early train from Highgate."

"Let me take you in," he said. "I've got an old automobile here."

"No, Tommy. I'd rather not." Seeing his look of disappointment, she laid a hand on his arm. "Mornings are bad times to say goodbye. They're so cold and impersonal. I'd much rather do it tonight."

"But that means I'm not going to see you again," he muttered. When she did not answer, he went on: "Did you say Hatfield is your base?"

"Yes. We move about a great deal but I can be contacted there."

"I've got two weeks leave coming up some time after Christmas. Can I come and see you?"

She hesitated. "But I might be away delivering an aircraft."

"That wouldn't matter. You'd be back in a day or two, wouldn't you?"

"Yes, but you'd waste so much of your leave. I wouldn't want you to do that."

"It's my leave," he said. "And I've no family over here. There's nothing I'd rather do. Give a guy a break, Carol."

She hesitated, then drew him into the shadow between two of the huts. From one of them a radio was playing 'All The Things You Are'. "All right, Tommy," she said quietly. "If you want to be so silly I'll leave a letter in the guardroom with my number and address. Then you can write and tell me when your leave is due."

Millburn found his voice had turned hoarse. "You will? That's wonderful, kid. Sure I'll write. Will you write me back?"

"Yes, of course I will."

There was just enough light for Millburn to see her eyes gazing up at him and he had the odd feeling he was sinking into them. As he gazed down at her, she raised a hand and touched his face. "I do like you, Tommy. Even if you are a dreadful flirt. So come and see me after Christmas if you still want to."

Millburn had never been more sure of anything. "I'll be there, kid. No question at all." Then, without his knowing how it happened, she was in his arms. For a long moment their lips clung together, then, with a low, breathless laugh, she drew back. "I must go now. Promise to take care of yourself."

Millburn wanted to say a hundred things and could think of none. "You do the same, kid. You really are something."

Before he could say any more he felt her lips, as light as thistledown, touch his own again. Then she was gone and Millburn was walking back to his billet, unsure of what had happened but with the feeling life would never be quite the same again.

Chapter 5

Millburn opened up the port engine of the pressurised Mosquito and lowered, then raised the flaps. Satisfied by the free movements, he repeated the procedure with the starboard engine. He then checked the take-off boost, the magnetos, and the remainder of the standard checks. Finally he glanced at Gabby alongside him. "OK?"

When Gabby nodded, he began taxiing towards the runway, checking brake pressures as he went. At the far end of the runway he swung the Mosquito around, set his trimming tabs and flaps, and waited for the Controller's clearance.

Ahead, the airfield was empty of Mosquitoes except for one being dragged across the grass by a tractor towards No. 2 hangar, for all flights of the squadron were once again in action against V1 sites. The Controller waited until the damaged Mosquito was dragged on to No. 2 hangar's tarmac apron, then Millburn's earphones crackled. At the same moment a green Very light arched from the Control Tower and fell sizzling into the wet grass along the runway.

Acknowledging his clearance, Millburn advanced both throttles, checking the aircraft tendency to swing to port by giving the port throttle an extra notch. The Mosquito began to pick up speed, her wheels splashing into puddles and throwing a haze of spray behind her. Stripped of all unnecessary weight and carrying only three .303 Browning guns, she was free of the runway before she covered half its length. Banking over The Black Swan, the old inn that stood on the road to Highgate, Millburn increased her speed to 200 mph and then turned to Gabby. "OK, kid. Let's see how high she'll go."

Gabby, suffering a hangover from the previous night's revelries, was in one of his darker Celtic moods. His voice sounded muffled through his high pressure mask. "She'll never make 43,000 feet. Davies was talking his usual bullshit."

Millburn shrugged. "I don't see why not. Carol thinks she can make it all right."

"And that's good enough for you, is it? A girl tells you about a kite and you believe everything she says."

"That girl's some pilot, boyo. Otherwise she'd never have found us last night."

"It wasn't her that found us, Millburn. It was her navigator. Pilots are only chauffeurs. When are you going to learn that?"

Millburn grinned. "What's wrong, kiddo? You having an attack of sour grapes because she passed you over last night for a real man?"

Gabby gave him a glare. "You probably lied to her and made her think because you're a Yank you're on a different pay scale to the rest of us. Wait until she finds out the truth, Millburn. You won't be looking so pleased with yourself then."

The two men were wearing high altitude flying suits as well as masks. Although the cabin of the adapted Mosquito was pressurised, the crews needed the added protection of suits and oxygen in case of a sudden drop in pressure caused by natural causes or enemy shells.

The slow minutes passed by as the Mosquito continued her climb. For the first eight thousand feet the sky was clear, then dense cloud closed in. It had been brought in by a low pressure belt that had crossed the British Isles early that morning and was multi-layered in its composition. By the time the Mosquito's altimeter was showing 18,000 feet, blue fire could be seen playing around her. Nudging Millburn, Gabby removed his gloves and reached out to metal parts of the cockpit. As long sparks flew from his fingertips towards them, Millburn grinned. "What's our little boy doing? Playing games? Didn't you know that can happen in a cumulo-nimbus cloud?"

Gabby took immediate umbrage. "Of course I bloody well knew. You think you're the only one who's seen St. Elmo's fire?"

The cloud closed in even tighter. In the grey, unreal world in which time seemed to stand still, Millburn found his thoughts drifting back to Carol Manning. A clock in his mind had awoken him at 5 a.m. that morning and the temptation had been strong to see her a last time before her departure. In the end he had respected her wish but his mental struggle had made certain he remained awake until his morning call.

The Mosquito's sudden emergence into the sunlight broke up his thoughts. The sudden contrast was dramatic, with the sun a molten ball above and great castles of cloud below. By this time both men were feeling slightly lightheaded, with the drone of the engines a neutral murmur in the background. Feeling as if his ears were full of cotton wool, Millburn found himself shouting into his intercom. "I think we're going to make it. We're already at 37,000 and she's as steady as a rock."

Ahead of him the altimeter was creeping on ... 39,000 ... 40,000 ... 41,000. For a moment he felt the Mosquito yaw slightly, but she replied to his correction and continued her climb. At 43,800 she began to pitch as well as yaw and he knew she had reached her ceiling. "That's it, boyo. 43,800 in 34 minutes. If she'll always do that, we ought to nail that Junkers."

Gabby's voice sounded miles away. "I'm cold, Millburn. Let's get back home. I want a cup of char."

Millburn allowed one wing to drop. "That's where we're going, boyo. Hold on to your dentures."

"Have you got him?" Henderson asked.

The young WAAF telephonist nodded. "Yes, sir. He's on the line now."

Henderson took the telephone from her. "Hello, sir. Yes, I'm calling you from the Control Tower. It's all right. Millburn has just got her up to 43,800 feet and he thinks on a good day he might squeeze a bit more out of her. What do you want us to do now?"

Davies's somewhat high-pitched voice sounded irritable. "I suppose we have to do what London wants. How soon can you get the two of 'em away?"

"They can leave any time, sir. They know the score."

"Then they'd better go this afternoon. Not that I foresee any haste. It might be weeks before we get a clear day. But it'll allow Simms to tell 'em we've got things moving."

"All right, sir. I'll see to it when they get down. Where are they to go?"

When Davies told him, Henderson gave a start. "But that's near enough for them to operate from here."

"That's what I told them. But I think the Admiralty are calling the tune on this one and they know as much about aircraft as I know about Nelson and his mistress. Keep in touch and let me know what happens. Bye."

Gabby, still wearing his high pressure suit, looked like an overdressed gremlin presented with a stick of rock. "Leconfield! Are you sure?"

Adams nodded. "That's the message Davies gave the CO. You're to go there after lunch. I've been in touch, so they're expecting you."

Full of triumphant sarcasm, Gabby swung round on Millburn. "Where did you say we were going, Millburn? Scapa Flow? We're going to Leconfield, boyo. And Leconfield's not far from Hull, a big city. Didn't I tell you this was going to be a piece of cake?"

Adams had to smile at Gabby's enthusiasm. "I wouldn't get too excited about it, Gabby. We've heard a great deal about the bombing of Coventry and London but the fact is Hull has been the worst bombed city in Britain. So don't expect too many amenities there."

"There'll be cinemas and girls, won't there?" Gabby demanded.

Adams glanced at the smiling Sue Spencer. "I don't know about cinemas but I suppose there'll be girls."

"Of course there'll be girls. And good looking ones too. I read once that Hull had the prettiest girls in England."

Millburn gave him a look. "Where did you read that?"

"I don't know. Probably in our local newspaper."

"That fits. Your village had so many Olive Oyls any girl would seem good looking beside them."

"Funny, funny," Gabby grunted. Then he gave a chortle of malice. "I know what's wrong with you, Millburn." He turned to the amused Adams and Sue. "The Yank fell for that ferry pilot who flew in yesterday. He was talking about her all night in his sleep. So now he's pretending he's on the water wagon and girls don't interest him."

Sue laughed. "Is that true, Tommy? Have you really turned over a new leaf?"

Millburn scowled at the grinning Gabby. "It's this high altitude flying. It always makes gremlins talk a load of bullshit."

Seeing he had touched Millburn on a tender spot, Gabby rubbed the spot with relish. "Look at his face. There's guilt written all over it."

The look Milburn gave the small Welshman would have killed a normal man at a thousand yards. The American turned to Adams. "Have you got all the gen you need, Frank?" When Adams nodded, Millburn turned to Gabby and gave him a shove. "Then let's go. You and I have things to talk about."

Chapter 6

There was a cold wind blowing down Highgate station when Adams arrived. He bore it for a couple of minutes, then, suspecting Valerie's train was going to be late, took shelter behind a pile of wooden crates. For a moment he fumbled in his greatcoat pocket for his pipe. Then, as the wind sent the telegraph wires singing, he withdrew his hand. Valerie had always disliked his pipe smoking, so perhaps it was wiser not to confront her with it today after their long separation.

Always one to analyse his behaviour, Adams could not decide whether it was a decision based on consideration or want of courage. Certainly, as a thin-skinned man, he found his wife's carping a painful infliction that less sensitive men would have shrugged off or ignored altogether. Nor was Adams helped by highly developed self-critical faculties which made him a soft target for those who needed a victim for their discontent.

This vulnerability that complicated Adams's psyche was never so evident as in his relationship with the slim, waspish woman that was his wife. He had little if any illusions about her feelings for him. He was a provider of her expensive tastes and little else. At the same time Adams was a man in whom a long relationship created its own sentiments: a feeling of responsibility, a loyalty, and even sympathy based upon one's awareness of the other's limitations. Adams had never been able to decide whether these feelings constituted love or not but in their compulsion to aid and protect, they seemed to bear a kinship. In a world where the great majority of people lived and died on their own terms with little tolerance for the imperfections of others, Adams was a victim of his forbearance and his loyalty, which explained why he was a lonely man.

A gust of wind, swirling round the crates, made him turn up his greatcoat collar and stamp his feet. A glance at the ancient, yellowed clock on the rafters of the station told him the train was ten minutes late. With the war playing havoc with timetables, Adams became resigned to a lengthy wait and was pleasantly surprised when a moment later a bell clanged and a uniformed railwayman appeared from nowhere with a flag in his hand.

Less than a minute later the train appeared round a bend in the track, puffing out smoke from its nostrils like a tired buffalo. As the carriages jolted to a halt and doors began clanging open, Adams moved forward.

He spotted Valerie halfway down the platform, a tall, elegant figure in an expensive maroon coat giving imperious instructions to a porter. Almost to his surprise Adams felt pleased to see her. As the porter vanished inside the carriage, he hurried forward. For a moment steam from the locomotive blew around him, giving a sulphurous taste to his tongue and hiding Valerie from sight. Then, as she appeared again, he waved his arm.

She had noticed him now and gave a somewhat languid flutter of a gloved hand. Then she turned to the porter who was heaving two large suitcases from the carriage. She was addressing him when Adams arrived and squeezed her arm affectionately. "Hello, darling. It's good to have you back here. How are you keeping?"

She turned and offered him a cheek, reminding him as he kissed her that she was the taller of the two. "Hello, Frank. It's nice to see you too. I'm all right except I'm cold. There wasn't any heating on the train and I'm half frozen."

As Adams muttered his regrets, her somewhat protuberant eyes ran over him. "You're looking well enough although I think you've put on a little more weight. Am I right?"

"Perhaps just a little," Adams admitted. "But you haven't changed at all. London must agree with you."

She shrugged. "London's all right but it's nice to get away for a while." She glanced at the porter who had put down her luggage. "Are we going by taxi or car?"

45

"Car," Adams told her. "It's at the front of the station."

She nodded at the porter. Seeing he was an elderly man, Adams took one of the heavy suitcases from him. Valerie stared at him. "What are you doing?"

Adams showed some embarrassment. "It's all right, Val. These cases are heavy."

"For God's sake, Frank. You're a Squadron Leader. Let the porter take them."

Adams tried to make light of it as he addressed the porter. "No, I'll take this one. I need the exercise." He turned back to Valerie. "Sorry you're cold, darling, but cheer up. It won't be long now before you'll be sipping tea before a warm fire."

Her lips had tightened at his refusal to surrender the suitcase but to Adams' relief she made no further comment on it. "Thank God for that. I'd forgotten how cold it gets up here." She handed her ticket to the collector, then pushed through the gate that led to the road outside. As Adams and the porter struggled after her, she glanced at Adams and motioned at the half dozen cars parked outside, "Which one is yours?"

Adams pointed to a Hillman. He helped her slide into the front seat before he and the porter loaded the luggage into the boot. As he climbed in beside her, she glanced round approvingly. "You never told me about this car. When did you buy it? It's rather nice."

Adams slipped in the clutch and pulled away. "It isn't mine, Val. I borrowed it from the Adjutant."

"Does that mean you don't have a car?"

"I'm afraid I don't. I hardly ever need a car, and when I do I can usually borrow one."

Her smooth forehead furrowed. "Isn't that going to make it difficult for me to get into town? If I remember right, it's an awful bus service into Highgate."

For a moment Adams believed he had done the right thing. "You won't need transport, Val. I've got you rooms in town."

She turned sharply. "In town. Why?"

"I thought you'd be happier here with cinemas and shops to go to. You remember you did find the inn too austere and old-fashioned. And you're right. It is a poor bus service into town."

"But I don't know anybody in Highgate. I'll be bored out of my mind here."

"You'll soon get to know people. And I'll come as often as I can and perhaps bring a few of the boys with me."

Her frown died. "Who's still left that I know? I know Grenville's a prisoner. What about Jack Richardson? Is he still with you?"

Adams kept his eyes on the road that led him deeper into the small market town. Richardson, the red-headed Equipment Officer, had been one of the squadron personnel Valerie had liked and encouraged during her stay in The Black Swan and Adams had never been sure how far her encouragement had gone. "Richardson's still alive and well. As he isn't aircrew, there's no reason why he shouldn't be."

Her slim lips gave a smile that was half-mocking. "He's no different to you, darling. So you shouldn't hold that against him."

She's right, I shouldn't, Adams thought. Like Richardson, I'm as safe as if it were peacetime. Just the same I still don't like the ginger-headed, carnal bastard! Ashamed of himself, Adams dropped Richardson from the conversation. "Gillibrand's gone, Barrett's gone, Teddy Young's gone — in fact everyone who took part in the Swartfjord operation has gone except Harvey who escaped thanks to the Norwegian partisans. It's a different squadron to the one you knew."

She gave a slight shudder. "I know all that. The press were full of the losses. Which one was Harvey? I don't remember him."

"You probably didn't meet him. In the old days he used to go into town rather than drink in the pub. He's a big tough Yorkshireman who took Ian Moore's place on an important raid we carried out in late summer and got wounded during it."

She interrupted him. "Ian Moore! But surely he was shot down on D-Day."

"He was but the squadron helped him to escape."

"Really. So Moore's back with you?"

"Not with us. Davies has co-opted him, so he spends most of his time at Group Headquarters."

"Then who's your new squadron commander?"

47

"At the moment an American volunteer, Tommy Millburn. It really ought to be Harvey but after what he did before the mission, no one can guess what Davies will do."

She looked curious. "What did Harvey do?"

Adams suddenly realized he was being too talkative. With High Command unaware that to save Moore from the risk of further capture Harvey had drugged him and then tricked Davies by taking his place, Adams could only speculate on the Air Commodore's fury if the truth came out.

He steered carefully around a stationary truck before finding a lie to quell Valerie's curiosity. "Harvey persuaded the CO to let him take Moore's place. Davies didn't like that and has held it against Harvey ever since."

"But isn't Davies in overall charge?"

"Yes, but the CO felt Moore would be in too much danger if he were shot down a second time. Knowing everyone on the squadron felt the same way, Davies was persuaded to back down. But he didn't take kindly to it, and as he's never liked Harvey we're all waiting to find out what Davies'll do to him when he's recovered from his wound. I know Harvey would like the command but Anna, his wife, would hate it. She feels he ought to have a long rest."

Valerie's inveterate curiosity about the relationships of men and women was wide awake now. "Is Anna the German girl you've mentioned in your letters?"

Adams, who had never for one moment told Valerie that Anna was an SOE agent, knew he would have to tread warily again. "Yes. In the past she was quite useful to us in analysing photographs of German locations. That's how Harvey met her. She feels he's done enough combat flying, so was terribly upset when he took Moore's place on this operation."

"Where do they both live? Here in town?"

"No. They have a bungalow near Harvey's OTU."

"That's a pity. We could have called on them."

With Valerie possessing a gift for causing mischief, Adams was not sorry that contact was unlikely. As he braked behind a horse and cart, he saw her pull out an expensive-looking cigarette case from her handbag. For a moment he was tempted to ask how she had obtained it. Then his wish to avoid any friction that day prevailed.

She drew out a cigarette and flicked her lighter. Then, exhaling smoke, she turned to Adams again. "Why did Harvey do it?"

The question took him by surprise. "Do what?"

"Why did he want to take Moore's place?"

"Moore was his friend and Harvey couldn't stand the thought of his being shot down again and perhaps tortured. Harvey's that kind of man."

Her eyes were on his face as she spoke. "You admire him, don't you?"

"Yes, I do. I thought it a wonderful gesture, particularly as it was a very dangerous operation."

She gave a sudden, hard laugh. "You never change, do you, Frank. You're still an incurable romantic."

Adams slowed down as two cyclists appeared before him. "I suppose I am. But is it romantic to admire a man risking his life for a friend?"

"Of course it is. If every man took his friend's place, the armed forces would become a shambles. If a man is given a nasty job, let him do it. One's own nasty job will come soon enough."

She's probably right, Adams thought, as he accelerated past the cyclists. Realists usually are. But, oh God, what a cold, selfish, and uncharitable world they make it sound.

Suddenly feeling depressed, Adams turned the car down a side road and drew up outside a semi-detached house. "This is it," he said. "30 Wilberforce Street. A young pilot of ours called Marsh used to have two rooms here with his wife and child. Two elderly sisters own it. I remembered it when you said you wanted to come and found they'd just lost their previous tenant. So I suppose I was lucky."

Valerie stared at the small house with its lace-curtained windows. "It looks awfully suburban. Who are the old women?"

"Their name's Taylor."

"Does that mean they're spinsters?"

"Yes, I suppose they are."

"My God," she said. "Spinsters in market town suburbia. Is that the best you could do for me?"

Adams sighed. "Rooms are still hard to get, Val."

49

"What accommodation are they offering?"

"A bedroom, a small sitting room, and use of the kitchen." Seeing her move of distaste, Adams added: "Most people are only offering bedrooms. There are still a lot of evacuees here."

She exhaled smoke, an act of irritation. "I don't know why you tried. I'd have been perfectly happy at the inn."

"But you hated it there. You said so often enough. We even quarrelled about it."

She glanced back at the house. "I'm going to hate it here if those old spinsters start to interfere with my life." Before Adams could ask what she meant, she flung open the car door and swung out her shapely, silken clad legs. "Oh well, let's go and get it over. I've waited long enough for that cup of tea."

Adams began pulling the suitcases from the boot. Although a man who detested gossip, he could not help wondering how Valerie had obtained those leg-enhancing silk stockings in wartime Britain. Valerie's sharp voice interrupted the thought. "For heaven's sake, hurry up, darling. I'm absolutely freezing."

With a sigh, Adams picked up the two heavy cases and followed Valerie down the path to the house.

Chapter 7

The town had the toylike, nature-dominated appearance so common in Norway. Clinging perilously to the steep sides of the massive wooded valley that flanked it on both sides, its houses, cottages and barns were bisected by a narrow road and stream. Here and there along the valley the white vapour of waterfalls could be seen, sinking with the deceptive slowness of water falling from great heights. With winter coming early that year and a heavy snowfall covering its roofs and narrow streets, Rosvik had a picture postcard appearance beneath its frosty, starlit sky. But the impression of tranquillity was an illusion. Rosvik was living under the heel of the Nazis, and under their strict orders no lights shone from windows and nothing stirred in its streets except a single man who was darting furtively from one shadow to another. Every now and then he would pause to listen but could hear nothing in the deep silence except the occasional bark of a dog and the distant sound of a waterfall.

Although he was heavily dressed against the cold with a fur-lined cap, padded anorak and thick breeches, his agile movements betrayed he was a young man. Once he had to pause and hide in a doorway when he heard a loud clatter from a nearby building but it proved to be nothing but a bird disturbed from a chimney stack. Relaxing, he continued his progress down the empty pavements, wincing only at the crunching sound of his footsteps when he had to cross stretches of frozen snow.

He reached his destination at last, a small bakery at the far end of town. Slipping down a passage alongside it, he stopped for a moment to steady his heartbeats and gather his breath. Then, pausing first to listen, he tapped on a side door.

He waited for a full twenty seconds but no reply came. Steeling himself, he tapped louder. When no reply came again, he muttered a curse and gazed up at the double-storied building. Seeing a window directly above him, he fumbled down the passage way for pebbles. Finding a few beneath a pile of snow, he threw one at the shuttered window.

The rattle it made sounded loud in the silence and afraid it might have awakened neighbours, he drew back into the shadows, only to try again when the silence returned. This time, to his relief, the shutters above opened and he heard a woman's voice, speaking in little more than a hoarse whisper, "Who are you? What do you want?"

He kept his voice as low as her own. "My name's Eiliv. Are you Mrs Helgenstrom?"

"Yes.'

"Then I need to talk to you. Steen sent me."

"Steen?"

"Yes, it's urgent. Please let me in."

"Why should I?"

"Steen needs your help. Hurry up, please."

The hoarse whisper hesitated but only for a moment. "Stay out of sight while I come down."

The door opened a minute later and the man had only a brief glimpse of a huge woman wrapped in a dressing-gown before a brawny arm pulled him inside and closed the door. "What's Steen's nickname to his friends?"

"Grizzly Bear," he muttered.

Her hoarse voice relaxed slightly. "Come with me."

With the house in darkness, he needed her grip on his arm to steer him towards a second door. As he reached it a wave of warmth struck him and he caught the smell of baked bread. A moment later, as the light was switched on, he saw he was in a bakery, with two large ovens banked against the opposite wall. A tug on his arm turned him round to face the woman whose voice was still suspicious. "You say your name is Eiliv. Why haven't I seen you before?"

He saw she was even bigger than he had realised, a massive woman with her mottled feet thrust into slippers and her iron-grey hair in rollers. "I've been down in the south for the last few months. But I know Rosvik. I worked in the timber mill here in 1937."

"Where did you leave your skis?"

"Up the mountainside."

"How old are you?"

"Twenty-five."

"Take your cap off."

Frowning at her orders, he obeyed, uncovering a mop of straight brown hair, a lean face, and a nose that was slightly askew. His blue eyes challenged her. "Satisfied now?"

"You don't look like a labourer," she grunted.

"I wasn't a labourer. I worked as a clerk in the mill's office before I got a job in Oslo. Look, Steen sent me and I've got to get out of town before the garrison wakes up." A plump tobacco-stained hand silenced him. "How did you get involved with Steen?"

"The Nazis were going to conscript me, so I did a bunk. I was hiding in a mountain hut when a man came to see me. I think he must have spoken to my friends and found out where I was. When he said the *Linge* would feed me if I worked for them, I jumped at the chance. After I was interrogated, I was taken to meet Steen and he took me on. It's because I used to work in the saw mill and know the layout of the town that he's sent me to you. For Christ's sake, Mrs Helgenstrom, can't we get down to business now?"

She studied him a moment more, then motioned to a flour dusted chair. "The Nazis pay their informers well. Only fools take chances." Drawing out a pack of cigarettes from her dressing gown, she offered it to him. "They're German but beggars can't be choosers. Sit your arse down and tell me what Steen wants."

Relieved by her friendlier tone, he took the match she shared with him and drew in smoke. "He wants to know if there has been any extra enemy activity round here lately. Or if you have noticed anything different in your dealings with the Germans."

Crossing the bakery, the woman flopped down into another chair, her bare mottled legs wide apart. Coughing, she took another drag on her cigarette before answering him. "Yes, there's been some. To start with, the bastards have put up a security fence on the way to the old cutting so no one can find out what they're doing. Then for some weeks now there's been an increase in the number of trucks running up there. People say a few have been carrying heavy equipment."

Eiliv showed interest. "What do you think it means?"

Mrs Helgenstrom shrugged her massive shoulders. "Anything or nothing. It might be they've opened the old quarry again. Or they could he building something and their construction work needs more equipment."

"Has there been any increase in manpower?"

"If men come in, they bring them at night when the curfew's on. But I'm sure there has been."

"Why?"

"Because of the bread I sell the bastards. Their orders have increased by nearly a third in the last two months. Other food shops say the same. So unless the sods are stuffing themselves silly, there must be more of 'em up there."

"You mean at the quarry?"

"Unless they've increased the strength of their town garrison. Folks think there are a few more of 'em strutting about but it still wouldn't account for all that extra food. There's another thing too. We've all been hearing a lot of blasting recently. It's coming from the old tunnel or thereabouts so you'd better mention it to Steen."

Eiliv looked reflective. "Are those the only changes you've noticed?"

The woman's hoarse voice turned sarcastic. "What do you want me to say? That the bloody Jerries are building up a bridge to invade England?" Then her tone changed. "Do you want anything to eat before you start back? You've got time. My helper doesn't start until four-thirty and it'll be another two hours before those sods at the garrison start pissing and scratching themselves."

Eiliv was showing both surprise and amusement at the woman's turn of phrase. "No, Steen wants our reports as quickly as possible, so I'd better start back. But thanks anyway."

Nodding and switching off the light, Mrs Helgenstrom led him to the outer door where she paused before opening it. "Give Grizzly Bear my love and tell the old sod I'll keep my eyes and ears open. I sometimes get Jerry construction workers in here and they're not likely to get suspicious of a fat old woman like me. If I get anything out of them I'll let Neilson in the village know and he'll do what's necessary."

With that, ignoring her thin slippers and the snow outside, she walked out into the darkened passageway and glanced up and down before waving Eiliv to follow her. "It's all quiet but be careful. There's usually a patrol to make certain the curfew's kept. So get out of town as quickly as you can."

Eiliv nodded. "I will. Thanks for your help."

She eyed him a moment, then pulled him towards her and planted a kiss on his lips. "You're my sort of man, lad. I wish we'd time to go to bed together." Then, seeing his startled expression, she gave a low chuckle. "That'll get you moving like nothing else will. So piss off."

Her words brought a grin to his lean face. "You're quite a woman, Mrs Helgenstrom."

"I'm a hell of a lot of woman, lad. I'd eat you alive. Now get off while you can."

He started down the passageway, turning back to wave before disappearing. She waved back, then, with a deep chuckle, re-entered the house and closed the door.

The reindeer hunter's hut, with its snow-covered roof, was hardly visible on the mountainside. Outside a heavily-clothed man was keeping watch, although winter gloom was already beginning to cloak the vast stretches of snow that reached out in all directions. As a rising wind sighed around the hut, the man stamped his feet and moved to the other side for protection.

Inside the hut eight partisans and a woman were grouped around a huge bearded man wearing the uniform of a Norwegian Army captain. Nearly all were smoking and the hut stank of cigarettes, wet clothes, fish-oil and other less definable odours. With the hut's wooden shutters closed, a lamp was providing light and every now and then the wind would find a gap between the moss-filled logs and send its flame flickering.

The furniture was as austere as the hut itself. Two pallet beds were drawn up against either wall, wooden crates served as chairs, and an unlit metal stove was set beneath a stone chimney. A few tools, with axes among them, stood alongside one wall and canvas packs, anoraks, and snow smocks were scattered around the bare wooden floor.

The Norwegian captain, presiding over the group like a sixteenth-century buccaneer, had a voice as fierce as it was loud. "So, except for Eiliv, none of you has anything unusual to report? You're sure about this? You haven't been sitting on your arses and letting the British, the Russians, and the Yanks do all the work for us?"

Men grinned and shook their heads. Some, like Steen Jensen, were wearing uniforms, indicating they were members of the Norwegian *Linge* Movement. Others were dressed as skiers or reindeer hunters. When engaging the common enemy in the mountains or on the high *viddas,* Norwegian freedom fighters chose to use their national uniforms beneath their anoraks and leggings but those acting as agents or saboteurs were forced to dress as civilians so they could merge with the indigenous population. Whatever their dress, most of those in attendance were trimmed down to bone and gristle by the rigours of their life in the inhospitable mountains.

Only one man, thin and wiry with a humorous face, answered the giant as his fierce blue eyes travelled over them. "Maybe the bastards have given it up, Steen. Maybe they're going to surrender as soon as Montgomery cuts off Denmark from Germany."

The giant's eyes challenged him. "There's no evidence of that, is there?"

"No. But what can they do if their communications are cut?"

"They can do a hell of a lot. What about all their submarine pens along our coasts? They can keep on sinking Allied shipping for years. And they can put up a hell of a defence with these mountains to help them. Isn't that what we'd do in their place? We'd make it so bloody expensive that our enemy would cut his losses and give us a better deal."

The wiry man grinned. "Speak for yourselves, Steen. I go for the easy life."

Someone laughed. The giant's hatred of his country's invaders was legendary among Norwegian freedom fighters. Although no one had ever heard him discuss the tragedy, at the beginning of the war his wife and only child had been killed in a bombing raid. From that moment a gentle giant had been transformed into an avenging Nemesis whose one aim was to punish the invaders and drive them from his homeland.

Jensen was scowling. "Stop talking bullshit, Olsen. I hate the Nazis like the devil hates holy water but I have to admit they don't quit easily. Anyway, Germany's still intact and some of their rockets are still raining down on London. Who's to say they won't pull out more secret weapons from the hat? London's told us they've been working on 'em since Christ knows when."

Someone coughed uneasily. "Do you think they've still time left?"

"Of course they have. A new weapon could change the scene overnight. That's why London is asking partisans everywhere to keep their eyes open. They're clever bastards as those V2 rockets have proved."

The woman broke in at this point. She was sitting on one of the pallet beds. Unlike most of the men she was bare-headed, a girl with thick blonde hair, strong features, wide-set eyes and a firm chin. Her voice was low pitched and cultured. "Steen's right. Most of our scientists have that fear. If we hadn't managed to destroy those IMI stocks, they might have already won the war. As it is, there's a belief they're working on at least a dozen secret weapons. We aren't certain what they are but even one of them could make a massive difference to the Allied plans."

Knowing the girl, Helga Lindstrom, was a scientist herself, Olsen treated her words with respect. "But even if it's true, the Allies and the Russians will soon be in Germany itself. So is it likely they'd release a weapon when they'd know they'd pay an even greater price for using it?"

"It would depend on the weapon. If it were powerful enough, like the IMI threat, of course they'd use it, particularly against the Russians. They fear a Russian invasion more than anything, and haven't they every reason to fear it after all they've done to the Russians?"

As a silence fell, Jensen addressed the group again.

"People are getting the impression the war's nearly over but remember we haven't crossed the German frontiers yet. And they've still got a firm grip on us and Denmark. If I know anything about the bastards, they'll hang on and fight to the end." He glanced at Eiliv who was standing behind one of the pallet beds. "What about this news Eiliv's brought us? Does that sound as if they intend to quit?"

Olsen was not convinced yet. "You can't be sure it's a blockhouse or fort they're building. Didn't the old woman say they've blocked the road so that no one can get past and see what they're doing? Maybe they've just opened the quarry again."

"Why would they need all that security for the quarry?" Jensen demanded. "They're up to something and ten to one it's a fortification of some kind. Which can only mean they intend to stay here no matter what happens."

Olsen shrugged. "One swallow doesn't make a summer, Steen. I'd need to see 'em building a lot more blockhouses before I'd be sure they're staying on."

Jensen gave his fierce, bloodthirsty grin. "So they're not building a blockhouse and they're not building any secret weapons. So they intend to run like rabbits as soon as Berlin falls. What difference does it make? They're still here and, while they are, we harass the sods every second of every day in every way we can. Isn't that right?"

As the group of men laughed and shouted their assent, Olsen grinned back. "I never suggested we didn't bite their arses, Steen. That's a different ball game altogether."

"All right, then keep all your groups active and keep on looking for anything out of the ordinary. London doesn't usually ask questions without a reason. If you hear anything suspicious, let me know at once." As the men nodded and began picking up their skis and clothing, Jensen ended with a warning. "Tell your men to keep their eyes open when they're operating in the mountains. The bastards have brought more of their Austrian ski troops over and they're good. All right. Off you go before it gets too dark."

As the men picked up their packs and began filing outside, Steen glanced at a small man with an unsightly cluster of warts on one side of his nose who was about to pick up a portable radio. "Stay behind, Arne. I want you to send a message to London." His eyes moved to the girl. "As for you, I'm not letting you roam around the mountains on your own. I've got a safe billet for you tonight."

The girl laughed. "Since when have I needed protection?"

"You take too many chances as it is," the giant grumbled. "Don't argue," he went on fiercely as the girl started to speak. "You had to come a long way and I know you haven't eaten since this morning. So do as you're told."

Helga laughed and gave him a mock salute. "Yes, sir. Very good, sir. Just as you say, sir."

The giant's white teeth showed through his thick beard. "That's better. In another minute you'd have gone across my knee." He turned to the waiting Arne. "You got a pencil and paper?" When the man nodded, the giant cleared his throat. "Then this is what you send to London."

Chapter 8

Gabb yawned. "God, I'm bored."

Millburn raised his head. "I thought you told me this was going to be a picnic?"

Gabby scowled. "I didn't know we were coming to a place full of snobs and jokers, did I?"

"You're lucky, boyo. You might be in a place full of bloodthirsty matelots."

The two men were lying on their beds in a cubicle in the permanent brick-built quarters of Leconfield. Eight days had passed since their arrival but with a depression centred over the British Isles, they had been given no chance to intercept and attack the JU86.

Their inactivity had not made them popular among the Halifax aircrews who in spite of the weather were flying combat missions almost nightly. Some wit had dubbed them "Wingless Wonders" and the expression had been picked up gleefully by the rest of the crews. Although at first Millburn had taken the nickname with good humour, the days of inactivity had finally taken their toll. The previous day a Canadian navigator, whom Millburn had disliked on first sight, had used the expression once too often in the Mess and the aggressive American had put him on the floor. The result had been a verbal reprimand from the Adjutant and a further division between the 633 men and the local aircrews.

It would not have been Gabby if he hadn't pointed this out to Millburn. "You didn't make things any better for us yesterday, did you? Weren't we unpopular enough?"

"What the hell was I supposed to do?" Millburn retorted. "Pin a medal on him? Anyway, what about your performance last Friday? That didn't exactly put us on top of the popularity poll, did it?"

He was referring to the only social function the two men had attended since their arrival. The previous week, with rain washing out operations, a dance had been hastily organised in the officers' Mess and hospitality had demanded the two visitors were invited. Hospitality, however, had ceased when the small local dance band had struck its first notes. With only a modicum of single, attractive girls present, the Leconfield men had made certain that none strayed from her orbit. Whenever Millburn or Gabby made for a pretty girl, his route would be quickly intercepted or his target whisked away. With Gabby's hormones at an all time high because of his enforced celibacy, his frustration had grown as the night had worn on. Finally, it had snapped when, after half a dozen abortive efforts, he had managed to reach a buxom blonde. With a penchant for buxom blondes, Gabby had been leading her triumphantly to the dance floor when a large hand had spun him round to face a huge, grinning Australian pilot. "Sorry, flying arsehole, but she's ours. Any case, you aren't big enough for a real woman."

With half a dozen gins inside Gabby, the outcome had been totally predictable. Taking a swing at the Australian's face and finding it out of reach, Gabby had kicked him on the shins. As the man gave a howl and the girl a scream, Millburn had run forward and grabbed at the truculent Welshman. "What the hell are you doing? The bloody CO's here."

It had taken all Millburn's considerable strength to drag Gabby from the floor and back to their billet. Reminded now about the incident, Gabby's complaints changed direction. "You know your trouble? It's that bloody ferry pilot. You've shown no interest in women ever since she flew that kite in."

"Don't talk bullshit. A blind man could have seen that all the women were spoken for."

"Then why did they invite us?"

Millburn shrugged. "To rub it in, I suppose. They're jealous of Mosquito crews and they think we've got a cushy number. Come to think of it, they're right. We'll probably be here for Christmas."

Gabby groaned. "Christmas! Can't we do anything? Tell Davies we've shot the bloody thing down or something?"

"Stop waffling and give me a cigarette. I smoked my last one ten minutes ago."

Gabby rolled over on his bed. As he tried to reach his tunic there was a tearing sound. Millburn stared at him. "What was that?"

Gabby was feeling the back of his trousers. "It's my slacks. I've torn the seam."

Millburn grinned. "You're getting fat, boyo. It's all this sitting around on your arse and doing nothing."

Gabby stood up and turned his backside to the American. "How bad is it?"

Millburn chortled. "It's bad. Four inches bad. If you were back at Sutton Craddock, Gwen Thomas would have her hand up there. But you're safe enough here, boyo."

Gabby had picked up a mirror and was trying to view the damage. "These are the only pair I've got. I left my best pair back at the station."

"Then you'll have to wear 'em, won't you? The guys in the mess are going to have another laugh on us. One of the Wingless Wonders splits his pants while sitting on his arse. You're in for a happy dinner, boyo."

Gabby was showing dismay. "Where do you get repairs done?"

"I don't know. The clothing store, I suppose. Don't they keep a tailor to make adjustments to uniforms?"

Gabby presented his backside again. "Can I walk over like this?"

"Only if you keep your cheeks together. You'd better take short steps too. One or two of that Halifax bunch look a bit suspect to me."

"What about lending me yours while I go over?"

The grinning Millburn shook his head. "Oh, no. A guy who can't look after his trousers isn't wearing mine. You tore yours, you wear 'em."

"You're a bastard, Millburn. A bastard through and through."

"I am, kid. I'm such a bastard I'm not letting a short ass like you drag my pants through the mud."

"I'll keep 'em hitched up, Millburn. I promise."

"No. Get over there before dinner but keep away from the WAAFs. This lot are so prim they might report you for indecency."

Muttering his disgust and giving Millburn a final glare, Gabby threw on his greatcoat and marched out. On his return three quarters of an hour later, his mood had clearly changed. Hearing him whistling beneath his breath, Millburn laid down his book. "What's happened? Are you sewn up again?"

Gabby nodded. "Yes. Everything's fine."

"Why are you looking so smug?"

Still whistling, Gabby threw himself back on his bed. "Everything went well, that's all."

"C'mon. I've seen that expression before. You've got some good news, haven't you? Or else you're up to something."

"Can't a man whistle without he's up to something?"

"Not you. You were in one of your Welsh moods when you went out. Is it a WAAF?"

Gabby smirked. "It might be."

"What do you mean, it might be? Stop farting about and come clean."

"What's it to you, Millburn? You don't share your girls with me?"

Millburn grinned. "I shared Susan with you, didn't I?" Gabby's face darkened at the memory. "That was a foul trick, Millburn. You've done some rotten things to me, but that was the worst."

"OK, kid, I'm sorry. Now tell me what's happened."

Gabby, who secretly wanted Millburn's participation, pretended to hesitate. "I can't see the point. Not with you head over heels for that ferry pilot."

Millburn was growing impatient. "Stop clowning around and get on with it."

"It'll cost you money if you come in with me," Gabby warned."

"Why?"

"Because I've had to pay out a couple of quid myself."

"Who to?"

"The Flight Sergeant in charge of the clothing store. He was in my flight at Wilmslow."

"So?"

"We got to know each other quite well there because we were both chasing the same girl."

"What — with little legs like yours?"

Gabby smirked. "Little legs or not, I still won."

"Why? Was her sight bad?"

"No, it wasn't. She was gorgeous."

"So why does this guy want to help you?"

"For old time's sake, I suppose. We aren't all like you, Millburn. Some people forgive and forget. When I told him how things were for us here, he said he'd help us out for a couple of quid."

"I can see now why the two of you were friends," the American muttered.

Gabby ignored the gibe. "It seems he knows four girls in Hull who are friends and fond of airmen. So when I gave him the two quid he said he'd get in touch with them and fix up a date for us."

"Did he give you their address?"

"Yes, I've got it here." The Welshman pulled out a slip of paper and handed it to Millburn. "It's in a street off Hessle Road. That's one of Hull's main roads."

Millburn handed the paper back. "Are you taking it on?"

"Of course I am. Why? Aren't you coming?"

Millburn shrugged. "I'm not that keen. You go and tell me what happens."

The Welshman, who wanted the use of Millburn's car, was showing dismay. "You've got to come. I lashed out two quid to get that address. What's the matter with you? Can't you forget that girl Carol for one night?"

"It's nothing to do with her. I just don't like blind dates, that's all."

Gabby, who knew his man well, fell back on cunning. "Don't give me that. Millburn. She's made putty out of you. It stands out a mile."

Millburn frowned. "Belt up, you little fart. I keep telling you — there's nothing between us. Carol's just a nice kid, that's all."

"Then prove it and come to see these girls. It could be a great evening."

Frowning, Millburn took back the piece of paper. "When's the guy going to fix up this date?"

Gabby relaxed. "As soon as he can. I told him to do it before the weather clears. Tomorrow night if possible."

Millburn sank back on his bed. "I suppose I'd better go or four of 'em might eat you alive. Now drop it and let me get back to my book."

Gabby hesitated, then took the plunge. "There is just one thing else. Sammy says we ought to change our uniforms."

Millburn sat up on his elbows. "Change our uniforms? What the hell for?"

"Sammy says they're a bit stuffy on this station about officers who go out womanising. So he feels we ought to go in non-commissioned uniforms. He'll lend us two for the night."

Millburn showed instant suspicion. "Since when has the RAF stopped a guy having a woman? He's pulling your leg, you Welsh twit. Forget the whole thing. The guy's making a monkey out of you."

Afraid he had blown it, Gabby made a vigorous protest. "No! Sammy says it has to do with this camp once being a permanent peacetime RAF station. It's kept up the old bullshit about all officers being gentlemen. That's why they were so stuffy at the dance last week." Seeing Millburn was still unconvinced, Gabby added a cunning caveat. "You must know the upper-class English by this time, boyo. They love to pretend they're different from the rest of us."

Millburn's suspicious frown slowly cleared. "Yeah. They are a tight-arsed lot. What uniforms do we get?"

"Sammy found a sergeant's tunic for me and he thinks he's got a corporal's for you."

"You out-ranking me? You're kidding."

Gabby's innocence shone like a beacon. "I couldn't help it. The sergeant's uniform was the only one that fitted me."

Grinning, Millburn leaned forward and prodded Gabby in the stomach. "Let's get one thing clear right now. If you think you're getting your own back on me by using your extra stripe, forget it. Or I'll bounce you right into that big River Humber."

Gabby looked hurt. "You ought to work on that suspicious mind of yours, Millburn. It could bring you a lot of unhappiness one day."

Millburn settled back on his bed. "I'll take my chance on that, boyo. Right now it's the only protection I've got against sneaky little Welshmen who'll do anything for a bit of nookie. So you watch it tomorrow."

The army captain knocked on the library door and then opened it. "Air Commodore Davies is here, sir."

Brigadier Simms, bending over a box of files, turned and saw Davies entering the library. "Hello, Davies. It's good of you to call round."

Davies, wearing his greatcoat and cap, saluted and then walked forward to take the soldier's outstretched hand. "Hello, sir. I had to pass this way today, so thought it would give us a chance to catch up on our news."

"A splendid idea. Can I get you a cup of coffee?"

Removing his cap, Davies shook his head. "I can't stay long. I just wanted to find out if you'd any news from your agents. I'm afraid there isn't a thing from my end."

Simms glanced at the French windows against which rain was beating. "I guessed your two boys would be grounded. I suppose our one consolation is that the enemy can't have been doing any reconnaissances either."

"Not a chance," Davies said. He hesitated, then went on: "I hope things break soon, sir. I can hardly go on keeping my acting squadron commander and his navigator plus a serviceable combat aircraft out of action indefinitely."

Simms, who had been expecting the complaint, sighed. "I wish it wasn't necessary, Davies. But our Lords and Master seem very concerned about this German surveillance."

Davies frowned. "Now I've had the time to think about it, I don't see why. It can't be because of Russian convoys, not now the

Russians are driving into Finland and northern Norway. So what's all the fuss about? And why have my men been posted so far south?"

"I wish I could tell you, Davies. But I don't think London knows yet what is going on. That's why I was instructed to contact our agents in Norway and Denmark. And why London wants these spy flights terminated. Until we can find out more, they feel we must play safe and do all we can to upset the enemy's plans."

"But you do feel this reconnaissance has something to do with shipping, don't you?"

"I can't see what other reason it can have. Although we are puzzled why the enemy seems to be concerned only with eastern ports."

"Could it have anything to do with submarines?"

"I suppose it's possible. But I have the impression London is more concerned about the secret weapons the enemy is developing and wondering if there is any connection."

Davies frowned. "What sort of weapon other than submarines could threaten our shipping?"

Simms raised his slim shoulders. "What else but aircraft could threaten London and yet look what the V2s are doing to it."

Davies took the point. "What about your agents? Have they come up with anything yet?"

"Only one thing," Simms told him. "And on the surface it seems to have nothing to do with our secret weapon fear. Steen Jensen sent us news of it two days ago. You remember him, the big *Linge* partisan?"

Davies had every reason to remember the giant Norwegian. "Yes, he helped us during Operation Valkyrie. If I remember right, he hates Nazis like a mule hates horseflies. So he's still alive?"

"Very much so. He controls a number of cells along the western coast. He's received a report that the Germans might be building a fort or blockhouse in or around an old quarry near Rosvik. From our point of view a fort would pose no threat but as they've sealed off the area, Steen has promised to keep an eye on it and report back."

Davies grimaced. "A fort must mean Jerry intends hanging on to Norway."

"It might if it is a fort. That's the question."

The Brigadier's tone made Davies lift an eyebrow. "What else could it be in a place like that?"

"We don't know. It's the security measures that are puzzling us. One wouldn't have thought such precautions were necessary for a mere strongpoint."

With something tangible emerging at last, Davies became his old positive self. "There's one way to find out. I'll get Benson to send a recce plane over. A few photographs should clear it up one way or the other."

The Brigadier considered the offer for a moment. "I wouldn't want to alert them if it was something important. Could your pilot make it look as if he were just flying over the valley towards another target?"

Davies nodded. "That's no problem. Benson is used to tricks like that. In any case they'll fly at high level. Where is Rosvik?"

Simms opened a drawer in the big mahogany table and pulled out a large map of Norway. Spreading it out, he laid a finger on a fjord on the western coast. "This is the Nelsfjord. Rosvik's a small town in a steep valley that runs a couple of miles parallel to it. Its only industries are forestry and a timber mill. But it did have a quarry once under this mountain, Helsberg. As you see, the road ends there. Because of this, it's been easy for the enemy to seal off the road between the town and the quarry without totally destroying the town's economy."

Davies was studying the map. "It's an odd place to build a fort, isn't it?"

"Not altogether," Simms told him. "The map doesn't show it but there is a road cutting and tunnel through the northern flanking mountain to a couple of jetties on the fjord. Before the war the Norwegians used it to transport timber and stone to barges on the fjord but blew up the tunnel in 1940 to prevent the Germans landing troops there. This forced the closure of the quarry and means timber has to be transported back along the road to Lillestad on the coast, an expensive process that might have put the town out of business had not the German work force and garrison provided some relief."

Davies glanced at him. "How big is their work force?"

"According to the Norwegians, it has been strengthened recently. At first they thought the extra men were brought in to open the cutting and tunnel to the fjord. It made sense that the enemy wanted to ship timber to Germany via the fjord. But since the war has gone against the Germans, the Norwegians are wondering if they're building a fort to prevent the Allies putting an invasion force through the cutting."

Davies was looking more puzzled than ever. "But why go to all the trouble of building a fort? Wouldn't it be far easier to blow up the tunnel again?"

Simms smiled. "You've hit the nail on the head, Davies. Why bring in more workers when a simple demolition charge would do the trick? That's why London is showing interest in Rosvik since Steen drew it to their attention. So, yes, I would appreciate your offer to have the site photographed, providing it can be done without making the enemy suspicious."

Davies picked his cap from the table. "It's a pity Millburn and Gabby aren't available. They'd be ideal men for the job. But don't worry. I'll brief Benson personally and stress the importance of secrecy. I'll be in touch as soon as the photographs are ready."

Chapter 9

Millburn drove his car down the side street and pulled in at the kerb. "Get out and look for the place," he told Gabby. "I can't read the numbers in this goddamned blackout."

Gabby returned a minute later. "It's further up the road. Leave the car there. It's only a few houses away."

Millburn followed him along the street. In the light of a waxing moon, he could see small unkempt front gardens with rows of semi-detached houses behind them. In the silence both men could hear the clank of cranes and the mournful wail of sirens from the docks. Like every other port in Britain, Hull was working night and day to win a war that seemed to have lasted for ages.

Millburn frowned as Gabby paused outside one of the featureless houses. "You're sure that's it? It seems quiet to me."

"What do you expect?" Gabby demanded. "A brass band and a row of dancing girls?"

"I expected something different to this. You sure that guy Sammy hasn't pulled your leg and sent us to an old ladies' home?"

"It's that bloody ferry pilot again, isn't it?" Gabby complained. "You've done nothing but find fault with everything I've done since you met her. Are you coming or not?"

Millburn eyed the shabby house and its equally shabby neighbours, then sighed. "Let's get it over."

He followed the Welshman to the front garden whose one-time iron railings had long been taken for the war effort. Crossing a broken concrete path, Gabby reached the house and paused. "Only a moment now, Millburn. And then it's girls, girls, girls."

"Stop gloating, you randy tom cat, and let's get inside. It's charpy out here."

Thirty seconds passed while Gabby fumbled at the door. Millburn stared at him. "What the hell are you doing?"

"I can't find a bell push," Gabby complained.

"Isn't there a knocker?"

"No, there isn't."

"Then rattle the letter box or something."

Finding a metal flap, Gabby lifted it, only to pause and turn triumphantly to Millburn. "Does that sound like an old ladies' home?"

Bending down, Millburn could hear swing music issuing from the house. He grinned at Gabby. "Maybe the old dears like Benny Goodman. Let's find out." Rattling the metal flap a few times, he then rapped his knuckles on the door. A few seconds later the door swung open and the two men saw the figure of a girl silhouetted against the muted light of a small hall. Her voice, slightly strident, had a strong local accent. "Yes. What d'you want?"

"Sammy sent us," Gabby told her. "Sammy from Leconfield."

The girl's voice cleared "Oh, yeh. Someone called Gabby and an American. Then yer'd better come in. Hurry up. We've got a right keen warden down this street."

Nudging Millburn's arm, Gabby led the American into the hall. The girl closed the door, then switched on the light. "Which wun of you is which?"

The two men saw there was a staircase at the back of the hall and a door on the left. The girl who had admitted them was tall, slimly built, and somewhat flashily dressed. Her features were not unattractive although they were half hidden by her Veronica Lake hair style which swept her blonde hair forward across her face. "I'm Gabby," the Welshman told her. "He's the Yank."

The girl's eyes ran with some favour over the tall, good looking American. "I'm Sandra. Tek your coats off and then come and meet the rest of the girls."

During this time the sound of Benny Goodman had grown louder. Turning after hanging their coats and caps on an old fashioned hall stand, the men saw three other girls, laughing and

71

tittering, crowded into the doorway. Sandra turned towards them. "All right. Don't panic. I'm bringing 'em in."

She led the way into a small sitting room where a hand-wound gramophone was playing records and waved a hand at the girls. "That's Betty, that's Joan, and that's Alison. This is Gabby and Tommy Millburn."

At that moment the Benny Goodman record finished and Gabby heard a low, disappointed voice. "I thought they'd be airmen. Real airmen, I mean."

Touched to the quick, Gabby responded without thinking. "What do you mean — real airmen? We are real airmen. We're ..." His indignant voice broke off as Millburn trod on his foot. "We're indispensable," he finished, somewhat lamely.

"Where are your brevets, then?" The questioner was Betty, a small neat brunette whose voice hinted at a better education than Sandra's.

Gabby sought and found an impressive reply. "We're gunners. We defend airfields against air attacks. Without us there wouldn't be any aircraft to fly."

Seeing a couple of the girls were looking impressed, Gabby went to gild the lily. "We shot a Jerry aircraft down only last week."

Betty, the original disappointed one, looked sceptical. "..I didn't think there were many German aircraft over the country these days."

"You don't know much about the Jerries and the RAF, do you?"

"No, we don't get many of you Brylcream boys around here. But we know how the air raids have fallen away and we can also read the newspapers."

Gabby was up to that. "That's what they tell you civilians. It's to keep your morale up. We in the services know better."

"That's not what Sandra's cousin, Sammy, tells her. He says things have been quiet over the country lately."

Gabby sniffed. "That's because Sammy's at Leconfield. Jerry's not interested in their bloody Halifaxes. Where Millburn and I come from, it's action twenty four hours a day."

"Where do you come from, Gabby?" The question came from Joan, a tall fair girl wearing a tight white sweater that

72

accentuated her large breasts. With the Welshman favouring girls of generous proportions, his eyes had picked her out from the moment they entered the room. But before he could reply, Millburn decided it was time to intervene. "We're not allowed to tell you that. It's a bit hush hush."

Alison, a small girl with a mass of curly black hair and the youngest of the four, was looking impressed. "You're an American, aren't you?"

"Yes, I am."

"Why aren't you in the American Forces?"

Millburn grinned. "I thought you Limeys needed a bit of know how. So I joined up before the Yanks entered the war."

Betty, the cynic, gave a disparaging sniff. "And you're still only a corporal. You haven't got very far, have you?"

Millburn grinned again. "That's just Limey jealousy. They prefer to give promotion to cocky little Welshmen and snooty Englishmen."

With his eyes on the Junoesque Joan, Gabby was taking no nonsense from Millburn. "Why don't you tell the truth, Millburn?" His eyes moved back to the big blonde. "It's his eyesight. He can't hit a barn door from ten yards." Seeing Millburn's expression, Gabby decided he might have gone too far. "But he's a nice guy just the same."

"If he's got bad eyesight, how can he be a gunner? And why doesn't he wear glasses?" It was the indefatigable Betty again.

Gabby nodded. "You might well ask. It's because I do the shooting and he loads the guns. The rest's pride. Just pride." Hearing heavy breathing from Millburn, his eyes moved back to Joan. "Anyway, why are we talking so much? Why don't we have a drink?" Slipping his hand into his battledress pocket, he pulled out two half bottles of Scotch and set them down on the table alongside the portable gramophone.

Sandra gave a whistle, then turned to the delighted girls. "C'mon. Help me to find glasses."

As the chattering quartet vanished into the kitchen, Millburn turned to the Welshman. "Where the hell did you get that whisky?"

73

Grinning, Gabby laid a finger alongside his nose. "No questions, no pack drill, Millburn. I want the big blonde, Joan. What about you?"

Millburn frowned, then lowered his voice. "I don't get this set-up. Why do three of them speak differently to Sandra? It looks too much like a brothel to me, with Sandra the madam. Maybe I'll sit it out for a while."

"It's that bloody ferry pilot again, isn't it?" As Millburn scowled, Gabby held up a contrite hand. "All right. You do as you like. But how about being a buddy and put in a few words for me with the blonde?"

"The way you've done for me? Like my eyesight?"

"That was just for laughs, Millburn. It's more serious business now."

Millburn grinned. "What do you want me to tell her? That you're the greatest stud since Casanova."

"It wouldn't do any harm, would it? Be a pal, Millburn. I'm dying for a bit of nookie."

"Why can't you do your own dirty work?"

"If you hadn't gone off women, I'd do it for you, Millburn."

Laughter was issuing from the kitchen as they spoke. Wondering what was being discussed, Millburn turned back to Gabby. "Like you've done in the past? You sonofabitch, you've tried to two-time me with every girl we've ever met."

"This is different, Millburn. You've got three others to choose from. So don't be mean."

"What if I fancy the big blonde too? What will you do then?"

Before Gabby could answer, the four girls were filing back and handing their glasses to Gabby. Pouring whisky into them, Gabby made certain he gave Joan the largest dram. As the girls began clustering around Millburn, Gabby drew the blonde aside and sat with her on a sofa. "You know something? You're just my kind of girl. Why haven't we met before?"

Joan, whose giggles suggested she was not Mensa material, gave another titter. "What is your kind of girl, Gabby?"

Emboldened by the reply, Gabby glanced down at her chest and drew two semi-circles with his hands. "I like big girls. You know, like this."

She tittered again. "You oughtn't to say such things."

"Why not?"

"It's naughty, that's why."

Gabby grinned. "Naughty but nice." With the big girl close to him on the sofa and exuding sex like strong perfume, the Welshman was finding his itch growing by the minute. He gazed round the small room. "Isn't there somewhere we can go to be quiet? What about your room?"

"I don't sleep here."

"Where do you sleep?"

"I sleep at home. But we can't go there."

"Why not?"

Before the girl could reply, Millburn's voice came above the chatter of the girls surrounding him. "Hey, Gabby. Remember that promise you made and take it easy."

Joan turned to the Welshman. "What does he mean?"

Not sure himself, Gabby threw back a non-committal reply. "Mind your own business, corporal."

Millburn's voice came back at him. "C'mon, sergeant. You asked me to remind you the next time you chatted up a girl."

The three girls surrounding the American were full of curiosity now. "Remind him of what?" Sandra asked.

"To let girls know his nickname's the Swansea Stallion. It's to warn 'em, you see. Isn't a guy like that really something?"

All the girls were staring at Gabby now and Joan's eyes were huge. "Do they really call you that? A stallion?"

Unable to decide whether the American had done him a favour or a mischief, Gabby prevaricated. "Don't take any notice of him. You know the stupid nicknames service men give one another."

Joan gave a small shiver. "But there must be reason for a nickname like that. And why did you ask Tommy to let girls know?"

Still unsure of her reaction, Gabby decided modesty was his best policy. "I don't remember. I must have had too much to drink. Anyway, it's all a load of rubbish."

Her knee touched his own as she spoke. "What happened? It seems such a funny thing to ask Tommy to do."

Seeing the other girls staring at him with interest and Joan's well endowed sweater brushing provocatively against his shoulder,

Gabby knew beyond any doubt that he owed Millburn a favour. His confidence returned along with his itch. "Never mind about that. What about that room? Won't one of the girls here lend you one?"

"I suppose I could ask Sandra. She lives here."

As their legs touched again. Gabby's voice turned hoarse. "Then hurry up and ask her."

Joan ran across and spoke into Sandra's ear. Sandra gave a strident laugh and pointed at the door that led into the hall. "Yes. Tek him upstairs and see if the lad deserves his nickname."

With whisky having taken its toll, the other two girls shouted encouragement. Too eager to feel embarrassed, Gabby followed the girl up the stairs to a small landing with a blacked out window and three doors. Seeing Joan open the far door, Gabby followed her into a small bedroom. It was full of old mahogany furniture but Gabby saw only the large double bed. Grabbing Joan's hand, he drew the girl towards it. "Sit down, love, and tell me how you got this figure of yours. I've never seen anything like it."

She gave an embarrassed titter as she sank down beside him. "What's so special about my figure?"

Gabby gazed down at her chest. "It's sensational, love. Hasn't anyone told you that before?" When she tittered, he slipped a hand down her back and began easing the sweater upwards.

She offered token resistance. "You mustn't, Gabby. It's naughty. And anyway it's too cold."

Gabby was feeling anything but cold as his hand slipped up higher and came into contact with smooth warm skin. "I'm just looking, love. There's no harm in that, is there?"

It seemed Joan decided there was not because after a couple of seconds her arms lifted, allowing Gabby to pull the sweater over her head. Goggle-eyed at the sights that appeared, Gabby tried to cup one huge breast in his hand while he sought to unfasten her overloaded bra with the other.

The girl's struggles were as much to aid him as to hinder him. "What are you doing? You're choking me."

"The bloody strap's too tight," Gabby panted.

Her arms were going back to help him when Gabby's patience ran out. Clutching the bottom of the bra, he heaved it upwards, bringing a gasp from the girl. "What are you doing? Go steady."

Gabby was too far gone for advice as two huge breasts heaved out and quivered before him. Fondling them and burying his face between them, he tried at the same time to remove her skirt.

The result was a tangle of arms and legs as the two of them fell back on the bed, each one struggling to unbutton the skirt. Success came when the girl pushed the panting Gabby back and did the task herself. Seeing she had only panties on beneath the skirt, Gabby flung himself back and in seconds her last garment slid to the floor.

With eyes glowing like star shells, Gabby hurled his tunic away, tore off his boots, yanked off his slacks, and launched himself on top of the girl. It was only when she moaned and moved to receive him that he realised that in the heat of his libido he had forgotten to remove his underpants.

Rolling off Joan, he yanked the guilty underpants down to his knees. He would have settled for that if the tight garment had not pinned his legs together and prevented his climbing on the girl again. Cursing, he rolled back once more and began tugging and kicking while the aroused Joan stared at him in bewilderment. "What on earth are you doing?"

With his heart pounding like a trip hammer, Gabby decided it was not a question that called for a reply. Clad only in his socks now, he threw himself back on the pulsating Joan. As he kissed her neck and slid down to her breasts, she gave a moan and slid her hands down to his buttocks. As Gabby prepared to enter nirvana, she suddenly stiffened. "What's that? Listen!"

With his face buried between her lush breasts, Gabby was beyond listening or even hearing. Bracing his feet on the floor, he pushed upwards and felt the girl's nails dig sharply into his back. As he thrust again and again, the girl's nubile body began to move in unison and the creaking of the bed filled the room. It was only when distant, raucous laughter sounded that the girl stiffened again. "It's them," she panted. "They've come tonight instead of tomorrow."

Gabby had no idea what she was talking about. With nirvana's greatest joy close upon him, nothing was going to rob him of victory be it Genghis Kahn or Ivan the Terrible. "Relax, love," he gasped. "Relax and enjoy yourself."

For a few seconds Joan obeyed and the creaking of the bed began again. Then it happened. The door crashed open and a familiar voice hurled icy water over the entwined couple. "Gabby! The bloody Navy's here. Get dressed."

Joan let out a scream at Millburn's appearance and grabbed a blanket to cover herself. As she was bigger than Gabby, her convulsive movement shot the Welshman out of nirvana like a cork from a bottle. Rolling over on the bed he stared with dazed eyes at Millburn. "What's going on? What's happened?"

Millburn had their greatcoats in his arms. "The Navy's here, that's what's happened." His voice rose as Gabby stared at him. "What're you waiting for, you moron? Move!"

Gabby, pitched from paradise to purgatory in one cruel moment, was still floundering. "What's the Navy doing here?"

"They're here because we've been conned by that bloody friend of yours, that's why." Grabbing Gabby's clothes from the floor, Millburn threw them at him. "Move it or they'll make meatballs of us."

Realising his danger at last, Gabby began dragging on his trousers and boots. As he reached for his shirt and tunic, Millburn jerked them away and tossed him his overcoat. "You haven't time for them. Just put that on.

As Millburn climbed into his own greatcoat, Joan, who had been watching their antics with astonishment, broke in at last. "What's the matter? The Navy boys are friends of ours. Only we didn't expect them tonight."

A loud burst of laughter downstairs checked Millburn's reply. Instead he grabbed Gabby's arm. "They don't know we're here yet. So we've still got a chance."

With black memories of the Navy, Gabby was showing panic now. He turned to the shivering Joan who had the blanket tucked up under her chin. "What are they? Men or officers."

"I don't know what you mean. Of course they're men."

Groaning, Gabby jabbed at the stripes on his greatcoat. "I mean are they sailors? Non-commissioned sailors. Not bloody officers," he hissed as the bewildered girl stared at him.

"They're all sorts but I don't think any of them are officers."

Gabby showed relief as he turned back to Millburn. "Then we're all right. They won't dare to attack officers."

Millburn showed his disgust. "Are you kidding? What about that big matelot who wanted to eat you for breakfast at Scarborough. Anyway, who's going to believe we're officers? That bloody Sammy of yours took care of that, didn't he?"

Gabby looked faint. "I'd forgotten that. What are we going to do, Millburn?"

The American went to the window, pulled back the blackout blind, and gazed out. He shook his head at Gabby. "No way down there." He turned to the frightened Joan. "Are there any outhouses? Something we can jump down on?"

"I don't know. I've never been outside."

Millburn grabbed Gabby's arm. "Let's try the other windows."

They ran out, leaving the bewildered Joan collecting her scattered clothing. On the landing the noises of the drunken intruders in the sitting room was at least two decibels louder. As Millburn threw open the other two doors, revealing a bathroom and another bedroom, Gabby peered down the stairs and saw the dimly-lit hall was empty. "I don't get it. If Sammy's framed us, why haven't the girls told 'em we're here?"

Finding no escape route from the bathroom, Millburn was making for the landing window. "The girls didn't know the Navy were coming. When we heard the transport, I asked 'em to keep quiet and they said they would." Then, seeing Gabby was looking as frozen as a rabbit threatened by a stoat, his tone changed. "Don't just stand there! Do something!"

Gabby was still finding the transition from bliss to adversity hard to handle. About to join the American at the window, he gave a start. "There's one of our caps, Millburn. On the stairs."

Slapping his greatcoat pocket, Millburn realised it was his own and cursed. About to creep down the stairs to collect it, he changed his mind. "They'll be coming up here sooner or later, if only for a pee. There's an outhouse below this window. That's our way out."

Peering from the landing window, Gabby could see a dark sloping roof directly below. He sounded faint again. "You mean we have to jump down?"

"No, we fly down, you moron," Millburn hissed. "Help me to open the window."

To Millburn's relief the lower pane slid upwards, although not without an effort from both men. As an icy wind blew in, a timid voice made both men start and turn, to see Joan had emerged from the bedroom. "Shall I go down?"

"You got a friend among them?" Millburn asked. When the girl nodded, he went on: "Then you'd better go or he might come up looking for you. But look natural. OK?"

Looking anything but natural, Joan nodded, then turned to Gabby. "Goodbye, Gabby. Be careful."

The Welshman's eyes followed her as she walked unsteadily down the stairs. Reading his mind, Millburn jerked his arm. "Stop thinking about it and get out of that window. Or it'll be the last bit of nookie you never had. Are you listening?"

Below, the decibels of raucous shouts and laughter rose to new levels as the sitting room door opened and closed. Reminded again of their peril, Gabby swung his legs over the window sill, only to pause as he gazed down at the slate roof below. "It's a hell of a way down, Millburn. I'll break my leg again, for sure."

"You'll have more than your leg broken if you don't," Millburn hissed. "There must be a dozen of the bastards down there."

Between Scylla and Charybdis, Gabby dithered. Then, as Millburn was about to take desperate measure and push him out, the decibel count soared again. As heavy footsteps sounded on the stairs, Millburn swung round on Gabby. "One of the sods is coming for a pee! Jump!"

Below the footsteps paused for a moment. Then a yell came that lifted the hairs on Gabby's neck. "Hey! Come and look at this, you guys! There's a bloody RAF cap here."

Knowing their cover was blown, Millburn gave a loud yell. "Gabby! Go!"

Closing his eyes, Gabby slid from the window and disappeared with a howl into the night. Hearing footsteps pounding up the stairs, Millburn knew a desperate delaying action was necessary. Running to the head of the stairs he saw a huge tattooed matelot with a flattened nose and thick beard pause to goggle at him while below the hall filled with his astonished shipmates. At the sight of Millburn's uniform a bloodthirsty howl broke out as if an enemy submarine had been sighted. The first sailor's grin was a mixture of disbelief and unholy pleasure. Spitting into his hands and hitching up his bell bottoms, he let out a joyous howl and came bounding up the stairs like Bluebeard attacking a merchantman.

With only seconds to act, Millburn grabbed the head of the balustrade and swung up a leg. As his foot caught Bluebeard in the middle of his chest, he kicked out with all his strength. Caught by surprise, the massive sailor toppled backwards and crashed into the men following behind him. As they fell down the stairs in a cursing tangle of arms and legs, Millburn ran to the window, swung out his legs, and jumped.

He had a momentary sensation of icy air on his face, then his feet crashed down on the roof below. His momentum slid him forward along the sloping roof and, accompanied by the clatter of broken slates, he dropped another seven feet to the shadowy ground.

He found Gabby groaning and nursing his leg. "I think I've broken my ankle, Millburn."

In the window above heads were appearing, followed by bloodthirsty cries. Seeing one sailor already swinging a leg out, Millburn grabbed the Welshman's arm. "Forget your ankle and get out of here. They'll be coming from all sides soon."

With the small garden untended and unkempt, the two panting men had to fight through prickly bushes and unseen obstacles before they reached a low wooden fence. Finding its gate locked and hearing a clatter of slates behind them, Millburn heaved the groaning Gabby over the fence into a narrow alley and then vaulted over himself. Panting hard, he pushed Gabby forward. "Keep going! We've gotta reach the car."

"My bloody ankle's killing me, Millburn."

"Sod your ankle. Run!"

Ferocious shouts from the garden were the spur Gabby needed. Although full of groans, he kept up with Millburn as the American ran down the narrow alley. Behind them a yell told them their escape route had been discovered. As they reached a side alley and heard the clatter of boots behind them, Millburn yanked Gabby into it. "This ought to get us back to the street."

"What if they're out there too?" Gabby panted.

"Then it'll be too bloody bad, won't it? We'll just have to hope they don't know it's our car."

They reached the moonlit street fifteen seconds later and to their relief it appeared empty of sailors. But as they flung themselves into their car, a vengeful yell sounded from the alley behind them and half a dozen sailors came pounding up the road. Cursing, Millburn switched on the starter, only for the engine to turn but not fire. Gabby's cry was pure dismay. "What're you doing? Get her off the ground!"

The sweating Millburn tried the starter again. To his immense relief the engine fired this time but only when the pursuing sailors were a few paces away. Slamming in the gears, Millburn sent the car accelerating up the street just as a dozen hands were outstretched to grab her.

Sinking back, the panting Gabby gave a sigh that came from the heart. "Oh, my God. I thought we'd had it, Millburn."

Millburn's eyes were fixed on the Bedford transport ahead that stood outside Sandra's house. "We're not clear yet," he panted. "The bastards might give chase."

Groaning, Gabby sat upright in his seat again but neither man could see any sailors around the transport. Reaching the end of the street Millburn reduced his speed to match the vision of his masked headlights and began making his way back to the main road. By the time he reached it, he had recovered enough to give vent to his feelings. "You moron. Do you realise what would have happened if those sailors had caught us?"

Gabby stared at him. "Why do you think I jumped from that window? Of course I know. The bloody Navy's never liked us. They're jealous because we get all the girls."

"You think that's all that would have happened? Just a beating up? We'd have been cashiered, buster. Stripped of all rank. And maybe been drummed out of the service too. And all because you wanted your nookie so much we had to wear NCOs' uniforms."

Gabby's expression showed the enormity of their danger was sinking home. "I suppose we might have got into trouble," he admitted.

"Trouble? They'd have hanged, drawn, and quartered us. And used the bits for dog meat. Don't you ever come to me again with any of your ideas. That's it. Finish! Final! The End!"

Traditionally resilient, Gabby had now got over his fright. "You agreed to it. So why put all the blame on me?"

The reminder did nothing to improve Millburn's state of mind. On an impulse he slowed the car. "I ought to drop you off and let you walk back in just your trousers and overcoat," he gritted. "Why should I worry if you're cashiered? Come to think of it, it's the best way of getting rid of you."

Startled, Gabby gave a sudden pitiful groan and bent forward. Millburn stared at him. "What is it now?"

Gabby groaned again. "It's my ache, Millburn. "It's getting worse."

"What ache? Your ankle isn't broken or you couldn't have run all that way."

"It's not my ankle, Millburn." Gabby clutched himself and groaned again. "It's something I always get when I can't finish, like tonight. It can be terrible, Millburn."

Millburn stared at him, then a slow, gratified smile began to cross his face. As Gabby groaned again, he began to roar with laughing. "So that's it. You've got lovers' ache, have you? Serve you bloody well right, you little tom-cat. I hope you ache right through to Christmas."

Chapter 10

To her two-man crew, the Mosquito hardly seemed to be moving. With heavy mist pressing on her on all sides and her engines muffled by the crews' high-flying equipment, she seemed to be suspended in a grey and endless limbo.

Gabby, who had slept badly the previous night after his near disaster with the Navy, gave vent to his feelings as the altimeter reading moved to 12,000 feet. "What Jerry's going to be crazy enough to try to take photographs today? It's a bloody leg pull. Those bastards at Leconfield have decided we've sat on our arses long enough and got their Navigation officer to come in on the act. When we get back — if we can find our way back — they'll be standing out there laughing their heads off. You've been conned, Millburn."

Millburn, who was beginning to have secret doubts himself, glared at the scornful Welshman. "What was I supposed to do when he said a hole in the clouds was drifting across? Tell him his weather ships and his aircraft were talking rubbish?"

"The only hole around here is your arsehole, Millburn. Look at the stuff. It's as thick as butter."

Millburn fought to hold his temper. "The Navigation Officer said there was a small anticyclone drifting in between two low pressure belts. It ought to last around three to four hours before it drifts on eastwards. That'll give Jerry plenty of time to take his photographs."

"How the hell is Jerry going to know that? Back at Borkholm or wherever he is, it'll be ten-tenths cloud."

"Don't you know anything, you Welsh moron? Jerry's got subs all over the Atlantic and they send weather reports back every hour or two. That means the JU crews will know as much as we know about the high pressure belt. All they have to do is fly out here and wait for it to arrive."

"How can they do that? They're as limited with fuel as we are."

"The Nav officer reckons they ought to get news of the drift in time for them to reach our coast before it drifts over. So there'd be no waste of fuel. If they're on the ball — and Jerry usually is — it's their chance, perhaps their last chance, to get more photographs before the winter closes in again."

Although secretly impressed, Gabby could not let the matter drop without a final grumble. "It's still a dozen to one chance. What if they make for Newcastle instead of Hull?"

"Davies suspects there's only one kite taking the photographs. If he's right, it'll be routed over all the eastern ports. So if we orbit over Hull we ought to run into it sooner or later."

As Millburn was speaking, the Mosquito broke free of the thick blanket of cloud into a world of brilliant sunlight. As the plane continued to climb, her contrails could now be seen, huge circles that quickly elongated in the westerly wind. Adjusting his smoked goggles, Gabby indicated the limitless azure bowl above them. "It's a big sky up here. How are we going to find him even if he does come this way?"

"Ground Control are watching out for him. And he'll be flying at his maximum height to avoid our fighters. If we keep at that height we've got a good chance." Millburn's voice turned sarcastic. "At least we have if you stop moaning and get the sleep out of your eyes."

"There's nothing wrong with my eyes, Millburn. I don't lie awake thinking about a ferry pilot like someone else I know."

The Mosquito suddenly dropped a wing and side-slipped almost vertically, causing Gabby to grab at his seat straps. As Millburn righted the aircraft and began climbing again, Gabby stared at him indignantly. "What did you do that for? Or are you still learning to fly?"

"Just a warning, you little fart. One more crack about Carol and you're outside without a parachute."

Below, the huge castles of cloud began to merge together as the Mosquito continued climbing, a white plain that stretched from horizon to horizon like some fissured Antarctic landscape. Knowing the break would come from the west if it came at all, Millburn kept an eye in that direction as the Mosquito continued climbing in wide circles that kept her above the hidden city of Hull.

The altimeter was reading 32,000 feet when Gabby gave an exclamation and pointed a gloved hand. "I think it's starting to clear, Millburn."

The American saw he was right as he came round the northern crescent of his orbit. Ahead the white plain was beginning to resemble a massive ice field that had floated into warm water, with cracks appearing on its fringes and separate iceflows breaking off and drifting away. Far below and beyond it Millburn could see a hazy vision of green and silver which he knew were the western reaches of the River Humber. His voice expressed his satisfaction. "So the Navigation guys were right, boyo."

Gabby wasn't going to admit defeat that easily. "All right, but do the Jerries know about it?"

As Millburn continued his climb, the cloud plain drifted on eastwards. By the time he reached 40,000 feet, he could see the tributaries of the Humber below him. Realising he had flown too far west, he turned and followed the main river to the point where it swung at right angles before continuing towards the sea. Although covered with a brown haze of smoke, the city of Hull with its huge dock complex was now visible. Staring down, Millburn could understand why Hull had been the most heavily bombed city in the British Isles. Even when the city was blacked out and the moon was down, enemy bombers had only to follow the river from its outlet in the North Sea to its angled bend and bombs dropped anywhere around it were certain to hit an urban target.

Gabby's voice interrupted his thoughts as the Mosquito yawed for a moment. "Has she reached her ceiling?"

Millburn glanced at the altimeter reading. "I think she'd make another thousand or two but they say the JUs come over at 43,000. So we'll stay here."

Minutes passed while the Mosquito orbited the city below. In spite of their pressurized cabin, the crew's need to wear high altitude equipment in case of combat damage was causing both of them discomfort. It was also giving them a sense of remoteness. The roar of the two Merlin engines was reduced to a mere ticking and their voices sounded muffled and unreal over the intercom. In an attempt to counter the effects, Millburn resorted to humour. "How's your lover's ache this morning?"

Gabby scowled. "That's not funny, Millburn. I'd a hell of a job getting to sleep last night."

"Don't expect any sympathy from me. If you hadn't told every lie in the book to get that girl in Wilmslow, Sammy wouldn't have framed us."

"Who said I told lies? Sammy wasn't there last night. He's gone on leave."

"Sure he has. He had it all tied up so we couldn't bounce him when we got back. His sergeant gave me the griff this morning. He said Sammy had often told him about the dirty tricks you'd played on him and if he ever ran into you again he'd fix you."

Gabby tried to change the line of attack. "How do you know Sandra hadn't something to do with it? Maybe she wanted to keep well in with the Navy."

"It was Sandra who told the girls to keep their mouths shut when she saw the Bedford arrive. No, it was Sammy all right. Somehow he fixed it so the Navy came the same night. You were framed, boyo, and deserved it. It's just a pity I was there to help you out."

With his defences in tatters, Gabby decided there was nothing left but to attack. "You were enjoying it as much as I was until the bloody Navy arrived. You said yourself the girls were great."

"What's that got to do with it? You think I'd have gone with you if I'd known the dirty tricks you'd played on this guy Sammy?"

Silenced for a moment, Gabby asked the question that had been puzzling him all night. "Did the sergeant know anything about the girls?"

"Know what?"

"Why three of them seemed so different to Sandra."

"Yeah, he knew that too. It seems Sandra recruits wives who're lonely because of the war. With naval ships always coming into port, she arranges visits. The girls do all right because they not only get their missing nookie but lots of food rations as well."

"So that's why they talked differently to Sandra?"

Millburn grinned. "And that's why you made it with Joan. Not because you're God's gift to women hut because that's what she came for. In other words any port in a storm would have done just as well."

Below, the anticyclone was right over the British Isles now, giving a panoramic view of its winter countryside right up to Durham and beyond. With no news from their controller and no enemy aircraft in sight, Millburn was becoming concerned about his fuel reserves. To allow for the Mosquito's three Browning guns and ammunition, an equal weight of fuel had been omitted, a loss that would put an end to the operation if the JU was not sighted soon.

A sudden sound and crackle in his earphones made him pause and listen. He addressed his microphone but was rewarded only by more indecipherable static. He shook his head as Gabby gazed at him. "Perhaps we're too high. Or perhaps something's wrong with the equipment."

"Do you think they've picked something up? Or are they telling us to abort?"

Millburn shrugged. "Who knows?" His eyes moved back to his fuel gauge. "I'll give it another fifteen minutes. Then we'll have to quit."

Discomfort was bringing back Gabby's irritability. "It's all a waste of time, Millburn. I'll bet that JU crew are drinking their Steinfurt and laughing their heads off at us silly buggers up here."

"Stop moaning and keep your eyes open," Millburn told him. "If the JU comes at all, it'll come either from the north or the east."

The Mosquito continued its wide circles. Long minutes passed and Millburn was becoming as convinced as Gabby that they were on a wild goose chase when suddenly the Welshman gave an exclamation. "What's that? Over by the coast?"

Millburn grabbed the binoculars from him. For seconds sky and coastline swung dizzily in the lenses. Then, as he steadied the Mosquito, he caught a glimpse of an elongated black speck.

Although it swam out of his vision a second later, it was enough for him to thrust the binoculars back at Gabby, swing the Mosquito's nose round, and ram open his throttles. "That's it. Let's go."

Both men had the same thought as the tiny black speck grew larger. If its crew spotted them, they still had time to dive into the clouds over the sea and escape. But Millburn had one thing in his favour: the position of the sun. A blazing orb at that altitude, it was almost behind him and there was the chance its dazzling glare would hide his approach.

As the vectors shrank between the two aircraft, it became clear to Millburn his hope was realised. From an elongated speck the JU had become an ever-growing dot between two horizontal lines, which could only mean it was approaching Hull to take its photographs. As the dot turned into an aircraft's curved nose and two yellow haloed propellers, Millburn's shout was that of a huntsman close on his quarry. "We've got him, boyo. He can't escape now."

Caring no longer whether he was seen or not, Millburn swung round in a wide arc to close on the JU's tail. Still unaware of his peril, the enemy pilot continued flying straight and level towards the Hull docks that were now visible below. Slower than the Mosquito, the Junker's twin-finned tail and streamlined body began growing larger in Millburn's windshield. Beside the American, Gabby was urging caution. "Watch the rear gunner, Millburn. He must open up soon."

Although the aggressive Millburn would have taken little notice if the gunner had begun firing, no tell-tale tracer came arcing towards the Mosquito. Waiting until the Junkers filled the range bars of his reflector sight, Millburn opened fire.

The effect was immediate. As the stream of .303 bullets struck the tail of the Junkers, the aircraft turned sharply and went into a steep dive. Thinking at first he had crippled it, Millburn held back his fire as he followed it down, then realised it was still under control. Cursing the inferior hitting power of the .303 Brownings as against 20 mm cannon, Millburn was about to open fire again when Gabby gave a chortle. "There isn't a rear gunner, Millburn. The poor bastards are unarmed."

Millburn realised he was right. In order to reach the altitude that the Germans believed would render their aircraft safe, the JU's armament had been sacrificed for fuel. If Millburn continued his attack, he would be killing helpless men.

At the same time he realised that unless he took action quickly, the Junkers might escape. Knowing where his chance of survival lay, the pilot had swung east, and with the two aircraft's natural speed being augmented by their dive, they were both over the sea already. A few more miles and the thick cloud cover would appear again and the Junkers would be safe.

Taking aim again, Millburn pressed his firing button and saw his harmonised burst of tracer zip past the JU's port wingtip. Beside him, Gabby gave a howl of scorn. "That's terrible shooting, Millburn. Get your finger out or he'll get away in those bloody clouds."

Still the Junkers continued its dive. Secretly admiring the crew's courage, Millburn aimed this time at the JU's starboard wingtip and fired another burst. Gabby gave another yell. "What the hell are you doing?"

Knowing he would have to shoot to kill soon if the Germans ignored his warning, Millburn fired one last burst past the Junker's port wingtip. For a long moment the aircraft continued its dive for the clouds, forcing Millburn to set its fuselage in his range bars again. Then, to his relief, the Junkers came out of its dive and waggled its wings. Beside the relieved American, Gabby gave a shout of surprise. "He's surrendering, Millburn! You see that? The bugger's surrendering!"

As Millburn swung the Mosquito alongside the Junkers, he could see its pilot waving at him. Waving back, Millburn indicated the pilot to change course. As the German obeyed and Milburn took station on the Junker's port quarter, the excited Gabby turned to him. "Where're you taking them? To Leconfield?"

Millburn grinned. "Where else? I want to see those guys' faces when we come back with a nice, undamaged Junkers in our pocket."

Gabby hugged himself at the thought. "We'll have the buggers on toast, Millburn. I can't wait."

Ten minutes later Leconfield came into sight. Increasing his speed again to come alongside the Junkers, Millburn jabbed his finger at the airfield. For a moment, as if having second thoughts, the

Junkers pilot made no response and swung east towards the sea. Immediately Millburn fell back and fired a long burst over the aircraft's cabin.

It was enough. Accepting the inevitable, the Junkers' pilot began to circle and lose height. As Millburn followed the aircraft down, Gabby gave a delighted chortle. "Look at 'em all. They don't know whether to man their guns or call out a welcoming party."

Millburn saw he was right as the airfield loomed larger. Fire trucks were speeding hither and thither and mechanics working on parked Halifaxes were either diving for cover or stared up in amazement at the enemy aircraft orbiting down towards them. As a burst of tracer soared up from one of the gun pits, Millburn realised some of the gunners were equally bemused and he made swift contact with the Station Controller. A few seconds later, as the station tannoy spread the message, the firing ceased and men began pouring out on the airfield from hangars and flight offices.

A minute later the Junkers completed its last orbit and touched down on the runway. As trucks of MPs screamed up alongside the aircraft to take its crew captive, Millburn winked at Gabby. "What do you say, boyo? Shall we rub it in?"

Before the exultant Welshman could answer, Millburn put the Mosquito into a dive, pulled out at little more than a hundred feet above the airfield, and did a slow victory roll. As he circled back to land and Gabby saw some of the spectators picking themselves from the ground, the Welshman's chortle was pure wickedness. That did it, Millburn. Look at 'em eating dirt."

Knowing his man, Millburn issued a warning. "Don't go overboard down there. You know what a line shooter you can be."

For once Gabby was prepared to ignore criticism as his generous tribute showed. "For an American, you've done all right today, Millburn."

Millburn, who knew that if the war lasted another hundred years, he would never receive higher praise from his navigator, gave a grin and made his preparations to land.

Adams tapped on the CO's office door and then opened it. "You wanted to see me, sir?"

Henderson glanced up from his desk which was littered with papers. "Hello, Frank. Come in and sit down."

As Adams took one of the two spare chairs, the big Scot grimaced at the papers before him. "As you'll gather, Laura is still on leave and with her assistant sick, things are getting out of hand."

"Would you like Sue to help out?" Adams asked. "She wouldn't mind and I could spare her for a day or two."

Henderson shook his head. "No, Laura is back in a couple of days. I can struggle on with this bumph until then. No, I wanted to see you about Valerie. The Adjutant tells me you haven't applied to live out yet. You're going to, aren't you?"

Adams hesitated. "I haven't decided yet."

Henderson showed surprise. "Why not? There's no problem as far as I'm concerned. All you need do is ask. So why don't you?"

For a private person like Adams, it was an awkward moment, no less because he was unsure of his own mind. "Thanks. But it would present problems. To begin with I haven't a car and the bus service is very ropey."

"We'd get round that. Our transports go into Highgate daily for supplies, so it wouldn't be difficult to fit you in somewhere."

Adams shifted uncomfortably. "I appreciate that, sir. But while we're being used as a front-line squadron, I'm working all hours, so it would make difficulties."

The big Scot was about to argue when he remembered the domestic problems Adams had suffered during Valerie's last stay at The Black Swan. Taking warning from the memory, he shrugged his wide shoulders. "If you'd rather billet here for the moment, that's fine with me. But if you change your mind later, just let me know."

Adams was about to thank him when the red telephone on the desk rang. The Scot picked up the receiver. "Henderson here. Oh, hello, sir. No, I haven't heard yet. What happened?"

Adams could hear a faint but excited voice coming from the receiver as Henderson listened. A moment later the Scot gave a start. "Is that official, sir? It is? Then it's a bloody fine show. Aye, he must be delighted. So I can expect them back today? Thanks for telling me, sir."

Replacing the receiver, Henderson gave a loud laugh and turned to Adams. "Guess what, Frank?"

Curious at the Scot's elation, Adams shook his head. "I can't. What's happened?"

With another delighted laugh, Henderson walked across his office and pulled out a bottle of Highland Dew from a filing cabinet. Picking up a glass from a shelf, he offered it to Adams. When Adams shook his head, Henderson poured himself a stiff dram and drank it straight back. Then he grinned at Adams. "It's that kind of news, Frank. Do you know what those two buggers Millburn and Gabby have done?"

"Shot down the Junkers," Adams ventured.

Henderson poured out another dram. "A damn sight better than that. They captured the bloody thing."

Adams gave a start. "Captured it? how?"

"Apparently it was unarmed, so Millburn forced it to land at Leconfield. Davies is over the moon and you can guess why, can't you?"

Adams' quick mind and intelligence training saw the possibility immediately. "The crews will be interrogated and with any luck we'll find out the reason for their reconnaissances."

"Bang on, Frank. Davies says Simms was thrilled to bits when he spoke to him. It's a leg up for us, Frank. Davies is even talking about giving the lads another bar to their DSOs." Henderson gave a loud, self-deprecating laugh. "And to think only yesterday I was moaning to Davies that I wanted Millburn back. Who'd have guessed this would happen?"

"Did I hear you say they'd be back today?" Adams asked.

"That's right." The Scot paused. "Isn't it Machin's birthday around this time?"

Adams nodded. "Tomorrow. He's having his usual party."

"Then let's celebrate and make it a big one." The Scot's expansive mood knew no limits or impediments at that moment. "I'll throw in a few bottles, you can invite Valerie, and the lads can bring their girl friends. Let's make it a night to remember."

Chapter 11

Davies looked disappointed. "Nothing at all?"

Simms shook his head. "Nothing. We had an expert team interrogate them, so I'm sure the fault's not there. I don't believe they know why they were sent to take photographs."

Davies was forced to admit the likelihood. "Because Jerry must have believed we hadn't a kite to reach them, I was hoping they might have been let into the secret. But as there was always a chance of engine failure, I suppose it was prudent to keep the crews in the dark. We'd do just the same."

Simms walked to the French windows of the library and stared out. In the dusk of the late autumn afternoon, a few hungry birds were picking at the wet lawns. His voice suggested he was talking to himself as much as Davies. "That's always supposing there was something to keep in the dark."

Davies stared at him. "Wasn't that the whole point of the exercise?"

The elderly Brigadier sighed. "London certainly thought so. But I suppose it was possible the enemy was just keeping a prudent eye on our shipping movements without any special motive."

"But in that case why couldn't the crews be told? There's nothing very hush hush about watching enemy shipping movements, is there?"

Simms gave a slight start, then turned from the window. "Thank you, Davies. You might have solved the mystery."

"I have? How?"

"By stating the thing that was too obvious for me to see. If the JU was only carrying out routine reconnaissance patrols, why didn't the crews say so. They'd be giving nothing away and have got our interrogation team off their backs. Their keeping silent means one of two things: either they know and had been told to keep silent at all costs or, much more likely, they've not been told anything. Whichever it is, it could only mean the enemy is up to something, as we first suspected."

"Unless Jerry wants us to think that. Otherwise the crews had only to say they were watching shipping movements and we'd have been satisfied, as you suggested."

Simms smiled. "I think you ought to move over into Intelligence, Davies. You're quite right. Anything is possible in this cat and mouse game. But from what I saw of the crew I don't think the enemy would involve them in subtleties like that. No, I believe there is a deeper reason for this surveillance."

"If you're right, what's the next step?"

Simms sighed. "I've been thinking about it for days and have got nowhere. At the moment I can only wait and hope we get more information from our agents in Norway and Denmark."

The German Kubelwagen drew up outside the bakery with a squeal of brakes. Catching sight of it through her front window, Mrs Helgenstrom saw a middle-aged man in overalls climb out and walk warily across the icy road. She spoke to a pimply-face youth who was stocking freshly baked loaves into a row of shelves behind her. "It's the bloody Jerries again, Ole. They haven't put in another order, have they?"

As the youth shook his head, the woman glanced back at the driver. Needing to step across the snow drifts that lined the road, he paused before entering the bakery to kick snow from his boots. Unused to such consideration from her German customers, Mrs Helgenstrom felt this might just be her day. As the man opened the door, she put on her best smile, *"Guten tag, mein Herr.* What can I do for you?"

The man looked surprised. "You speak German, *meine Frau."*

"I do. Quite fluently, or so your friends tell me."

"How is that, *meine Frau?"*

Mrs Helgenstrom shrugged her huge shoulders. "I used to take my holiday's in Germany before the war. I had many happy times there. So I learned the language."

The man looked relieved at finding at last a Norwegian who showed some liking for his country. "What part did you go to? Anywhere special?"

She had been assessing his appearance as they spoke. In his late forties, somewhat fleshily built, he had an educated voice and features that contained none of the arrogance so many of his military counterparts displayed. Although he was wearing thick overalls whose bulk suggested pullovers beneath them, the shiver he had given on entering the shop hinted at a man unused to the cold. Mrs Helgenstrom decided it was worth a try. "I went mostly to Bavaria. I liked the scenery down there and the people."

His face lit up. "That's where I come from. Munich's my home town."

"It is? Oh, I liked Munich." She gave her massive bosom a comical pat. "As you see, I also liked your beer and cream cakes."

He laughed with her. *"Ja,* I miss them too. I miss many things there."

"But you like our bread, don't you?"

He returned her smile. "Oh yes. Your bread is good. That's why I have come this morning. As the damned soldiers control the food supplies, the bread is often stale when we get it. So my men and I have decided to buy fresh bread ourselves."

"So you're not part of the Army?"

Her chatter was relaxing him. "No, I'm not a soldier, thank God. My job kept me out. But I never expected to be sent over here." He gave a shudder. "I knew it would be cold but not as cold as this."

Mrs Helgenstrom decided the signs were propitious. "What about a hot drink before you start back?"

He hesitated. "Do you mean it?"

"Of course I do. Or haven't you the time?"

He glanced at his wrist watch. "I think I've got another fifteen minutes."

"Then come in my sitting room and I'll make you some coffee. I got some from one of your soldiers last week. It's ersatz, of course, but it's drinkable."

As she waddled into a room behind the shop she had the feeling he had accepted her offer more as a gesture towards a Norwegian's hospitality than for the drink itself. As he followed her into a sitting room full of pine furniture, she waved him to a chair. "It won't take a minute. My names' Gerde Helgenstrom, by the way."

"Mine's Holstein," he told her. "Michael Holstein." She held out a packet of cigarettes. "Have a fag while you wait."

She returned five minutes later with two cups of hot synthetic coffee. As he rose she waved him back into his chair. "Don't stand on ceremony with me. Here. Drink this down. You looked frozen when you came in. What are they making you do out there? Sit on the mountain tops and look out for British planes!"

He laughed as he sipped at the hot liquid. "No, it's not that bad. It's reasonably warm underground."

She felt her heart give a huge throb. To hide her excitement, she lit a cigarette herself. "Underground? What are you doing underground? Digging an invasion tunnel to England?"

"Not quite. Although it's a pity we can't."

"It's a hell of a pity. If you could knock the Tommies out, we might get things back to normal again. So what's your job?"

"I'm a mining engineer. That's why I wasn't called up into the Army."

"A mining engineer? Do they need mining engineers in quarries?"

He looked surprised at her question. "The quarry's long closed. It was shut down when your people blocked the way to the fjord. Didn't you know that?"

"How could we know? The road up there has been cordoned off for months. Like the rest of us I've been thinking all this time your people had opened it again. So what are you mining? Gold?"

He took another sip of his drink. "No, it's something else we've discovered there. There was one other mine in Norway but it was shut down some time ago."

She could hardly believe her good luck. "What is it? Or can't you tell me?"

For the first time he showed caution. "We're supposed to keep it quiet. I can't see it matters but you know what the military are like. They make a secret out of anything. I find it all so damned childish."

Her heart was beating so fast she was afraid he would notice it. "I suppose they have to be careful. But who cares what it is. I'm just glad it was found. It's been damned good for business."

Draining his cup, he rose. "I'd better get back with my bread and cakes now or I'll be in trouble. We've got a pig of a supervisor. Thanks for the drink and the chat."

She took the cup from him. "My lad in the shop will attend to you. Drop in again soon. There'll always be a cup of coffee for you."

He touched his cap. "Many thanks, *meine Frau.* It's good to know we still have some friends in Norway."

As he walked back into the shop, she pulled out a notebook from a table drawer, tore out a page, and scribbled on it. Seeing her young assistant helping the German to load bread loaves on to the van, she waited until the van had driven away before calling the youth into the sitting room. "I want you to go and give this to Neilson right away." As the youth was taking the scrap of paper, she snatched it back and tore it into fragments. "No, it's too dangerous. Tell Neilson to come and see me as soon as he can. Tell him I've got important news for Steen."

Number One hangar at Sutton Craddock that same night was a shock to the senses. At one end, a group of the station personnel were clustered round a piano that had been brought in from the officers' Mess. The pianist, a new navigator called Arthur Pearson, had once played in a London dance band and he was extemporising every request thrown at him. At the far end some of the aircrews were playing 633 Squadron's version of the Eton Wall Game with a football borrowed from the PT instructor. Full of the vigour and high spirits of the young and equally full of the tension of aerial combat, they were surging back and forth like waves against granite cliffs. Every now and then their forays would take them as far as the piano but the imperturbable songsters would regain their cohesion as soon as the wave had receded.

But it was not all confusion and mayhem. With the foresight born of long experience, Henderson had ordered the section opposite the piano to be cordoned off as a bar and issued a directive that if any drunken officer or WAAF entered it with malicious intent, he or she would be docked a week's pay. As a result it was possible to obtain a drink without too much hassle although conversation still needed good lungs or explicit sign language.

Among the male officers standing at the bar, there were a number of WAAFs of all ranks. With 633 Squadron something of a law unto itself, it was a common practice for certain non-commissioned personnel to be invited to officers' parties.

There were also a number of civilians, Valerie among them. A few ground staff officers had managed to find rooms in Highgate for their wives and although Henderson had remained puzzled about Adams' relationship with Valerie since his conversation with the Intelligence Officer, he had thought it circumspect to invite her.

At first Adams had received the invitation with mixed feelings and the eagerness Valerie had shown to visit the squadron again had done nothing to dispel them. But Adams was Adams, and in no time was reprimanding himself. After London, she must find Highgate quiet and boring, and living with two old ladies could hardly be a ball of fun either. Surely it was natural she would look forward to the colour and excitement of a squadron party.

In this frame of mind he had borrowed a car and fetched her that evening. She had chosen to wear a blue evening dress that emphasised her tall, elegant figure, and although she had complained there had been no time to have her hair styled, she still had drawn many approving glances when Adams had brought her into the Mess. Almost to his surprise, Adams had felt a twinge of pride that he was the husband of the most attractive woman present.

To make things even better she had been in an expansive mood and seemed to be enjoying herself as he pointed out members of the squadron she had not known at her last visit. When she asked whose birthday it was, he pointed to a lean officer who was standing alongside the improvised bar and having a furious argument with a red-faced warrant officer. "Machin. He's from Eire."

"I didn't think Eire was in the war," she said.

"It isn't. Machin's a volunteer." Adams smiled. "He's the one they say belonged to the IRA and used to throw bombs at us."

She stared at Machin again. With the Irishman's collar torn open and his tie askew, he was not a pretty sight. "I'm not surprised," she said. "He looks as if he could do it again."

Adams laughed. "He's one of our best pilots. It seems there's nothing like a war to bring one time enemies together."

"I still don't see why you should throw a party this size for him. Has he just won the VC or something?"

Unable to give the real reason for the occasion, Adams shook his head. "It's become something of a tradition to give a party on his birthday."

As if she was seeing through his deception, she pointed at Millburn and Gabby who were arguing with one another at the near end of the bar. "Who are those two?"

"They're two of our characters, although Millburn is acting squadron commander at present. He's an American."

"Which is he?"

"The taller one with the dark hair."

She eyed the American with interest. "He's very good looking."

Adams smiled. "So all the WAAFs think."

"Why? Is he a womaniser?"

Adams shrugged. "Not really. He's just a young man full of life, as so many of them are."

"What about that assistant of yours? What's her name — Sue something? Isn't she here?"

"No. She's standing in for me tonight."

Valerie lifted an eyebrow. "That's noble of her. Couldn't you have given someone else the job? I'd like to have met her." When Adams, sensing cattiness, made no reply, she went on: "What about your big names?"

"Big names?"

"Yes. Your CO, Ian Moore and Harvey."

"Moore couldn't make it. But Harvey was invited and I expect Henderson to drop in later on."

She looked disappointed. "It's a pity about Moore. Why couldn't he come?"

With the young and wealthy Ian Moore a byword in the newspapers for his achievements, decorations, and good looks,

Adams was not entirely surprised at her disappointment but he kept his council. "He's at Group Headquarters now that he's not allowed to fly over Europe again, and Davies couldn't spare him. But no doubt you'll meet him one of these days."

She turned her eyes to the floor again. "I recognise some of your specialist officers but I don't see Squadron Leader Richardson. Has he been invited or is he on duty?"

Although her question had a casual sound, Adams had been expecting it ever since their arrival. "No. But I expect he'll be here soon. He's not one to miss a party."

She gave him a sharp look and seemed about to give an equally sharp reply when a tall officer and a slim attractive girl entered the hangar and made their way past the songsters around the piano. Missing nothing, particularly that the girl outshone her in beauty, Valerie nudged Adams' arm. "Who are those two? The couple who've just come in?" When Adams gazed around, she jerked his arm. "Over there! The officer has a slight limp. Is it Harvey?"

Following her pointed finger, Adams gave a start of pleasure. "Yes. And his wife Anna. I was hoping they'd be able to come."

Valerie's voice turned impatient as the couple neared the bar. "Well! Aren't you going to invite them over?"

Nodding, Adams moved forward. Catching sight of him, the girl said something to the tall officer. As he turned, the girl took his hand and drew him towards the smiling Adams. Before Adams could speak, the girl reached up and kissed his cheek: "Hello, Frank. We were hoping you would be here."

Conscious of Valerie's stare, Adams was feeling some embarrassment. "It's good to see you again, Anna. You're looking wonderful. How's that wounded husband of yours?"

"He's much better, thank you. But he still needs a long rest."

The tall officer grinned at Adams. "She talks like my old mum. I'm as good as new." He held out a big hand to Adams. "It's good to see you again, Frank. How's tricks?"

Valerie had missed nothing during the brief exchanges. As tall as herself, Anna was wearing a simple green velvet dress that set off to perfection her shapely figure. Wearing only a cameo brooch for jewellery and with her luxurious dark hair swept up in a French

101

roll, she was a woman of distinction and great beauty, as Valerie was acutely aware.

Her companion was puzzling her. Tall and powerfully built, Harvey had a face as craggy as the Yorkshire fells from whence he came. His accent and gruff voice gave some evidence of his working class background and yet he wore on his tunic sleeves the rings of a squadron leader and had a wife who would have graced a prince. Remembering what Adams had told her about the man, Valerie was intrigued.

Her sharp cough reminded Adams of his duties. Turning, he drew Valerie forward. "I'd like you both to meet Valerie, my wife. Val, this is Frank Harvey and Anna, whom you've heard me talk about."

Smiling, slender hand extended, Valerie stepped forward. "You have, dear. So often I feel I know them both."

Anna shook hands with her, followed by Harvey, whose brusque voice carried little warmth. "Hello, Mrs Adams. I believe you've been here before."

"Yes. Although it seems a long time ago now."

"Are you glad to be back?"

"Yes, of course I am. I just wish I were living a little nearer, that's all. By the way, do call me Valerie."

"Frank tells me you've got rooms in Highgate."

Valerie pulled a face. "Yes, with two old spinsters. I think I'd rather be in The Black Swan, as I was the last time. Then I could see more of Frank's friends."

Harvey's courtesy went no further than a brief smile before he turned back to Adams. Knowing something of Valerie's infidelity, the Yorkshireman's puritanical northern background had little tolerance for it, particularly as Adams was his friend. The warmth returned to his voice when he grinned at Adams. "Intelligence officers don't have any friends. Do they, love?" he said to Anna.

She pretended to punch him, her voice carrying the accent that Adams had always found attractive. "This one has." She glanced back at Valerie. "Your husband is a lovely man, Mrs Adams. We all think the world of him."

Harvey's coolness had not gone unnoticed by Valerie who was wondering how much Adams had confided in him. The possibility was enough to stir the cat's claws within her. "Really. It must be nice to be loved. How do you like mixing with all these Air Force types, Mrs Harvey?"

Anna smiled. "I like them. But then I would, wouldn't I, *Liebling?*" she said, smiling at Harvey and hugging his arm.

"Don't you sometimes feel strange among them? You are a German, aren't you?"

The girl gave a faint start of surprise at the question but her grey eyes did not falter. "Yes, Mrs Adams. I am German."

Valerie nodded at the sole Mosquito resting in the centre of the hangar. "Then doesn't it upset you to think these planes and these men go out daily to bomb your homeland?"

Adams winced as the German girl's voice went quiet. "I would hardly have married one if it upset me, Mrs Adams. No, I don't see it that way at all. To me they are bombing the Nazis, the enemies of my country. Of course it makes me sad if innocent people are killed. But for that I blame the guilty men who started this war."

Secretly impressed by the girl's dignity, Valerie gave a short laugh. "You've more tolerance that I would have in your shoes, I must say." She turned to the embarrassed Adams. "Aren't you going to get us all a drink, darling?"

As Adams hesitated then moved towards the bar, Harvey checked him. "Not just now, Frank. I want to have a word with Millburn and Gabby. Later on perhaps. All right?"

"Are you sure?" Adams muttered.

Harvey slapped his shoulder. "Sure. We'll have one later." Turning, he glanced at Valerie. "See you, Mrs Adams." Then, taking Anna's arm, he drew her towards the bar.

Valerie stared after him. "He doesn't like me, does he?"

"Why did you have to make those remarks about Anna being German?" Adams muttered.

She stiffened. "Why not? It's true, isn't it?"

"That's not the point. You didn't need to emphasise it, did you?"

"I didn't emphasise it. I was just curious how she felt about being among her country's enemies. Anyway, Harvey didn't like me before I made any mention about her being German."

"That's silly. Why shouldn't he?"

Valerie's slightly protruding eyes stared at him. "That's what I keep asking myself." Then, with an impatient gesture, she thrust her empty glass at him. "Get me another drink, please."

As Adams sighed and turned to the bar he noticed the scrum at the far end of the hanger was starting to break up, partly out of exhaustion and partly because the Adjutant had called for a little more decorum now that all the station guests had arrived. As young officers broke into ribald, laughing groups, the adjutant spoke to the pianist who broke into the latest popular dance tune. It was a signal for young men to make a dash across the floor for the prettiest girls present. By the time Adams had received his drinks from a sweating barman, the floor was full of couples dancing a quickstep. Turning with his drinks, Adams saw the rope cordoning the guest enclosure had been removed and Valerie had disappeared.

He spotted her a few seconds later, swinging round in the arms of a young B flight pilot. Standing with drinks in both hands and feeling slightly foolish, Adams was about to return to the bar when a familiar voice checked him. "You look lost, Frank."

Turning, Adams saw the tall figure of Henderson alongside him. "Hello, sir. When did you arrive?"

"A few minutes ago. I came in the back way so not to disturb the party." The Scot nodded at the twirling couples. "It seems to be going well."

"Yes, sir. I think it is."

Henderson pointed at the far end of the bar where Machin was having a fierce argument with two equally drunken Englishmen. "Not that our birthday boy knows much about it. Do you think he's plotting to blow up the bomb dump?"

Adams smiled as he laid his drinks down on a table. "If he is, I hope he waits until the guests have gone."

"Talking about guests, I'm looking forward to meeting your wife. You have brought her?"

"Yes." Adams searched through the crowd, then pointed. "That's her. In the blue dress."

104

Henderson gave a grunt of approval. "She's a handsome woman, Frank. You're a lucky man."

"Yes, sir. Can I get you a drink?"

"Aye, I wouldn't mind one."

"Whisky?"

The Scot hesitated, then shook his head. "No. Better make it beer tonight. Someone needs to keep a clear head."

As Adams reached the bar again, he heard the music cease, only for a waltz to follow immediately as an impatient shout rose from the dancers. Hoping Valerie would return now, he searched for her among the milling couples. For a moment he could not spot her, then her blue dress showed at the far end of the Mess. She was still dancing but her partner was no longer the young pilot. Laughing and talking animatedly, she was in the arms of a burly ginger-headed squadron leader.

Adams took a tankard of beer back to Henderson. "Do you like dancing, sir?"

The Scot grimaced. "I did once. But my feet seem to get in my way these days. What about you?"

"I'm much the same. But Valerie likes it."

The Scot grinned. "So you've no choice, you poor bastard."

Minutes passed, the music changed, but still Valerie stayed on the floor. As she passed by, laughing and chatting to the squadron leader, Adams tried to catch her eye but she either never saw him or ignored his signal. Henderson laughed. "You're right, Frank. She does like dancing. And Richardson's not bad, is he?"

Adams was feeling both hot and cold by this time. "She doesn't know who you are, sir. I'll go and tell her."

Before the Scot could answer, he made his way through the dancers and tapped Valerie on the shoulder. "I'm sorry, Val, but you'll have to break it up now."

She gave him no time to explain his reason. Her animated face changed into anger as, still held in Richardson's arms, she turned towards him. "What do you mean, break it up? I'll finish when I want to finish."

About to explain, Adams was interrupted by the burly Richardson. By nature a belligerent man, his reaction was compounded by the attention Valerie was giving him. "For Christ's sake, Frank, what's the matter with you? Val and I are old friends. And you know you don't like dancing. So what's wrong with Val dancing with someone who does?"

Adams took a deep breath. "I don't mind her dancing, Jack. It's the CO who wants to meet her. He's been waiting with me for the last fifteen minutes."

Richardson glanced across the floor and his belligerence died. "You'd better go, Val. We can have another dance later."

All Valerie's spiteful elements were on the surface now. Her arms tightened around Richardson. "No, I want to finish this dance. I can meet the CO afterwards."

Richardson hesitated, then grinned at Adams. "You heard the lady, Frank. I guess she knows her own mind."

Adams made his shamefaced way back to Henderson. "She'll be along in a moment, sir. Can I get you another beer?"

The Scot, whose keen eyes had missed nothing of the encounter, emptied his tankard and set it down on the table. "Not at the moment, Frank. I'd better circulate among the guests for a while. But I'm bound to run into the two of you later."

Adams watched Henderson's tall figure mingle with the crowd at the far end of the bar. He was thinking about the drive back to Highgate when the party was over. With Valerie in her present mood, it was a prospect that made him return to the bar for another drink.

Chapter 12

Henderson's red telephone rang just as the Scot was having his early morning coffee. "Yes, sir. What can I do for you?"

Davies sounded eager. "Can you be ready in half an hour, Jock?"

"Is it important, sir?"

"It might be. That's all I can say at the moment."

"Then I suppose I must be. Are you coming here?"

"Only to pick you up. I shall want Adams too."

"Where are we going, sir?"

"To High Elms. You'll learn the rest later. Half an hour, Jock. Bye."

Henderson put the receiver down with a groan. In the past, appointments at High Elms had invariably meant unusual and dangerous missions and although Henderson was fully aware they were the *raison d'être* for his squadron's existence, the Scot had never become accustomed to the losses the missions incurred.

Perhaps inevitably these losses coloured his opinion of Davies. Although Henderson respected the small Air Commodore's tenacity and enthusiasm and his foresight in creating a Special Service Squadron, and although the Scot was a professional airman who knew wartime flying was a highly dangerous occupation, he had never been able to decide how much of Davies's enthusiasm was due to personal ambition and how much to a dedicated and ruthless determination to win the war at all costs.

That Davies had been successful so far went without saying. The enemy threats that his special unit had eliminated — the deadly IMI stocks, the anti-aircraft rockets, the poison gas menace, the vital

107

D-Day bridge, and the super jet-propelled fighter — had made it pound for pound the most successful unit in British military history and made Henderson justly proud of being its commanding officer.

But as each operation had inflicted its sickening losses, Henderson had found himself moving a little nearer to Adams' view of the mercurial Davies. Not all of the way, Henderson thought, correcting himself. Adams was a civilian at heart and in spite of his half-baked wish to be a flier himself, no one could imagine Adams going out every day bombing and killing his fellow men as routinely as a postman delivering letters. Adams saw war as a monstrous obscenity and so found it difficult to face any mission that involved the loss of his friends. A professional serviceman such as Henderson could accept the necessity but even so there were limits and these days he was asking himself if Davies was reaching beyond them. Sighing and wondering if his nerve was going, Henderson lifted the receiver and asked for Adams' office.

Davies's staff car was winding its way down narrow country lanes. Davies, seated at the rear with Henderson and Adams, wiped mist from his side window and gazed out at a fine drizzle and a mist covered landscape. "We're lucky today, Jock. All flying scrubbed, so we can be spared for an hour or two."

His tone, almost lighthearted, made Henderson nudge Adams, who was squashed in between the two men. The prospect of an important mission seldom failed to raise Davies's spirits and although Henderson had learned next to nothing about the reason for their trip to High Elms, he had noticed a difference in the Air Commodore's mood on his arrival at Sutton Craddock to his earlier attitude when discussing the JU's flights.

Knowing Henderson had failed to extract any details from him, Adams decided there was no harm in his trying. "Haven't you any idea why the Brigadier wants to see us, sir?"

"Not a clue," Davies told him. "But he must have his reasons for asking all three of us out here."

"Do you think it can have anything to do with the Junkers?"

"Maybe. Maybe not. Let's wait until we get there." Closing the subject, Davies glanced across at Henderson. "I heard you'd a good party last night, Jock."

"Yes, sir. It's a pity you couldn't have come."

Davies turned to Adams. "I hear you've got your wife down here, Frank. Did she enjoy herself?"

Knowing that Davies had been closeted in Henderson's office for a few minutes before they had driven off, Adams wondered how much had been said. "Yes, she did, sir. Very much."

"I believe you've got rooms for her in Highgate. Are you going to move out there?"

"I might, sir." Adams got in quickly before the next question could he asked. "Only we've been so busy lately it's more convenient to billet on the station."

At that moment the car slowed down and Adams saw the huge stone pillars of High Elms approaching. As Davies was about to reply, the car swung round and stopped as a sentry approached for their identification. When the car drove on through the gates and towards the car park, Davies's mind was on other things. Relieved, Adams followed the two men up a flight of stone steps and into the library.

As always the elderly Brigadier was full of courtesy. "Thank you for coming so promptly, gentlemen, but as you will see in a moment the matter is urgent. If in the meantime you wish to smoke, please do so."

Showing excitement at this introduction, Davies followed him to the long mahogany table. As Adams followed the two men he saw a large map of Norway and some photographs spread across it. With his memories of the Swartfjord and Operation Valkyrie brought sharply to life, his curiosity was almost painful as Simms took a position at the head of the table, his eyes on Davies.

"As you might have guessed, Davies, my reason for asking you here is connected with these recent Junkers reconnaissance flights over our eastern ports. We were hoping that your brilliant capture of this plane might have given us a reason for them but unfortunately its crew plead ignorance and repeated interrogation has convinced us they are telling the truth.

"We were equally hopeful that photographs taken by your Benson unit would give us a clue or two, but as you will have seen already, whatever the enemy is up to, he has hidden it under elaborate camouflage." As Simms pushed the pile of photographs towards the curious Henderson and Adams, he glanced at Davies. "By the way, thank you for getting these processed so quickly. I hadn't expected them so soon."

Davies was frowning. "I'm only sorry to hear they haven't helped you."

"They have helped in one way, Davies. The very fact the enemy has gone to so much trouble with camouflage means he has something to hide."

With neither Henderson nor Adams yet privy to the suspicions SOE had about German activities in Norway, both men were puzzling over the large prints. Taken from different angles and from a great height, they showed a section of a steep valley with a small town straddling the flanking mountains and the thread of a road leading towards a wood and cul-de-sac at its landward end. Henderson raised his head and indicated the map on the table. "I take it this valley is in Norway, sir?"

Seeing from Davies' expression that he had said nothing to the Scot about the affair, Simms nodded. "Yes, it is. Let me put you in the picture quickly. These Junkers flights over our eastern ports made us think the enemy might be up to some mischief in either Denmark or Norway. We've made enquiries and our Norwegian agents suggest something in this valley might be worth investigating. Since then we've had information that makes us certain it is."

Davies jumped at his words like a terrier at a bone. "You've got some facts, then?"

"Yes. London had a radio message from Steen Jenson last night. It seems he has a woman agent in Rosvik who managed a conversation with a German miner yesterday."

"A miner?"

"A mining engineer, to be precise. He didn't say what was being mined but we feel the trouble the enemy is taking to hide the mine suggests it is some mineral of considerable value."

Davies was looking disappointed. "Only a mine? I thought Jerry was up to something important."

110

"Don't underestimate the importance of minerals in this war, Davies. Think what a shortage of oil could do to the enemy's war effort."

"Is that what they're digging for?" Henderson asked. "Oil?"

"No. As far as we know there's no oil in Norway. But according to the German miner this mineral is almost as scarce. He told the woman there had been only one other mine in Norway and it had been closed some time ago."

"So you don't know what the mineral is yet?" Davies asked.

Simms smiled. "Yes, we do. The mention of the other mine being closed was the clue. London passed the word on to one of its research teams and they had the answer within an hour. The other mine wasn't closed. It was at Knaben and was blown up by Bomber Command."

Davies was beginning to think Simms had a natural talent for drama. "You haven't said what the mineral is yet, sir."

"Molybdenum, Davies. Atomic number 42. Atomic weight 95.95. A very rare metal indeed."

Davies was looking anything but impressed. "Molybdenum. Why is it so important to the Germans?"

"Because it is used in high speed steels. An absolute essential for the *Vergeltungswaffen,* the highly secret reprisal weapons the enemy is developing, which they hope can still win them the war. The Knaben mine was supplying four fifths of Germany's needs before Bomber Command destroyed it. This discovery at Rosvik must have sent the enemy scientists dancing for joy."

Henderson's concern for his squadron's role in the equation was growing. "But isn't this still supposition, sir?"

"To a very fine degree, I suppose it is, Henderson. But if you put all the facts together — the introduction of mining experts, the security cordon, the size of the army garrison, the miner's disclosure, and the elaborate camouflage — I think we can be ninety-nine per cent certain our guess is correct. In fact the tight security is a betrayal. If it weren't there, our agents might have been less suspicious."

Adams spoke for the first time. "Where do the Junker's reconnaissance flights fit into this, sir? Could they have some other connection and have only served by accident to bring about this discovery?"

Simms turned to him. "I agree it's possible, Adams, although I've a feeling in my bones there is a link. If there is, only time will tell. But in the meantime SOE's task is to find a way of destroying this mine."

"Where exactly do you think this mine is?" Henderson asked.

"We're almost certain it's somewhere in the wood at the end of the valley, with elaborate camouflage hiding its position from the air."

"Couldn't it be destroyed like the other mine was? I realise its position is camouflaged but couldn't Lancasters or Fortresses do a saturation raid? If they carried heavy ordnance they'd surely do severe damage even if they didn't obliterate it."

Adams passed the Scot a photograph. "I think you'll find that small town is too close, sir. There'd almost certainly be heavy civilian casualties."

Simms gave Adams an appreciative nod. "You're right, Adams. We'd never get permission from the King of Norway or his Government in exile for such a raid. There are other factors too. Not only is the wood close to the town and the valley very narrow, but the wood lies beneath a particularly unpleasant mountain called Helsberg. It all makes high level bombing difficult if not impossible, particularly as at this time of the year the sun never reaches the valley floor."

Seeing Davies's excited expression, Adams was quick to ask his question. "How narrow is this valley, sir?"

"Very narrow, I'm afraid, with two nasty looking bluffs that constrict it even further."

"And how long?"

"Around fifteen miles from its entrance at the sea to Helsberg, which makes it a cul-de-sac."

"And there isn't any exit to the fjord that runs parallel to it?"

"Yes." Simms handed Adams another photograph and explained the history of the cutting and its tunnel. When he finished, Adams took another look at the photograph. "Do you know how badly this cutting is blocked, sir?"

112

At this point, Davies broke in impatiently. "What's all this about, Frank?"

Adams turned to him. "I was thinking that if the cutting was negotiable, a party of commandos might be able to land there and blow up the mine before the Germans could call for reinforcements."

Before Davies could answer, Henderson broke in eagerly. "That's it! A commando raid. Well done, Frank."

Fully aware that Henderson wanted to keep his squadron away from a task that looked highly dangerous, Davies showed irritation as he listened to Simms's reply. "We have given a seaborne attack thought, Adams, but we do welcome any ideas you might have. That was one reason I asked you to be here today. Your Air Commodore has always said you have a fertile mind."

Flattered and with the thought his idea might keep his aircrew friends from a dangerous mission, Adams pursued his idea with enthusiasm. "It would have to be at night, of course. The Jerries might have guns commanding the fjord. But it would ensure the safety of the town."

"What about mines?" Davies interrupted. "Jerry's sure to have thought about them. And if this molybdenum is so precious, won't he have considered a sea and commando attack himself and have guns guarding the cutting as well as the fjord?"

Simms, who gave the appearance of a man appreciating the advice he was being given, nodded thoughtfully. "You could well be right, Davies. These are all the points one has to consider before deciding on a method of attack."

With suspicions growing that they were being led up a garden path by the gentle but astute Brigadier, Adams felt no surprise at Davies's reply. "This all shows there's only one raid that's likely to work, doesn't it? A low level precision attack by Mosquitoes?"

This time Simms allowed himself a smile. "I had hoped you might see it that way, Davies. But because of the unusual circumstances I preferred you first eliminated the other alternatives."

Henderson, lulled into believing the use of his squadron had been ruled out, gave a grunt of alarm. "We can't fly down that valley, sir. It doesn't look wide enough for a flight of birds. And anyway, what would we bomb? The wood seems quite large and we couldn't saturate it the way a hundred heavies could."

Davies held up a hand. "One thing at a time, Jock. It's the partisans' job to locate the mine. Let's first see if the valley's negotiable. We'll send a Mossie down it. The crew can tell us the score."

Simms shook his iron-grey head. "That's something we mustn't do, Davies. At the moment we don't believe the enemy is aware we know about the mine. If we send an aircraft through the valley he'll be alerted and take every precaution possible."

As alarmed as Henderson at the way Davies's mind was working, Adams added his own protest. "If he hasn't guns already in the valley, he'd bring them in, sir. If he'd any sense he'd also bring in smoke generators."

Davies gave a start. "Smoke!"

"Yes. Even if agents found where the mine was hidden, that's all he'd have to do. Smoke would be sheltered from the wind down there and could drift back as far as the town. In fact he might even use smoke in the town itself. That would put the inhabitants in even greater danger."

Seeing Davies bite his lip, Henderson threw his own weight behind Adams' warning. "Equally, if we can't do a recce first, it would be suicide to send an entire squadron into a valley like that. We could lose half of our lads from collisions alone."

Scowling, Davies picked up another photograph. "What about this cutting that runs from the fjord? Couldn't we go in that way and avoid the valley altogether?"

Adams examined a few more photographs before replying. "One really needs to see the cutting and the valley first hand, sir. But from all I see here, there would be an even greater risk of collisions. If aircraft made an attack down the valley, at least they could escape via the cutting. But if they came through it, they'd have too little air space to clear the mountains and so would have to circle round and return back through it. In dense smoke that would be highly dangerous. It would also mean, of course, a lengthy delay between each aircraft's attack, otherwise there would certainly be some collisions in the cutting."

Henderson was quick to add his own endorsement. "There are the bombs too. I know we'd have to use time delays but we don't know their effects in a confined space like that. Our kites might get blown up by them if they have to circle back before getting out."

Davies muttered a curse. The tug of war between his urgent need to use his squadron again on an important mission and his fear of its being wiped out, was playing havoc with his mercurial temper. "For Christ's sake, do you think I don't know the risks? Keep quiet, both of you, and let me think."

As the two men fell silent, Davies lit a cigarette — an act significant in itself — and gazed around for an ashtray. As Adams pushed one towards him, Davies dropped his match into it, then turned to the waiting Brigadier. "I'll be honest with you, sir, and admit I find it hard to believe a mine is that important, even if the mineral is so scarce. Are you certain London isn't exaggerating?"

Something in Simms' expression drew all three men's attention as he nodded. "A fair question, Davies, and one that deserves an honest answer." As his gaze moved round all three officers, the Brigadier dropped his bombshell. "I didn't tell you earlier because I felt it might affect your thinking. But the truth is Churchill is demanding that this mine is destroyed."

Davies jumped as if a dog had bitten his leg. "Churchill?"

"Yes. When he was told last night the mine was almost certainly producing molybdenum, he issued one of his ACTION THIS DAY directives. You all know what that means. One way or the other that mine has to go."

Davies was finding it hard to believe what he was hearing. "But why is he taking it so seriously?"

"You're forgetting the V2s, Davies. They've come as a massive shock to everyone, and no one more than Churchill. If the enemy can produce them, he can produce equally deadly weapons and the next one might be worse, even fatal. So Churchill intends taking no chances. His orders are that the enemy gets no more molybdenum."

Shaking his head, Davies turned to Henderson. "This changes the entire picture, doesn't it, Jock?"

Henderson was having none of that. "No, sir. It's not going to help Churchill or the war effort one jot if my lads commit suicide.

And it would be suicide if they flew into that valley without any prior reconnaissance."

"All right. Then let's give 'em reconnaissance."

Henderson threw a glance at the Brigadier. "And if we do that, Jerry makes a death trap of the valley. Heads we lose, tails we lose."

Although Davies was scowling again, he made no reply. It was Simms who broke the silence. "It is asking a great deal, I know. Might I suggest we leave it for the moment while I see what my team comes up with: they've been working on the problem ever since London sent us the directive."

"What will happen if they don't find one?" Davies asked.

Simms gave a sigh. "Someone will have to do the job, Davies. Churchill will see to that."

Davies nodded, then turned to Henderson. "I want you to keep your squadron on alert until further orders, Jock." Then, picking up his cap, he addressed the Brigadier. "You'll keep in touch, sir?"

"Oh yes, Davies. You can rely on that."

Five minutes later Davies and his party were descending the stone steps to the car park. Davies, moody and irritable, barely spoke a word until they reached Sutton Craddock. Then, as Henderson and Adams climbed from the car, he wound down his window and called them back. "Listen. I don't want you two to let this thing drop. I want you to rattle your brains and come up with something."

Henderson looked dismayed. "What can we come up with? If we're forbidden to send in a recce plane, what's left?"

Davies's epithet made his WAAF driver turn in protest. "If I knew that I'd tell you, wouldn't I?" His glare, swinging on to Adams, almost knocked off the Intelligence Officer's cap. "You're supposed to be the gen man of this outfit, Frank. So how about proving it?"

"I'll do my best, sir. But I can't promise anything."

"I don't want your bloody promises. I want an answer. In the meantime I'm putting Moore in the picture to see if he has any ideas. If this metal's so important to Churchill and we can't come up with something, everyone from the Cabinet down is going to ask what the hell's the point of keeping this squadron in food and shelter."

116

The two men were saved from a reply by Davies snapping an order to his driver. As the car turned and drove at speed out of the airfield entrance, Henderson turned to Adams. "What's the point of keeping the station on alert? What's he hoping for? There's no way we can operate in that valley without prior reconnaissance. The very sight of it put the fear of God into me."

Adams nodded. "It made me think of the Swartfjord too. But I can understand why Churchill wants that mine destroyed. The V2s are a major breakthrough in technology. If Jerry's production of new weapons isn't slowed down or stopped, who knows what he might come up with the next time."

"You really believe it's as serious as that?"

"There's no question about it. Supposing Jerry had been able to build four or five thousand V2s and release them all on London in a single day. What would that have done to our war effort or to the morale of our armies in Europe? It's probably what he would have done but for the shortage of raw materials."

Henderson grimaced. "You're a bloody Cassandra today, aren't you, Frank?"

Adams looked almost apologetic. "I know it's looking on the dark side but aren't the Jerries going to get more and more desperate as we and the Russians close in on them?"

"All right. The molybdenum mine has to be destroyed but not from the air because of the risk to civilians. So that makes it London's problem. They'll come up with something. They always do."

"Unless we beat them to it," Adams said, semi-humorously.

Henderson glanced at him, then his voice turned hoarse. "Now you listen, Frank. Don't you dare get us into this. Not unless you want to be dropped over Berlin without a parachute."

Adams smiled. "I shouldn't worry. Without a thorough reconnaissance I can't see any way we could take it on. Even Davies knows that."

"Then mind you keep it that way," the Scot grunted. "I want my lads to live into the New Year, not to be splattered all over a bloody Norwegian mountainside."

Chapter 13

The blackout in Wilberforce Street was complete that night, causing Adams to stumble on an uneven section of the pavement as he searched for number 30. Wishing he had brought a torch and wishing even more the inhabitants of the prim, semi-detached houses used honest to God numbers instead of absurd appellatives like Dunromin and Bella Vista, he finally found number 30 and tapped on the door.

The barking of a dog down the street broke the silence but his tap remained unanswered. Bracing himself, Adams tapped harder and this time heard an impatient cry. A moment later a key was inserted in the lock and the door swung open.

The woman's voice that greeted him was anything but friendly. "Yes. What do you want?"

"I'm sorry," Adams apologised. "But my wife has the only key. May I come in?"

The woman's tone modified as she drew back. "Oh, it's you, Squadron Leader Adams. Yes, I suppose you can come in if you want to."

Inside the hall, Adams saw now that he was speaking to the elder of the two Taylor sisters, an apparition wrapped in a blue dressing gown, with curlers in her frizzled hair and skinny legs thrust into a pair of fluffy slippers. "I'm sorry," he said. "I didn't know you would be in bed."

The woman had a wheedling voice that made her sound as if she had a permanent cold. "My sister and I often go to bed in the evenings. We have to. Our coal ration wouldn't last out otherwise."

Adams nodded sympathetically. "That's a shame. May I go up to my wife's room now?"

The woman gave a little sniff. "You can but you won't find her there."

Adams paused. "Why? Has she gone into town."

"Yes. About an hour ago. With another RAF officer. Didn't you know?"

Knowing a gossip when he saw one, Adams trod carefully. "I did ask a friend to come round. Can you describe him?"

"Yes. He was a broad stocky man with ginger hair. Your wife seemed to know him very well. They were laughing and talking ten to a dozen when they went out."

Adams managed to smile. "Yes, that's Jack. If you don't mind, I'll go up to her rooms and wait for them."

The woman gave her little sniff again. "I just hope you haven't to wait too long. It was gone eleven the other night when they came home."

Aware her curiosity was white hot, Adams hoped she did not notice his start. "I'll be all right. Valerie has a wireless I can listen to."

Miss Taylor followed him up the stairs. "You won't play the wireless too loud, will you? Your wife had it on so loud the other night that we couldn't get to sleep."

Promising he would not, Adams entered the small converted bedroom that served as a sitting room and closed the door. Small items of Valerie's lay around the room, an alarm clock resting on the mantelpiece, a cardigan slung across a utility chair, a pair of high heeled shoes standing beside the chintz-covered sofa, a half-finished cigarette with lipstick traces on a small table. Valerie had never been a tidy woman.

Adams was about to walk through the opposite door into the bedroom when he hesitated and turned back. To Adams it was no victory over distrust. He saw it as rank cowardice, the act of a weak man who preferred not to know the facts than face the truth, whatever the truth was. Sighing, he walked over to a bakelite radio, switched it on, and sank into the threadbare armchair alongside it.

As music filled the room, he turned down the volume. He listened for a few minutes, then rose and switched off the light.

Crossing to the window, he drew aside the blackout curtain and gazed out. The half-moon had momentarily broken through heavy clouds and was silvering the slate roofs of the houses opposite. He could see the shape of his borrowed car down the street and two dark figures on the pavement approaching it. For a moment he felt his heartbeats quicken but then the couple walked on and disappeared. A few minutes later a shower of rain began beating against the window.

Leaving the blackout curtain drawn aside, Adams returned to his chair. Sitting there in the dark, listening to the music, he felt the chill of the room sinking into him and he switched on the small electric fire, the only means of heating available to Valerie. Finding it inadequate and that he still needed to keep on his greatcoat, Adams found himself making excuses for Valerie. After her heady life in London, was it fair to expect her to spend night after night alone in this chilly box of a room? Shouldn't he have applied to live out with her or at least made arrangements to see her more often?

About to light his pipe, Adams remembered where he was and pushed it back into his pocket. Lost in his thoughts, with the glow of the electric fire the only light in the darkness, he noticed the lateness of the hour only when the music ceased and an announcer's voice took its place. "Good evening, ladies and gentlemen. This is the late evening news read by Alvar Lidell. In Germany over twenty million people are reported to be homeless after the Allied air attacks. In Moscow General de Gaulle and Marshall Stalin have signed a treaty of alliance. If a plan proposed by Professor Patrick Abercrombie is accepted by Parliament, express highways, satellite new towns, and an encircling green belt of countryside will form part of a master plan for the future of London. Tonight Lancasters of Bomber Command made a heavy raid on the German town of Cologne. Twenty of our bombers are missing ..."

Wincing, Adams switched off the radio and went to the window again. The rain had ceased and the rising moon was now shining on the wet road and pavements. As he stood there he heard a car approaching and saw it draw up below him. As a man and a woman climbed from it, Adams felt his heartbeats quicken again.

Closing the blackout curtain again he heard the front door open and low voices in the hall below. As footsteps ascended the stairs, a man's voice and a woman's low giggle suggested the couple were making a heroic effort not to waken the Misses Taylor. The sounds were followed by Valerie's whisper. "All right, darling. You can turn the landing light off now."

The sitting room door opened. It was followed by Valerie's puzzled voice. "That's funny. I must have left the fire on."

A moment later the room light switched on and Adams saw Valerie, wrapped in a musquash coat, standing in the doorway. As he moved forward, she gave a violent start. "Frank! What are you doing here?"

Behind her Adams had a glimpse of Richardson, whose low exclamation sounded like a curse. Adams, whose dislike of scenes amounted almost to paranoia, motioned Valerie to be quiet. "Come in and close the door or you'll wake up the old ladies."

Valerie hesitated, then turned to Richardson who was showing some embarrassment. "Come in, Jack, or those old cows will he moaning again." She turned back to Adams. "How long have you been here?"

Adams was trying to decide on his correct behaviour and failing on every count. "Sometime after seven, I think."

She opened her handbag and pulled out her expensive cigarette case, a clear effort to regain her composure. "Why didn't you tell me you were coming?"

"I didn't know I could get away until this afternoon. It left me no time to tell you."

She applied a lighter to her cigarette and exhaled smoke. "Couldn't you have phoned?"

"How could I? The Taylors don't have a phone."

Remembering he was right, Valerie decided to take the initiative. "That's what happens when you put me into a dump like this. What made you decide to come tonight, anyway?"

"I thought you might like to go to the cinema."

"Did you now?" She turned her hard, attractive face to Richardson. "We've been to the cinema. Jack's been kind enough to take me."

Adams, unable to make up his mind whether protocol demanded a greater show of censure on his part, glanced at the clock on the mantelpiece. "You're late back, aren't you? I thought the cinema closed at 10.30."

Richardson, certain now that Adams wasn't going to play the affronted husband, spoke for the first time. "I took her to some friends of mine afterwards, Frank. They gave us a drink and a bite of supper."

Adams found courage in his dislike of the burly Equipment Officer. "Did you take her there the other night too?"

Richardson threw a glance at Valerie. "What other night?"

"The other night when you brought her back late. Don't say you didn't," Adams went on as Richardson opened his mouth. "Old Miss Taylor was only too happy to tell me when I got here tonight."

Nothing else was needed to stir Valerie's guilt into anger. "Are you saying you've been talking about me to those two old crones?"

"I didn't say anything about you. I didn't need to. Don't you realise the gossip there is in a small town like this?"

Valerie's shapely lips curled. "Do you think I care if a pair of old biddies gossip about me? If you were anything like a man you'd tell them to mind their own business."

"I think they'd tell me it was their business, seeing you're living in their house."

"And paying them a damned good rent for it. I'm not going to live here like a nun in a convent, Frank. Let's get that straight here and now."

Recognising the signs of a first class quarrel, Richardson moved towards the door. "I'll have to be getting back, Val. Thanks for your company and the evening."

Giving Adams a defiant look, Valerie followed him. "I've enjoyed it too, Jack. Let's do it again soon." With that she leaned forward and kissed his cheek.

Until that moment Adams believed he had gone too far but the defiance of her act was too much. His voice seemed to come from a stranger rather than himself. "It's time you and I had a talk, Jack. I'd like to see you tomorrow. What about in my office at 14.00 hours?"

Trapped until now by the legal and moral inequality of his position, the aggressive Richardson found his escape in Adams' challenge. "What do you want to do, Frank? Beat me up?"

Valerie's eyes were bright with excitement now. Her sarcastic laugh made Adams fight for control. "We've things to talk about, Jack. So please be there."

Richardson grinned. "I'll be there, Frank. Don't worry about that." Relieved the sparring was over, he caught hold of Valerie's arm, drew her close, and kissed her full on the lips. Then, with a laugh, he pulled open the door and ran down the stairs.

For a moment Valerie stood with her back to Adams. Then she turned, her attractive face flushed and spiteful.

"How dare you spy on me? And how dare you treat my friends this way?"

Adams took a deep breath. "Richardson's no friend of yours, Val. He's no friend of any woman. All he does is take what he wants."

Her lips curled into a sneer. "What a fool you are and how little you know about women. Some of us like a man to take what he wants. It makes us think we've something worth taking." When Adams stared at her, her voice rose. "With your gentlemanly ways, you've never understood that, have you?"

Adams took off his glasses and wiped them. "I'm sorry I've disappointed you, Val. But I couldn't be a Richardson in a hundred years. What do you want? A divorce?"

She gave a start. "Divorce? What the hell are you talking about?"

"Let's face it, Val. Richardson's just happened because he's here. What about London? You've been playing around for years."

"Prove it," she sneered.

"I can't. So why don't you divorce me?"

She gave her hard laugh again. "What are you going to do? Have an affair with that pretty little assistant of yours? Or have you already?"

Adams took another deep breath. "Don't be a bitch, Val. Just say the word and I'll do all that's necessary."

Her eyes appraised him. "You haven't got the guts." Then as he replaced his glasses her tone changed. "What a stupid fuss about nothing. All I did tonight was go to the cinema with one of your colleagues. Anyone else would be glad I hadn't to stay alone in this damned icy room."

Adams knew only too well what her change of manner signified. He had always given her a generous allowance and since joining the RAF he had allocated her most of his senior officer's salary. While in the heat of the moment she would provoke and insult him, upon reflection she always remembered which side her bread was buttered on.

He sighed. "Let's stop all this bickering and get a divorce, Val. In the long run it'd be better for both of us."

She gave a tut of impatience. "Don't be so silly. It's just a storm in a tea cup. Tomorrow you'll realise just how silly you've been."

"Val, it's not just tonight. I'm not the right man for you. You said it yourself only a few minutes ago."

She gave a self-deprecating smile and came to his side. "I say stupid things when I'm angry, darling, just as we all do. Give me a kiss and let's forget all about it."

He drew back as she pressed against him. "It's no good, Val. I want a divorce."

Her switch of mood was instant. Her voice rose stridently. "Well, you're not getting one. Now or ever. So put that in your damned pipe and smoke it."

At that moment Adams heard a cry of protest from the adjacent bedroom. The thought of the two Miss Taylors joining in the fray made his heart sink. He went to the door. "We'll talk about it another time or the whole town will hear about it."

He never heard Valerie's reply. Another indignant cry and a bump from the adjacent bedroom turned his blood cold. Closing the sitting room door, Adams hurried down the stairs and ran out into the street.

Adams had a nightmare that night. In it he was running a gauntlet between two ranks of tormentors who were striking him with sticks. If he kept in the centre of the lane the sticks could not reach him but because the narrow lane zigzagged like a snake and because it was dark, he kept veering off course and then one or the other assailant would strike him.

In spite of the darkness he knew who the assailants were by their taunting voices. They were Valerie and Richardson, multiplied a hundred times along the seemingly endless gauntlet he was being forced to run.

Relief from the pain came only when he stumbled round a bend and saw lights shining on either side of the gauntlet. As they silhouetted the threatening figures, he was at last able to avoid their punishing sticks. Hearing his assailants' taunting cries turn into cries of frustration, Adams stumbled out of his nightmare into consciousness. As he lay in his bed, wet from perspiration and trying to make sense of his dream, he gave a violent start and sat upright. With little or no effort on his part, Adams knew he had been given the answer to the problem that was defeating both Davies and Simms.

Chapter 14

Sue Spenser took another glance at Adams. Although he gave the appearance of studying a pile of prints recently brought to him by a WAAF from the Photographic Section, she could see from his expression that his mind was far away.

She had noticed his preoccupation earlier. With the squadron still working closely with the Allied armies in Europe, there had been a constant influx of aircrews into the "Confessional" that morning and although Adams had conducted his interrogations with his usual thoroughness, there had been slight lapses of concentration, perhaps only noticed by her, that suggested he was having difficulty in keeping his mind entirely on his work.

If that were the case, it had become more obvious after lunch. By then dense clouds and drenching rain had forced a cancellation of flying for the rest of the day. It had brought a respite for the Intelligence Section as well as for the aircrews, but its effect had been only to increase Adams' preoccupation.

Sue watched him rise and walk restlessly to the iron stove that stood near a window. As he gave a shiver and held out his hands, she smiled. "Are you cold?"

He nodded. "It's raw today, isn't it? We could do with two of these stoves in here ." Turning, he gazed through the rain-streaked window from which a few parked Mosquitoes could be seen. "It's a filthy day but at least it's giving the boys a rest. And that's no small thing."

She nodded. "If the Met report is right, it could last for the rest of the week."

"Let's hope so," Adams said. Giving his hands a final warm and rub, he returned to his desk, a somewhat untidy figure in his well-worn tunic and slightly baggy trousers. She watched him fish out his pipe, gaze down at it a moment, then replace it in his pocket. As he sighed and began gazing at the photographs again, she could control her curiosity no longer. "What's the matter, Frank? Your mind's been elsewhere all day, hasn't it?"

He gave a start, then a grimace. "Has it shown that much?"

She smiled. "No, but I've learned your little ways." Knowing he had gone into Highgate the previous evening to see Valerie, she felt certain there was a connection. "Do you want to talk about it or not?"

Because of the confidences he had exchanged with her in the past, his hesitation surprised her. "I'm not certain that I should, Sue."

She tried to conceal her hurt with a laugh. "Then you mustn't. I wasn't prying. I just thought it might help to talk."

He sighed again. "It would help. But ..."

She broke in quickly as he hesitated again. "Frank, you don't need to explain. Your private life is no one's business but your own."

At that he showed surprise. "Oh no, it hasn't anything to do with Val. It's true we did have a quarrel. Jack Richardson had taken her out and I acted like a damn fool when they got back. But this has to do with the squadron and a problem Davies has."

"Then you mustn't talk about it," she said. "Not if it's classified information."

He shifted restlessly, a man torn with inner conflict. "It's a tactical problem, Sue. Davies seems to think I'm good at solving such problems and more or less ordered me to find an answer to this one. It seemed insoluble at first but last night, after I got back from Highgate, I think I got the answer."

"Isn't that good news?" she asked as he paused.

He shook his head. "No, it isn't. In fact I wish to God I'd never thought of it."

Her attractive face showed her surprise. "But why, Frank? Isn't anything that'll help win this war a good thing?"

He turned sharply away. "Damn the war. Damn the entire bloody business."

127

His intensity puzzled her. "I don't understand. Can't you tell me a little more?"

A full ten seconds passed before he turned back to her. "It's a simple choice, Sue. If I say nothing, then it's likely the squadron won't get the job. If on the other hand I tell Davies my idea, it's quite possible a third or more of our boys will be killed carrying it out. Now do you see my problem?"

For a sensitive man like Adams, she understood only too well. "Are you sure it would he that dangerous?"

Adams jerked his head. "Yes."

"How important is the target?"

"According to Simms, very important."

"Would it save many lives if it were destroyed?"

Adams' voice was bitter. "Who can ever say in this mad business? But Simms and others above him seem to think so. At the extreme, they think it might even be critical."

"You've always found Simms a man of sound judgement, haven't you? Also, a man who doesn't exaggerate?"

Adams' nod was reluctant. "Yes, I suppose I have."

"Then at least you can assume any sacrifices called for wouldn't be in vain."

For a moment Adams' glance was full of dislike. "You're saying I should go ahead and tell Davies, aren't you?"

"If you believe everything Simms tells you, it doesn't seem you have any choice."

"For God's sake, Sue, these boys are my friends."

The girl's voice was quiet, reproachful. "They're mine too, Frank. Don't forget that."

Adams gazed at her, then rose heavily to his feet and walked back to the window. She had to strain to hear his words. "There's no question that Davies will jump at the idea. He can't wait to get the squadron another major operation. I'll be like an executioner. I wonder what the boys would think of me."

His pain was so real she could feel it. "The boys would never blame you. They'd know you were only doing your duty."

"Duty!" He spat out the word like an epithet. "How many good lives has that damned word cost?"

Although she had long learned that there was much more to Adams than his tolerance and mild manner suggested, she had never seen him in this state before. "I know it's an awful decision to take. I'd feel just the same. But if an attack can save many lives or even influence the course of the war, what alternative do you have?"

He threw her a resentful glance. "You're talking like Davies now."

She bit her lip. "I'm sorry. But you did want my opinion, didn't you? Or why did you tell me about it?"

His state of mind was self-punishing. "Because I'm a damned coward, that's why. Because I hadn't the courage to face it myself."

She jumped up and went to his side. "Now you're being silly. A problem like this has to be shared."

He turned towards her and to her distress she saw that behind his glasses his eyes were moist. "Why are you so different?"

"Different?"

"To her. To Valerie. She wouldn't understand this in a thousand years."

She wanted nothing more than to take the pain from him. She took both of his hands in her own. "Listen, Frank. Aren't you being a little unfair to her? How can civilians understand? They're a thousand miles away from all these decisions and sacrifices."

With the rain hammering down on the tin roof, neither of them heard footsteps approaching on the path outside. It took a loud laugh to make them start and turn towards the door. Richardson, wearing his greatcoat and soaked cap, was standing there. As Sue drew sharply back from Adams, he laughed again. "Don't stop for me, Sue. I'm no spoilsport."

The girl's cheeks went pink with embarrassment as Richardson turned his grin on Adams. "Sorry if I broke things up, Frank. But you did ask to see me this afternoon."

Adams, whose personal problem had been pushed to the back of his mind by this greater one, had wished earlier that he had not asked Richardson to see him. To handle the truculent, over-sexed Equipment Officer would have been difficult enough in normal circumstances; to decide on the right action when his mind was fully occupied with a life or death decision was too much. In other words Adams had no idea what he was going to say to Richardson.

As it happened the need was taken from him. Before he could speak, Richardson made a mocking gesture at the embarrassed Sue. "I don't think this is the right time for the two of us to have a tête-a-tête, do you, Frank? A rainy day ... flying scrubbed ... just the two of you in here. The chances can't come that often." His close-set, prurient eyes moved back to Adams. "As I say, I'm not a spoilsport, like some people I know. I'll leave you both to it and we can talk some other time."

Seeing Sue's embarrassment, the tightly strung wire inside Adams quivered to the point of snapping. "Don't talk to Sue that way! You know damn well there's nothing between us."

With the situation conveniently slanted his way, the burly Richardson took full advantage of it. "You could have fooled me, Frank. But don't worry about it. Relax and enjoy yourselves. I'm not going to spread it around the station."

"There's nothing to spread around, damn you. Keep your dirty thoughts to yourself."

Richardson grinned. "There's as much to gossip about as there was last night. And that didn't stop you throwing your weight about, did it? You know what you are, mate? You're a damned hypocrite. You expect your wife to behave like a Vestal Virgin while you enjoy your little love nest here. Valerie's always suspected it and now I see she's right."

Adams heard Sue give a gasp and the wire within him snapped. "You filthy minded bastard! Get out of here. Get out before I throw you out."

With Richardson feeding on aggression as he did, Adams could not have said anything more calculated to please him. The words had barely left his mouth before a heavy thump on his chest sent him stumbling back. "You'll do what, Frank? You'll do what?"

A second thump dislodged Adams spectacles and sent him reeling. As he tried frantically to set the glasses back in place, he heard a frantic cry from Sue. "Leave him alone! Leave him or I'll tell the Adjutant what you've done."

The grinning Richardson turned to her. "Why don't you do that? I'm sure he'd like to hear about the goings-on you have in here."

With his sight restored, Adams took a swing at the burly figure, only for Richardson to catch his arm and twist it behind his back. "Now that's naughty, Frank. You can get hurt doing things like that. Sit down and be a good boy."

With Richardson both stronger and heavier, Adams found himself unable to struggle free as he was pushed towards a bench. As he was forced down on it, Richardson gave a final spiteful twist of his arm and then stood back grinning. "That's better. Now I'm going. And if you two have any sense, you'll forget all about this afternoon."

As the Nissen hut door slammed triumphantly behind him, the white-faced Sue ran over to Adams. "Are you all right, Frank? Did he hurt you?"

Adams, panting heavily, turned away. She dropped on one knee alongside him. "Frank, look at me!"

Adams' only reply was a muted sob. She threw her arms round his trembling shoulders. "Frank, listen to me. It doesn't matter what a disgusting brute like Richardson says. We know it's only a pack of lies."

When he made no reply, she shook him, hardly knowing what she was saying. "You did all you could, Frank. You've nothing to be ashamed of."

His cry made her realise her mistake. "God, I hate myself, Sue. Look how I handled myself. Valerie's right. I've no right to call myself a man."

She tightened her grip and pressed her cheek against his own, her voice fierce. "Valerie's a bitch. She's also a fool. If it wasn't for Tony, you'd be sick and tired of me chasing you all over the station."

She felt him give a faint start. For a moment he sat motionless, then he removed his glasses and wiped his eyes. She bent forward and kissed his cheek. "I mean it," she said quietly. "I've never known a lovelier man. I'd be proud to be seen with you anywhere. If you haven't guessed that, you must be blind. So stop all this self-punishment."

He felt back for her hand and squeezed it. Then, although desperately embarrassed, he replaced his glasses, turned to her, and attempted a smile. "I've made a fool of myself, haven't I? But thanks. I'm all right now."

Embarrassed herself, she drew back. "You're just a sensitive man with too many problems, that's all. I only wish I could help you."

He rose to his feet. "You have, Sue. More than you know." Gripping her hand again, he turned and made for the red telephone on his desk.

She wiped her own eyes as she watched him. "What are you going to do?"

He picked up the receiver. "I'm going to phone Henderson and ask him to convene a meeting with Davies at High Elms."

"Does that mean you're going to tell them your plan?"

Adams took a deep breath. "Yes, God help me. You're quite right. The way things are I just don't have any choice."

Chapter 15

Hearing the sound of an engine, Simms went to the French windows of the library and drew back the blackout curtain. Seeing car headlights in the forecourt below, he glanced back at Adams and Henderson. "Yes, it is Air Commodore Davies. I must say he's wasted no time getting here."

He turned back to glance again through the rain-streaked windows. Three figures were emerging from the staff car and being greeted by a young army officer. Satisfied, the elderly Brigadier drew the blackout curtain back into place. His smile was at Adams. "You couldn't have solved our problem at a better time, Squadron Leader. As you'll hear later, we have suddenly discovered that time is not on our side."

Adams showed his anxiety. "I'm not sure it is the answer yet, sir. It's only a suggestion as it stands."

"Quite, Adams. Quite. But from what you've told me I think Air Commodore Davies is going to like it."

It was not what Adams wanted to hear but he held back his reply as Davies and Ian Moore entered the library. Moore's presence was due to Adams. Conscious of the ex-squadron commander's vast low-level experience and knowing he was a supreme judge of the Mosquito's spacial requirements, Adams had requested the distinguished young officer be present in the hope he would be a counter to the over-enthusiasm he felt certain Davies would show.

Making no comment on the absence of the third man who had arrived with the party, Simms welcomed the two officers with his usual courtesy. "Thank you for coming so promptly, gentlemen. Take off your overcoats and come near the fire." As they obeyed and followed Simms to the long mahogany table, the Brigadier nodded at Adams. "As I've just explained to your Intelligence Officer, we in SOE have discovered today that we have no time to lose. So in every way this meeting is fortunate."

Bursting with energy and enthusiasm after hearing Adams had come up with an idea, Davies responded like a terrier sighting a tom cat. "Why? What's happened?"

Simms smiled. "In a moment, Davies. First I suggest you let Adams tell you about his idea. Although I'm no airman, I do think it has great promise."

Davies gave Adams an impatient scowl. "About time too. I don't know why Jock couldn't tell me over the phone."

"We thought it safer not to, sir," Adams told him.

Davies's scowl faded. "It's that hush hush, is it? All right. Let's have it now."

A silence fell as Adams pulled a sheet of paper from his tunic on which he had made notes. Acutely aware he was putting forward an idea that, if taken up by Davies, would almost certainly cost the lives of some of his friends, Adams had a sudden feeling of unreality. The artificial light in the library and the uniformed figures gazing at him made him feel he was an actor in some grotesque play rather than a leading figure in a life and death situation.

Pulling himself together, he explained his idea. It took him little more than a minute but before that short time was over Davies's eyes were glowing. When he finished Davies gave a hoarse, delighted laugh. "Frank, you've cracked it. It's marvellous. Bloody marvellous in fact. How do you do it? Is it those monkey glands again?"

Adams lifted a protesting hand at the small Air Commodore's enthusiasm. "Hang on, sir. We still don't know it'll work."

After his initial disappointment at being unable to use his squadron, Davies was in no mood to find flaws in the opportunity now offered to him. "Of course it'll work. It's too simple not to work. That's the beauty of it."

It was not what Adams wanted to hear. "No, sir. We still don't know the valley is wide enough."

"Of course it'll be wide enough. It was those bluffs and that damned smoke that was the problem." The excited Davies turned to Moore. "Don't you agree, Ian?"

Moore's good-looking face was showing neither disappointment nor encouragement. "I have to agree with Frank, sir. Although his idea might counter the smoke defences, we do need to know the width of the valley from end to end, particularly where those two bluffs jut out. Firstly, though, are you quite certain you can't dive straight down at the wood from the mountain tops?"

Davies shook his head. "Not a hope. The valley's too narrow and it's also a cul-de-sac. We'd be fighting for height to clear the opposite mountains before we got near the wood. Also, as you know well enough, you can only bomb from a Mosquito in a shallow dive. A low level attack coming through the valley is the only way."

Moore grimaced. "It's a hazardous business flying between mountains as steep as this, sir."

It was not the statement Davies wanted. "For Christ's sake, Ian, I know all that." He swung round on Simms. "Now we have a way of countering the smoke, we'll have to lay on a proper reconnaissance. I know there's a risk Jerry might bring guns in but if Churchill demands the job has to be done, what alternative is there?"

Henderson's protest came immediately. "Guns would make a death trap of that valley, sir. You know it as well as I do."

Davies glared at him. "What are you saying, Jock? That we've got this great idea from Adams and we can't use it?" When Henderson made no reply, Davies made a grudging concession. "All right. Now we know how to handle the smoke we'll do the rest ourselves from medium high level. That way we can do a more thorough job than the Benson boys. Pretend we're going somewhere else and take photographs as we pass over. Our photo-recce people are clever at working out heights and distances from photographs."

Moore shook his head. "You couldn't rely on that, sir. They'd only have to miss some crag or misjudge some distance and it could be mayhem for our boys."

Davies's patience was fast running out. "It's a risk we'll have to take, Ian. We can't drop it now Frank's solved the main problem."

Adams knew it was the right moment to make his move. He gave a cough. "There is one way that might not alert the Germans, sir."

Davies swung round on him as sharply as a terrier snatching a rat. "Yes. Go on."

"Instead of using the partisans to overcome the smoke problem, we could send one of our own men over there. Someone who knows the capabilities and limitations of our aircraft. If he were to examine the valleys from the ground, take photographs, and work with one of the partisan groups, they could radio back his findings and send back his photographs."

Davies let out an epithet and then slammed a fist into his palm. "That's it! An RAF ground observer! Frank, what would we do without you? Who do we use? An RAF Regiment man?"

"No, sir." Adams took a deep breath. "You use me."

Eyes widened and then a loud murmur broke out. Davies looked half amused and half incredulous. "Come on, Frank. This is a job for a fit young man. It would be murder climbing over those mountains. Don't forget the time of the year. It's as cold as hell in Norway now."

Adams nodded. "That's what you said to me last year, sir, before Operation Valkyrie. But I still did the job, didn't I?"

Davies was taken aback by the reminder. "Yes. You did well. But this is a different job altogether."

"I don't see why. I'd plenty of climbing to do the last time."

"Frank, we've got loads of younger men who can do the job." Davies glanced at Simms who inclined his head. "We can get somebody from SOE who's experienced in clandestine operations of this kind."

"But not acquainted with a Mosquito's capabilities, sir."

"All right, then a younger man from the squadron."

"You're going to need every pilot or observer you have, sir. And there aren't that many specialist officers younger than me."

Although secretly sympathetic with Adams' case, Davies tended to over-compensate when his commonsense clashed with his emotions, a habit that tended to support his critics' assertions that he was a hard man. It showed now as he cast an unkind eye over

Adams' figure. "There are fitter ones, though, aren't there? Come on, Frank. You and I are past this kind of lark."

No one could be more dogged than Adams when he wanted something as badly as this. "I think I deserve it, sir. After all, it is my idea."

Moore's pleasant voice broke in before Davies could reply. "There is an alternative, sir. As I'm not allowed to fly against the Germans any longer, why don't I go? I think I'm as qualified as anyone about the Mossie's capabilities."

Seeing from Davies's expression how tempting the suggestion was, Henderson gave him no time to speculate. "Don't be a fool, Ian. You'd be in far more danger of being captured than if you flew over there."

Although Davies scowled at the Scot, he could do little else but agree. "Jock's right. Since CRISIS I've been given express orders not to use you against the Jerries in any active capacity. So that's out."

As silence returned, Adams made his appeal again. "I'm the right man to go, sir. The Brigadier says that Steen Jensen and his group are involved. They're the ones I worked with during Valkyrie and I've an excellent relationship with them. I know they'd help me in every way possible." Seeing from Davies's expression that the point had gone home, and knowing how much he respected Moore's opinion, Adams turned to the young Wing Commander. "What about you, Ian? You backed me over Valkyrie. What's the difference here?"

Moore hesitated. "It's going to be very dangerous, Frank."

"No more dangerous than Valkyrie. And I handled it all right, didn't I?"

Acknowledging his case with a smile, Moore turned to Davies. "You can't deny he did a fine job, sir. You said it yourself. So why shouldn't we use him again?"

As Adams' heart leapt, Davies gave a sarcastic grunt. "Friendship wouldn't be involved here, would it, Ian?"

Moore's lips quirked wryly. "Friendship? For a job like this? No, sir, my views come from Frank's record. We all know what he did last year."

Henderson, who had been studying Adams with curiosity, broke in at this point with his usual bluntness. "Why do you want to go so much, Frank?"

Wondering if he knew himself, Adams said the first thing that came to his mind. "I want to see my idea put into practice."

"You're sure it's nothing personal?"

Adams gave the Scot a look of reproach. "Why should it be?"

"I just don't see why at your age you should want to go climbing big, icy mountains, particularly when you might be caught and handed over to the Gestapo as a spy."

Simms gave Adams no chance to answer. Although by nature a patient man, he had been showing a growing restlessness as the argument over Adams' participation had dragged on. "Forgive me, gentlemen, but if you are taking on this raid you need to choose your agent tonight. Since he was alerted about the mine, Steen has been giving it his full attention and his woman agent has discovered something that makes our raid far more urgent than we suspected."

All eyes were on the slim, elderly Brigadier now. "What discovery's that?" Davies asked.

"It seems the mine is no longer our only target. Because of the narrowness of the valley, enemy transports moving along it are vulnerable to partisan attack and since our armies invaded Europe, Norwegian partisan activity has greatly increased, particularly in this valley. As a consequence, the enemy has been storing his recent output of molybdenum near the mine itself."

Davies was looking puzzled. "But I thought you said molybdenum is essential for his new weapons."

"It is, Davies. That's why the enemy is being so careful. His thinking would go this way. If a small consignment of ore were captured and the ore examined, it would have told us about the mine and what it was producing."

"But if the metal's so important to Jerry, isn't he defeating his purpose by keeping it there?"

"Like so many things in this war, Davies, it's a balancing act. The enemy wants the ore badly but can't risk losing its source. So London believes he will soon be sending in a large armoured convoy that the partisans will be unable to attack. As this could be sent any day, we have far less time to launch our raid than we previously believed."

Adams did not waste his opportunity. "So the sooner I go, the better."

Davies shook his head. "On the contrary it counts you out, Frank. If the job has to be done so quickly, there'll be no time to give you parachute training."

Adams' quick brain was not caught out so easily. "No, sir. I can go by fishing boat. The Norwegian's run their Shetland Bus service almost every day."

Simms nodded at Davies's questioning glance. "He's right, Davies. I can get him on a fishing boat without any problems. So can I take it you are going to settle on Adams?"

With the Brigadier showing impatience at his quibbling, Davies knew he was defeated. His disgruntled eyes moved to Adams. "All right, Frank. If you believe you can handle it, you've got the job." Before the excited Adams could reply, he turned to Simms. "I take it you'll organise Frank's trip, sir?"

"Yes. But I'll want him ready early tomorrow morning." As the other officers gave a start, Simms looked apologetic. "I know it's short notice but this news from Norway has changed everything." He turned to Henderson. "I'm afraid it means you and your colleagues will have to work tonight to get Adams' equipment ready. It'll be taken with him up to Scotland where a fishing boat will be waiting. Are there any questions?"

Although looking dismayed at the time allowed him, Henderson bit back his complaint and addressed Davies instead. "What about the raid itself, sir? I take it you're leaving me to choose its leader?"

Full of eagerness again now that the matter of the ground observer was settled, Davies gave him a grin. "You hate my interfering, don't you, Jock? But this time I must."

The Scot tried to stifle a groan. "Who, sir?"

"It's going to be Harvey, Jock."

For a moment both Henderson and Adams looked too shocked to reply. Then Adams found his tongue. "You can't use Harvey again, sir."

Although normally intolerant of criticism, Davies took the protest well. "I'm not using him again, Frank. He used himself the last time."

"I know that, sir. But you did make a promise to Anna."

"And who broke that promise? Harvey, not me. In fact the insubordinate bugger broke every rule in the book."

To Adams' relief, Henderson joined in the protest. "He did that for Ian, sir, not for himself."

"What's that to do with it? He still struck a superior officer and then drugged him. I ought to have court martialed him and you both know it. He's the luckiest man alive that I didn't."

Moore, who looked as shocked as anyone, added his own protest. "I still don't think it gives you a right to break your promise to Anna, sir."

Although Davies's sharp face darkened at the comment, he chose not to take offence from it. "You all keep on talking about Anna. Have you stopped to think what Harvey wants?"

Adams looked puzzled. "I don't follow you, sir."

"You ought to, Frank. You were one of the few who were at Sutton Craddock after the Swartfjord job and saw how badly Harvey took it when Moore was given command of the squadron afterwards. Isn't that true?"

"Yes," Adams admitted. "He felt he'd deserved the promotion."

"And so did you, Frank, and most of the other lads. Come on. You can't deny it."

Adams had to agree. "Yes, sir. We did. Although, as it happened, a better man couldn't have been brought in than Ian."

"That's by the bye. Harvey felt cheated and it's been smouldering in him ever since. So, as Ian can't lead the squadron any longer, I'm giving it to Harvey until this mission's over. And you know something? He's as pleased about it as a dog with two tails."

Although Davies was giving the impression he was making up for a past injustice, Adams was too aware of the long standing feud between the choleric Davies and the stubborn but dedicated Yorkshireman to believe his reasons were entirely altruistic. Davies believed this new mission was going to require the highest qualities of leadership and without Moore to call on, he was seeing Harvey as the rightful successor. "Does Anna know this yet?" Adams asked.

"I don't think so. I only told Harvey he was getting the job today." Davies glanced at the Brigadier. "I think we'll have him in now, sir."

Henderson showed surprise as Simms pressed a button on the table. "Is he here?"

"Yes. We brought him with us." Guessing the Scot's unspoken question, Davies answered it with some sarcasm. "I knew there'd be a lot of moaning and grumbling about my using him on this operation, so I thought he'd better stay out until the squabbling was over."

The door opened at that moment and the tall figure of Harvey appeared. Davies turned to him as he saluted. "All right. You can come in now."

Harvey walked forward. His rugged face showed pleasure as he saw Adams standing by the table. "Hello, Frank. They said you'd be here. What's this plan you've come up with?"

Adams avoided Davies's eyes. "I'll tell you in a moment. How's the leg coming along?"

Harvey slapped his thigh disparagingly. "It's as right as rain. I walked a couple of miles yesterday without any problem. How's Valerie finding Highgate? Is she settling down?"

To Adams' relief, Davies's testy voice saved him a reply. "When you two have finished with your pleasantries. do you mind if we get on with the war? You've been called in, Harvey, because your promotion is confirmed. From today you are the squadron commander with the acting rank of Wing Commander. This means you'll lead the squadron on this new operation that we're planning."

Although the tall Yorkshireman showed no emotion, Adams could sense his deep satisfaction at achieving his ambition at last. At the same time Harvey ran to form in the bluntness of his reply. "In that case I'd better know all about this new idea Adams has come up with, hadn't I, sir?"

For a moment, Davies forgot where he was. "Give us a bloody moment, for Christ's sake." Then, with an apologetic glance at Simms, he turned to Adams. "Give it to him as quickly as you can, Frank. We've got a busy night ahead of us."

141

Adams glanced across the table at Harvey. "It's very simple really. We're going to send a man into the valley to check for any dangerous obstacles and report them back to London. But his main job will be to fix lights on the worst obstacles in case Jerry uses smoke. As for the problem of avoiding bombs falling on the town, he'll rig up a light or lights at its far end so crews won't drop their bombs too soon."

"You mean they fly between lights and use the ground light as a target marker?"

"That's right. So if Jerry uses smoke, the lights should still shine through."

Harvey's first reaction, bringing a glare from Davies, was a derisory laugh. "Frank, it's crazy! It's pure bloody Heath Robinson!" Then, seeing Moore's expression, his tone changed. "You don't think it'll work, do you, Ian?"

Moore shrugged. "If the valley isn't too narrow, I think it just might. Mind you, it'll test your boys' reflexes."

Harvey turned back to Adams. "But isn't Jerry going to shoot out the lights as soon as they're switched on? And how does your man find out where the target's hidden?"

Adams nodded. "The first depends on the kind of lights we use. If they're electric, they'll have to be focused upwards and shaded at ground level. They'll also have to be as far away as possible from any machine gun nests. Alternatively we might use long-lasting magnesium flares which couldn't be shot out. As for the location of the target, the Brigadier says the partisans are working on that at the moment."

Shaking his head, Harvey glanced at Davies. "Are you going ahead with this, sir?"

Davies gave him a scowl. "Yes, we are. So you'd better give it all your attention."

In his forthright way, Harvey said the thing Henderson and Moore were thinking. "I wouldn't like to be the poor devil who does this job. He'll have to work right under Jerry's nose. Who's he going to be?"

Adams' voice was almost sheepish. "I'm going, Frank."

Harvey's rugged jaw dropped. "You're kidding?" When Adams made no reply, Harvey swung round on Davies. "Who had this idea, sir? Frank can't be sent on a job like this. It's crazy."

Seeing Simms's impatient expression, Davies was quick to snuff out any further argument over Adams. "Frank volunteered and that's all there is to it." As Harvey opened his mouth to protest again, Davies closed it with a sharp, peremptory order. "That's enough, Harvey. In fact that's enough from the lot of you. We're leaving now, so get your coats on. We've a ton of work to do back at Sutton Craddock before Frank leaves in the morning."

Chapter 16

Orderly chaos reigned in a section of Number Two hangar that night as Davies, rendered urgent by Simms' news, led a small team in a frantic rush to collect the equipment and stores Adams would need during his Norwegian adventure.

His party consisted of the same men who had been with him at High Elms plus two specialist officers, both sworn to high secrecy. One was the Armament Officer whose co-operation was necessary both for advice and for the procurement of suitable pyrotechnics. The other was Richardson, the last man Adams would have wanted in normal circumstances, but in his role of Equipment Officer, Richardson was needed to advise what other artefacts might be needed and what was readily available.

Even so, with the hazards of the Norwegian valley still unexplored, men could only guess at Adams' requirements. The bomb store and the armoury were plundered for long duration magnesium flares, coloured markers, a miscellaneous selection of pyrotechnics, Very pistols, Sten guns, a revolver, and boxes of ammunition. At the same time Richardson provided a petrol driven generator, cans of petrol, coils of electric cable, and cold weather clothing for Adams. As each item was added to the pile, one man or another would suggest a further item and the search would begin again. Long before the collection was over Adams was resigned to the belief that in a few days he would be bitterly kicking himself for forgetting some vital artefact while most of the equipment taken over would prove useless.

It was 02.00 hours before men ran out of ideas and Davies turned to Adams. "Anything else you can think of, Frank?"

Adams shook his head. "No, sir." Then he paused. "Perhaps I should take a bottle or two of whisky. Jensen has a taste for it."

Davies gave a grunt. "Then we'd better send some." He turned to Henderson. "Have you any in the Mess?"

Henderson was trying to hide his dismay. "I think the Mess Officer got a few bottles the other week, sir."

"Then wake him up and tell him we want them. All of them. We're going to need all the co-operation we can get from Jensen and his group before this business is over."

As Henderson gave a deep sigh and made for the hangar door, Davies winked at Adams and followed him. "I'll come with you, Jock. Just to make sure the Mess Officer doesn't hold out on us."

As the two men disappeared from the hangar, Harvey turned to Moore. "He's in his bloody element again, isn't he?"

Moore smiled. "It's relief, Frank. He's always scared the squadron might be disbanded if there's a long gap between operations. And this time it seemed likely."

The Yorkshireman had no intention of letting Davies off the hook so lightly. "He's a bloodthirsty little bastard. He's never happy unless he's planning some mischief or other."

"What are you complaining about?" Moore asked. "He's given you my job, hasn't he?"

Harvey's rugged face grinned with malice. "Not before bloody time, mate. I'd have had it two years ago if you hadn't gone to the right schools and had all that brass in the bank."

Moore laughed. Then his tone changed. "Anna doesn't know about it yet, does she?"

Harvey grimaced. "No. And she's going to play hell when she does. I haven't worked out yet what I'm going to say to her."

For a moment Moore's voice was condemning. "You should have turned it down. For her sake if not your own."

"What, and be court-martialled instead? After Crisis, the little bastard was probably hoping that's what I'd do."

Moore's dismay on hearing Harvey was to lead the mission was not only based on his friendship for the Yorkshireman. In love with Anna himself, he wanted her happiness above all else and he had been hoping Harvey would get the rest he deserved on leaving hospital. To hide his feelings he fell back on the mordant humour of the RAF.

"I'd been hoping he would cashier you. You damn nearly broke my jaw, you crazy tike." Then, as Harvey grinned, he went on: "Personally I don't think Davies intended to punish you. He'd have had you as soon as you left hospital if that had been his intention. He's put you in charge because he thinks you're the best man for the job."

"I'd have expected he'd use Millburn," Harvey said.

"Perhaps he would have if you hadn't done such a good job in Austria. That Crisis operation really impressed him."

Harvey grinned. "I must do something like it again. Maybe if I clouted him on the jaw too, he'd promote me to the Air Council."

While the two men were talking, Richardson had moved across to Adams who was down on his knees sorting through the pyrotechnics. Until then, conscious of Davies's presence, both men had kept an icy courtesy to one another. Now the burly Richardson, frowning heavily, stared down at Adams. "What the hell are you up to, Frank? Why are you doing this?"

Adams glanced up at him. "Does it matter?"

"Is it to impress Sue?"

"Sue? Don't be a fool."

"Then what's it for?" Richardson's close-set eyes ran over Adams' figure. "You'll never pull it off, you know. You're too old and flabby. You'll get yourself killed or captured. Davies must be crazy letting you go."

Adams shrugged. "You could be right. You feel like taking my place?"

Richardson's face tightened at the gibe. "What about Valerie? She'll have to be told. Do you want me to do it?"

Adams realised he had given no thought to Valerie since offering his services to Davies. "You won't tell her anything. You're sworn to secrecy, remember."

"But she's going to ask where you are. She has to be told something."

As he spoke Adams was conscious of the irony that this man could endanger his life if he let his tongue run loose. "Tell her I'm busy at the airfield. She won't bother if she believes that."

There was more than curiosity in Richardson's expression now. "You still haven't told me why you're doing it. Is it to get your own back on her?"

For the first time since he, Valerie, and Richardson had clashed, Adams felt in command of the situation. He found the effect elating. "You wouldn't understand if I told you, Jack. So stop wasting your time."

The man's voice turned aggressive. "You're enjoying all this, aren't you? Playing the big hero. I'd lay odds you'll be scared to bloody death over there."

It was a prediction Adams could accept. "You'd win your bet. I'm scared now, so God knows how I'll feel later."

Richardson stared at him, a hint of desperation in his voice. "Then why the hell are you going?"

Adams got up from his knees. "If you want the truth, I don't know. Perhaps I like snow and ice and big mountains. Or perhaps I'm just tired of a wife who uses me to provide for her extravagances and her affairs. Whatever it is, what does it matter? I'm going."

Richardson's frown deepened. "So you're blaming me and Valerie?"

"I never said anything about you, Jack." As he turned and faced Richardson, Adams was delighted both by his courage and his choice of words. "From my viewpoint you aren't worth a beggar's spit in a heap of sand. So will you piss off now and let me get on with my job?"

With Richardson's face turning thunderblack, it was perhaps fortunate for Adams that Davies and Henderson returned to the hangar at that moment, the latter carrying a cardboard box. Motioning him to set it alongside the other artefacts, Davies gave him a grin. "Sorry, Jock. But it is important we keep that big Norwegian happy."

Henderson's silence said it all. Winking at Adams like a mischievous elf, Davies walked over to him. "Have you thought of anything else, Frank?"

"No, sir. Although I'm sure I will later."

"No question you will once you've seen the valley. But don't worry. We'll either drop it by air or send it by boat. That's something we'll have to play by ear. In the meantime Jock's

147

arranging for this stuff to be sent tonight to High Elms. There it'll be loaded on to one of Simms's transports and taken up to Scotland to the fishing boat Simms is getting for you. As you'll be going along with the stuff, Simms wants you to be at High Elms no later than 07.30 hours. Sorry you won't get much sleep but that's the way it goes. By the way, you don't get seasick, do you?"

The question caught Adams by surprise. "I don't know, sir. I've never been out in a fishing boat before."

Davies looked sympathetic. "I'm told it can be a bit hairy in Norwegian waters. So try to get some of these new seasick pills I hear they dished out to the Army on D-Day. Simms might have some. He's full of surprises."

When Adams made no reply, Davies drew him aside. "I have to go in a few minutes, Frank. So I might not see you before you leave. I'm sorry it's turned out this way. I was hoping we'd have a couple of days to get prepared. But that's war. The first thing I want you to do over there is check whether our kites could dive in over the town and release their bombs without colliding with those mountains at the far end. If we could do that and avoid flying along the lower reaches of the valley, it would enormously simplify the job. It would also make it easier for you because we'd only need markers at the far end of the town."

As Adams nodded, Davies went on: "The thing you'll have to remember is that the Mossie can only drop bombs in a shallow dive. So you'll need to make a fine judgement because you can't have 'em swooping up and down like a flight of swallows. Personally, from the height of those mountains, I think it's low level or nothing but it's the first thing to decide. All right?"

Adams nodded. "I'm just hoping the mine isn't right at the foot of Helsberg. If it is, I don't see any way we can bomb it, even at low level."

From his expression Davies had the same fear. "Yes, that bloody camouflage is a nuisance. If the mine's that close, I don't know what we'll do because with that town lying there the Norwegians will never give permission for a saturation raid by heavies. So we'll just have to hope for the best. Have you any more questions before you go?"

148

Adams shook his head. "I probably would have if there was more time to think but, like you, I hadn't expected things to move so quickly."

Davies's nod was sympathetic. "It's possible we might have more time, of course. Jerry might not move his stocks for another week or two. But Simms can't afford to take the risk. So there's nothing else you want to ask?"

"Not at the moment, sir. I take it if I get any problems I can radio them back to London?"

"So Simms says. I know there's always a danger Jerry might break into the code but that's a risk we have to take."

Davies paused. "What about your wife? Do you want to go and see her tonight?"

Adams had a vision of the two Miss Taylors being awakened in the middle of the night and hid a shudder. "No, sir. I think it's better I go without saying anything."

"Fair enough but your wife will have to be told sometime. I thought we could say you've been posted to an airfield in Scotland for a few weeks. How does that sound?"

It took only a moment for the better side of Adams to prevail. "It would be best if someone would do that. Perhaps my assistant might go."

"No need for that, Frank. I'll go myself when I have a moment."

Adams could not believe his ears. "You, sir? Are you sure?"

"Why not? It's the least I can do. I suppose the Adjutant has her address?"

As Adams nodded, he was thinking nothing could have stressed the danger of his mission more than Davies's offer. "Yes. As you know, she has rooms in Highgate."

"Right, then I'll see to it. I'll tell her you'll be back in two or three weeks. Mind you are."

Adams managed a smile. "I'll do my best, sir."

Davies held out his hand. "Pave the way for our kites and you'll be the toast of the squadron when you get back. Good luck, Frank."

* * *

149

The rain had ceased when Harvey reached the small village of Heselton but the swelling moon was having the greatest difficulty in breaking through the drifting mass of clouds. As Harvey braked his car, it succeeded for a moment in silvering the small bungalow that flanked the road but it was hauled ignominiously back just as Harvey had reached the door and was fumbling in his greatcoat pocket.

Cursing under his breath, the Yorkshireman had to feel for the Yale lock before he could insert his key. Hoping Sam had recognised his footsteps and wouldn't bark, Harvey gently eased the door open. As he stepped into the small warm hall, he felt Sam's wagging tail strike his leg and the dog's wet nose press against his hand. Patting the animal's shoulder and whispering for it to keep quiet, he felt his way into the sitting room. Removing his greatcoat and sinking down on the sofa, he was about to remove his shoes when he noticed a faint line of light beneath the main bedroom door. A moment later the door swung open and the slim figure of Anna appeared. Although she was wearing a dressing gown, her voice told him she had been long awake. "Frank! Do you know the time? It's almost morning. Where on earth have you been?"

Harvey sighed. Since receiving his promotion and during his long car ride back from High Elms, there had been no other thought in his mind than how he could break his news to Anna. But although he had approached the problem from a dozen angles, he knew there was no way to lessen her shock. Now, facing the moment he dreaded, the Yorkshireman met it in the only way he knew, bluntly and openly. "Sorry, love, but Davies phoned through this afternoon saying he wanted to see me at High Elms. As we didn't finish until 2 a.m. I couldn't get back any sooner."

She had switched on the sitting room light as he was speaking and he saw her face was full of alarm. "High Elms? Why did he want to see you there?"

Harvey took deep breath. "He wanted to talk to us all about a new operation that's coming up. Frank Adams and Ian were there, along with Henderson and Simms."

She reached out a hand to the back of an armchair, an unconscious act to brace herself "Why did he want you there?"

150

Without Harvey knowing it, his voice turned defiant. "Now Moore can't do the job any longer, he's made me squadron commander."

Her lovely face turned white. "Squadron commander!"

"Yes. It's something I hadn't expected."

She lowered herself into the armchair as if her legs would not support her. *"Mein Gott.* I don't believe this."

He took her hand and found it was cold and trembling. "Don't get upset, love. Just sit tight and let me explain."

She snatched her hand away. Her grey eyes were full of shock and disbelief. "What are you saying? You promised me you would take a rest from combat flying months ago. Then you flew to Austria in place of Ian. Now you tell me you are going to be squadron commander. Why do you keep on lying to me in this way?"

Harvey winced. "I couldn't help it this time, love. After what I did the other month, Davies had me over a barrel. He could have court-martialled me if he'd wanted to."

She stiffened. "Davies is in our debt, not we in his. I only went to Austria because he promised not to use you on active service again. So how can he cheat us both like this?"

"He's not cheating us, love. It's because of CRISIS. He could have punished me but he didn't. Instead he's given me this chance to put things right."

"Put things right!" In her anger and distress, she fell back on her native tongue. *"Mein Gott, Er ist in deiner Schuld, nicht du in seiner.* You led a successful mission for him and got wounded doing it. So why do you have to put anything right?"

Harvey looked almost sheepish. "I did break every rule in the book, love. To be honest I expected to be cashiered."

Emotion brought a cry from her. "I wish to God you had been. At least you'd be safe." When he shook his head but made no comment, she went on: "Davies is just using you. Otherwise why should you be punished for what you did?"

His laugh was meant to calm her. "I'm not being punished, love. He's promoted me."

She stared at him, then her eyes opened wide. "You're pleased, aren't you? You're pleased you've been put in charge of the squadron at last."

Harvey had never been a good liar. "Let's face it, love. It's a damn sight better than a court martial."

"You're pleased," she breathed again. "Damn you, you're pleased. It's something you've always wanted, isn't it?" When he made no comment she suddenly jumped to her feet, ran into the bedroom and flung open her wardrobe door. As she began dragging clothes from it, he ran after her and caught her arm. "What are you doing?"

She was sobbing bitterly. "I'm leaving you. I can't go through all that hell again." As he tried to draw her to him, she fought him with her fists. *"Lass mich gehen!* I can't take any more. I can't. I can't."

All Harvey's worst fears were alive now. He caught her wrists and locked her arms behind her back. "Calm down, love, for God's sake. You can't leave me."

She tried to break free but his strength was too great. "I am leaving you. I told you the last time I couldn't take any more."

"But this might be for only one operation."

She began struggling again. "Stop lying to me. If you're the squadron commander you'll have to fly every mission the squadron is given. Let me go. I don't want to stay with you any longer."

With Harvey universally regarded as a hard if just man, it would have astonished aircrews and erks alike to have seen his expression at that moment. "For God's sake, don't talk that way, love. You're my whole world. I'd fall apart if you left me."

"What do you think I will do if you go back on operations again? Davies promised me the last time you wouldn't fly but you still did. You all broke your promises to me and you're doing it again. I don't trust any of you any longer."

Thinking of the times this courageous and disciplined girl had faced hideous danger in Nazi-dominated Europe without faltering, Harvey knew he was frightened. He pressed her tear-drenched face into his shoulder to hide his expression. "I had to go the last time, love. I couldn't take the risk of Ian being shot down. But there was something else as well. There was you?"

For a moment her struggling ceased. "What does that mean?"

In Harvey's hard world a man rarely admitted his emotional weaknesses in case his predators used them against him. It was a measure of his distress that he admitted them now. "I hadn't known you were over there until Ian told me. That made a hell of a difference, love. You see I couldn't leave you alone to face ..."

As he broke off she lifted her face to him. "Are you saying you couldn't bear not to take part because I was involved?"

His voice turned gruff. "That wouldn't be so surprising would it? Wouldn't any man feel the same way?"

Suddenly her arms were around him instead of fighting him. *"Lieber Gott,"* she breathed. "I love you, Frank."

Harvey had never known such relief. "Then you won't go?"

"No, I won't go. I can't go. But I don't know how long I can bear it. Perhaps it is my nerves ... Oh, *Liebling,* you should never have agreed to be squadron commander."

While her words brought Harvey comfort, they also left him in no doubt what he must do. "After this one operation I'll ask Davies if I can come back to the OTU. How does that sound?"

Her voice sounded weary now, without hope. "Davies won't let you go once you've accepted his offer. It's too late."

He kissed her dark hair. "I think he might, love. I believe he just wants me for this one operation. After that I think he'll keep his word."

"What is this operation?"

Harvey had no qualms about telling her. If she could not be trusted, the whole bloody world could go up in smoke for all the Yorkshireman cared.

She listened intently but gave a gasp of shock when he mentioned Adams' role. "Are you saying that Frank Adams is going over to Norway?"

"Yes. I understand he insisted on it and because it was his idea and because he did so well last year, Davies agreed."

Her grey eyes, still moist with tears, showed bewilderment. "But Frank's such a gentle, kindly man. He should never be given a dangerous job like this."

He drew her forward and kissed her. "He's not the only gentle person who's done dangerous jobs in this war, love."

"But why is he doing it? Is it because of his wife?"

Harvey shrugged. "That could be a part of it, I suppose. But knowing Frank, I think it's more than that. Until he came up with his idea, the squadron wasn't being used. That made it all too much for Frank's conscience."

"Conscience? I don't understand."

"He couldn't bear putting the lads in danger with his idea and then sitting here on his backside doing nothing. So his conscience made him volunteer. Ian thinks that and so do I."

Tears returned to her eyes again. "Yes, I can believe it of Frank too. When will this operation begin? Do you know?"

"It'll start for Frank as soon as he lands in Norway. We have to wait until he gets things ready for us."

"You do realise I shall want to stay in The Black Swan again until it is over?"

Although expecting her demand, he made a token protest. "I wish you wouldn't."

"You wanted to be close to me when I was in danger!"

He sighed at her reminder. "Aye, that's true. All right. I'll make the arrangements with Joe Kearns. Now don't you think you should try to get some sleep?"

"When have you to report to the station?"

"Henderson doesn't expect me there until 10.00 hours. He knows I've things to settle here."

She touched his cheek and felt his night's growth rough against her fingers. Feeling a lump form in her throat, she reached up and kissed him. "Then you must get some rest too, *Liebling.*"

But they did not rest. They made love with the passion and intensity they always felt when either of them was facing danger. And although Harvey fell into a deep sleep afterwards, she was still awake when the first light of a grey winter morning showed round the edges of the blackout curtain. It brought her nothing but misgivings and fear, for with Harvey breathing quietly and peacefully by her side, she had wished the night would last forever.

Chapter 17

The bearded fisherman in sou'wester and oilskins bent down and shook Adams. "Sir! Wake up."

With an enormous effort, Adams rolled over on his hard hunk. "What is it?"

The man grinned. Lifting a hand and displaying five outstretched fingers, he waved them twice before Adams' bloodshot eyes. "Ten minutes, *ja?*"

Adams' voice was incredulous. "You mean we're there?"

"*Ja. Norge. OK?*"

Adams wanted to go on his knees and thank God but doubted if he had the strength. For what had seemed an eternity but in fact had been forty-one hours, he had retched, vomited, and retched again. Every now and then he had tried to fight his nausea by crawling up to the wet slippery deck where the three fishermen manning the boat had shown him amused sympathy, but each time the sight of the grey, tossing sea had been too much and he had been driven back into the small, claustrophobic cabin that reeked of fish and diesel fumes. Before half the journey was over, Adams had only one wish, that a German patrol boat would sight them and blow them to hell.

But with the perversity Adams expected of the world, there had been no such reprieve. As the waves of nausea had swept over him and his stomach had threatened to rupture or eject from his mouth, Adams in delirium had begun to wonder if Simms and the SOE were all they seemed. Could they be part of the Fifth Column, sponsored by the enemy and involved with the black arts? Had Simms, with Mephisthophelean cunning, transformed a fishing boat

155

into The Flying Dutchman, so dooming him to sail back and forth across the tossing North Sea until the end of time?

As the skipper climbed back on deck, Adams managed to swing his legs down from the hunk. Feeling the floorboards still heaving, he was about to abandon the effort when the pitching and tossing suddenly eased. Not daring to hope, Adams clung to the side of his bunk and waited.

No, it was not his desperate imagination at work. The pitching was less violent and the lurching was now a gentle roll. Thanking God and every one of his angels, Adams thought about climbing back on deck, then shook his head. Let the damned boat reach its berth first before he put any trust in his shaking legs.

A few more minutes passed and then the note of the two-stroke diesel changed. As shouts were heard from the crew above, Adams could feel the bows of the boat swinging. A moment later there was a vibrating clang of metal against metal and the chugging of the engine died.

Hearing more shouts from above, Adams knew his ordeal was over. Giving yet another benediction, he straightened and made his unsteady way up to the deck.

He was totally unprepared for the scene that met him. Dark skerries lay all around the boat, rocky islands through which the fishing boat had slipped to receive the protection of a natural harbour. To the north and south high, snow-covered mountains rose into the night sky.

But Adams' eyes were on the berth the fishing boat was using. Until that moment he had expected a jetty of some kind, even if only a small one. Instead, in the moonlight, he saw the boat was lying alongside the wreck of a beached ship. It appeared to have driven on to rocks under its own power for it had remained upright, although the impact must have torn away its hull because its deck was almost level with the fishing boat. Two medium-sized gun turrets, rusting and eroding, showed it had once been a naval vessel, probably a patrol boat.

Half a dozen shadowy figures were on the wreck's deck, belaying ropes that the fishing boat's crew had thrown to them. Noticing Adams' appearance, the bearded skipper grinned at him. "You feel better now, *ja?*"

156

With his heaving stomach beginning to settle at last, Adams managed a smile. "Much better." He pointed at the men on the wreck. "Who are they?"

"They're your men. They take your things. You go to them now, *ja?*"

By this time some of the partisans had leapt aboard the fishing boat and were helping its crew to haul out Adams' equipment from the hold where it had been hidden during the voyage. Feeling he ought to help them, Adams was about to cross the deck when a gust of wind, sharp enough to cut through the ship's riggings, reminded him he was wearing only battledress. Collecting a duffel coat from the cabin, he had just climbed back on deck when a yell of delight almost burst his eardrums. "Frank! It's you, you old bastard. How're you doing?"

Adams knew there was only one man in Norway with a voice like that but before he could reply a blow across his shoulders almost sent him flat on his face. "They said you were comin' but I didn't believe 'em. But here you are. That's good, Frank! That's bloody splendid!"

Still gasping for breath, Adams now had his hand caught in a steel trap. "Hello, Steen. I hadn't expected to see you so soon."

The giant grinned, his atrociously pronounced English booming over the sound of the wind. "You hadn't? Why not? Aren't I always here when you Tommies need me?"

Although acutely aware he was now in enemy occupied territory, Adams was thinking the very size of the man and his exuberance seemed to diminish danger and to make all things possible. "I suppose it's because I didn't know where we were going to make our landing."

Jensen, who had a Sten gun strapped across his back, jabbed a finger at the rusting wreck. "A good place, *ja?* They steal our ports and harbours, so we use one of their goddamned ships. What do you call it? A fair exchange?"

Adams pointed at the rocky beach that lay at the far side of the wreck and the bank that rose beyond it. "How are you going to get my stuff away? There's a lot of it."

Jensen put a sly finger alongside his nose. "We've got ways, Frank." Then he gave Adams a nudge in the ribs. "What about Scotch? You bring any with you?"

"Yes. I managed four bottles."

Adams took quick evasive action as Jensen let out a howl of delight. His reply reminded Adams that the Norwegian's one-time days at sea had taken him to the States as well as Britain. "You're a bloody fine guy, Frank. We'll have a party when your stuff's packed safely away."

Adams, who had been wanting to ask a question since meeting the giant, decided he could ask it now without seeming too hasty. "How is Helga? Is she safe?"

"*Ja*, Helga's fine. She liked it when she heard you were coming."

"Doesn't she work in Rjukan any longer?"

"Naw, it was getting too risky. She works for us now." The giant grinned. "The Jerries don't suspect her. She's too pretty, *ja?*"

Seeing two partisans heaving a large crate on to the deck, Adams was reminded of the work yet to be done. "I'd better go and give your men a hand."

Steen's teeth showed whitely through his beard as he took Adams' arm. "Naw. I'm told you puked all the way across from Blighty. You go over to the beach and sit your arse down. We'll see to your stuff."

Adams' protest sounded as weak as he felt. "I ought to help. It's my equipment."

A playful shove sent him stumbling towards the wreck. "Go and sit down. You can help us later."

Adams stepped gingerly over to the rusted deck of the patrol boat where a chain of men were passing his equipment down to another party of men on the beach. They in turn were manhandling it up the steep bank. Curious where they were taking it, Adams was about to climb the bank when his legs decided otherwise. Finding a suitable rock, he sank down on it, wondering how long it would be before nausea left him.

Watching the partisans, all armed and dressed in thick anoraks or white snow smocks, he was impressed by their discipline. Now and then one would cast him a curious glance but from the few words that passed between them it was obvious they were well trained in clandestine operations. Less than ten minutes passed before Steen leapt down on to the beach. His loud laugh boomed out in the icy silence. "That's the lot but what's all this stuff for, Frank? A generator and a motor? You goin' to light up a town or something?"

Adams climbed to his feet. "It was all done in a hurry, Steen. We didn't know what was needed so we brought anything that came to mind."

"You've sure done that, Frank." For a moment the giant's voice changed. "But why only three Stens and two boxes of shells? And why no anti-tank ammo? Don't those silly buggers back there know the more Jerries we kill the easier job it's goin' to be when they invade?"

"We'd no choice," Adams explained. "With only hours to work in, we could only get equipment from our own bomb store and armoury."

Steen's scowl faded. "It's a goddamned shame we only got the news after you left."

"What news?" Adams asked.

The giant was grinning again. "Two days ago I managed to get one of my men taken on by the Jerries as a labourer. He told us yesterday that the blasting we keep hearing isn't coming from the quarry or from anything else they're building but from the old cutting that used to run to the fjord. You see what that means? They aren't goin' to send the ore by armoured convoy but by water once they've cleared the cutting and tunnel. My guy says they've been given five more days to finish the job. That's why the bastards have brought in extra men."

Adams' relief was profound. "Thank God for that. We're going to need all the time we can get."

Throwing a massive arm round the fragile Adams, Steen steered him towards the rocky bank. "We'll be OK, Frank. First you need some grub, *ja?* So let's get moving."

Adams began to climb the slippery rocks. "Have we far to go?"

"Not tonight. Only ten or eleven miles."

Adams' heart sank. "On foot?"

Steen's laugh was full of good-natured sarcasm. "Naw, Jerry's providing transport for us." As Adams paused in his climb for a moment, he received a playful push. "Don't worry. If you get tired you can always ride on one of the sledges."

As Adams reached the top of the bank he saw a moonlit landscape, interspaced by clumps of dark trees, stretching out before him. Half a mile ahead, it tilted upwards in a series of snow-covered foothills, woods, and fissures, to end in a high mountain plateau.

By this time the partisans had finished loading his equipment on half a dozen hand-drawn sledges. Some men had already begun their journey and could be seen dragging their sledges towards a distant wood. Others were waiting for Steen and as he climbed over the bank a partisan addressed him in Norwegian.

Replying, Steen turned to Adams. "Johannson says you brought too much stuff for the sledges. So the lads have hidden some of it in the wreck and will collect it tomorrow. OK?"

"I suppose so. As long as the Jerries don't find it."

"Naw. We're a long way from Jerry outposts here. The stuff'll be safe enough from the bastards." The giant's eyes assessed Adams. "You OK to go now?"

Hiding his doubts well, Adams nodded. "Where are we making for?"

Steen jabbed a finger at the high plateau. "Up there. Where the Jerries hate to go."

"Why?" Adams asked.

Steen gave his wicked grin. "Because in the winter it's too cold and bleak for the bastards."

Adams took another look at the distant plateau and wondered if he could reach it, much less climb it. "All right. I'm ready to start when you are."

Steen's voice was sly. "That's good, Frank. You don't want Helga's meal to go beggin', do you?"

Adams gave a start. "You mean she's here?"

"Not here. But not far away either." As the giant noticed Adams' expression, his grin spread. "When she heard you were coming, she said she wanted to welcome you. That's why she came half way with us tonight." He turned to the other partisans. "OK you guys. Let's go."

160

* * *

Unsteady with fatigue, Adams slipped and fell to his knees. As Steen bent down to assist him, he pushed him angrily away. As he stumbled forward again, Steen exchanged a glance with Johannson who, along with two other partisans, was helping the giant to drag a sledge. "We're nearly there, Frank. See that lake and the wood? That's where we're going."

Adams, whose lungs were burning from his exertions in the bitter cold, peered painfully ahead. The party were now travelling across the high, icy plateau, and the frozen lake to which Steen was pointing was little more than a snow-covered circle surrounded by sloping banks. In the moonlight Adams saw that one of the advance parties had already crossed it and were heading for a cluster of huts scattered around the fringe of a large wood on its far side.

Adams was finding it difficult to speak and when he managed a question it was hoarse and breathless. "What are they? Holiday huts?"

Steen shrugged as he hoisted a trace from the sledge back over his shoulder. "Some might be. But with the lake there I'd say most belonged to fishermen. You find huts like them all over Norway. Thank God you do. We'd be in a bad way without 'em."

Adams knew he meant they gave cover to the Resistance. He wanted to ask if the Germans had ever carried out a national search of the huts but decided it was a question that would have to wait for another time.

The truth was Adams was near to exhaustion. Afraid of showing weakness in front of the tough, battle-hardened partisans, he had somehow kept up with them through the foothills and up the ever steepening slope to the top of the high plateau. He had not offered to help with a sledge: he had known that would be foolhardy. But he had refused, at first politely and then angrily, Steen's suggestion that he took a rest on one. Instead, as his lungs burned for air and his legs screamed for a rest, he had gritted his teeth and stumbled forward on will power alone. Now, with his body at last threatening to take no more punishment, he was afraid Helga would be greeted by an inadequate creature travelling on the backs of men who had suffered a harder ordeal than himself. In spite of his gentle

161

disposition, there was a pride in Adams that Valerie had never known or bothered to recognise.

His eyes kept blurring as he stumbled forward. For some time he had found it a help to count his steps to one hundred and then begin again. One, two, three, four ... thirty, thirty-one, thirty-two ... ninety-eight, ninety-nine, one hundred. One, two, three, four, five ... By this time every step was a small triumph for Adams. In front of him the snow turned into the pallor of dead skin and he believed it was his eyes again until he saw a large bank of black cloud had slid over the moon.

He never remembered crossing the lake. All his concentration was needed to keep his legs moving. As the far shore was reached and climbed, and his sobbing breath threatened to tear his lungs, he felt a hand on his arm again. A surge of anger engulfed him. He wanted to scream obscenities at his would-be helper but his anger gave him only enough strength to shake off the hand and continue his counting.

By the time he reached the hut he was too far gone to know a hand was guiding his steps. He was aware only of a sudden wall of warm air that felt like balm on his half-frozen face. A few seconds later the screaming pain in his legs magically eased. Freed from the tyranny of walking and counting, realising he was seated at last, he became aware of voices around him speaking in Norwegian. As they became clearer and he realised one was a woman's voice, blood started to pump back through his veins. Straightening on his wooden chair, he saw Steen and a woman standing before him. Seeing his movement, the woman sank down and threw her arms round him. "Frank! Oh, it's so good to see you again."

His cheeks felt stiff as he tried to smile. "Hello, Helga." She kissed his cheek, then gazed at him anxiously. "How do you feel?"

The warmth of her welcome was like a stimulant. "I'm all right. Just a little tired, that's all."

She turned and gazed up accusingly at Steen. "Didn't I tell you? It was much too long a walk for someone not yet acclimatized."

The giant made no attempt to answer her. Instead he offered her a cup. "Give him this, *kjaere.*"

162

She held the cup to Adams' lips and he felt the burn of neat whisky as he swallowed. It quickened his life force and sharpened his vision. As Helga came into focus he saw she was wearing a thick fisherman's jersey and warm slacks. Her thick blonde hair was free, however, and longer than when he had last seen it, making a frame for her intelligent and attractive face. With his perceptions alive again, Adams was reminded of his thoughts during his last visit to Norway: that Helga Lindstrom was a woman who seemed to radiate both sexuality and competence in equal measure.

He pulled his eyes away from her and began taking in details of the hut. With wooden shutters in place, its only light came from a fish-oil lamp standing on a pinewood table. Two pallet beds, two wooden chairs and a wire-meshed food cabinet comprised the furniture. A glowing wood stove, supporting a pot of simmering water, stood beneath a stone chimney, with piles of birch on either side. A miscellany of tools and fisherman's tackle was scattered in one corner, in a second were two large canvas packs. One was opened and as Steen moved across to it Adams recognised it as one of the packs he had brought over with him.

Rummaging into it, Steen turned to Helga. "I think our friend has a good memory."

Smiling at Adams, she moved over to the Norwegian. "Why?"

He held out a small packet to her. "He's brought you some chocolate."

She clapped her hands together in a way that Adams found delightful. "Chocolate! *Real* chocolate?"

"*Ja.* And some real coffee and cigarettes too." Steen turned his grinning, bearded face to Adams. "Maybe we won't hand him over to the Jerries after all."

Partially restored now, Adams was able to ask the questions denied him before. "When I was last here you said the Germans were going around Norway emptying the huts of everything your Resistance might find useful. Did they miss these huts or have you re-equipped them?"

Helga, busy making coffee, answered for the giant. "There are too many. They couldn't check them all. These are some they missed."

Steen's fierce blue eyes gleamed with malice. "And even the ones they've checked we sometimes use again. The bastards haven't the manpower to be everywhere. And, as I said, they hate it up here in the winter."

Adams was wondering why the German Army, ruthless in its treatment of partisans, had not burned down the huts.

He pushed the question aside as pointless. War, as he knew too well, was full of such anomalies.

Steen, with a whisky bottle in his hand, moved over to Helga as she poured hot water into three cups. "Here. Put a shot of this in. We've all earned it tonight."

Laughing, she obeyed. Ignoring the coffee that was scalding hot, Steen drained his cup, gave a burp of satisfaction, then set the whisky bottle on the table. "I've gotta go to my guys now," he told Adams. "You stay here and have the meal Helga's prepared for you. After that get some sleep. You're goin' to need it tomorrow."

Adams was confused. "Do you mean sleep here?"

"Ja. Where else?"

"But what about Helga?"

As Steen glanced at the girl, she gave an amused laugh. "This isn't peacetime England, Frank. We sleep where we can these days."

"I was thinking of you," Adams muttered.

"I know you were, Frank. You were always the proper English gentleman. But Steen and his men will be working through the night and you must get some rest." A dimple appeared in the girl's wind-tanned cheek. "In any case you're not really in a state tonight to play games, are you?"

As Adams reached for his cup, he realised she was right. For a moment the hut did a half turn to the left before steadying itself. As he sank back, Steen nodded at Helga and left the hut.

Left alone with Adams, the girl walked over to the food cabinet and drew out a covered plate. "I've got a meal here for you, Frank. I'm afraid it's cold because I didn't know what time you'd arrive."

Adams held out a protesting hand. "No, thanks. I couldn't eat anything. I was sick on the boat and I'm starting to feel sick again. I think I'll just lie down."

She hesitated, then replaced the plate in the cabinet. "It's the altitude and the cold. It happened to you the last time you came over here. So perhaps you had better sleep and eat later."

Adams suspected the whisky on an empty stomach was not helping him either. Seeing his dizziness as he rose, she ran forward and helped him to the nearest pallet bed. As he sank down on the hard mattress, Adams found himself wondering why he had accepted her help after refusing all aid from the partisans.

He lay back, gazing up at her face and its halo of golden hair. Muddled with whisky and weariness he imagined for a moment he was back in the previous year when they had shared a similar hut together.

But all such speculations and imaginings were wiped away like writings in sand as a huge wave of exhaustion swept over him. As its darkness closed in he did not see the girl draw up a chair beside his bed or feel her cool hand rest on his forehead. Enemy territory or not, the girl of his dreams or not, Adams was fast asleep.

Chapter 18

The phone in Henderson's private quarters rang at exactly 03.00 hours the following morning. Henderson, who was enjoying an excellent night's sleep, thought at first the ringing was part of his dream.

It had begun with a wild aircrew party attended by most of the station's WAAFs. Laura, his Junoesque assistant, had been present and been paying him the kind of attention station commanders fantasise about but seldom receive. After two or three erotic dances with him in which she made certain her nubile body pressed against all the right places, she had whispered a suggestion in his ear.

Henderson had made all the correct military noises but had clearly lost control of the situation because in a flash he was in his office with the pulsating Laura doing a Salome strip tease in front of his desk.

To his credit Henderson had made an initial effort to preserve the dignity of his office but by the time the girl was down to her fifth veil the Scot had decided it would be cruel to spurn such generosity. Better by far to let her work off her inhibitions in a manner befitting to her needs.

It was when the sixth veil had fallen away that one of his desk telephones had rung. With the girl's proportions enough to make any self-respecting airman's eyes goggle, Henderson had decided the war could wait a few minutes longer. But when the girl had complained the ringing was inhibiting her and she couldn't let the seventh veil slip until it was silenced, Henderson had been stirred into action. Jumping from his chair to silence the offender, he had seen the nubile Laura disappear before his eyes and found himself in bed with his phone ringing as if the world were coming to an end.

Cursing, wondering what he was doing having schoolboy dreams, the Scot climbed out of bed and fumbled for his light switch. Then, scowling at the spoilsport telephone, he snatched it up and barked into the receiver. "Well. What is it?"

A WAAF's timid voice answered him. "It's Air Commodore Davies, sir. He's been trying to get hold of you for ten minutes."

Serve him right, Henderson thought punitively. Doesn't the little bastard ever sleep? "Put him on," he muttered.

Davies's high-pitched voice sounded immediately. "For Christ's sake, Jock. Where have you been?"

The Scot was tempted to tell him until prudence took over. "I've been asleep, sir."

"I know you've been asleep but does it take ten minutes to wake up? Or are you with a woman?"

"No, sir," Henderson said patiently. "I'm not with a woman. What can I do for you?"

"We can't talk over this bloody phone, Jock, but I can say this. Your squadron can stand down until further orders."

"Stand down, sir?"

"Yes. You know what stand down means, don't you?"

"Yes, sir. I know what it means but I don't understand it."

"And I can't tell you over an ordinary phone, can I? I want you over at High Elms at 09.00 hours prompt. You'll get all the gen there."

Henderson sighed. "All right, sir. Shall I come alone?"

"No, bring Harvey." Davies paused, then his tone changed. "Unless you want to bring that woman over with you."

Knowing Davies and his sense of humour, Henderson knew that, whatever the news was, it suited the Air Commodore's plans. Although unsure it would suit his own, the Scot replied in kind. "Then I will bring her, sir. She might make better coffee than that girl at High Elms."

Davies chuckled. "Good thinking, Jock. See you at nine."

* * *

167

Although cold, it was a bright clear morning when Henderson and Harvey arrived at High Elms. After going through the usual security checks, they were led into the library where Davies and Simms were waiting for them. Davies's cheerful greeting confirmed the Scot's impression of the previous night. "Sorry to get you here so early, Jock. But we might as well take advantage of all the good news we can get."

To Henderson good news would have been the cancellation of the operation but he knew that was the last thing Davies's behaviour signified. "What good news is that, sir?" he asked as the Brigadier led them to the long table where a detailed map of Norway was lying.

Davies indicated the smiling Simms. "I think I ought to leave that to the Brigadier. He's the one who got the message through from London. But first can I take it you've stood the squadron down?"

Henderson nodded. "I've told the ground crews they can fall back on routine procedures and the aircrews they can put their feet up and relax. But I haven't lifted the restriction on phone calls or movements outside the station. I thought I'd better find out what all this is about before I took things any further."

"Fair enough, Jock. We can talk about the station's readiness after you've heard the latest news from the Brigadier."

Simms looked almost apologetic as he faced the two curious officers. "It was only a short message from our contacts in Norway, gentlemen. But because it could be very significant in the context of our preparations, the Air Commodore felt we should meet to discuss it."

"The operation isn't cancelled, is it, sir?" Henderson asked, more from hope than belief.

"Oh, no, Henderson. Churchill wants the mine destroyed as urgently as before. It is just that we have more time to plan our attacks than we originally believed." Leading the two officers to the map, Simms told them about the partisan Steen had managed to plant inside the German security zone and his discoveries. "If the enemy is clearing the tunnel it can only mean they intend to transport the stocks of ore to the fjord, where they will probably ship them in barges to Lillestad where there is a rail terminal. It makes sense because that way they'll be hoping to avoid any partisan activity."

Henderson was gazing down at the map. "How much longer does this give us? Clearing a cutting and tunnel through a mountain range will take quite a time, won't it?"

"No, Henderson. It seems the enemy has been working on the cutting and tunnel for weeks. Indeed the job must be nearly finished because our contact tells us it's scheduled to be open in four days."

"That soon?" Henderson said.

"Yes, but at least we know the stocks won't be moved during that time."

Harvey was frowning. "It's a pity Jensen couldn't have got his man in earlier. It would have given Adams time to assemble the right equipment instead of the bits and bobs he had to take with him."

With oil and water never intended by nature to mix, the tough Yorkshireman had only to open his mouth and make a criticism for Davies's mood to change. "Do you think Jensen wouldn't know that? It's a bloody miracle he got a man into that cutting at all."

Simms, unperturbed by Harvey's brusque comment, nodded. "I'm afraid that's true, Harvey. They're playing a highly dangerous game over there and can only make their moves when the opportunities arrive. But at least it gives Adams more time to examine the valley and set up his markers."

It took more than Davies's irritation to shake Harvey. "Have you heard yet if Adams has arrived safely?" he asked Simms.

"Yes, a radio message came through this morning. He's safely in the hands of Jensen and his men."

Harvey visibly relaxed. "That's something, I suppose."

Davies glared at him. "Do you mind if we go on now?" When Harvey, silenced by the kick Henderson gave him beneath the table, went quiet, Davies turned to the Scot. "You have an inventory of the equipment Adams took with him, haven't you?"

"Yes, sir, Richardson took one."

"Good. Then I'm going to lend you Moore for a day and I want the two of you and Harvey to run over the list to see if there's anything else Adams might need. If there is, we'll use an air drop."

Harvey stirred. "Using our Mossies?" he asked.

"I suppose so," Davies snapped. "Or have you a better idea?"

It appeared Harvey had not because he addressed Simms instead. "I've been thinking about the markers Adams took, sir. You said this character Steen has men who're used to handling explosives but are you certain they can adapt our flares? Most if not all of them are ignited either by barometric pressure or percussion. How will the partisans ignite them. With electric detonators, fuse wire or what?"

Simms' nod showed he appreciated the question. "I have to assume they'll find a way. Fortunately, if any problems arise they'll now have time to get in touch with us."

Davies, whose silence suggested he had seen the point of the question, broke the short silence that followed. "Any more questions before we get on with our jobs?"

"When do you intend to brief the crews, sir?" Henderson asked.

"If possible I want to wait until I've got sketches or photographs from Adams. So we'll have to wait a day or two."

"Then what about the stand down? Is it full or partial?"

"You can let the boys out for a drink but they're to keep within call. No leave on any account. But you can restore communications. We don't want Jerry to get the idea we're up to something. Anything else?"

Harvey raised a hand. "Now we've got a breathing space, are you going to organise air cover for us, sir?"

"I've already done that," Davies snapped. "Lancs with Mandrels are going to give you radar cover on your way out."

"I said air cover, sir. We might need it when we come out of that valley."

"You're going to Norway, Harvey, not bloody France."

"I know that too, sir, but long range Mustangs could operate there. And General Staines has a pretty useful wing of 'em."

Henderson hid a smile. There had been a time when Harvey would have scoffed at the value of American help. But after Staines's wing of Mustangs had given the squadron such excellent service during its last three operations, it seemed that even the tribal Yorkshireman was converted.

170

Davies answered without looking at him. "That's something we can think about. Maybe I'll have a talk to General Staines. All right, if that's all your questions, let's get back to work."

An icy wind was sweeping the courtyard when Henderson and Harvey made their way to their WAAF driven car. As a gust made Harvey turn up his greatcoat collar, he gave a short laugh. "This weather makes me think about Frank. At the best of times he hates the cold. He'll be over the bloody moon in Norway."

Although aware of the friendship between Harvey and Adams, Henderson knew it was only the comment of concern he was likely to get from the taciturn Yorkshireman. "He'll be OK. Jensen seems to be well organised over there."

Hearing Harvey's grunt of disgust and afraid he was going to bring up the matter of an aerial reconnaissance again, Henderson changed the subject as the two men slid into the car. "Did you say your wife was arriving today?"

Harvey nodded as the WAAF driver started the engine. "Aye, she's taking the train to Highgate. One of my lads is picking her up."

Henderson glanced at him. "You don't sound too pleased."

"I'm not," Harvey said bluntly. "I don't like her too close to the airfield."

Henderson offered him a cigarette. "How did she take your promotion?"

Harvey blew out smoke before replying. "Badly. Worse than I thought."

"Perhaps you shouldn't have taken it, Frank."

"You think I'd any choice, sir?"

The Scot frowned, "I don't know. But I know Davies wanted you for this operation." When Harvey made no reply, Henderson tried to lighten his mood. "Do you think Anna will be at the pub by the time we get back?"

"She ought to be. Her train was due in twenty minutes ago."

Henderson was wondering why he always felt like a drink after a session with Davies. Deciding to kill two birds with one stone, he waited until the car entered the suburbs of Highgate. Then he turned back to Harvey. "I know how you feel but just the same it's good to have Anna back. Let's stop at the pub and have a dram with her."

171

Chapter 19

Adams edged forward along the icy rocks and drew in his breath at the sight that opened out before him. Far below, clinging like tiny limpets to the steep sides of the valley, the houses of Rosvik straddled two threads of river and road. Dominating the town and crushing it with their immensity, the wooded sides of the valley rose in a huge V. Disfigured here and there by scree or the fan-shaped scars of waterfalls, they were like the walls of a gigantic prison. As Adams stared down he saw a bird winging along the valley at least four hundred feet below him.

The sight brought on a wave of vertigo and he turned to the girl alongside him. "How do people live down there? I'd feel crushed by these mountains."

Helga smile. "People all over Norway live like that. You'd get used to it."

"But sunlight can't ever get down there."

"No. They get a few hours during the summer. But not in the winter."

Shaking his head, Adams turned back to the valley. In the thin winter sunlight he could see that a couple or more miles past the small town the valley ended in the massive barrier of Helsberg. A part of the plateau around it, Helsberg turned the valley into a long cul-de-sac. The twin threads of river and road could be traced running towards it until both vanished into the huge featureless wood that covered the valley floor almost from town to mountain. The configuration made Adams think of a spring onion, with the narrow valley its stem and the wood its bulbous root.

One thing could be told London at once, Adams thought. With such high mountains surrounding the wood on three sides, there was no way Mosquitoes could dive into it and hit their target. Only a flat, low-level run in, which meant flying through the valley, would give them a chance of dropping their bombs with any accuracy and escaping collision with the heights above.

Knowing the mine and its accumulated stocks were somewhere in the wood, Adams took his binoculars and searched the dense trees but the camouflaged area was too expertly done to be detected. The only activity he could see were three army trucks travelling along the road. As they vanished into the wood Adams took note of the odd feature of the plateau opposite. Before reaching the barrier of Helsberg, the rock-strewn plateau sloped downwards and was severed by a ravine, giving the valley an unexpected access to the fjord which lay deep and sullen a couple of miles to the north.

Adams lowered his binoculars. "You wouldn't call this valley a fjord, would you? It's surely far too steep."

"You're right, she told him. "The fjords were caused by glacier action. When Steen told me London were interested in this valley, I asked a geologist friend of mine about it. He said it is believed the entire plateau was uplifted by volcanic action some millions of years ago and this valley is a crack between two sections of the rock plate. I suppose the ravine that runs off at right angles is a secondary crack."

Her reply reminded Adams the girl was a scientist in her own right. "Could that be why molybdenum was found here? The split in the plateau could have brought it to the surface?"

"Yes. That's very possible."

Adams lifted his binoculars again to the huge wood. "One thing is for sure. Heavy bombers could never plant explosives down such a narrow valley and so near to Helsberg without threatening the town. Particularly when it's not going to be real daylight down there for another few months."

He shifted his gaze to the distant ravine. Although its depth and his angle of sight prevented his seeing the work being carried out inside it, a sudden cloud of brown smoke and the far-off sound of an explosion made him turn to Helga. "They're still blasting. So they can't have opened a way through it yet."

173

She nodded. "I expect it's the blocked tunnel that's holding them up. Steen's man says they've no intention of building a road."

"But then how will they get the ore through?

"Probably with tracked vehicles," she told him. "If it wasn't for the tunnel, they'd probably have been able to get through already."

With this reminder that time was not on his side, Adams rolled over and tried to gaze along the western length of the valley. Finding his vision was impaired by a clump of rocks, he wriggled forward. Still unable to gain a clear view, he was pushing himself still further forward when Helga caught his ankles. "Be careful, Frank. If the snow begins to slide, it could take you with it."

Realising she was right, Adams wriggled back a few feet and then rose to his knees. The extra height he gained enabled him to see the plateau had not fractured cleanly but had splintered into two huge bluffs that jutted out like massive chins into the valley. Half-bearded with trees, the nearer bluff was little more than a mile from the town, forcing the threads of river and road to wind round it. With little space between the bluffs and the opposite wall of the valley, Adams knew that if visibility was poor or if smoke protection was used, the bluffs would make an air attack along the valley suicidal unless he could plant lights on them. Realising for the first time the enormity of the task facing him, Adams sank back, to see Helga drawing a pad from her white anorak. "I'll do the sketching while you take your photographs."

Adams hesitated. "Isn't it too dull for photographs?"

She laughed. "Frank, you're in Norway in winter time. For us this is a beautiful winter day. Tomorrow you might not be able to see four hundred yards. So take your photographs while you can."

Realising she was right, Adams pulled out a small camera from his duffel coat pocket. It had been given him before his departure by an officer at High Elms who had spent a precious half hour instructing him in its use. Adams, whose previous photography had been limited to the use of a Kodak Box on his peacetime holidays, had done his best to listen but with the excitement of his forthcoming adventure occupying his mind, precious little information had filtered in.

It had only been during his sea journey, when sickness had depressed his every thought, that he realised how inadequate he was to supply intelligence of the fateful valley. For not only had he forgotten the requirements of the special camera but his sketching powers were no better than those of a child.

Too weary to think about it the previous night, he had made the admission to Helga that morning while Steen had been dividing out his band of partisans, one third to return to the wreck for the remaining supplies, the rest to trek to the new headquarters the giant had set up near the Rosvik valley. Adams had barely made his admission before Helga had clapped her hands together in the gesture Adams had always found so attractive. "Your troubles are over before they begin, sir. I will do the sketching for you."

Adams had started. "You can sketch?"

"Yes. I'm very good. If you were in my home, you would see some of the sketches my parents framed. When I was young I wanted to be an artist."

"But you can't come with me," Adams protested. "It might be dangerous."

She laughed. "Frank, I was going to come with you in any case. Steen and his men will have enough to do today sorting out your equipment and hiding it away."

Adams, who until now had believed his venture meant a hundred per cent involvement with tough, hard-nosed partisans, found the prospects of her company more than agreeable but being Adams he had his doubts. "But what if there are German patrols about?"

"As they've no suspicions we know anything about the mine, why should there be? In any case you need someone who knows this plateau?"

"I realise that. But I expected Steen would provide help."

"Steen is providing help. He's sending me with you." When Adams still hesitated, she had caught his arm and shaken it playfully. "Stop looking so worried. Steen wouldn't let either of us go out on our own if he thought it was dangerous. As long as we're sensible, we should have no trouble."

Steen's first move had been to take his entire advance party on a six mile trek over the frozen plateau to a small cluster of huts that he had previously earmarked. After allowing Adams a short rest, he had then allowed Helga to guide him to the Rosvik valley but not before he had given them both a lecture. "You take no risks. OK? It's not likely there'll be any German patrols up here but if they get suspicious the place will swarm with the bastards." His fierce blue eyes had turned on the smiling girl. "So you be careful. You hear me, *kjaere?*"

She had curtsied. "Yes, master."

His big voice had risen in mock anger. "No funny stuff or you'll go over my knee." He turned to Adams. "You'll take one of our portable radio sets so you can get in touch. But don't use it unless it's absolutely necessary because the bastards will pick up your transmission. Now off you go but be back in two hours. Remember it is dark by 16.00 hours."

It had taken Adams and the girl another twenty minutes to reach the valley rim. Although weary again and breathless in the bitter cold, Adams had found it a psychological help to have the girl with him. Although he had noticed she made subtle allowances for his lack of fitness and acclimatization, at the same time he found her femininity was a stimulant that aided him to overcome his aches and pains.

Forgetting his photography for the moment, Adams watched her now, sketching the distant bluffs with sure, swift strokes. Prone to irrelevant thoughts in moments of significance or high drama, Adams thought of Valerie in such a situation and the contrast became ludicrous. Valerie for whom a fifty yard dash in the rain from a taxi to her front door was a hardship ... Helga, almost the same age, risking torture and death every day of her life with a courage that Adams found astonishing. Not for the first time in his life he wondered whether it was circumstances that made men and women what they were or whether they were just born with the right genes.

Helga's laugh brought him back to the present. "Why are you staring at me like that?"

"I was thinking what an extraordinary person you are," Adams said. "I thought the same the last time I was here."

"Me? Why? Because I can sketch a little?"

"No. For a dozen reasons."

She laughed again although her cheeks had coloured slightly. "Stop talking nonsense and take your photographs. We'll have to get back in a few minutes."

Stirred into action by her warning, Adams opened his camera and tried to remember his instructions. Finding he could not, he peered through the viewfinder at the wood and clicked the release. Hoping against hope the settings were right, he then took pictures of Helsberg and the cutting that ran to the fjord. Finally he turned his attention to the twin bluffs to the west. By the time he had exhausted the spool, he found his hands were half frozen and he was shivering. The girl noticed it and her voice became concerned. "We must go back now. It'll be bitterly cold this evening." When Adams protested, she offered him her pad. "It's all right. I've finished the sketches."

Adams found she had sketched the cutting and Helsberg as well as the twin bluffs. The latter, jutting out across the valley, were in perfect proportion and perspective. "These are wonderful. Davies'll go over the moon with them."

"You'll see for reference I've put the names in," she said. "There nearest one is Trollhorn, the other is Kaldhorn."

"They're wonderful," he said again. "Davies'll think I'm Picasso."

She laughed. "What about your photographs?"

"I've taken a full spool. Although I doubt if they'll be any good, so these sketches will be invaluable."

"When will you send them over?" she asked.

"Steen said he'll have a fishing boat ready tonight. The sooner Davies has them the better."

"Will you need any more sketches?"

"Yes. I'd like a couple taken from the other side of those bluffs."

"They'll have to wait until tomorrow morning," she told him. "We must get back now or Steen'll send out a search party." As he paused to glance down again at the camouflaged wood, her voice turned impatient. "Frank, you're looking white with cold. The snow probably soaked through your clothes and that could be dangerous. So pick up the radio and let's get back before you catch a chill."

* * *

Steen was livid. With his beard bristling and his fierce eyes blazing, the imaginative Adams thought of Giant Fury in a Grimm fairy tale. "The stupid bastards. Don't they know the tide rises? I ought to shoot the sonsofbitches."

Adams felt he ought to pour a little oil on the wild waters. "I suppose part of it's my fault. I ought to have made sure they were in marked boxes. But it was such a mad rush at the airfield there wasn't time to classify everything."

Steen's snarl would have made a rutting grizzly bear envious. "Don't excuse the sods, As far as they knew, all the stuff was valuable. So why didn't they put everything out of harm's reach?"

The two men were standing in a hut containing Adams' stores. Built of split logs, with moss and earth packing the joints, it was standing within a circle of rocks. Its roof, low enough to force the raging Steen to keep his head and shoulders bent, was little more than a frame of birch laid over by frozen earth. It had no furniture or equipment, only Adams' stores and a smoking oil lamp that kept flickering in the icy draughts that sliced in from the night outside.

There was a third man sharing the hut, a thick-set nuggety partisan who was kneeling on the earthen floor beside three crates covered in melting snow. One crate had been opened and while Steen was venting his anger, the man was examining its contents. As he glanced back, Adams knelt down beside him. "What do you think? Are they all ruined?"

The man nodded. *"Ja.* Salt water. They'll never light now."

As Adams silently cursed his luck. Steen's anger burst out again. "I tell you, I should shoot the sonsofbitches. Any bloody fool would have thought about the tide. Maybe the sods are working for the Boche."

Surprising himself by his nerve, Adams rose to his feet. "It's no use making too much of a fuss about it. It's happened. The thing is, what are we going to do now?"

As Steen glared at him, the wooden door creaked open and Helga appeared. Looking startled, she gazed at Steen. "What on earth's going on? You can be heard a hundred yards away."

178

Before the giant could answer, Adams pointed down at the three crates. "It's the markers I brought. By accident they were among the things left to be collected today. Apparently they weren't stored high enough inside the wreck and the tide got to them. Larson here says they're ruined."

She showed dismay. "But they're vital, aren't they?"

"I must have them," Adams admitted. He turned to Steen. "Can you get a radio message through to London tonight?"

He received a scowl. "Of course I can."

"Then will you get one off as quickly as possible? Tell them I want at least a dozen more markers. No, make it two dozen, just in case." Pausing, Adams swung round on the nuggety partisan who had now climbed to his feet. "You're my expert, Larson. Is there anything more you need for igniting the flares? I'm going to ask for an air drop."

The man, who had a square, pleasant face, nodded. *"Ja.* Ask for more electric cable. Plenty of it. And another electric generator and at least two dozen electric detonators."

Adams was thanking God the man could speak such good English. "You can fix the markers to go off electrically, can you?"

"Yes. That shouldn't be a problem."

"Is that all you want?"

"Ja, I think so."

Adams turned back to Steen. "Have you got that? Tell London we need them as quickly as possible. Can I leave it to you to decide where you want the air drop?"

The giant's voice was sarcastic. "I think you can safely leave that to me, Englishman. But remembering one thing. I can't get a message off under two hours. Maybe even three."

"Why is that?"

"Because I'm not a bloody magician, that's why. In case you don't know, the Germans have D/F stations all over the country and if they once fix a bearing they come in like a swarm of wasps. So I can't have my radio operator too close to the Englishman that London has sent us to win the war."

Although he flushed at the sarcasm, Adams was not a man to wilt if he felt his case was right. "I wasn't trying to teach you your business, Steen. And it wasn't my fault the markers got damaged.

179

I'm just asking if you'll please get the request for new ones off to London as quickly as possible. That's all."

The giant scowled at him for a few seconds, then turned for the low entrance. Although he ducked down even more, his head struck the lintel and his thunderous curse brought snow tumbling from the roof. As he stomped away across the frozen ground, Helga gave a wicked chuckle. "He's really cross, isn't he?"

Hoping Steen didn't hear her, Adams grinned ruefully back. "One thing's for sure. He's not too happy with me."

"Oh no, it's not just you. He's angry with himself. Isn't that right, Johann?" she asked, turning to the grinning Larson.

"*Ja,* that right. He hates things to go wrong with his planning. Even though things might not be his fault, he takes the blame."

"Maybe," Adams said. "But he didn't take well to my asking for a radio message. He thought I was giving him orders."

Larson shook his head. "No. That was because you stood up to him. And that was only because he was angry. Tomorrow he will respect you all the more. You wait and see."

Adams decided he was going to like working with Larson. "Let's hope you're right. Because I'm going to need him more than he needs me."

"You're safe with Steen," Helga said. "He's the most honest and reliable man in the world." As he smiled at her, she took his arm. "That's enough for one day. I've got your meal ready. Come over before it gets cold."

Chapter 20

The news that galvanised 633 Squadron into action came that evening when Henderson was exchanging a few drams with half a dozen of his senior officers in the Mess. A young WAAF telephonist ran up to him and exchanged a few hurried words. Thanking her, and muttering an obscenity after she had gone, Henderson hurried to his office and picked up his red telephone. "Hello. Put Air Commodore Davies on, please."

A buzz and crackle sounded and then Davies's impatient voice. "Jock, we've got an emergency."

Henderson hid a groan. "What is it, sir?"

"How many markers have you got in store?"

"I don't know off hand, sir. I'll have to contact Greenwood. But after Adams' raid on them the other night I don't expect we'll have many."

"That's what I thought. So I've put in an urgent order for you. They'll be arriving sometime during the night."

The Scot gave a start. Taking no chances of a security leak, even over the scrambler telephone, he chose his words carefully. "The big show isn't on yet, sir, is it?"

"No, but there's been a bloody unfortunate accident and Adams needs more markers. It's going to mean an air drop tomorrow morning, Jock. As it's a rush job your boys will have to do it."

"How many kites, sir?"

"That's something we'll decide when I arrive. In the meantime get your MPs out and round up everyone who's out of camp."

The Scot gave another start. "You're not thinking of sending the entire squadron out, are you?"

"Of course I'm not. But there's a lot of decisions to be made in the next few hours and I want all my options open. So get to it, will you, Jock? I'll be over before 23.00 hours."

Shaking his head, Henderson replaced the red telephone and made contact with his duty officer. Within minutes truck loads of MPs were speeding up the hill to Highgate where indignant airmen were shepherded from pubs, dance halls, and in some cases the beds of their girl friends. Although speculation ran high as men were driven back to Sutton Craddock, only a tiny minority, and they were senior officers, could guess the urgency involved Norway. Thanks to Davies and to a lesser degree Henderson, no unit in the RAF was better at keeping its cards close to its chest than 633 Squadron.

While all this was happening, Henderson had sent a messenger over to The Black Swan. Fifteen minutes later Harvey entered his office. From his appearance, his tie askew, his rain-stained tunic half unbuttoned, and a dark shadow round his rugged chin, the Yorkshireman had been in bed when the order had reached him. His brusque voice hinted he was not pleased at having to leave it. "I got your message, sir. What's the problem?"

Henderson indicated a chair. "Sorry about this, Frank. But Davies has just been on the blower. It seems there's been some kind of accident over in Norway and we've got to air drop more markers to Adams."

"When?"

"In the morning. Which means we'll have to leave some time during the night if we're to make it."

"How many kites are we supposed to use?"

"I suppose that depends on what Davies wants us to carry."

"Did he give you the co-ordinates?"

"No. It was too risky on the phone. He'll be bringing them with him."

Harvey gave a grunt. "So he's coming?"

"What do you think? Of course he's coming."

"If we've got to be airborne in a few hours, we can't sit around waiting for him. I take it you've alerted Chiefy Powell?"

"Yes. But he wants to know how many kites to get ready."

182

Harvey gave another grunt. "I'm not surprised. Why couldn't the little bugger have told you when he phoned?"

Henderson decided he had not heard the last comment. "He wasn't sure how much stuff to send over. However, he'll be here soon and then we can get cracking. In the meantime the duty officer's making sure everyone's on their toes." The Scot paused, then went on: "I'm wondering who we should send. Norway's a hell of a place for aircraft at this time of the year."

Harvey made the question sound superfluous. "I'll be one of 'em. I've been to the bloody place."

"Everybody's been, Frank. At least all the old sweats have."

"Aye, but I've seen it at its worst. That's what counts."

Henderson knew he was being reminded that Harvey was the sole survivor of the Swartfjord disaster. "We'll have to leave that for the moment and see what Davies has in mind. What I'd like you to do now is get all the crews into their flight offices. We'd better look ready and willing when he arrives."

As Harvey nodded and rose, the Scot lifted his hand and indicated his tie and tunic. "Talking about ready and willing, what about a wee wash and brush up before he arrives? Otherwise we could start off on two left feet."

Harvey slanted a look down at himself, then gave a short laugh. "Why take his fun away? He enjoys chucking stones at me."

"Just the same, I don't want any friction tonight. So see to it, will you?"

As Harvey nodded and left, Henderson picked up a telephone again and spoke to the guardroom. "As soon as Air Commodore Davies's car arrives, send it straight round to the Administration Block. Tell him I'll be in my office waiting for him."

In fact Henderson didn't have to wait long. Wearing a mackintosh that flapped about his knees, Davies entered his office less than fifteen minutes later. "Not bad going, is it, Jock. Forty minutes flat. Mind you, I wouldn't like to do it again in that bloody blackout. We nearly hit a lorry without lights and damn nearly ran over a cyclist."

Henderson knew that loquacity of this kind meant Davies was as tense as a greyhound in the slips. "Just what has happened, sir?"

183

Davies told him about the ruined markers. "Bloody careless on some one's part but it doesn't sound as if Adams is to blame. Anyway, as we've no idea how soon he's going to need 'em, we have to get more over to him tonight. Also some other bits and pieces like cable and detonators." Davies glanced round the office. "Where's Harvey?"

"Over in the flight offices, I think." Henderson reached for his telephone. "Shall I get him?"

"Yes. We're going to need him tonight."

Harvey came in two minutes later. As he saluted Davies, Henderson saw the small officer's eyes focus on the Yorkshireman's chin which was still in shadow. To his relief Davies made no comment on it. "I understand you've been told about the air drop over in Norway so I won't go over all that again. What I want us to decide right away is who to send. Now I've had time to think about it, I believe we can get all the stuff into two Mossies but we'd better get a third one ready to be on the safe side."

"Are they going unescorted, sir?" Harvey asked.

Davies glanced at Henderson. "I put out a few feelers before I left but from what I was told it's going to be hellishly difficult to arrange anything in time. What are your views on this?"

Harvey answered for the Scot. "An escort might alert Jerry. Two Mossies will have a better chance."

Davies looked relieved. "You think so? Then who will you pick?"

The Yorkshireman shrugged. "Just Machin. He can go as my wing man."

Davies gave a start. *"Your* wing man. You can't go."

Harvey's voice turned brusque. "Why not?"

"Isn't that obvious? I need you to lead the squadron later."

"I can still lead the squadron later. I don't intend to be shot down."

"You could be. This operation isn't going to be a picnic."

Harvey shrugged. "All the more reason why I should go. Norway's a tough place to navigate in. If those supplies don't get to Adams, there mightn't be an operation for me to lead later on."

Privately conceding Harvey had a point, Henderson half-expected Davies to hesitate but the small officer remained adamant.

"It's the navigators who get you to your targets and yours is no more experienced than any of the others. So stop arguing and give me a couple of names."

Afraid Harvey had not given up yet, Henderson intervened quickly. "What about Millburn and Machin? They've both got experience of Norwegian conditions."

When Harvey made no comment, Davies swung back at him. "Well?"

The Yorkshireman shrugged. "Yes. You couldn't use better men. But do you want to risk a flight commander on the job?"

"I'd rather risk a flight commander than my bloody squadron commander," Davies snapped. "So it's decided?" When both Henderson and Harvey nodded, he went on: "Then get the two of 'em and their navigators into the briefing room. We'll also need your armament, navigation, and weather specialists too. I want the crews thoroughly briefed and the kites ready to leave the moment those markers arrive. So let's get on with it."

Illuminated in the light of storm lanterns, the wings of the two selected Mosquitoes quivered as a bitter night wind blew across the airfield. Frozen-fingered armourers cursed as they clipped tanks of shells on to the aircrafts' short barrelled cannon while their equally frozen colleagues loaded markers into the open bomb bays.

The markers had arrived at 02.15 hours and Davies had made certain no time was wasted before they were packed into padded containers and rushed out on to the airfield. The containers carried no parachutes. With the risk the containers could be lost in a high wind, it had been decided at the briefing that the drop should be carried out at low level.

The two crews, along with Davies, Henderson, Harvey, and the Navigation Officer, Deakin, were waiting in A flight office. Although word came that the Mosquitoes were ready, Deakin, a small Welshman with a pencil thin moustache, glanced at his watch and shook his head. "Give it a few more minutes. Then you should be about right.'"

Millburn, looking large in his padded flying suit, grinned at Gabby. "You sure you don't want another pee before we go? All this waiting can't be doing much for your bladder."

Gabby sniffed. "There's nothing wrong with my bladder, Millburn. Or my nerves either."

Machin overheard them. "After six beers in the Mess tonight, Oi wish Oi could say the same." He threw an accusing glance at Davies. "Someone should warn us beforehand about these night shenanigans."

Baldwin, his black navigator who was the ex-Barbados lawyer, answered in his slow Caribbean drawl. "Mon, you keep all that beer to yourself. We've a long ways to go tonight."

Overhearing them, Henderson stole a glance at Davies but the small Air Commodore's smile told the Scot he was appreciating the crews' need to relieve their tension.

Five minutes later Deakin gave a nod. "That's it. I think you can go now."

As the four men picked up their parachutes and moved towards the door, Harvey walked forward with them. His words were addressed to Henderson. "I'll go as far as the kites with them, sir."

As Henderson nodded and the five men disappeared outside, Davies swung round on the Scot. "What's all that for?"

Henderson raised his eyebrows. "I don't understand, sir."

Davies was looking suspicious. "Why is he going to the kites with them? He's not going to do another Crisis job and knock out Millburn, is he?"

Henderson never knew how he held back a grin. "No, sir. He probably wants to give them a last bit of advice. Harvey's a protective character and doesn't like his men doing things he's not doing himself. That's all."

Davies frowned but said no more. Outside a motor started up and gears meshed as the transport detailed to take the crews to their aircraft began moving away. Davies listened to it for a moment, then muttered something under his breath before turning to the Scot. "I suppose that's all we can do for the moment."

"Yes, sir, I think it is. What are your plans now?"

"I want to hear those markers have arrived safely, so I'm going to spend the night at High Elms. You do realise if anything should go wrong, we'd have to send two more kites out, don't you?"

Henderson sighed. "Yes, sir. I suppose we would."

"Good. Then keep your fingers crossed." All bustle and urgency, Davies crossed to the door. "I'll have to go now, Jock, but I'll be in touch as soon as Simms gets his message from Norway. Let's hope for everyone's sake it's good news."

The sudden crackle and roar of a Merlin engine sounded loud in the quiet bedroom of The Black Swan. Anna, sitting up in bed with a quilt tucked around her and a book on her lap, felt her heart contract. As a second engine fired, she jumped out of bed and turned off the light. Turning towards the window, she saw the blackout curtain glow as the airfield landing lights were turned on. Drawing aside the curtain, she gazed out.

The twin row of lights were dazzling in the darkness and at first she could not see the two Mosquitoes. Then one came into view, moving slowly down the runway away from her as the pilot blipped his engines.

A second one appeared a few seconds later, following the path of the first. They reached the end of the runway and for a long moment disappeared into the darkness.

The girl waited as she had waited since Harvey was recalled to the airfield three hours earlier. With no knowledge of the reason, she had hoped against hope that his recall was not for some urgent combat mission.

But her knowledge of RAF procedures was not her ally for she knew that station communications were seldom cut unless operations were involved, and she had discovered the line was dead two hours ago when she had tried to phone Harvey. After that, unable to sleep, she had tried to occupy her mind with reading but with little success.

The first Mosquito had now appeared again at the far end of the runway. For a few seconds it paused like a bird sensing danger. Then, as a green Very light soared up in a huge arc from the Control Tower, it began to move forward, slowly at first then with ever increasing speed, its twin propellers glinting yellow in the lights and its wheels throwing up spray from the wet runway.

She watched in fascination as it raced towards her. It bounced one, twice, thrice, then it was airborne and its black shadow was passing like a giant bat over the inn, the roar of its engines rattling the mullioned windows.

The second Mosquito followed less than fifteen seconds later. It had barely lifted from the airfield before the runway lights switched off, leaving the airfield in almost total darkness.

Anna found she was ice cold as she replaced the blackout curtain and switched on the light. It had been Frank, she was convinced of it as she climbed back into bed and drew the quilt around her shivering body again. Otherwise why would he have been recalled at that time of night? And in all probability his destination was Norway, that frightening land of jagged mountain peaks that had nearly claimed him twice before. Not for the first time she felt herself racked with both anger and fear at his willingness to accept Davies's offer.

A full fifteen minutes passed before she heard quiet footsteps in the hall below. Listening, thinking at first they belonged to Joe Kearns, she heard the stairs creak and realised someone was coming upstairs. A moment later the door swung open and she saw Harvey standing there, his shoes in his hand. He looked almost shamefaced as he gazed at her. "What are you doing? I thought you'd be sleeping." Then he noticed her expression. "What's wrong? You look as if you've seen a ghost."

She did not want him to know her fears. Now the die was cast, he would have enough to worry about. "I didn't expect you back. When they recalled you, I thought it meant you were flying tonight. So this has come as a nice surprise."

He looked unconvinced. "You look pale. Are you cold?"

She laughed. "Yes. Very cold."

"Then why are you sitting up in bed like that?"

"I couldn't sleep after you left so I've been reading. And when I heard your footsteps I thought someone had broken into the pub. That's all."

Realising his shoes were still in his hand, he lowered them to the floor. Then, too tired to see through her act, he sank down on the bed. "No, Davies just wanted my advice. There's been a cock-up in Norway over Adams' equipment and Millburn and Machin have gone out to do an air drop."

Thank God it was them and not you, she thought, and immediately felt shame at her selfishness. "Frank isn't in any trouble over there, is he?"

"No, I don't think so. But it's a hell of a nuisance. It's a bad trip for those four lads."

Now he was back, she wanted him beside her. "It'll soon be morning, Frank. Come to bed now and try to get some rest."

Chapter 21

Millburn addressed his intercom. "How are we for time?"

With his oxygen mask and thick flying suit making him a weird sight in the faint blue cockpit light, Gabby peered at his chronometer. "We go down in four minutes. Then we change course." He turned to the American. "Do you think it'll work?"

Millburn shrugged. "It depends what we can see down there. If it's too dark I'd rather hit the Heinies than the sea."

Halfway across the North Sea the two Mosquitoes were graceful silhouettes as moonlight frosted their wings and edged their propellers' arcs with silver, their speed only detectable by the massive banks of cloud that were drifting beneath them. Feeling T-Tommy yaw slightly, Millburn was glad he had taken the precaution of having the two aircrafts' wings rubbed with glycol while re-fuelling at Sumburgh in the Shetlands. Even so he knew it would not be long at their present altitude before ice became a serious problem.

Since leaving Sumburgh they had been climbing steadily. They knew the German Freya long range radar would have picked them up and be monitoring them, so they had set a compass course that would take them to the southernmost province of Norway if it were maintained. For nearly ninety minutes they had kept to this course. Now it was nearly time to drop down below the cloud base and then turn on a new leg that would take them to the co-ordinates sent them by Steen. If they could fly low enough to disappear from the enemy monitoring system, the Germans would have no idea which part of the long Norwegian coastline they would strike. They might even believe the aircraft had frozen up and crashed.

The plan had been Harvey's and he and the Navigation Officer had worked out the details of time, airspeed, and compass bearings. But it had one flaw and no one had known it better than the Yorkshireman. To avoid the German monitors when they changed course, the two Mosquitoes would have to fly at low level, and at night, even in bright moonlight, only pilots of the highest skill could avoid collision with the sea. This was the reason Millburn and Machin had been chosen.

Millburn felt a tap on his knee and saw Gabby jerking a thumb sideways. Flying under strict radio silence, the American glanced at Machin's M-Mother in station on his starboard quarter and waggled his wings. Seeing Machin respond in kind and keeping the same compass course, Millburn eased his control column forward.

A few seconds later the moonlight dimmed and died. Knowing the danger of collision or loss of contact was far greater than that of enemy action, Millburn switched on his recognition lights. A quarter of a mile to his right a faint glow told him Machin had done the same.

Satisfied, Millburn watched the thickening cloud. "Keep your fingers crossed it doesn't go all the way down to the deck."

"What if it does?" Gabby asked. "Do we go home?"

Millburn grinned. "Yes. After we've dropped our load."

"You can't go in blind, Millburn. Don't you know what Norway's like? There are bloody great mountains everywhere. If we can't see the bastards, we'll end up like flies on a flycatcher."

Millburn knew he was right. "Let's see what it's like on the deck before you start your moaning."

Outside the cloud was like smoke as it pressed against the Mosquito's cupola. In M-Mother Machin turned to Baldwin. "You still with me?"

With Baldwin ebony black, it was an old joke in the squadron that Baldwin disappeared during night flying. Blessed with a rich sense of humour, Baldwin took it all without turning a hair. "Ah'm still here, mon. And aren't you glad I am."

A few moments more and a sudden white wall swept out of the darkness, smothering the Mosquitoes' windshields and hurling hail like bullets against their engine nacelles and wings. Bringing

191

freezing cold with it, both aircraft began to slither about like men losing their reflexes and the pilots knew their control surfaces were being rapidly iced up. The anticyclone that had favoured the British Isles the previous day had now moved eastwards and given way to a huge cold depression that had swept in from the Western Approaches and was now drifting towards Norway. Knowing this and the hazards it brought, Deakin and his planners had banked on the two Mosquitoes flying through it and catching up with the junction of the two weather fronts before the depression reached Norway.

The hailstorm took one last spiteful blow at T-Tommy and then the white hell died away. In the faint cockpit light, Millburn was keeping his eyes on the altimeter. 10,000, 8,000, 6,000 feet ... To his relief rime ice was now shredding from T-Tommy's wings and restoring its stability.

For a moment the Mosquito swept into a huge valley flanked by towering mountains of cloud. Glimpsing the grey sea below, Millburn felt his hopes rise but ten seconds later clouds closed round him again.

T-Tommy finally broke out of cloud at two thousand feet. The light was sepulchral, the horizon less than a mile away and the sea a grey shapeless plain flecked by spindrifts, but Millburn knew that for even that amount of moonlight to have filtered through he must be close to the junction of the two weather fronts. Heartened, he turned to Gabby. "Can you see Machin?"

They spotted the lights of M-Mother a few seconds later and waited until Machin was back on their starboard quarter. Then Millburn eased his control column forward again. "How are we for time?"

"It's hard to say," the Welshman told him. "We're probably a few minutes out."

"Try to allow for that when we start our new leg, will you?"

Tension was making Gabby irritable. "For Christ's sake, Millburn. Leave the bloody navigation to me."

Millburn watched his altimeter again. 1,000 feet . . . 800 feet ... The sea was now an icy pitiless waste that could freeze a man's blood in minutes. As Millburn took T-Tommy down to 500 feet,

Gabby turned to him. "That's enough. We might run into another hailstorm."

Millburn hesitated. "You think we're under their monitor screen?"

"We'd better be. If we go any lower we could end up fish food."

Below a bank of fog hid the sea for a few seconds. Deciding Gabby was right, Millburn waggled his wings at Machin again. When the Irishman replied, the American gingerly swung T-Tommy on the new compass course.

The next sixty minutes were a massive strain on both crews. Although they were now in the fringe of the depression and the moonlit sea lay below them, fog banks kept sweeping in, leaving the two aircraft suspended in a grey limbo. At such times, with horizons disappearing, pilots were flying blind and forced to rely entirely on their instruments, in particular their altimeters. In peacetime, flying at such a low altitude would have been considered suicidal. In wartime crews were trained to take such risks but the effect on their bodies and nerves was intense. With pilots straining their eyes to avoid collision with the sea, the need to watch instruments fell mainly on the navigators and soon all four men were suffering from eye strain and irritability.

In T-Tommy, leading the mission, tension was growing by the minute. Millburn, his eyes reddened from strain, was peering at the grey horizon. "Where's the bloody sunrise? Deakin didn't get the time wrong, did he?"

By this time Gabby was in an unforgiving Celtic mood. "He probably did. Which means if we keep going we'll run slap into one of those bloody great mountains."

The sunrise Millburn was referring to was part of the strategy Deakin and Harvey had worked out. As there was no way the two aircrews could fly in darkness at low level within Norway, much less find their dropping site, their airspeeds on the two legs of their journey had been governed by the time of sunrise in central Norway. Providing no heavy winds were encountered over the North Sea — and none had been reported — sunrise should occur when the two Mosquitoes were within a hundred miles of the Norwegian coast.

Thus by the time they reached the coast, there should be enough light for them to complete their mission.

But Millburn could see no lightening of the eastern horizon no matter how hard he peered. It was Gabby, a Cassandra on such occasions, who came up with the reason. "I'll bet Deakin forgot about the mountains. He forgot they'll screen the sun until it clears them."

Millburn realised he was probably right. "How much difference will that make?"

"I don't know. Maybe too much. Our ETA comes up in thirty minutes."

But to Millburn's relief the horizon began to brighten ten minutes later. "It's OK, boyo. Get your maps out. We're in business again."

Another ten minutes and rocky skerries began to appear below. Able to sink lower now that visibility had improved, the two Mosquitoes looked like phantoms as they raced through the shredding fog banks towards the coast. A fishing boat appeared ahead. As the Mosquitoes roared over it a man jumped from its wheelhouse and waved a hand. Relieved now their mission seemed attainable, Millburn grinned. "At least the natives are friendly."

"You always say that," Gabby complained. "How do you know he's not already radioing the Jerries that we're on our way?"

"Because I'm an optimist and not a pessimist like you, you little fart. Have you worked out yet where we are?"

The Norwegian coastline was clearly visible now, its hills and mountains silhouetted against the brightening sky. Busy examining his maps, Gabby shook his head. "We're not close enough yet."

Two minutes later the Welshman tapped Millburn's knee. "I think we're too far south. Turn north and run along the coast."

"You're sure you know what you're doing?" Millburn asked.

Gabby scowled. "I think that hailstorm drifted us off course. Turn north."

Waggling his wings at Machin, Millburn obeyed. The two aircraft were now near enough to the coast to see waves breaking against its rocks and cliffs. Thirty seconds more and then Gabby gave a relieved exclamation and pointed ahead. "There it is. The plateau Davies mentioned."

Millburn followed his finger and among a row of serrated mountains saw a distant snow-covered plateau silhouetted against the rising sun. Waggling his wings again he swung towards it. Thirty seconds later a rocky beach and breaking waves flashed beneath T-Tommy. With the Mosquitoes' real speed now apparent, a white plain, fractured by shadowy ravines and dotted with woods, scrolled beneath them like a rapidly moving film. Flying now at zero height, the air blast of the Mosquitoes' propellers sent snow sprinkling down from trees as the plateau took shape and height before them.

In less than two minutes T-Tommy cleared its crest and under Gabby's instructions swung northwards. Peering across the snowy heights, the Welshman gave a sudden yell. "There they are! At two o'clock!"

Millburn spotted the huts and waving men a second later. "See any bandits about?" he asked Gabby.

The Welshman, who had already scanned the bright sky, shook his head. "No. I think we're in the clear."

"OK. Then we'll do the drop on my next pass. Get the bomb doors open."

T-Tommy quivered as Gabby obeyed. Sweeping round in a wide circle, Millburn headed back towards the waving men. As they swept beneath him, he gave a yell to Gabby. "Now!"

Three huge containers toppled from T-Tommy's belly, hit the snow, and skidded to rest. As Millburn swung the Mosquito round he saw the excited partisans, who had run forward to grab the containers, draw back as Machin's Mosquito released its stores. A moment later Millburn swung T-Tommy northward. "Did you see Frank?" he shouted to Gabby.

"I was too busy dropping our load," Gabby complained. Then his tone changed. "Where the hell are you going?"

"Where's this Rosvik valley?" Millburn asked.

"Why?"

"Never mind why. Where is it?"

"Straight ahead. But we're supposed to keep away from it."

Ignoring Gabby's reminder, Millburn held T-Tommy on its course. Ninety seconds later the plateau fell away beneath him and although the shadows were dense in the valley he caught a brief glimpse of the small town below before his speed carried him away. He was banking over Helsberg to take another look when Machin broke radio silence. "Bandits, Blue One! Five o'clock high!"

Drawing back on the control column Millburn searched the pale winter sky. "See them?"

Gabby was craning his neck round. "Yes. Four of the bastards. Coming straight towards us."

"What are they?"

"Focke Wulfs, I think. Yes, they are."

"Do you think they could have seen our air drop?"

"Not unless they've got binocular vision?"

Millburn saw the Focke Wulfs as he was completing his orbit of Helsberg, four hornets high in the winter sky that were growing rapidly larger as he watched. "Listen, Blue Two. Follow me down into the valley. OK?"

"OK Blue One. Oi read you."

The Focke Wulfs could be seen clearly now with their huge radial engines and long transparent cupolas. Old enemies of the squadron, they had a slight edge on speed on the Mosquitoes but were slightly less manoeuvrable. As Millburn turned on a wingtip over Helsberg and made for the valley, their noses dipped and they came down like gannets.

With the Focke Wulfs having the advantage of height, Millburn knew desperate measures were required. For a few seconds the rocks and snow of Helsberg flashed beneath T-Tommy. Then, as the valley sprang towards him, Millburn pushed his control column right forward.

The effect was like a man stepping from a sunlit room into a cold, dark cellar. From the corner of his eyes Millburn saw Gabby draw back sharply in his seat. In the sudden gloom the southern side of the valley could be seen streaming upwards, its towering walls fined smooth by the Mosquito's descent. Black rocks flashed upwards and past ... a plunging waterfall ... a dense mass of trees ...

Flown by pilots with experience in both Russia and North Africa, the Focke Wulfs had peeled away into two sections, one plunging down after Millburn and the other after Machin. Diving still deeper, Millburn caught a glimpse of houses, of narrow pastures

196

lining a road, and of the green strip of a river. Beside him, Gabby was trying to evaluate the threat behind. At first the two Focke Wulfs had swooped down in line abreast. Now, forced by the narrow valley to fly in line astern and confronted with the chance of shooting down a Mosquito, a rare prize in Germans' eyes, the flight *kittenführer* had made certain he was leading the chase.

With all six aircraft now inside the valley, the massive reverberations of engines was bringing down avalanches of snow from the heights above. With the Focke Wulfs' speed augmented by their dive, they had become within range of the Mosquitoes almost before they plunged into the valley and their leading pilots were already opening fire. In T-Tommy, Millburn's brain was working like an overloaded computer as he eyed the massive bluff that jutted across the valley ahead and tried to work out ways of avoiding the vicious cannon shells that were already searching for the Mosquito's fuel tanks.

As T-Tommy shuddered under the impact of a shell and another made a two foot hole in its starboard wing, Millburn knew he had to go down to zero height. To ensure Focke Wulfs flew low enough to avoid the fire of tail gunners, their guns were set up at two degrees. If he could get low enough he might protect T-Tommy and even cause the enemy fighter to crash. Making the decision, he dived steeply again, bringing an alarmed yell from Gabby as he levelled out only a few feet above the valley floor. "What the hell are you trying to do? Land on the bloody road?"

The sweating Millburn had no time to answer. Trees flanking the river were almost brushing his wing tips. A cyclist on the road, seeing the Mosquito howling towards him, collapsed in a tangled heap of legs and wheels. Birds nesting in a tree rose in a minute explosion, one smashing into a mass of blood and feathers against T-Tommy's port wing. For a split second the Mosquito shuddered as a wingtip sliced off the upper branches of a willow.

But the deadly shells had stopped. Too wily to allow his lust to kill to overcome his prudence, the Focke Wulf pilot knew he could no longer bring his cannon to bear on the darting Mosquito. He would wait until conditions forced his prey to fly at a saner altitude.

The breathless Millburn knew that moment was only seconds away. The huge shadowy bluff, bearded with dark trees, was rearing ahead, forcing the road and river into a wide detour. As the road climbed round the lower slopes of the bluff, Millburn believed it unlikely he would be able to hug it tightly enough to stay protected.

Instead, in another split second decision, he swung from the road and headed right at the towering cliff. Ignoring the despairing cry from Gabby, he held his course for three or four seconds, then swung T-Tommy over on its starboard side and heaved back on the control column.

T-Tommy groaned in agony as its wings bowed under the intense pressure. To the two men, driven down into their seats by the massive g, the black rocks and trees of the cliff seemed to be crashing right through the windshield before they swung dizzily away. Gabby tried to speak but his breath was driven from his lungs again as T-Tommy swung violently in the opposite direction to avoid a collision with the far side of the valley.

Although unseen by either man, the violent manoeuvre had proved fatal to the pursuing *kittenführer*. With the Mosquito edging back into his gunsight, he had momentarily forgotten his caution and when T-Tommy had swung so violently away to starboard, his reflexes had failed him. Although he had swung his fighter over, his port wing had struck a protruding rock, spinning the Focke Wulf round like a child's toy before it crashed in flames at the foot of the cliff.

Unaware of this Millburn gave a shout as he levelled T-Tommy. "Is that sonofabitch still behind us?"

The shaken Gabby tried to answer but found his throat was closed.

Millburn's voice rose. "Answer me, damn you! Where's that sonofabitch gone?"

Gabby's legs were too weak to turn him round. "Can't you see in your mirror?"

Although Millburn could see nothing of either fighter, he found it hard to believe that neither had followed him. But unable to spot them and with the second bluff leaping towards him, he had no time for speculation. Seeing the bluff was as perilous an obstacle as the first, he made height this time before banking steeply round it. Then he addressed his radio. "Blue Two! Do you read me?"

There was no answer, only a crackle of static. He tried again. "Machin! This is Blue One. Can you hear me?"

When no reply came again, the American glanced at Gabby. "It looks as if Machin's bought it."

Before Gabby could reply, the crackle of static grew louder, followed by an unmistakable voice. "Hello, Blue One. Oi'm right behind yer."

Finding the strength had returned to his legs, Gabby twisted round on his seat. As he peered back he saw a battle-scarred Mosquito rounding the second bluff. When he informed Milburn, the American addressed his radio again. "What's happened to the bandits, Blue Two? Have they gone home?"

"One of the bastards has, Tommy. He missed his turn on that first cliff and went straight into it. It must have put the fear o' God into the others because they suddenly pissed off."

Fully recovered now, Milburn grinned at Gabby. "What was your problem back there? That fancy bit of flying saved your skin, didn't it?"

Gabby's indignation knew no bounds. "You're a mad fool, Milburn. We'd never have run into the bastards if you hadn't disobeyed orders and taken a look at this bloody valley."

"Don't talk out of your trousers. They must have picked us up when we went down to low level. I guess we weren't low enough."

"Then whose fault was that? You're the pilot, aren't you?"

As T-Tommy swept along the shadowy valley, Milburn's tone changed. "Take note of everything you see. It might save some of the boys' lives when we come back."

Gabby's suspicions grew. "Is that what Harvey was whispering to you before we took off?"

Milburn grinned. "No, he was wishing us *bon voyage.* Not a word about that to anyone, boyo, or I'll have your guts for garters."

Two minutes later the crews saw the valley was widening as it approached the coast. Catching sight of the sea, Gabby glanced at Milburn. "Do you think they'll be out there waiting for us?"

The American shrugged. "They could be." He addressed his radio. "Close up, Blue Two. Keep low and keep your eyes peeled."

Machin obeyed and like two swifts the Mosquitoes darted out of the valley and into a low fog bank that clung to the sea like a cobweb. As they emerged from it, Millburn glanced at Gabby. "See anything?"

"Not yet," Gabby muttered. "But there's still time."

Millburn gave a chuckle. "No, there isn't. Look over there?"

Following the American's pointing finger, Gabby saw the huge banks of cloud that had followed them across the North Sea were banking up like dark mountains on the horizon. Grinning at Gabby, still euphoric after their near escape, Millburn jerked a thumb at the bright sky above. "Someone up there loves us, boyo. What else can it be?"

With Gabby lost for an answer, Millburn addressed Machin again. "Keep your head down, Blue Two. We'll be OK in a few minutes."

And so it proved. Skimming like ghosts through the shredding fogbanks, the two Mosquitoes were beneath the oncoming weather front before any patrolling enemy fighter could sight them. As they soared upwards and the heavy clouds closed around them, Millburn grinned at the relieved Gabby. "That's it, boyo. We're going home and you're still in one piece for Gwen Thomas. Aren't you a lucky guy to fly with me?"

Chapter 22

Adams heard the distant thunder of engines and the drumming of cannon fire as he was helping two partisans to drag one of the containers into the storage hut. As he ran outside he saw the rest of the partisans had ceased working and were staring in the direction of the Rosvik valley. Gazing into the bright morning sky, the bespectacled Adams could see nothing but was only too aware his sight could not be relied on. Seeing Steen and Helga standing at the far side of the circle of rocks, he ran up to them. "They must have run into fighters. Can you see them?"

As Helga shook her head, Steen held up a hand for silence as another burst of cannon fire sounded. Then, as the roar of engines began to drift and fade away westward, he turned to Adams. "They've gone. Either down the fjord or the valley."

"Could you see them?" Adams asked again.

The giant shook his head. "No, thank Christ. Or they could have seen us."

In his concern for the two Mosquitoes, Adams had momentarily forgotten their own peril. "They took a big chance in flying out here without air cover."

Steen gave a grunt. "We'd be in trouble if they had. If there'd been a circus of 'em flying over here, Jerry couldn't have missed spotting us."

Seeing Adams' anxiety, Helga laid a hand on his arm. "Do you know who they were, Frank?"

Adams nodded. "I recognised Millburn's identification letters. He's our resident American. But I didn't spot the other. It could have been Harvey."

Far away, more a vibration in the icy air than a sound, there was another burst of cannon fire. The girl's voice was full of sympathy. "Harvey is your friend, isn't he?"

Conscious of the presence of the hard-bitten Steen, Adams tried to sound matter of fact. "I suppose he is. But then both of them are."

Her hand tightened on his arm, a silent gesture of sympathy. Then her tone changed. "Why did you get up so early? I told you last night you needed plenty of rest. You're not acclimatised yet."

Adams gave her a wry glance. "You think I could sleep when we heard an air drop was coming? I've been awake half the night listening for it."

Steen, satisfied by this time that the enemy fighters were well away from his hideout, turned and scowled at the girl. "Stop mothering him, *kjaere*. Frank's a tough guy; he proved that the last time he was here. Let him do what he has to do. Frank'll be OK."

Although secretly flattered by the big Norwegian's compliment and relieved he bore no ill will from the previous evening, Adams could not help a rueful smile. "Don't you believe it. I'd be lost without the help you're all giving me."

Steen showed impatience at his gratitude. "What're your plans today now you've got your markers?"

"Did you get Helga's sketches and my photographs off last night?" Adams asked.

"*Ja,* I sent a man down to the coast as soon as you gave them to me. They should be in Blighty today."

Adams showed surprise. "So soon?"

Steen grinned and laid a tobacco-stained finger alongside his nose. "We have ways, Frank. So what's your next move?"

"I just need to look at the bluffs from the other side. After that I can get to work setting up the markers."

"I think you should get your markers up today, Frank. The bastards might get that tunnel cleared any time now. We don't want to be caught with our trousers down."

Adams knew the giant was right. "The trouble is I must first let Davies know all about that valley. The boys can't fly up it blind."

"Perhaps your two aircraft flew along it just now?"

"We don't know that," Adams pointed out. "They might have dived into the fjord. For that matter, we don't even know if they weren't shot down."

"Get your markers set up first," Steen grunted. "If they're not in place, the job will be called off anyway. You can take half a dozen men and Larson: they'll do the climbing for you. We'll cover you with men at the top of the main paths that come up from Rosvik, although Jerry's search parties usually use the one that skirts Helsberg. I'll take care of that with the rest of my lads. OK?"

As Adams hesitated, Helga broke in. "Don't worry about the sketches, Frank. I'll do those while you're setting up the markers."

Adams started. "Would you?" Then he paused. "But will you be safe? There is a chance those fighters saw us."

"No. They were too far away and too occupied with what they were doing. In any case I intended coming with you. But this is a better idea. With any luck we can have both jobs finished today."

Winking at Helga, Steen clapped Adams across the shoulders. "Don't worry, Frank. I'll send a couple of my lads with her." As Adams gave a reluctant nod, the Norwegian's voice quickened. "OK, let's get moving. Tell Larson how many markers you want and he'll organise a work party. In the meantime you put a couple of extra pullovers on. London says there's some shitty weather on its way and you're going to be exposed on those cliffs."

Although Adams had often found Steen's choice of words bizarre if undeniably graphic, he had to admit that in this case no choice could have been better made. Standing on the snow-covered crest of the bluff that overlooked Helsberg, far out across the valley with a dazzling drop beneath him, Adams had never felt so exposed in his life. Not only did he feel he was visible to everyone in the town and the German garrison, but he felt the wind was driving through his white anorak and the layers of pullovers beneath it as easily as water through a sieve and stripping the goose-pimpled skin from his bones.

The weather had started deteriorating before Larson and his team had loaded their sledge and begun their trek to the two bluffs. Now the sky was a dirty yellow-grey and a razor-sharp wind was slicing over the valley and whipping up snow from the rocks that Adams kept stumbling over.

Kaldhorn, the bluff farthermost from Helsberg, had been planted with markers an hour ago. Adams' task had been to walk out as far as he dared along its treacherous crest and point out the sites he thought markers would be most effective.

It had not been an easy choice. The bluff did not end in a sheer drop but in two great wooded chins, the lower one jutting out fifty feet or more beyond the crest above. At first Adams' heart had sunk; he had believed his markers could only be set up on the crest itself and so perhaps not give sufficient warning to speeding aircraft of the threat below.

But to his astonishment Larson and his team had slid down on ropes to the ledge and set up markers on overhanging trees. In all five markers had been put in position, each adapted by Larson to be fired by electric detonators and each with separate cables that ran back up to the crest. Thus the operator, by using a portable electric generator, could fire each marker in turn. As each marker had a burning time of ten minutes, Adams had calculated that five ought to provide more than ample time for all the aircraft to carry out their mission.

In all the task had taken an hour and a half. Now it was being repeated on Trollhorn. Even before he had climbed out on the bluff, Adams had recognised the threat it presented. Now, as he and his party neared its outermost point, he could see that it jutted out across the valley even further than its companion, leaving a gap between its outer face and the valley wall opposite that was terrifyingly narrow for fast, low flying aircraft. Moreover, as Adams knew only too well, it was imperative that the attacking Mosquitoes took the correct line around it because, with Helsberg looming up ahead, they would have precious little time to fall into a straight and level bombing run before urgent evasive action was needed.

As Larson and his party paused to unload a sleigh, Adams pointed at the mountain side opposite. "I think I must have markers across there as well. Otherwise pilots might be dazzled by these lights, swing too far round them, and crash into the slopes opposite. Can we set some up there too?"

Larson, blowing on his hands, nodded. *"Ja,* we can do it. But not today. It would be too dark by the time we got over there."

After the work Larson and his party had put in already, Adams felt heartless in asking his next question. "Does that mean they can be ready early tomorrow morning?"

"Ja. An hour after sunrise. I will go myself. What about these markers? Where do you want them?"

Adams pointed to a thicket of windswept dwarf birch thirty feet below the cliff edge. "That's the ideal place. But can your men reach it? And have we enough cable left?"

Larson eyed the coils of cable still on the sledge. "It's a good thing you sent for more. *Ja,* I think we have enough for another five markers."

Adams was watching two of the partisans securing one end of a rope to a dwarf tree on the edge of the bluff. "Can't they be seen from below?"

Larson shook his head. "No. We'll keep out of sight. Will you be on this bluff when the Tommies come?"

Aware it was the critical observation site, Adams had already decided on it. "Yes."

"Then you look for a hiding place for yourself and we'll bring the cables to you."

While the partisans lowered themselves over the cliff edge and lashed the markers by wire to the trees, Adams found a small nest of rocks from which he had an uninterrupted view of the town and the wood beyond. By this time he was half frozen and was dancing up and down and clapping his gloved hands when Larson appeared over the cliff edge. He gave Adams a nod. "They're all tied to trees. So if any go out by accident, the trees should still burn and give light."

Adams, who was feeling shame as well as cold by his inactivity, indicated the circle of rocks. "Will the cables reach? I chose a place as near the edge as possible."

The cables did reach but had to be hidden with snow before the task was finally done. Able to assist at last, Adams also helped the partisans to load the sledges with surplus equipment. Still unused to the intense cold, he felt desperately tired by the time he and his party got back to their base.

He was relieved to find Helga waiting for him. "It's all done," she told him as she led him towards her hut. "I made the sketches and gave them to Neilson."

Adams was feeling dulled and stupid by the cold. "Neilson?"

"He's the young man Steen left behind to take the sketches to a fishing boat. They'll be going over to England by the morning."

"Where is Steen?" Adams asked.

"I expect he's still keeping an eye on the Germans. Don't worry about him. He'll be back when it suits him. You must come and have a hot drink now. I've never seen you look so cold."

At the very moment Helga was speaking, Steen and two other white-clad figures were crouched on Helsberg behind a pile of icy rocks that overlooked the fjord. Steen was gazing down the fjord through a pair of binoculars. His fierce voice, speaking in Norwegian, expressed both surprise and satisfaction. "So this is why the bastards were doing those reconnaissance flights over Blighty."

"But why have they sent her?" The question came from Arne, the radio operator.

"Isn't it obvious? She's going to collect this damned metal from the mine and cart it back to Germany."

The third man, gaunt and thinly built, was showing concern. "Isn't it an extravagant way of transporting it? You don't think that IMI business has started up again? That the Jerries have gone on accumulating stocks and she's come to take them away."

Steen shook his head. "No. London says that threat is over, thank God. No, she's come for these stocks of metal. You can see now how important they are."

The third man was still unconvinced. "Perhaps she's been damaged. Perhaps she's been attacked and is coming in for repairs."

"Repairs," the giant scoffed. "There aren't any facilities for repairs down there. There's only a jetty or two and a few old oil tanks." Picking up the binoculars again, he gazed down the long fjord. Between the mountainous slopes of dark pines, icy scree, and snow drifts, a huge German cruiser was sailing majestically towards them, its bow wave forming a huge vee in the sullen, icy water. "In any case, she's not damaged. She a Hipper class cruiser. A big strong bastard." Glancing at Arne, Steen gave his fierce grin. "You don't think London could send out a squadron to sink her, do you?"

Arne, who was wearing a balaclava against the icy wind, shook his head. "Not a chance. She'll probably anchor off the cutting but if she heard aircraft were coming she'd make for safety in the narrows further up." He glanced at the threatening sky that looked full of snow. "The weather's broken too. By the time the Tommies got here the visibility wouldn't allow an attack."

"Then what about when she's on her way out? If we could sink her when she loaded up, we'd get Uncle Tom Cobley and all."

Arne grinned. The giant's knowledge of English slang never failed to amuse him. "The Nazis will have thought of that. She's sure to leave at night. And the British can't risk ships close to the coast because of minefields and land-based bombers."

Steen scowled. "We've got to get the bastard one way or the other. Get back to your radio and tell London all about her. Ask 'em if they can do anything. And while you're at it, tell them we got the goods safely and thank 'em for the whisky."

Arne started. "Whisky?"

Steen grinned and pulled a half bottle out of his pocket. "Did you think I'd forgotten you? Take it back and drink to the downfall of Quisling and every bloody Nazi in Norway. Now I'm off before the sky falls on top of us."

Chapter 23

Davies stared at Simms. "The *Königsberg*? A Hipper class cruiser? What's happened to the barges?"

Simms looked apologetic. "It seemed a reasonable enough assumption at the time."

Davies was looking quite shaken. "A huge armoured cruiser. Now I see what those JU flights over our eastern ports were for. Jerry was trying to see if we'd any fighting ships big enough and near enough to clobber her."

The Brigadier nodded. "I suppose we should have put two and two together. But even we didn't imagine the enemy would take precautions as thorough as this. It certainly shows the value the Germans put on these molybdenum stocks."

"You can say that again," Davies muttered. "It must be worth more than gold for them to risk a cruiser of that size. What happens now? Does it affect our plans?"

"Not in itself. But it does mean the raid must take place before the loading is commenced. Otherwise you would need to sink the cruiser and even if that were successful, the stocks would almost certainly be retrieved. Our Norwegian experts tell us the fjord becomes progressively more shallow as it approaches the cutting. So divers could retrieve the metal fairly easily."

"The same thing would have applied to the barges." Davies pointed out. "We'd still have had to attack before the tunnel was cleared."

"That's true, Davies. But an hour ago we received an urgent message from London that might affect your planning. It's the reason I drove over to see you. It seems that Jensen hasn't heard from his agent since he sent in his message about the four day deadline. Jensen suspects he has been detected and captured."

Henderson showed immediate alarm. "That means the Jerries will find out about the raid, doesn't it?"

Simms shook his head. "The agent wouldn't know about the raid, Henderson. Jensen is too crafty a fox to let his men know more than necessary. But if he has been captured, the enemy must surely guess from his presence that the partisans know about the mine. It will also mean, of course, that the agent will no longer be available to find out where the mine is located."

Henderson swung round on Davies. "Surely that changes everything, sir. How can we bomb a target in a wood that size if we don't know where it is?"

Although secretly disturbed by the news he'd had to bring, Simms gave nothing of it away in his voice. "It is something of a crisis, gentlemen, I agree."

Harvey, the fourth man present in the CO's office, gave an exclamation of disgust but before he could speak, Henderson continued with his protest. "It's more than a crisis, sir. What about the markers? Adams lost a whole day because of that cock-up. He might find it impossible now to get them up in time."

Simms sighed. "Yes, that was unfortunate. No one was more angry or sorry than Jensen. But at least we know Adams has received the replacements and we do have his first photographs and sketches."

Davies, dismayed by the news and at the same time irritated by his junior officers' reactions, showed surprise. "Already?"

Simms drew out a file from his briefcase. "Yes. Jensen sent them by fishing boat last night and we arranged for a high speed launch to meet it outside Norwegian waters."

Impressed by the speed and efficiency of the SOE officer's organisation, Davies took the file from Simms and opened it. A moment later he gave a whistle of surprise. "These are marvellous. I never knew Frank could draw like this." As Henderson and Harvey peered over his shoulder, Davies turned to the Scot. "Did you know he was an artist?"

As surprised as Davies, Henderson shook his head. "I'd no idea." He glanced at Harvey. "Did you know?"

Harvey's reply showed little concern for Adams' imagined artistry. "No. But I don't like the look of those bluffs. If we do go, we'll need markers on 'em or we'll never get through."

Irritated that the practical Yorkshireman was emphasising that the substance was more important than the wrapping, Davies gave him a scowl. "We know all that. That's why Adams is over there." He turned back to Simms. "What about his photographs?"

The Brigadier handed him a dozen prints. "These aren't so good, I'm afraid."

Davies examined them, then passed them to Henderson. "He's no photographer, that's for sure," he muttered.

Henderson and Harvey thumbed through the prints. All were slightly out of focus and over-exposed but they did give a general if watery impression of the main features of the valley. As always Harvey's comments were right up to the point. "One thing for sure, there's not enough air space for us to go in through the cutting or from the mountain tops. We'd not only have to face that cruiser's fire power now but we'd be crashing into the mountains or into one another like wasps in a jam jar."

Secretly agreeing it wasn't a bad simile, Davies gave him a sharp look. "We never thought we could. So nothing's changed."

"Except it looks now as if we're not going to know where the mine is," Henderson reminded him.

Scowling, Davies turned to the Brigadier. "Can't Jensen plant another man into the compound?"

"I'm sure he's trying, Davies, but you can guess how difficult the enemy will make it when he's guarding something as precious as this mine. And if he has captured Jensen's agent he'll be even more vigilant now."

Henderson broke the heavy silence that followed. His question was addressed at Davies. "So what does this all mean, sir? Surely the raid must be off if we get no further news about the target?"

To the Scot's surprise it was Simms who replied. "I deeply regret this, gentlemen, but I think you will find the raid still has to go ahead."

Even Davies was looking surprised at the statement. "I don't follow you, sir."

Simms turned to him. "You're forgetting Churchill, Davies. In spite of the dangers involved, he was envisaging a seaborne strike until your scheme was put to him. Realising it would obviate a heavy loss of ships and men, he fell for it hook, line, and sinker. In other circumstances he might listen to a change of plan. But with the arrival of the cruiser, which must mean the tunnel will be clear any day now, no other strike can be laid on in time. I'm afraid you really have no option but to proceed with your plan."

Henderson could not believe what he was hearing. "Even if we don't know the location of the target?"

"I'm not an airman, Henderson, but I would imagine that in an emergency you could pattern bomb that wood. I know it would be a hit and miss affair but at least there'd be a chance of striking the mine. Certainly you could bomb the tunnel and delay the movement of the stocks. That would be something in itself."

Before Davies could answer, Harvey broke in. "What if the cock-up means Adams can't get his markers up in time?"

Simms nodded. "I'm afraid you'd still have to go, Harvey."

The Yorkshireman muttered an epithet beneath his breath. Even Davies was looking shocked now. "I couldn't agree to that, sir. It would be tantamount to asking men to commit suicide."

Simms took a deep breath. "I'm afraid it is one of those situations that arise in war from time to time, Davies. I had hoped you would have heard all this from your own masters before I came. But I assure you, you will get your orders from them very soon."

The silence that followed was full of questions and protests. Seeing the expressions of the three officers, Simms gave a slight cough before continuing. "Don't blame those in power, gentlemen. They have to weigh things up against the common good. Think of Churchill's feelings when the Bismarck was loose in the Atlantic. He knew the massive threat it represented to our convoys and our survival. So what choice was left him when he sent his message to the aircrews detailed to attack her?"

Only the cartilaginous sound of Henderson swallowing could be heard in the office as Simms paused, then went on: "In case you have not heard it, this was the message he gave them. 'Gentlemen, you are expendable. The Bismarck must be sunk.' I'm afraid he regards this molybdenum mine in the same light." His eyes turned to

Davies. "For my part I wish now you'd left the job to the Navy and Army. As it is, I'm afraid you are committed."

Henderson tapped Harvey's arm as Davies and Simms were leaving his office and motioned him to stay back. The Scot waited until the two senior officers had disappeared down the corridor, then closed his door and turned to Harvey. "Well, what do you think?"

As always the Yorkshireman' opinion was unequivocal. "It's bloody madness. They've all gone crazy."

"Do you really believe Churchill is demanding we go ahead?"

All Harvey's harsh social background came out in his reply. "Every word. That's what our upper class characters are like. They see us as expendable. They always have."

The shock Henderson had received was still evident on his square, honest face. "I can understand some jobs being so important they have to be done whatever the cost. But this one could be a sheer waste of life if the markers aren't up in time or we don't know the site of the target."

When Harvey made no reply, the Scot went on: "There's something else worrying me too. That flight of Millburn and Machin down the valley. I know Davies was going to bring it up tonight but I think he was too shaken by the news Simms gave us." Henderson looked straight into Harvey's face. "Did you tell Millburn to fly down it?"

With Harvey always finding it difficult to lie, his hesitation lasted less than a second. "What if I did? I have to lead the lads, remember? And I wasn't taking 'em into that valley until I'd an idea what's in it. Davies was a fool to expect it."

Henderson took a deep breath. "I hope you realise what you've done. If Jerry's twigged our game, he could already have a couple of dozen guns lining that valley. And all because you can't obey orders. What's come over you lately? First you pull that crazy CRISIS stunt and now you go directly against Davies' orders. You going dolally or something?"

The Yorkshireman's craggy face was showing defiance instead of contrition. "This is Davies's fault, sir, not mine. Simms as good as said so. If Davies hadn't been so keen to get another commendation, he'd never have offered to use us in the first place. Then we wouldn't have found ourselves in this mess."

Although secretly agreeing, Henderson felt protocol demanded some defence of Davies's behaviour. "It's not all ambition, Frank. He's genuinely proud of the squadron and Simms convinced him of the importance of this mine, quite apart from Churchill's orders for its destruction." Before Harvey could comment, Henderson went on: "Anyway, none of this has anything to do with your disobeying orders. You do realise you could be cashiered for it, don't you?"

Harvey wasn't giving an inch of ground. "Aye, I know that. I also know those mountains better than anyone here. They're murder at the best of times and we're going out in the winter. As I said before, I'd rather my lads faced guns than collision with great hunks of rock."

Knowing he was right, knowing he had his men's interest at heart, knowing everyone was right, and yet equally knowing the situation was chronic and seemingly insoluble, Henderson found his frustration coming to a head. "Davies should have left you at that OTU. You're becoming nothing but a bloody headache to me. All right, you can piss off now. I want to get some sleep before I jack the whole thing in and blow my brains out."

Chapter 24

Steen shook his shaggy head. "You can't do it, Frank. If you could speak Norwegian, maybe. But as you can't, it'd be madness."

Helga, who had looked horrified at Adams' announcement, added her own protest. "It's out of the question, Frank. You'd be committing suicide."

"I have to go," Adams told her. "I realised it when I was on Trollhorn and it's even more urgent now this cruiser has arrived and Steen thinks his agent has been captured." His glance at Steen was one of hope rather than anticipation. "You don't think there could be any other reason why he hasn't contacted you?"

The giant shook his head again. "Naw. He's missed two transmissions and he's not a guy to do that. I'm sure the bastards have got him."

Helga shuddered. "Poor Jocheim. Let's hope they don't suspect his real reason for being down there."

"If they do, *kjaere,* they still can't find out what he doesn't know." Steen turned to Adams. "It seems your squadron will make the attack even if we can't tell them where the mine is. How will that work?"

"I expect they'll pattern bomb the wood in the hope one of the bombs burns away the camouflage nets and exposes the mine," Adams told him. "It'll be a hit and miss affair but as London considers the mine's so important I suppose they're left with no choice."

It was the evening after Helga had made her second set of sketches and sent them to London. The two men and Helga were occupying the small hut reserved for the girl. Steen was showing scepticism at Adams' reply. "It won't work, Frank. If Jerry uses smoke, they won't know their arse from their elbow. It'll be bloody chaos."

Adams nodded. "If there's heavy smoke and no reference point, it will. That's why I must go down."

Before Steen could reply, Helga broke in. "Perhaps Mrs Helgenstrom might find out something more from her miner. Do you think there's a chance?"

Steen lifted his huge shoulders. "I sent a message asking her to do all she can. But she can't go too far without putting herself in danger."

"I'll be able to find out tomorrow," Adams said. "Do you think she'll let me use her house as a reference point?"

Steen's expression turned fierce again. "What's the matter with you, Frank? You deaf or something? You're not going down there. So forget about it."

Adams's doggedness had never shown itself more. "Listen. Once Jerry hears aircraft are coming he's sure to use smoke. On top of that the weather's worsening and the aircraft will be flying at nearly three hundred miles an hour. If I don't fix up a lighted reference point for the boys, they could drop bombs on the town. Or run straight into Helsberg."

Steen cursed. "OK. We'll give you a light down there. What sort of light do you want? I suppose markers wouldn't be any use?"

"No, I need a light that'll burn throughout the operation. I was thinking of a powerful electric light pointing upwards with a shade round it to hide it from Jerry."

"OK. If the bakery's the right place for it, Gustafasson and me'll go down tomorrow and set one up."

Helga gave a cry of impatience. "That's as stupid as letting Frank go. Every German in Norway knows what you look like. There's been a price on your head for over a year now. You wouldn't last five minutes down there."

"I'll go in disguise, *kjaere*. Perhaps cut off my beard and look like a forester."

"You'd have to cut off more than your beard. You'd need a foot or two off your legs to begin with. Don't be a fool, Steen. If you were caught it would be a disaster for the entire Resistance in this part of Norway. You'd be betraying all your friends."

Although Steen's face had darkened at her words, his silence told Adams he knew she was right. He broke in before the girl could speak again. "I don't want Steen with me, Helga. He'd be spotted and we'd both be caught." As Helga began arguing with him again, Adams held up a hand. "It's not just the light, Helga. I have to try to work out some kind of a compass course from the light and I need to be down there to do that."

"But supposing Mrs Helgenstrom has found out more from the miner. Can't you wait until we hear from her?"

"If she has, it'll be even more important that I'm down there to use her information."

"But you can't speak Norwegian. So how will you communicate with her?"

Realising the flaw in his case, Adams was forced to turn to Steen. "I would need an interpreter. Can I take someone with me?"

Steen was scowling. "No, you can't. Have you any idea what would happen if you were captured? They wouldn't treat you like one of your shot-down aircrews. They'd see you as a spy and if you didn't talk, they'd torture you until you did. Do you know what torture means? Have you any idea of the things they do? You'd talk — everyone talks sooner or later — and that would be the end of the bloody mission because they'd fill the valley with guns. You'll have to do your calculations from up here."

Adams had secretly flinched at Steen's outburst. For many servicemen during the war the activities of the Gestapo were little known, but Adams' role of Intelligence Officer had made him privy to the many tortures that vile organisation employed and the effect on him had been profound. Often, when hearing about an agent that had been captured, he had wondered how he would respond in the hands of a Gestapo torturer. With little or no confidence in his own courage, Adams believed the very prospect of deliberately inflicted pain would be enough to destroy him.

He hoped his voice disguised his fear. "Of course I've thought about it. But what choice do I have? If London are determined to send the squadron out under any circumstances, then I must do something or men might die for nothing."

"Men might still die for nothing," the Norwegian said grimly. "Lots and lots of 'em."

Helga turned to him. "As Gustafasson's an electrician, couldn't he go to Mrs Helgenstrom's bakery himself? He wouldn't be recognised and couldn't be caught out by not speaking the language."

The giant sighed and heaved his bulk from the crate on which he'd been sitting. *"Ja.* That's what I had in mind. I'll go and talk to him."

"I'd like Gustafasson because he'd know how to set up the light," Adams said. "But I'll still be going with him.'"

This time the giant's weather-beaten face suffused with anger. "You're not going, goddamn it. Don't you understand your own bloody language?"

Not for the first time, Adams was surprised by his own tenacity. "I'm still going. On my own if necessary."

As the infuriated Steen took a deep breath, Adams thought of a 1000 lb bomb with its safety pin removed. Expecting an explosion at any moment, he was relieved when the giant snarled some Norwegian expletive and shouldered his way from the hut. As the door slammed back in place, Helga gave Adams a rueful smile. "You know what's wrong with him, don't you? He is angry because he can't do the job himself."

"Well, he can't," Adams said. "They'd spot him in seconds and we'd all be taken with him."

"But what if he won't let Gustafasson go with you?"

"Then I'll do what I said. I'll go on my own." As the girl flinched, Adams went on: "Look, what have I done so far? Just shown your men where to put markers. They've done all the work. In fact, everything I've done so far could probably have been done without me."

"So now, to justify your existence, you've decided to put your neck in a noose. Is that the act of a rational man?"

Her accusation made Adams pause before replying. "It's not that, Helga. I'm the only one who knows the problems pilots have on a mission like this. Once they come round that last bluff our crews will have little more than seconds to swing into line and release their bombs before Helsberg is looming up before them. As it is, they'll never be able to clear its summit. They can only escape collision by swinging steeply to port and flying through the cutting. So it's vitally important they have a reference point and a bearing. Otherwise the valley could be a death trap for them."

Her mind was too sharp not to see the flaw in his argument. "But if they have to pattern bomb the wood, won't each plane need to take a different flight path? So all you need is the light in the bakery roof and Gustafasson doesn't need you to set that up."

Adams, whose main purpose in going down the valley himself was the desperate hope he would see or hear something that would give him a clue to the mine's location, knew her words laid bare the sophistry of his arguments. Unable to find a plausible reply in time, he listened to her quiet, perceptive voice. "This operation was your idea, wasn't it, Frank?"

Adams never realised how much his sigh gave him away. "Yes, I suppose it was. Why?"

Instead of answering him, she pointed at the bed that stood at the far side of the stove. "I want you to lie down for a while. You are still not used to this cold and altitude and you are looking very tired."

Although he hesitated for a moment, Adams did as she asked. Coming after an exhausting day reconnoitring the western sides of the bluffs, his argument with Steen had seemed to drain the last of his energy and it was a relief to sink back on the stout wooden bed. He lay supine for a moment, then rolled over and propped up his head with a bent arm. "What are you doing?"

"Sssh," she said. "I want you to rest."

"I can talk," he said. "I'm not too tired for that."

He saw she had two mugs resting on the pine table beside her. As he watched, she reached for a kettle that was simmering on the stove. Turning, she poured hot water into the mugs and then handed one to him. "Drink this. It will make you feel better."

He took a sip and then gave a grimace of pleasure. "Coffee *and* whisky. We're doing well tonight, aren't we?"

She smiled. "Both with the compliments of London. Some thoughtful Englishman included them in the air drop. So, after the four bottles you brought, we are well supplied now."

Adams took another sip and felt a comforting warmth spreading through his stomach. "God bless that man whoever he was."

She raised her mug. "Skol. To the thoughtful Englishman."

A silence followed, broken only by the crackle of wood in the stove and the spluttering of the fish oil lamp. She offered him a cigarette, then smiled and withdrew the packet. "No, you mustn't. You are a pipe smoker."

"You remember that?" he said.

"Of course I do."

He reached out for the packet. "Just the same, I'll have one. I broke my pipe crawling about on those rocks yesterday."

The silence returned. He exhaled and in the mellow lamplight saw the smoke spiralling upwards. "This is a warm hut. Most of the others seemed full of draughts."

"That's because of Steen. He always gives me the warmest hut. He has never accepted that I can take the cold better than most men." Before Adams could reply, she went on quietly: "But let us talk about one another while we have the chance. How is Valerie? You spoke about her the last time you were here, but this time you have said nothing. Is she well?"

Adams drained his mug before replying. "Oh, yes. Valerie's well. Valerie's very well."

"Does she know you are over here?"

"I shouldn't think so." Adams hadn't meant to say more but the whisky betrayed him. "Not unless Richardson has told her."

She looked puzzled. "Richardson? Who is he?"

Her sympathetic presence, allied to alcohol and the strange cosiness of the hut, began opening doors that Adams had intended to keep closed. "Her latest boyfriend. This time she's keeping it in the family. He's a member of the squadron."

She winced. "Poor Frank. I am so sorry. Do you want to talk about it or would you rather not?"

Adams was finding that as one door swung open, another followed it until the entire story was out. "Of course it was a mistake allowing her to come up from London," he ended. "But I think she'd got herself into trouble down there."

"So all this happened just before you volunteered to come over here?"

With alcohol and weariness dulling his faculties, Adams missed the point of the question. "I suppose it did. Just before or after. I can't remember which. But let's stop talking about Valerie. Tell me about Rolf. Have you had a chance to see him since my last visit?"

Instead of answering him, she reached for his mug. "Let's have another drink, shall we? Chances like this don't come very often."

Adams was showing concern. "What is it, Helga? Has something happened to him?"

She filled his mug and handed it to him before replying. "Yes, Frank, but it happened a long time ago. Rolf was killed at the beginning of the war when the Germans first invaded Norway."

Adams struggled to clear his mind. "But you told me he was serving with the British Navy. And that was only last year."

To Adams the short silence was filled with unanswered questions. He wanted to see the girl's expression but in reaching to pick up her cigarette from the table, she had turned her face from him. "Why did you tell me that, Helga?"

She drew on her cigarette. Then, crushing it out, she rose, crossed over to his bed, and sat beside him. As she gazed down at him, Adams tried to rise. "You still haven't answered me. Why didn't you tell me Rolf was dead?"

She pushed him gently back. "Have you forgotten what happened, Frank? How after my brother was killed you begged me to fly back to England with you?"

"Of course I haven't forgotten. How could I forget?"

"Then don't you see I had to lie? You were in such a state of turmoil. I had to make it easier for you."

Adams sank back. He felt her cool hand touch and rest on his forehead. "You were so mixed up, Frank. It seemed the only decent thing to do."

The lamp behind her was giving her thick blonde hair a golden halo and framing her face, a face that had fascinated Adams from the onset with its blend of strength and sensitivity. Her voice, with its attractive Scandinavian accent, was like warm balm entering

220

his mind. "I didn't like lying to you. But war forces us to do these things. War is cruel enough without making things worse for those we have grown to love."

Adams gave a violent start. "Love?"

Her eyes, reflecting his image, did not falter. "Yes. Didn't you know that? Steen did. That is why he keeps putting us together."

The astonished Adams was trying to find the right words. "I've often thought about us. Many times. Perhaps that was why I volunteered to come over. But I hadn't really hoped ..."

Her quiet voice interrupted him. "No, Frank. That wasn't the reason you came. Valerie had made you unhappy but the real reason was your conscience. Like Steen, you cannot throw others into danger and stand aside yourself."

Before Adams could speak she laid a finger over his lips. "Don't say anything. Just lie still and I will come back to you in a moment."

Rising, she went to the door and drew a bolt across it. Then she turned down the wick of the lamp and drew off her thick pullover and slacks.

Adams found he was trembling as she returned to the bed and sank down beside him. She kissed him on the lips, then drew back. "Are you nervous?"

Adams tried to smile. "Yes. Very."

Smiling back, she removed his spectacles and put them on the table. "So am I. It is a long time for a woman."

Adams stirred himself. "Are you sure you want to do this?"

She laughed to relax him. "Always the gentleman, aren't you, Frank? Yes. I have wanted to ever since I met you last year."

She removed her vest as she was speaking, revealing breasts that were full and shapely above a waist as slim as that of a young girl. A moment later Adams found her beside him and her hands taking hold of his own. "Hold me, darling," she whispered. "Hold me and tell me you find me attractive."

Adams found his hands had been drawn on her breasts. Beneath them her skin was warm, rounded, and firm. His voice was unsteady with emotion. "You're more than attractive. You're beautiful. I've always thought that."

She snuggled closer to him. "Truly?"

"Truly. I'd never met a woman like you before. So attractive and yet so brave."

She laughed and kissed him. "You are not wearing your spectacles. Perhaps you should never wear them when we are together."

He found her humour relaxing but still his traumas with Valerie were inhibiting him. Sensing it, Helga drew his head to her breasts and then guided his hand down her body.

Adams felt it brush her pubic parts and then dip between her smooth thighs. For a moment he felt her body stiffen, then she sighed and her thighs opened to his touch.

Adams could feel his own loins hardening and pressing against her long, smooth flanks. As she lay supine, his hand grew more confident and entered her. For a long moment she allowed him to caress her. Then she gently drew his hand away and began helping him remove his clothing. When he was naked, she eased him back on the bed. "Are you cold?"

Adams shook his head. As she held out her arms, he caught hold of her nude shapely body and tried to draw her beneath him. Instead she pushed him back. "No, my love," she breathed. "You are tired. I shall make love to you tonight."

Adams watched her bend over his groin. A moment later he gave a gasp and his body spasmed. With all his life energy seemingly drawn down to his loins, Adams felt his very body was being consumed by her attentions.

He barely knew when the transformation occurred. His first intimation was when she was kneeling over him and her lovely body was rising and falling to his passion. Adams, whose love life with Valerie had consisted entirely of the myth of the long-suffering woman giving supine service to the rapacious male, knew he had entered a new dimension of love. Seeing his expression, Helga reached down and drew his face to her breasts. "Are you happy?" she whispered.

Adams had barely time to nod before his swelling passion exploded into an orgasm of exquisite intensity. As Helga gave a gasp and a sob at the same time, it seemed to Adams their bodies had fused together in the moment of their union.

They clung together for a full minute before the shuddering of their bodies ceased and they sank back on the bed. When his world was steady again, Adams turned and kissed her, his voice thick with emotion. "Thank you. It was wonderful."

She looked surprised, then laughed and kissed him back. "How funny you are. It was just as wonderful for me too."

She jumped up a moment later and stoked up the fire. Then she drew on her pullover and handed Adams his own. "Put it on. You might need it later."

Greedy for her now, Adams looked disappointed. "I was hoping we were going to lie together."

Her voice softened. "We are, my love. Beneath this." and she threw a quilt over the bed.

She climbed into the bed a moment later and pressed herself against him. "Now go to sleep," she whispered. "You must be fully rested by tomorrow."

But Adams did not want to sleep. As he felt her steady breathing on his cheek, he knew beyond doubt that rewards and fulfilment bore no relationship to status or security. In that small snowbound hut on the icy plateau in Norway, with danger and perhaps death facing him on the morrow, Adams knew he was having the most fulfilling and rewarding night of his life.

Chapter 25

Adams was feeling excitement and disappointment in equal measure. "Is she sure that's all the miner told her? Tell her it's very important."

Eiliv, halfway through a warm breadcake, turned back to Mrs Helgenstrom and translated. As the woman said something and shook her head, the young man turned back to Adams. "No. He just said the mine workings were well off the main road and hidden under camouflage. The stocks are in sheds close by. She got the impression the entire workings and the garrison were in the wood to the right of the road but can't be certain."

"What made her think that?" Adams asked.

"She says it was from the gesture the miner made. But it's only a guess."

Knowing he would have to be satisfied with that, Adams gave the woman a smile. "Tell her she mustn't switch on the light until she sees a flare burning on Trollhorn. I can't say when that'll be but it should be sometime after daylight in the next two or three days. Also don't forget to tell her to be careful."

As Eiliv translated for her, the woman gave a deep chuckle. "I don't need an Englishman to tell me how to be careful. Tell him I've been living with the bastards for four years."

Adams smiled on receiving her reply. "I didn't mean to insult her. I'm very grateful for her help and I know my country will be equally grateful. I think she is a very brave woman."

Grinning as Eiliv translated, the woman's stout arm came out and gave Adams a friendly push. "Off you go, Englishman, before my lad arrives. But tell your Tommies one thing. Tell 'em not to drop their bloody bombs on my bakery."

Adams laughed at her warning. "I'll make very sure they're told. But, just the same, as accidents can happen, tell her she must go into her cellar until the raid's over." He turned to Gustafasson, the other member of his party. "Are we ready to go?"

Gustafasson, a middle-aged balding man, said a few words to the woman before turning to Adams. "*Ja.* She knows what to do. We can go now."

The woman glanced out into the lane, then waved the three men out. After the warmth of the bakery, Adams felt the icy air bite his cheeks as he followed the two Norwegians down to the road.

The light was poor, no better than twilight. The late arrival of the winter sun had made little impression on the small town living in the shadow of Helsberg. To Adams' surprise, until he realised it was mid morning, the sidewalks were now busy with local townsfolk. Muffled up in hats, worn coats or anoraks, they looked pinched and dejected as they tried to obtain food from the poorly stocked shops.

At that moment, however, Adams was feeling more relief than sympathy. On their arrival in the small town early that morning, only foresters and workmen going about their business had occupied the sidewalks. Although Adams and his two comrades were wearing overalls over their heavy clothing to look like artisans themselves, Adams had still felt vulnerable. Now, with housewives filling the ice-rutted pavements, he had a comforting feeling of anonymity.

As he had hoped, Steen's temper had been partially restored when an early reveille had awakened the small camp that morning. Although the giant had still argued that Adams' participation was too great a risk, he had finally given in but not with grace. "You know what this means to us, don't you?"

Adams had been puzzled. "You? I don't follow."

"We'll have to move camp until you get back. Just in case."

Adams had almost asked why and then understood. "Is that going to be a great deal of trouble?"

"Of course it is," the giant had grumbled.

Helga, present at the meeting, had squeezed Adams' arm. "Don't worry about that. We'd have had to move camp whoever had

225

gone into town. It's only a precaution and we can get back here quickly when we need to."

Steen had given her his ferocious scowl. "Stop being nice to him, *kjaere*. He doesn't deserve it. I ought to let him go alone but Gustafasson and Eiliv have both volunteered to go too. That's a lot more luck than he deserves."

Her eyes had shone their gratitude. "I knew you'd help."

"Only because I'm as crazy as he is, *kjaere*. Gustafasson and Eiliv are good men. I don't want to lose them."

Knowing how slim his chances of survival were if he went alone, Adams had felt profound relief. "I'm grateful, Steen. Gustafasson's the electrician, isn't he?"

"*Ja*, so he'll know how to fix your bloody light. He can also speak English like Eiliv, so you can tell him exactly what you want."

"Thanks. I know I'd have had trouble attaching a light to the mains myself."

"I'm glad you admit it. You see what a fool you were making of yourself last night?" When Adams said nothing, Steen drew him away from Helga. "Are you wearing your uniform beneath your overalls?" When Adams nodded, the big Norwegian thrust a revolver into his hand. "Here. Hide this inside your tunic."

Adams' voice was rueful. "You think I'll need it?"

"Who knows? Gustafasson and Eiliv are going armed too."

Before Adams left, Helga called him into her hut. Although looking pale and strained, she made no attempt to dissuade him. Instead she gave him a kiss and told him with a smile that he mustn't be late back that afternoon because she was preparing a special meal for him. Realising she had accepted his need to go and was determined not to make it harder for him, Adams thought again what a very special woman she was.

Gustafasson proved to be one of the men who had helped Larson set up the markers, a taciturn man with a quizzical sense of humour. Like the younger Eiliv, he was carrying a canvas bag containing a set of tools as well as a powerful electric bulb and a piece of cable. Handing a similar tool kit and bag to Adams, he gave his sardonic grin. "To fool the Jerries in case they question us. OK?"

With the plateau to cross and a seldom used path to descend, it had taken the three men nearly ninety minutes to reach the valley

226

floor. They had to skirt one enemy garrison post to reach the small town but by taking cover among the trees flanking the road they by-passed the hut without problems. It was true they passed a couple of patrolling German soldiers on entering the town but although the encounter had set Adams' heart hammering like a piston, the chilled Germans proved too busy stamping their feet and clapping their frozen hands to bother with just another party of Norwegian artisans going to work.

From then on the going had been easy. After Adams had established that the site of the bakery was ideal for his purposes, the only obstacle left had been obtaining Mrs Helgenstrom's permission to use her home and that had proved no obstacle at all. When Eiliv had told her they were working for Steen, Mrs Helgenstrom had given her deep chuckle and told them that if it meant the Nazis were going to get a bloody nose, they could light her place up like a Christmas tree, a contempt for the risk she was taking that had awed Adams. Less than forty minutes later Gustafasson had attached a shaded electric bulb to the roof chimney, connected it to the mains supply, and they had been ready to leave.

Although disappointed there had been no way of discovering the exact site of the mine, Adams was feeling satisfaction that at least the all important marker light had been positioned and safely installed. If the raid came, at least the town should be safe and, if smoke were used, crews would have some way of judging their distance from Helsberg. As the rutted ice crunched beneath his feet and he followed his two comrades past shops and shoppers, Adams began feeling almost euphoric with the thought that soon he would be back with Helga with at least part of his mission accomplished.

As they neared a road intersection he heard music interspaced by shouts and bursts of raucous laughter. As it grew louder and quarrelling voices could be heard, Gustafasson pointed at a lighted building on the street corner. "It must be some kind of canteen for off duty soldiers. By the sound of it they've had a skinful of drink."

"Should we go round it?" Adams asked.

Gustafasson shook his head. "We'd stand out more if we were seen round the back of the town."

With Eiliv agreeing with the older man, the three of them started across the intersection. A small crowd of civilians were standing outside the canteen, drawn by the light, the music, and the quarrelling voices. As the shouts and curses grew louder and a woman's scream was heard, Adams found his heart was hammering apprehensively again.

The three men had just reached the fringe of the small crowd when the front door of the canteen burst open and a struggling crowd of soldiers came tumbling out. With women spectators screaming and running from the scene and cursing servicemen wrestling and throwing punches at one another, the road became blocked for the three men. Wishing above all else not to be involved, Adams was about to suggest they took the side road when two soldiers broke free from the struggling mass and came reeling towards them. Slipping on the frozen road, both fell heavily but still continued their fight. As one soldier began kicking the other, the latter hooked a leg behind his knee and kicked out viciously. Flung backwards by the force of the kick, the soldier struck his head on the nearside kerb with a thud that made Adams wince.

Frozen on the spot by the suddenness of the fight, Adams felt his sleeve being urgently tugged. Seeing Gustafasson motioning him to take the side road, Adams turned to obey when a German Army Kubelwagen appeared and came speeding up the road towards the intersection. Forced on to the sidewalk, the three men saw the vehicle skid to a halt alongside them and three members of the German Feldgendarmerie leap out. As whistles shrilled and the military policemen dived into the mass of struggling men, Gustafasson tugged Adams' sleeve again. "Come on. We mustn't get involved."

As Adams turned to obey, an Oberwachtmeister, still sitting in the Kubelwagen, noticed their intention and yelled an order. *"Halt! Niemand gehtweg!"*

Freezing, Adams saw one of the MPs was bending over the prostrate soldier. After a few seconds he turned and shouted at the Oberwachtmeister, who jumped out of the Kubelwagen and knelt beside him.

Adams heard Gustafasson's whisper. "What's going on? Do you know?"

228

Although his German was barely adequate, Adams had heard enough to chill his blood. "They think the soldier is dead."

"Dead?" Gustafasson breathed. "Oh, my God."

By this time order had been restored and the servicemen, sobered by the news, were beginning to cluster round the stricken soldier. The Oberwachtmeister, an authoritative figure with his white metal gorget and mountain cap, rose and gazed at them. "Who fought with this man? Who did this?"

Nobody spoke.

"I asked who did this. If no one confesses you will all be put under arrest."

Murmurs broke out. Then a young soldier stepped forward and pointed at Adams and his colleagues who were trying to look as inconspicuous as possible on the sidewalk. "They were the nearest. They must have seen it happen."

The Oberwachtmeister swung round. His eyes fell on Adams. "You. Come here!"

Feeling a restraining tug on the back of his overalls, Adams did not move. As the Oberwachtmeister shouted at him again, one of his men whispered in his ear. Frowning at the reminder, the Oberwachtmeister turned back to the silent group of servicemen. "Do any of you speak Norwegian?"

A middle aged soldier stepped forward. "*Ja,* I do. A little."

"Then ask this dolt if he saw who was fighting with this man."

The soldier turned and addressed Adams. Unable to answer in Norwegian, the panic-stricken Adams could only stand and stare at him. To his infinite relief, he heard Gustafasson's voice. "He can't speak, sir. He has a throat injury. No, I'm sorry but we didn't see what happened."

As the soldier was translating Gustafasson's reply, a German voice came from the spectators. "He's a bloody liar. The soldier fell right at their feet. All three of them saw it happen."

Fully focused on the three men now, the Oberwachtmeister frowned. "Why are they lying?" He waved one of his military policemen forward. "Bring them over here. I want to see their papers."

As the MP started towards them, Adams heard Eiliv's whisper in his ear. "It's over, sir. We've got to run."

From that moment on, life became a series of dramatic and fragmentary impressions for Adams. He heard a revolver fire alongside him and saw the advancing MP clutch his stomach and drop to his knees. The next moment he was running frantically down a shadowy street with Gustafasson urging him on and Eiliv pausing to fire shots back along the road. Then, as the roar of an engine sounded behind them, Adams was dragged into a side alley.

His next memory was the hollow pounding of feet as he followed Gustafasson across a wooden bridge. As he reached the other side, gasping and choking for breath as if his heart would burst, he saw Gustafasson crouched down alongside the bridge waiting for him. Waving him to keep running, Gustafasson started firing at their pursuers who were now reinforced by half drunken soldiers. As bullets ricocheted from frozen rocks, the horrified Adams saw Gustafasson's head jerk back, split like a melon by a heavy bullet. As Adams stopped beside him, Eiliv appeared from nowhere and dragged him forward. Adams needed no knowledge of Norwegian to understand his frantic message. "You can't help him. Hurry up, for God's sake."

After that it was pure nightmare for Adams. Escape if escape were possible meant running up the steep mountainside to reach a belt of trees and Adams was almost spent. He managed to stumble on when the ground levelled for a moment and hid him from his pursuers, but when the steep slope returned and his legs bucked on the scree, Adams knew the end was near. As Eiliv tugged at him, he managed to lift his head. "Go," he gasped. "Leave me. Please."

As Eiliv hesitated, Adams managed to push him away. As he dropped back he heard a shout in German through the agonised wheezing and sobbing of his breath. "Don't shoot that one. I want him prisoner."

With a last glance at Adams, Eiliv ran on. Terrified at the thought of being captured, Adams rolled over and struggled to pull out his revolver. He had just disentangled it from his heavy clothing when a boot kicked it from his hand. Lifting his head, he saw uniformed figures everywhere, some running after Eiliv, others standing over him but firing at the young partisan. As he threw his arms round one man's booted legs to hinder his aim, a rifle butt drove down on him. A split second later Adams was unconscious.

Chapter 26

Consciousness returned to Adams slowly. Firstly brief flashes of light interspaced by throbbing darkness. Then bright arrows that pierced his eyes and drove into his brain. Finally a steady glare that seemed to emanate from a formless sky above him. As he tried to move his head, an explosion of pain momentarily paralysed him. After a few seconds he tried again and this time discovered the glare came from an electric bulb set in the centre of a white ceiling.

For a full minute he lay still regaining full consciousness. Then, realising his glasses had gone, he lifted a hand and fumbled inside his tunic. Discovering to his relief his spare pair had not been removed, he managed to open the case and set them in place. As objects came back into focus, he ignored the pain and lifted his head. The room, as white as the ceiling, was lined with glass cabinets and illustrated posters, mostly devoted to various parts of the human body. A desk, filled with medical implements, stood in the centre of the floor. As Adams managed to lift his head higher, he saw his overalls and warmer clothing had been removed, leaving him in his RAF uniform. Unsure what he was lying on, he felt down with one hand. Feeling a metal stay beneath him, he decided he was lying on the kind of bed doctors employ in their surgeries.

As memory returned to him, the discovery with all its implications brought on a surge of panic, doubling his heart rate and the sickening pounding of his head. Realising he was not bound, he tried to swing his legs to the floor, only for pain to check him. About to try again, he heard a movement behind him and, turning his head with an effort, saw a German sentry staring at him from a doorway.

A moment later he heard a shout, *"Der Gefangene is erwacht, major!"*

Footsteps sounded outside a few seconds later and a white-coated officer entered the room. Of average height, with iron grey hair and a lined, intelligent face, he had the air of a country doctor as he approached Adams' bed. "Good afternoon, Squadron Leader. How do you feel?"

With the man speaking such excellent English, Adams was lost and drifting. "Where am I?"

"You are in my surgery, sir. I am Major Vogel. A military doctor. You were brought to me nearly an hour ago. Unpleasantly concussed, I'm afraid. Let me feel your head, please."

Expecting rough treatment, Adams was surprised at the gentleness of the hands that probed the back of his head. "Yes, you have a nasty swelling there. Let me give you something to ease the pain."

Adams watched the major walk over to a cabinet on the opposite wall and extract a small bottle. Filling a glass with water from an adjacent tap, he offered the glass and two tablets to Adams. "Take these, please. They will make you feel better."

Feeling he had entered an Alice in Wonderland world, Adams swallowed down the two tablets. Vogel eased him back as he tried to rise. "No, wait a few minutes until your headache eases."

With relief Adams obeyed. "You say I'm in your surgery but where is your surgery?"

For the first time Adams noticed a slight hesitation before the German gave his humorous reply. "You are still in Norway if that is what you are wondering, Squadron Leader. Not so very far from where your accident occurred. More than that I had better not say."

Adams was now certain where he was. Although the daylight in the valley was not good, it hardly warranted artificial lighting unless the building lay beneath camouflage. The distant rumble of machinery confirmed his belief he had been brought to the hidden mine compound. "How do you come to speak such good English?" he asked.

Vogel smiled. "Probably because I worked in a hospital in Cheltenham for a few years before the war. How are you feeling now? Are you able to rise and come over to this chair?"

Adams swung his legs gingerly down to the floor, pausing as the room swung giddily round. He felt a hand on his arm steadying him. "Still a little dizzy, are you? Don't worry. It will soon pass."

Adams dropped into the chair facing the desk. His laugh was rueful. "To be honest, I hadn't expected treatment like this. Not after what happened."

Vogel sank into the chair opposite him. "We Germans are not all barbarians, Squadron Leader. To a doctor you are a patient like any other patient."

With his head clearing, Adams was beginning to wonder if he was facing a clever ploy to loosen his tongue. "Yet our countries are at war."

"Yes, sadly they are. But to a real doctor the only true enemies are sickness and disease. Unless, of course, you include war which gives strength to those two enemies."

"Does that mean you detest war as I do?" Adams asked.

"Of course. Don't all intelligent men?"

Still not fully himself, Adams, a lover of philosophical discussions, was beginning to feel he was having one instead of the brutal interrogation he had feared. "Yet the leader of your country uses war as an instrument of politics. Doesn't that make it difficult for you to serve him?"

The lined face before him gave another smile. "It is difficult for a doctor to serve anyone or anything but humanity, Squadron Leader. I'm sure that is the answer most of my colleagues would give."

Adams felt he had been neatly turned. "I shouldn't have asked that question, should I? I suppose like many of your people you've had no choice."

"Choice is a luxury that requires precise and honest information, Squadron Leader. How many of us are given such a luxury in this world of mass propaganda? Aren't we all victims of our businessmen and our politicians?"

With Adams sensing a man of his own kind, at any other time or place, headache or not, he would have continued the discussion like a dog enjoying a juicy bone. But his eyes had just settled on a large map pinned to the wall behind Vogel's desk. Large and detailed, it featured the Rosvik valley from Lillestad on the coast to Helsberg at its farthermost end and had red pins inserted into it at various points. Trained to read and interpret maps quickly, Adams was absorbing its details with all the speed of a fevered mind. The red pins, almost certainly first aid posts . . . the road and river snaking round the bluffs ... the small town that straddled both ... the road running through the town and towards the wood beyond ... the bald white patch near the cutting that had to be the old quarry . . . *the red marker pinned over the forest to the right of the road . . .*

Hoping his sudden distraction had not given him away, Adams forced his attention back to the doctor. "I suppose we are. I'm not happy with the propaganda we're given either. But there is propaganda and propaganda, don't you think?"

Vogel laughed. "You are thinking of our Dr. Goebbels."

Relieved his interest in the map appeared to have gone unnoticed, Adams nodded. "Yes, I am. From all we hear it's difficult to understand how an intelligent race like the Germans could believe the things he has said."

"On the whole people believe what they want to believe, Squadron Leader. Germany needed its confidence restored. Hitler and Goebbels provided that confidence — although some would say in excess. Ergo, Hitler the Chancellor. Ergo, the Nazis."

"You can't believe it was as black and white as that," Adams argued, his mind feverishly computing the distances and angles of the red pin to the map's other features.

"Nothing in politics is black and white, Squadron Leader. Things are just different shades of gray. You must know that as well as I. But let us return to your injury. How does your head feel now?"

"Much better," Adams told him.

Lowering his voice, Vogel leaned forward across his desk. "Then will you do me a great favour?"

"Favour? I don't understand."

"I don't need to know your name, rank, and the rest. They were obtained while you were unconscious. But I do need to know why you were in the Rosvik valley today."

Knowing the question must come sooner or later, Adams braced himself and tried to stall. "I didn't expect you would be my interrogator."

"Officially I am not, Squadron Leader. I have been asked to do this by my commandant. He has no English speaking staff and I take it you cannot speak German?"

Adams, whose throat was now dry, lied and shook his head.

"So the task falls on me. If you are truthful, you will be sent to a prisoner of war camp. I have the Commandant's promise and I believe him. He is a man of both honour and compassion."

"What happens if I don't talk?" Adams asked, his apprehension growing.

"Squadron Leader, you must know what Hitler's orders are. Your commandos were shot to a man when they were parachuted down near Rjukan the other year. And they were wearing military uniforms."

"So am I," Adams pointed out

"No, you were wearing overalls over your uniform. So it is easy to argue you are a spy. I am afraid that is what you will be called if you don't accept the Commandant's terms. Like all other military commanders over here, his orders are to hand any spies or partisans over to the Gestapo. If you collaborate he will do his best to have you treated as a prisoner of war, although frankly it is more than you deserve. If you do not, his own life will be in danger if he tries to protect you."

Adams' blood had run cold at the mention of the Gestapo. "How can you work under a system like this? How can any decent man work alongside murderers and torturers?"

Vogel shrugged. "I suppose the answer to that is human frailty. We want to live because we are afraid of death, and we also want to live for our wives and children. Are you sure that you would show greater courage, Squadron Leader?"

Certain he could not, Adams could only rack his mind in a desperate effort to avoid physical interrogation. "What do you want to know?"

"We need to know what you, an RAF officer, were doing walking in disguise through Rosvik with two armed partisans. What were you looking for?"

During their earlier conversation Adams had thought of an excuse for his presence in the town. It had seemed more than frail but he clutched at it now with the desperation of a drowning man. "I wasn't looking for anything. I came down for food."

Vogel lifted a greying eyebrow. "Food?"

"Yes. A Mosquito crew was flying me over to Sweden on a purchasing mission but we had engine failure and came down on the Hardangervidda. They decided to try to get to Sweden on foot but I thought it a better idea to head west and try to get a boat back to Britain. But I was half-starved and when I saw Rosvik I came down for food."

"And just happened to come across two armed partisans in the town?"

Adams had never known he could lie so glibly. "I know it doesn't sound plausible but that's what happened. I went into a shop for food and when these two men heard me speak English they said they would take care of me. After that you probably know what happened."

"Are you telling me these men risked their lives for a man they had only just met in a shop?"

Adams, who was clinging to the faint hope that Steen might somehow find a way of rescuing him, was wondering if Eiliv had escaped. "I know it sounds implausible but they did. I suppose they saw me as an ally. I know one of them was killed. Do you know what happened to the other?"

Vogel shook his head. "No, I have not been told about him. But you say your airplane crashed on the Hardangervidda. That is many miles away. Are you telling me you walked all this way without food or shelter?"

"No. I found mountain huts to sleep in. And sometimes there were tins and scraps of food."

"Where did you get your warm clothing and overalls from?"

It was now Adams made his mistake. "The two partisans gave them to me."

"You mean they were carrying them when you met?"

Realising his error, Adams compounded it in his panic. "No. They took me to a house. We had recently left it when we ran into your men."

"I see. Where in this house, Squadron Leader? We shall have to know."

Adams tried to give himself time to think. "How can I tell you that when one of those men died for me?"

Vogel gazed at him for a moment, then sighed. "You can't tell me because there isn't such a house. You came into Rosvik with those two men, didn't you?"

"No. I've told you what happened."

"Then tell me where the house is."

"I can't. I've told you why."

There was a long silence, then Vogel rose to his feet. "I'm sorry, Squadron Leader. I'm truly sorry because I believe you are a patriot doing your best for your country. But you are either lying or defending a gang of terrorists and either way I can't allow my Commandant to be compromised. If he were to send you to a prisoner of war camp and there were repercussions, he could be punished as a collaborator or even a traitor. If you refuse to be honest with me, then I have no option but to hand you over for military interrogation."

Adams was sweating freely now. "You mean to the Gestapo?"

"Regrettably, yes. When you were captured our zealous Feldgendarmerie commander notified the Gestapo headquarters at Lillestad that they believed you were a spy. As a result they said they were sending out two of their agents. We were hoping to get you away before they arrived but ..." Vogel finished the sentence with a regretful shrug of his shoulders.

Adams was knowing real fear now. "You can't turn me over to those inhuman bastards. You're a civilised man and a doctor too. After all, I was only doing my duty to my country."

"Then tell us what that duty was and we might still be able to save you."

Adams was frantically trying to weigh up the consequences if he talked. Would London still order the attack on hearing of his capture? If London did and he, Adams, betrayed his trust, massed guns would certainly await the crews as they flew up the valley. Then there was Helga, Steen and the partisans. Would his confession endanger them? Almost certainly if the Germans threw a huge cordon around the plateau. Adams' shoulders slumped. "I can't, major. I'd like to but I can't."

"But you will talk, Squadron Leader. The Gestapo will see to that. So is it not more sensible to talk here and now and save yourself all that pain and your likely execution too?"

As Adams was taking in his words, a young officer came into the surgery and whispered something in Vogel's ear. The doctor nodded, then, with a look of regret, turned back to Adams. "It seems we are too late. The Gestapo agents have arrived and are demanding to see you. So I must ask you to go along with this officer. I am truly sorry about this, Squadron Leader, as my Commandant will be. *Habt Mut, mein Freund.*"

Chapter 27

While aircrews were filing into the Operations Room that morning, the squadron was obeying Davies's order and preparing for action. In its photographic section gun cameras were being checked and loaded with film. In the parachute section WAAFs were checking packs and in some cases re-folding the huge silken canopies. In the armoury men were testing the springs of the 20 mm gun magazines and filling them with shells, for 633 Squadron's Mosquitoes were unique in being adapted to take short barrelled cannon. In the Intelligence Office Sue Spencer was preparing escape equipment for all the crews detailed for the mission. In half a dozen other rooms specialist officers not required for the crews' briefing were issuing requisitions or checking their calculations.

Similar activity was evident on the rainswept airfield. Transports were running round the perimeter tracks, dropping off ammunition drums and spare parts. Petrol bowsers were trundling round the field from hard standing to hard standing.

The sleek Mosquitoes, picketed out on the airfield at their dispersal points, were the objects of this activity. With engine cowlings and spring loaded panels removed, drenched mechanics were servicing their Merlin engines, checking their airframes and radios, and arming their cannon. The only stores not being loaded at that moment were the incendiaries, bombs and rockets they would eventually carry, although these were ready on trailers to be wheeled out the moment the order was given.

While these preparations were being made, the aircrews had taken their places in the Operations Room and listened to an introduction by Davies. The room had then been darkened and the light behind the huge map of Europe switched on. As Davies pointed out details and features of the forthcoming operation, the illuminated map had made the rows of massed faces look pale and apprehensive. When Davies finally nodded at Henderson and the map light was switched off, a couple of bold souls could be heard muttering their protest. "Bloody Norway again! Jesus Christ, don't they know it's winter!"

Silence returned as the main lights came on and Davies moved to the front of the platform. Knowing it was going to be one of the most difficult briefings he had ever made, he was wearing his most genial hat as he gazed down at the dismayed crews. "What's wrong with Norway? It's a beautiful country. You're a lucky lot to be having a free trip over there."

As a low groan sounded, Davies grinned. "Just think if you were one of those civvy street characters in grey suits or overalls. You could be clocking in some dreary office every morning or crawling on your belly along some coal seam. Instead you have all the glamour and all the girls and a free trip to Europe every now and then. So why all the moans?"

As Davies hoped, Machin didn't let him down. "Bugger the glamour, sur. Just stick me in some nice warm coal mine and Oi'll pass on the rest."

"You'd never make a Bevin boy, Paddy. You'd be bored out of your socks in a week. This flying game's got everything, so make the most of it. You'll miss it after the war."

As groans and laughter sounded, Davies, ever the actor, knew he had the audience in his hands and his tone changed. "All right, let's get back to Norway and our target. It's vitally important it's destroyed, so listen carefully and keep your questions and comments until I've finished. Understood?"

As men nodded and nervous coughs broke out, Davies proceeded to discuss the problems involved in the target's destruction. Although as always he made light of the dangers, it did not prevent an arm being raised the moment he finished speaking. "This is another Swartfjord job, isn't it, sir?"

With Harvey the only pilot present who had returned from the Swartfjord and the questioner a "fresher" who had joined the squadron only a month ago, it was another reminder to Davies how

241

far the shadows of that operation had spread. Knowing for the sake of morale the impression must be scotched in the bud, Davies did just that. "It's nothing like the bloody Swartfjord, lad. What I haven't told you yet is that we've got men over there lighting up the valley for you. One of them is Squadron Leader Adams and you all know what a reliable officer he is."

Gasps came from all sides at this revelation. Until now the story had been sent round that Adams had gone up to Scotland on a course. Davies took full advantage of the crews' surprise. "You see how we look after your interests. When you enter that valley, it'll be lit up like Piccadilly Circus. All you'll have to do is follow the lights, find the reference point that I've mentioned, and Bob's your uncle. It'll be like a paper chase except the paper will be a succession of flares to guide you on your way and the finish a steady fixed light to take your bearings from."

After a short pause, hands shot up from all sides. Knowing the question before it was asked, Davies allowed a "fresher" to ask it. "But if we don't know where the target is in the wood, sir, how can we bomb it?"

"That'll be explained to you, lad, when your squadron commander takes over. Just be patient and all will be revealed."

As a loud hum of puzzlement and speculation broke out, Davies put up a hand. "Never mind the target for a moment. Have you any other questions?"

An arm rose. "You haven't mentioned flak, sir."

"I haven't mentioned it, Mason, because we believe Jerry thinks his mine is a secret. So we're not expecting flak inside the valley. That's why, with lights to help you, it should be a piece of cake."

Another raised hand suggested Davies's reassurances had their sceptics. "Are you certain of that, sur? You were hoping the same thing when we raided Bavaria, weren't you now?"

This time Davies looked less pleased with Machin. "We're not bloody prophets or magicians, Machin. All we can tell you is what we're told by our Intelligence people. And they think the valley's unguarded."

Machin's expression said as clearly as words what he thought about Military Intelligence. But the Irishman was a survivor and knew when silence was golden. As he nodded and returned to his seat, Davies transferred his glare to the rest of the crews. "Any more questions?"

A hand raised at the back of the room. "Have you got a model of the valley to show us, sir?"

"No. We haven't had time to have a model made but we do have sketches and photographs sent to us by Squadron Leader Adams." At this point Davies stared pointedly at Millburn who was seated on the front bench below. "We've also had drawings done from the impressions of two pilots who had their reasons for flying down the valley recently. They flew its full length with no flares to help them, so you lot have it made. When this briefing is over I want you all to examine the sketches and photographs and to memorise every detail."

Another hand rose. "When do we go, sir?"

"I thought I'd explained that. We can't go until we're sure Mr. Adams has his lights in place. There's also the weather factor. We must arrive in daylight and the cloud base mustn't be any lower than three thousand feet on our arrival. As you'll appreciate, these factors might come together at any time or not for days. That's why you're being briefed today and why you are to stay in readiness after this briefing. In other words there'll be no forays to The Black Swan or going out to see any popsies in Highgate. The station will be closed until further notice. Any more questions before I hand you over to squadron commander for the battle details?"

A hand was half raised, then quickly lowered again. Davies frowned. "Yes. What is it?"

"Sorry, sir. I've just realised it's an operational question."

When no one else spoke, Davies glanced back at Harvey who was seated at the rear of the platform along with Henderson, Moore, and a group of specialist officers. His voice was terse. "All right, Wing Commander. The platform's yours."

Harvey nodded, moved forward, and took his place. Watching him and the crews lined up along the benches, Henderson found himself comparing the moment to past briefings when Moore had been the squadron commander. Moore's style had been particularly his own, an easy, light-hearted approach to danger that had been very much public school and very much English. With aircrews drawn from many social levels, it might not have gone down too well in other circumstances but with every man having experienced Moore's qualities of leadership as well as his courage, the effect had always relaxed the crews and aided their confidence. Henderson was wondering whether the Yorkshireman, a different man in so many ways, would have the same effect on his young crews.

Henderson soon realised he need not have worried. The tall, craggy, no-frills Yorkshireman had less style than Moore, his voice was brusque, his humour more mordant, and yet the crews were clearly hanging on his every word. While everyone knew Harvey was a strict disciplinarian, they also knew no man on the squadron had greater experience, no man was more forthright, and no man was more sparing with the lives of his men, as Harvey had proved many times. If anyone could bring them back home, Harvey would, but at the same time he wouldn't bullshit them by hiding unpleasant facts. Satisfied his new squadron commander held the confidence of his crews, Henderson sat back and listened to a question being put to Harvey.

"Why can't we enter the valley at the far end, skipper? Wouldn't that save us having to fly all the way along the valley?"

Harvey scowled. "If you'd listened to the Air Commodore, you'd know why, Donovan. Although the valley opens out at the eastern end, it's too deep to dive into and not wide enough to swing Mossies around, not when there are high mountains on all sides. There's also that bloody big cruiser. She's shoot your arse off if you went in over her."

Millburn in his flight commander's seat on the front row, was grinning at Harvey's graphics. "Won't she still shoot our arses off when we've dropped our eggs? You said it's our only way out."

"She'll do her best," Harvey admitted. "But we haven't forgotten her. As I've told you, we're going out in two sections, red and blue. If we don't get the co-ordinates of the target before we leave — and it's unlikely we will — I'll be carrying the inflammable spray in my SCIs that we used in CRISIS. That's the way we're hoping to burn away the camouflage nets and expose the mine and its stocks. Machin, my No. 2, will drop incendiaries on it. If that doesn't work, we'll repeat the procedure. By the time we've finished, with any luck at all, the rest of you will have a clear sight of the target. All right?"

At the rear of the platform, Greenwood, the armament officer, leaned towards Henderson and gave a dubious whisper. "Do you think it'll work, sir?"

Henderson's whispered reply was fervent. "Christ knows. It's the only thing we could come up with."

Before them Harvey was filling in the rest of the briefing. "Both sections will be carrying rockets as well as bombs, so once we've pranged the mine and the stocks we'll be able to blow up the tunnel on our way out in case any of the stocks have survived. But Blue section, led by Squadron Leader Millburn, will only send aircraft through the valley on my orders. On arrival they'll stay just under the cloud base to give us air cover. That's unless we need help with the cruiser, in which case I'll order some of them down."

With cruisers possessing awesome firepower, Millburn's protest was understood by every crewman. "You're going to need her harassed all the time, aren't you, skipper? Shouldn't my Blue section take her on straight away?"

Harvey's reply was brusque. "No. If we all buzz around her, we'll end up having collisions. If we need help, we'll ask for it. Next question."

It was all so typical of the man, Henderson was thinking. First into the valley to test its dangers, first to attack the cruiser. If ever a man led from the front, it was Harvey. The Scot's eyes moved to a fresh-faced navigator who had risen from a rear bench. "Won't Jerry pick us up on his monitors when we're going out, skipper? And if they do, how will we reach the valley?"

"They won't pick us up, Prescott, because we've made the same arrangements as we did on Operation Valkyrie. We've got two flights of Lancaster equipped with Mandrels standing by to fly up and down the Norwegian coast once we're on our way. For you freshers who don't know, Mandrels are radar jammers. So although Jerry will know something's up, he won't know where or why."

"What about fuel, skipper?" It was Larkin, the New Zealander. "It's a hell of a long way to Norway."

Harvey scowled at him. "You think we're a bunch of clowns, Larkin? We've arranged to refuel in the Shetlands. We're also going to pick up drop tanks as well. Satisfied?"

Larkin grinned back. "Satisfied, skipper."

"There's one more thing, Larkin. Every man has to help in rubbing his kite's wings with glycol when we get to Sumburgh. We don't want any icing up on the way."

Harvey's reminder that the winter could prove to be their worst enemy brought an immediate question from Machin's navigator. "How often are we getting weather reports, skipper?"

There was a hush in the room as Harvey motioned at the two specialist officers involved in the associated problems of weather and navigation. "We're getting 'em hour by hour, so navigators will get an up to date plot before we leave. Going out we'll fly at high level to avoid losing contact. After that we might have to play it by ear, depending what the weather's like over there."

"What about fighter cover, skipper?" It was Van Breedenkamp, "Are we getting any?"

From the way the Yorkshireman's face darkened, it was clear the question had touched a raw nerve. As he glanced round at Davies, the Air Commodore rose to his feet and answered the question himself. "Because of the range, we can only call on Mustangs and all of them, ours and the Americans' are involved in the current ding-dong in Europe. The Americans would like to help but the trouble is we can't give them a definite date to make their arrangements. So if Jerry should arrive before you've finished, you'll have to rely on your Blue section and cloud cover. There ought to be plenty of that at this time of the year.''

Obviously suppressing his feelings, although his rugged face still showed discontent, Harvey turned back to the silent crews. "There is one thing to remember before you examine the sketches and get down to specifics. Once the target is identified, you must keep a full fifty seconds between your kites when you enter the valley. We don't know the effect of blast in a valley like this and your bombs are going to have a ten second delay fuse. So if you cut it too fine, you could be in trouble. All right. You can look at the sketches now and listen to your specialist officers."

A puzzled voice came from the back row just as Harvey was about to resume his seat. "What if the spray doesn't work, skipper, and we still don't know where the target is?"

Harvey's disgust in the entire operation was betrayed by his tone. "Then we'll have to pattern bomb the bloody wood, won't we? But don't worry about that now. Hopefully Squadron Leader Adams will be in radio contact during the action and I'll be acting as Master of Ceremonies. So if any problems arise, we can hopefully sort them out at the time." With that, ignoring the look Davies gave him, Harvey waved the Navigation Officer to take his place.

It was another hour before Henderson was able to complete the detailed briefing. "These are your code-signs. The operation will be called Thor. Your call sign will be Dragonfly and the station's will be Troubleshooter. As your squadron commander has told you, with any luck Squadron Leader Adams will be in radio contact with you when you reach the valley which, along with the flares, ought to be a great help in guiding you to your target."

Pausing, Henderson glanced back at Davies. "I know you're all late for lunch so unless the Air Commodore has anything else to say, that's about it for the moment." When Davies shook his head, the Scot turned back to the crews. "After you've eaten you can put your feet up until midnight. Then you'll be on standby until further orders. As you've heard, we can't fix a time until all our necessary factors come together but once they do we mustn't waste a minute. So stay sharp and alert. Any final questions?"

A hand rose immediately. "What about the bar, sur? I take it you won't be closing it today, will you?"

Henderson grinned. "No, but I'm rationing your booze, Machin. If the green light comes after midnight I don't want anyone pie-eyed and paralytic. The ration for the day will be five pints a man."

A groan rose from the benches. As Henderson was about to make a humorous remark, an MP entered the doorway at the far end of the room. Seeing the Scot on the platform, the man ran up the aisle towards him. Puzzled, Henderson leaned forward. "What do you want, corporal?

"There's a Brigadier to see you, sir. He says it's urgent."

247

Overhearing the message, Davies jumped up and hurried forward. "Where is he, corporal?"

"He's in the CO's office, sir. W.O. Bertram took him there."

Davies swung round on Henderson. "Come on, Jock," he muttered.

The Scot turned to Harvey, his voice low. "Dismiss the men when we've gone and then come straight to my office. OK?"

Harvey nodded. As Davies and Henderson hurried towards the far door there was a rumble of benches as the assembled crews rose to attention. A moment later when the two officers disappeared, the Operations Room became alive with a loud buzz of curiosity and speculation.

Chapter 28

Henderson looked horrified. "They've captured him? Frank?"

Simms, who looked a frail figure that morning in his army greatcoat, nodded. "I'm afraid so, Henderson. The news came through an hour ago. I thought I had better drive over here right away."

"I suppose there can't be any mistake?"

"No. The message came from Steen himself. It seems one of the partisans he sent with Adams escaped, although he was wounded. He said the enemy seemed to want to capture Adams alive."

"So he'll be tortured?"

Simms sighed. "If he doesn't talk, I'm afraid it is very likely."

Henderson dropped into his chair as if his legs would no longer hold him. "God, that's awful. Frank tortured." For a moment his voice was condemning. "We should never have sent him. He was too old for the job."

Davies, who until that moment had looked as shocked as the Scot, took the implied criticism to heart. "He asked for it. In fact he begged for it. And he did a fine job in Norway last year."

Henderson was too upset to care how Davies took his protest. "That's not the point, is it, sir? This was a more dangerous and strenuous job. It needed a younger man."

"For Christ's sake, we had to send someone who knew the requirements of the squadron. Anyway, I don't remember you putting up such a strong case against using him."

With Simms so normally composed, his sharp reply was an indication of his own dismay at the news. "I hardly think this is the time to argue who is to blame, gentlemen. Not when we are faced with the urgent problem of what to do next."

Henderson's reply was unequivocal. "There's only one thing we can do. Once Frank talks, they'll fill the valley with guns. We must cancel the operation at once."

Davies scowled at him, then turned to the SOE officer. "Do you know if the markers are in place?"

"Yes, Steen says they are. So is the reference light. Adams must have done all that before he was captured. But there seems no possibility now of finding out where the mine is."

At that moment Harvey entered the office. On hearing the news from Henderson, he gave a violent start. Then his craggy face set in censure. "I'm not surprised. It was far too risky sending him in the first place."

Davies glared at him. "Don't you start as well!"

It was not easy to intimidate Harvey. "The poor devil's going to talk, you do realise that, sir? You've only to ask my wife what the bastards do to people they think are spies. So what happens to the operation now?"

"We'll have to cancel it whatever London says," Henderson said again. "We've simply no choice."

Davies was breathing hard and there were two red spots high up on his cheeks. "Will you remember who is in charge of this squadron, Henderson, and let me make my own decisions?" When the Scot opened his mouth but then went silent, Davies swung round on Harvey. "We never expected any co-ordinates, so nothing's changed there. The first two kites can still spray the wood. If that doesn't work, the rest can fan out and bomb on different tracks. Unless we're desperately unlucky, someone must land a bomb on the camouflage netting and that should leave a target for the others."

Henderson shook his head. "You're forgetting about the flak, sir. As soon as Frank talks, they'll jam pack the valley with guns. That won't be difficult. They only have to run 'em up the road. Then it would be worse than the Swartfjord."

The Scot could not have used a more effective simile. Seeing Davies's expression, Henderson moderated his tone. "We all want to pull it off, sir, but this way wouldn't be a gamble, it would be suicide."

Davies glanced at him, then turned and walked to the window. His subdued voice barely reached the desk. "Aren't you both forgetting something? Churchill wants this job doing. If we refuse to take it on, it'll not only be a massive disgrace but it'll be the end of this unit. And that won't just be a loss to us. It'll be a loss to the country too."

Knowing what the squadron meant to Davies, Henderson was wondering what proportion of his fears were due to self-interest and what proportion to genuine distress. "I know all that, sir. But would Churchill want us to throw away our boys' lives on a hopeless mission?"

Harvey, the cynic, gave a bitter laugh. "He told the Bismarck boys they were expendable. So what's the difference here?"

Davies gave the Yorkshireman a look of dislike, then turned to Simms. "It's your operation, sir. What are your feelings about it?"

Simms sighed. "What can I say, gentlemen? I can't make you go. If you feel the job is impossible, I can only let Churchill know and ask the Navy if they will risk a major fighting ship to attack the cruiser when she sails out with the ore. But even that will depend on whether they have one available, which I doubt."

Davies glanced back through the window. A long, tense silence followed, broken only by the distant roar of a Merlin engine under test. When Davies finally turned to Simms, his expression betrayed his shame and the cost of his decision. "I'm sorry, sir, but unless we get better news from Steen it would simply be a waste of young lives. So I've no choice but to put a hold on the operation."

For a moment, Henderson felt immense relief. Then he looked puzzled. "A hold, sir? Why a hold?"

At that, all Davies's pent up feelings broke to the surface. "Because I'm hoping for a bloody miracle, that's why. Maybe Steen's agent hasn't been captured and still gets word to him. Maybe Adams holds out and doesn't talk. Maybe pigs start flying or Jerry sends us a cable and tells us where his bloody mine is. Until the situation's completely hopeless I want the station keeping on standby."

Seeing the Scot about to protest, Davies slammed the door in his face. "You've got what you wanted, Jock. Don't push your luck any further. You can relax your bar restrictions but I still want the station on standby for two more days."

"And after that, sir?"

Davies made no attempt to hide his bitterness. "Then you can stand the station down and we can all say goodbye to the finest fighting unit this country ever had."

Anna was showing her delight and surprise as Harvey entered her room. "How did you manage it, *Liebling?* I thought the station was closed down."

Harvey kissed her, patted the frisking Sam for a moment, then sank down on the bed. "We are, officially. But as the pressure's off, Henderson let me out for the night."

She moved to his side, her voice full of curiosity and hope. "Why is the pressure off? What has happened?"

Harvey lowered his eyes to Sam as he replied. "Frank Adams has been captured."

She gave a gasp of horror and a slim hand rose to her throat. "What did you say?"

"They've got Frank. This morning, I think."

Her lovely face was chalk white as she dropped on the bed beside him. "Oh, *Liebling,* that's terrible news. Poor Frank. *Oh, mein Gott! Wie schrecklich!"*

Harvey kept his eyes on the tail-wagging Sam. "Yes. It's not good, is it?"

She glanced at him, then threw an arm round his broad shoulders. "I'm so sorry, my love. You and he are such close friends, aren't you?"

For a moment he allowed her to draw him close. To the German girl, who knew Harvey better than he knew himself, no act could have betrayed the Yorkshireman's grief more movingly. Then, as she kissed his cheek, he pulled away. "Aye, I like Frank. We've had some good chats together. They never should have sent him."

She was torn between fears for Adams and the effect of his capture on the squadron. "What will happen now?"

"I don't know. As there's just the possibility Steen's agent might still give us more information, Davies has put the operation on hold. But neither he nor Simms know how Churchill will react to a postponement."

Her eyes were wide with fear now. "But surely Churchill couldn't order you to go now? Not now they have Frank. They're sure to make him talk and then they'd make the valley a death trap."

In his bitterness at Adams' capture, Harvey's thoughts were that the High Command and their ilk could do anything without a smattering of remorse. But wishing to keep the worst aspects of the operation from her he controlled himself. "Personally I doubt if they'd have enough guns in that area to get them in quickly. It's a hell of a country for transporting heavy equipment. And that's assuming Frank was to talk. He might not."

A shudder ran through her. "The Gestapo are devils, *Liebling.* Poor Frank won't have a chance."

Flinching, Harvey tried to change the subject. "If we don't go, Davies is sure he'll lose the squadron."

"Lose it? I don't understand."

"He's always known he has enemies jealous of his success in forming a special service unit, and if we let Churchill down he's certain we'll be disbanded."

"Disbanded? Does that mean the end of these special missions?"

Harvey gave her a lopsided grin. "You'd like that, wouldn't you?"

In spite of the news about Adams, her grey eyes had lit up with sudden hope. "Oh, yes. I would like that more than anything in the world!"

He cuffed her cheek. "I thought you were on our side. You ought to be hoping we get our information and wipe that mine off the face of the earth."

She gave a little ashamed laugh. "I know I should. I shouldn't want anything to happen that might prolong the war by a single day." Then, with a cry, she threw her arms around him. "But I can't. I can't bear you flying on these missions any longer. I hope Frank talks and tells them everything so that he doesn't have to suffer. And I hope Davies has to cancel the operation and that his squadron is taken from him forever."

Adams saw his spectacles being taken away, replaced into their case, and returned to his inside pocket. "There, Squadron Leader." The clipped voice, speaking in excellent English, was mocking. "In case you remain stubborn we mustn't deny you sight of all the pleasures we are going to provide for you, must we? Now I will ask you again. What were you doing in the valley this morning? What were you looking for?"

Adams, who was slumped in a chair and whose left arm had been twisted back until he feared his shoulder would break, answered through a haze of pain. "I've told you. I crashed on the Hardangervidda. I came down into the valley looking for food."

The uniformed Gestapo officer, a tall man with blond hair and narrow shoulders, glanced at a leather-coated civilian standing alongside Adams. "Our spy seems to need more persuasion, Edrich."

The man, bulky of build, with close-cropped dark hair and a fleshy prurient face, grinned and stepped in front of Adams. A moment later Adams felt as if a bomb had exploded inside his head. The clipped voice came again, fractured and distorted by surging waves of pain. "Your reason, Squadron Leader. Why did you enter this valley?"

Adams could taste blood and knew he had lost teeth. Unable to speak, he shook his head. A moment later he was hauled from the chair and thrown face down over a desk. "You are wasting my time, Squadron Leader. You are a spy and you are going to tell me everything you know. Edrich!"

From the corner of his eye Adams saw the man was now holding a rubber truncheon. As he tried to squirm away, a brutal hand drove his face down against the desk top. The next second the truncheon came down on his kidneys.

If Adams had felt pain before, it had only been the threshold of pain. This time it surged up from his lumbar regions in wave after wave of agony that travelled to his very fingertips before exploding. As his legs drained of strength, he slumped heavily down to the floor.

A brutal foot threw him over and pinned him face down. "Just a small taste of what is to come, Squadron Leader. At the moment you may pass a little blood but it is likely your kidneys will recover. But if you insist on being stubborn, we shall have to do things to you that will be far more painful and will destroy your body forever. So isn't it good sense to talk before that happens?"

In some untouched cell of his mind Adams was trying to equate Helga's love and gentleness of the previous night with this brutal nightmare. Terrified of more pain, he tried to stall for time, only to find his bruised jaw and mouth made speech difficult. "What does it matter? You will kill me anyway."

"Not necessarily, Squadron Leader. We might let you live if you are co-operative and tell us all we need to know."

Although Adams knew the officer was lying, the temptation to avoid more pain was massive. His voice seemed to come from a stranger, not his own terrified self. "What can I tell you other than what happened? My plane crashed and I came down here for food. That's all there is to tell."

The officer sighed. "You insult our intelligence, Squadron Leader. Edrich will have to teach you better manners."

A foot rammed down on Adams' back again. The first blow did not come immediately and Adams knew why. The Gestapo were refined sadists and knew anticipation could sometimes be a more potent instrument of torture than pain itself. As his body cringed and the temptation to talk became overwhelming, Adams found his mind suddenly flooded with fierce protests. What kind of men were these who could enjoy inflicting pain on their fellow creatures? How could they sanctify the beast that dwells in all men and allow it such freedom and gratification? What devils had they become and how could they be allowed to dominate the earth?

A moment later the beating began again. Through the thud of blows and the excruciating pain, Adams heard a thin high-pitched sound and knew it was himself screaming. But to his astonishment Adams suddenly found he had an ally. Suddenly pure, undiluted, white-hot hatred was surging through his arteries to every muscle, every fibre, every tiny vein, every cell of his mind. Adams, the gentle man who found war an obscenity and believed cruelty was the one unforgivable sin, was now hating his torturers with an intensity

255

that matched and even dominated his pain. He could hear his sobbing voice mingled with his screaming.

"Fuck you to hell, you scum. You're filth, you're slime. I'll burn in hell before I tell you anything." Adams, who seldom swore, found his ally was dredging up words from his mind whose existence had gone unsuspected.

Instead of the beating intensifying, as Adams expected, it suddenly ceased. He understood why a moment later when a sharp voice from the doorway penetrated his blanket of pain. "You will stop this, Mannheim. Immediately."

The clipped voice above Adams was haughty with defiance. "I shall do as I please, Colonel. You have no jurisdiction over me."

"You are wrong, Mannheim. I have authority over everyone in my unit."

"But I am not of your unit, Colonel. Please remember that."

By this time Adams had managed to squirm round and could see Vogel and a German Army colonel standing in the doorway. The colonel, a man in his early forties, of medium height and build, was looking pale with indignation and anger. As Adams tried to sit up, the colonel stepped forward towards the Gestapo officer. "As far as I'm concerned you are in my unit while you stand in one of my offices. And I will not allow you to abuse a prisoner of war in this way. You tarnish the honour of the German Army."

"Don't talk like a fool, man. This prisoner is a spy."

"He is still a man and a brave one at that. I tell you again. You will not abuse him while I am the commandant of this station."

There was a second of silence. Then Mannheim motioned to his assistant. "Then we will question him elsewhere. Perhaps it is for the best. We have more persuasive instruments in Lillestad. Pick him up, Edrich, and take him to the Kubelwagen." As Adams was lifted painfully to his feet, Mannheim turned back to the incensed Army officer. "You will hear more of this, Colonel. In the meantime I shall want an armed escort as far as Lillestad. If the partisans were to attempt to rescue this spy, you would be in even deeper trouble than you are already."

For a moment it seemed the colonel would refuse. Then his lips tightened. "Very well. But please arrange to go quickly. It offends me to have people like you on my station."

The clipped voice was full of menace now. "You take offence easily, Colonel. I wonder what offence you will take when I file my report."

Seeing Adams' difficulty in standing, the colonel waved a sentry forward to help Edrich remove him from the office. As the three men reached Vogel, the doctor broke his silence for the first time, speaking to Adams in English. "I am desperately sorry about this, Squadron Leader. Please believe that."

The German's obvious sincerity moved Adams more than the sentiment warranted, making him realise that compassion after brutality could be a greater threat to security than pain. To control himself, he gave Vogel only a nod of his swollen face before being led out into the corridor. As he was dragged down it, Mannheim made certain his voice could be heard by the two officers standing in the doorway. "Don't think you have been done a favour, Squadron Leader. On the contrary, we have enough gadgets in our headquarters to ensure you tell us the very birthmarks on your wife's body, much less the information you will give us."

Chapter 29

The icy air was slicing through Adams' uniform like a razor through tissue paper. He was seated in the rear seat of a Kubelwagen alongside the heavily clothed stocky figure of Edrich. In front of him was a driver and the narrow-shouldered upright figure of Mannheim.

Adams had been driven from the military compound fifteen minutes ago. Although as a precaution he had been blindfolded until the Kubelwagen had reached Rosvik, he had been able to judge from the map in Vogel's surgery the distance he had travelled from the compound. Now, with the blindfold removed, he could see the huge bluff of Trollhorn ahead and the armoured personnel carrier provided by the compound some fifty yards in the rear. Although in the way a drowning man clutches at every floating plank around him, Adams was hoping a rescue attempt would be made before he reached Lillestad, but every time he glanced back and saw the size of his escort and the guns mounted on the personnel carrier, he knew it would be suicide for Steen and his lightly armed partisans to face such odds.

As the note of the engine changed and the cutting wind varied its direction, Adams saw the Kubelwagen was now approaching the steep bend that ran round Trollhorn. Although the road was coated with woodash to combat the low winter temperatures, it was rutted by ridges of ice and sluices of water draining across it, causing the Kubelwagen to jump and rock as if it were alive. As Adams was thrown about in his seat, he was reminded of the hard object he had felt beneath him earlier when he had been thrown roughly into the vehicle. Waiting until the scowling Edrich was looking the other way, he felt down and discovered the object was a heavy adjustable spanner some mechanic must have overlooked when servicing the vehicle.

The Kubelwagen was now following the rutted road round the wide bluff. As Adams took another glance back he saw the personnel carrier suddenly skid on the rutted ice, slide to the road edge, and drop a rear wheel over the irrigation ditch. The huge vehicle did not turn over but from the way men were jumping out it was obvious it would be some minutes before it would be under way again.

In following his gaze Edrich had seen the accident and his guttural voice gave a warning to Mannheim. Glancing back, the major told his driver to slow down. The driver obeyed but was unable to brake sharply because of the ice. As a result the armoured carrier was hidden by the bluff before he brought the Kubelwagen down to a steady crawl.

Adams knew that fate was offering him one last chance and if he failed to take it through cowardice or indecision, he would soon be entering the gates of hell. With desperation motivating him, sweating freely in spite of the cold, he felt beneath him again and clutched hold of the heavy spanner. Then, as the wagon jolted on another rut of ice, he jerked the spanner out and hit Edrich on the head with all the hatred within him.

The blow cracked the man's head like an eggshell. As he sagged sideways and the startled Mannheim turned and tried to draw his pistol, Adams struck him first across the face and then on the back of his head with another crushing blow. As the startled driver braked, Adams grabbed the pistol from Mannheim's belt and pointed it at him. "Drive on! Quickly!"

It is doubtful if the driver understood his sobbing order but the waving pistol was a message in itself. As the Kubelwagen began accelerating, Adams risked a glance back, only to see the road around the bluff was still clear. Ahead trees were sweeping down to the road and Adams pointed at them. *"Haltet an!* Stop there!"

As the Kubelwagen neared the trees, the driver braked sharply, an effort to throw Adams off balance. Expecting the ploy, Adams hung on tightly and as the vehicle came to a halt he reversed the pistol and struck the driver over the head. Then he swung open a door and tried to climb out on the road.

For one terrifying moment he believed his back would not allow him to walk. Supporting his upper body with hands on thighs, he managed a few faltering steps and found the pain begin gradually to ease.

A minute later, with the road still clear behind him, he managed to cross the irrigation ditch and reach the trees. Glancing at the slope towering above him, Adams knew he would need to call on every ounce of his strength and courage if he were to reach the summit. Before beginning to climb he took one last look back at the Kubelwagen. He knew he had killed Mannheim and his agent but he could feel neither remorse nor contrition. The driver he believed might still be alive but as he was still slumped over the steering wheel he presented no threat. Satisfied and yet wondering what kind of man he had become, the half-crippled Adams began the climb and the greatest test of his life.

The sudden hammering on the door brought a minor avalanche of snow from the roof of the hut. An excited bellow added its own contribution. "Helga, I've got news! Bloody marvellous news! Can I come in?"

The girl, sitting on a wooden chair and nervously smoking a cigarette, jumped to her feet. "Yes, of course. What's happened?"

The door was flung back and Steen appeared. Wearing a snow smock, breeches and a grey woollen cap sprinkled with flakes of snow, he looked weary but intensely excited. Grinning all over his bearded face, he grabbed hold of her and hugged her. "Guess what?"

She was struggling to control herself. "Is it about Frank?"

He gave her another bear hug before drawing back. "You're not going to believe this. I don't know I believe it myself."

She struck his shoulder with her fist. "Stop doing this. Tell me what's happened."

"Frank's here, *kjaere!* He's escaped!"

Her face went deathly pale and her voice sank into a whisper. "This isn't a joke, is it? Because if it is I'll kill you."

"No, *kjaere*. It's true. Frank escaped and we've brought him to these new quarters." As she sank down on the chair, with her pale, disbelieving face gazing up at him, his big laugh made the lamplight flicker. "He did it all himself. He smashed in the skulls of two Gestapo bastards to get away. Frank's one hell of a man, *kjaere*. Didn't I always say that?"

She was still believing it was all a dream. "But how and where? And how did you find him?"

"Down in the valley. I'd posted a couple of men with radios to let us know when the escort was coming so we could know what the opposition was going to be like when they reached us. It looked bad after the first guy said they were using an armoured carrier and I couldn't see how we were going to handle it. But then the second guy contacted us. He'd seen what Frank had done and after checking he'd finished off the bastards in the wagon, he followed him into the trees. We got the message, found 'em both, and helped carry Frank up here."

Belief was beginning to filter into her mind like blood from a released tourniquet. "Carry him? Is he badly hurt?"

"Naw. He's a bit bruised here and there and needs a rest. But he'll be OK in a few days."

She jumped to her feet. "Where is he?"

"He's in our HQ hut. Magnus has been giving him some painkillers and strapping up his back." The giant gave his huge grin and laugh. "We thought we'd better do that before you saw him. But I reckon the sight of you will be the best medicine he can get."

They entered the large HQ hut a minute later. Adams was lying on a pallet bed with the partisan completing the strapping of his back. Seeing Helga, he tried to rise, only to give an involuntary gasp of pain. Seeing his bruised and swollen face, she gave a distressed cry and ran to the bedside. "Oh, my love. What have they done to you?"

Adams did his best to smile. "I'm all right. At least I will be when my back's strapped up."

Ignoring the other partisans who were in the hut, she kissed and kissed his swollen face. "I've been going crazy about you. Are you sure you're not badly hurt? Are you telling me the truth?"

He reached up and put a finger over her lips. "Stop worrying. I'm just bruised, that's all. Truly."

She brushed tears from her cheeks. "I want to hear everything that happened. But first you must have something to eat.

I'll go and prepare something for you. Soft food that you can manage. Then you must rest for the next few days."

Adams, who was having difficulty in speaking, shook his head. "I have to go back to the valley in the morning, Helga."

She gave a violent start. "Are you mad? You're in no state to travel."

Wincing with pain from his bruised jaw, Adams motioned at Steen to help him explain. The giant nodded and turned to the girl. "He wants to go because he got the bearings he needed when he was held in the Jerry garrison and he wants to be on Trollhorn when the Tommies come. Don't worry," he went on when the girl continued to protest. "We'll take him by sledge to Trollhorn so he won't have to do any walking."

"But why must he go at all? Can't our men set off the flares?"

"They can but he's taking one of the radios with him so he can speak to the crews. Larson's taking the other one to Kaldhorn so Frank can let him know when to fire his flares."

"But Frank's been tortured. Can't the operation wait one more day?"

"No, *kjaere*. The weather conditions are right at the moment. And Frank's afraid the Jerries might have guessed why he was in the valley and be rushing guns into it." Steen motioned at Arne who was sitting with a portable radio at the far side of the hut. "That's why I sent for Arne when we found Frank. He's going to send Frank's instructions and call-sign back to London. And I've already sent some of our men to their stations by the flares. We can finish the job tomorrow morning."

"But if you've sent men to the flares and the squadron receive their instructions, I still don't see why it's necessary for Frank to go?"

Steen's pride in Adams' achievement showed in the grin he gave him. "Ask the Englishman that question, *kjaere.*"

"Why?" she demanded of Adams. "Why must you go?"

Adams motioned Magnus to help him put on his shirt. "Anything could happen, Helga. They might need my help on the radio. In any case, after all that's happened, I want to see it through."

One look at his swollen but determined face told her any further argument would be useless. "Then I shall go with you in the morning. You will need help out there."

Adams shook his head angrily. "That's stupid." His eyes switched to Steen for help. "Tell her she can't go."

The giant grinned. "I'm too scared of her to tell her anything. Let her go with you, Frank. I'm going to need all my men and she might be a help in handling those flares."

"But aren't the Germans going to rush up patrols as soon as the flares light up?"

"If they aren't kept busy by your aircraft, maybe. But if they send up any troops, we're going to give 'em a surprise when they come up the hillside."

The giant's words eased Adams of one worry. At that moment Arne said something in Norwegian to Steen. The giant nodded and turned to Adams. "Arne's going to transmit in a moment and wants to know what call-sign you want to use."

Adams thought for a moment, then gave a painful grin. "Tell him it's Guy Fawkes."

Helga looked puzzled. "What is Guy Fawkes?"

Adams, whose escape and deliverance had left him almost light-headed, started to laugh until the pain became too severe. "He's someone who once tried to blow up our Houses of Parliament. I think it's a call sign our new squadron commander will appreciate."

A light sleeper, Anna was awakened by the sound just before 3 a.m. the following morning. It seemed to be coming from the hall below, a rhythmical sound that was muffled by the woodwork of the old inn. As she listened, the noise ceased and a man's low voice took its place. Immediately, the girl's heart surged and began to race.

Beside the bed, Sam had now awakened and gave a low enquiring growl. Whispering him to be quiet, Anna listened intently. The man's voice ceased and for a few seconds there was silence. Then a heavy creak on the staircase confirmed the girl's worst fears. A moment later there was a tap on the door and Joe Kearns' voice. "Mr. Harvey! There's a telephone call for you from the airfield."

Sam leapt to his feet and began barking. As Harvey awoke, Anna called out to the innkeeper. "Thank you, Mr Kearns. Please tell them my husband will be down in a moment."

By this time Harvey was awake, although still drugged with sleep. "What did Kearns want?"

Her mouth was dry with apprehension as she switched on a bedside lamp. "The airfield are on the phone. They want to talk to you."

Cursing, Harvey shouted at Sam to keep quiet, then climbed from the bed and threw on his dressing gown. As he left the room, closing the door to stop Sam following him, she sat listening to his muffled voice as he reached the phone. Although unable to hear his words, she felt her heart pounding again as his voice grew louder and more excited.

He burst into the bedroom a minute later, his rugged face, shadowed by a night's growth, full of surprise and delight. "You're not going to believe this! Frank's all right! He's escaped!"

She could not believe her ears. "Escaped? But how?"

"I don't know but he did. Henderson got the news from Davies a few minutes ago."

"But how? Did the Norwegians free him?"

"No, Henderson doesn't think so." Harvey's laugh infected Sam who leapt up at him in excitement. "They think he did it himself. Isn't it bloody marvellous?"

Sharing his delight, she held out her arms to him. "It's wonderful news, *Liebling.* More than we could ever have hoped for."

As Harvey crossed the floor towards her, Sam leapt up at him again. Laughing, he picked the dog up and gave it a hug. For one who kept his dog under strict control, no act could have expressed his delight more. Lowering the animal to the floor, he dropped down on the bed and hugged her. "Can you believe it? Frank of all people. Davies is doing cartwheels at the news."

His mention of Davies was like a sudden cloud crossing a bright sun. She drew back to see his face. "Why is he so excited?"

"Why? Because Frank somehow got the information we needed and had it radioed through."

Suddenly her smile felt tight and frozen. "What does that mean? That the operation can go ahead now?"

He kissed her again and then crossed over to a chair on which his uniform was lying. "Yes. Davies wants us ready in fifty minutes. It seems the weather conditions are O.K. over there at the moment, so he wants to take advantage of them."

All the sunlight had vanished now. In seconds she had been dragged from high summer to bitter winter. "So you'll be flying out tonight?"

Harvey was dragging on his clothes. "That' right." Blinded for the moment by his euphoria at Adams' escape, he suddenly realised what his news meant to the girl. "I'm sorry, love, but it shouldn't be a problem now. Not with the information we need and Frank out there to help us."

She knew he was lying but knew she must also keep up the pretence. "When do you expect to be back?"

He was buttoning up his service tunic. As he reached for his greatcoat, which was hanging on a wall peg, she thought how threadbare his tunic elbows had become. Puzzled by the triviality of the thought, she heard his answer. "Probably sometime tomorrow afternoon. Unless they keep us up in Sumburgh. If they do, I'll ask Henderson to let you know."

Although the bedroom was unheated, she was sitting upright in bed with only her thin nightdress as protection. As he walked towards her, he thought how beautiful she looked with the bedside lamp illuminating her pale, lovely face and giving a sheen to her bare neck and arms. Yet when he bent down and kissed her, she felt as cold as ice. He tried to draw up the bedclothes around her. "Cover yourself up," he said. "Or you'll catch cold."

Sinking back, she allowed him to cover her. As he kissed her again, she gazed up at him, her eyes huge in the lamplight. "You'll come back, won't you?" she whispered. "You will come back?"

He grinned down at her and touched her cheek with a calloused hand. "Don't talk daft, lass. You can't get rid of me this easily. Of course I'll come back."

She wanted to clutch and hold his hand but knew she must not. He patted and spoke to Sam, then walked to the door, where he paused as if about to glance back. As Sam gave a low whimper, a Judas thought broke into her mind. "Is this the last time I shall see him? Is this our last goodbye?"

The thought terrified her. To counter it before it could take shape and determine the future, her mind screamed its denial. *No! He will come back! He must come back! Gott wird ihn zuruckbringen!*

A moment later the door closed and she heard his footsteps descending the stairs. Whimpering again, Sam ran to the door and began scratching at it. Seeing the dog's behaviour as an endorsement of her Judas thoughts, her fear of them returned as she called him back to her bedside.

Less than thirty minutes later the first Merlin engine coughed and broke into life over on the airfield. It was soon followed by others until the bedroom window was rattling with the noise. A few moments later the blackout curtain glowed as the landing strip lights were switched on but this time she did not run to the window. Instead, lying in a cocoon of fear, she drew the bedclothes around her ears and tried to stifle the sound as one after the other of the Mosquitoes climbed into the icy night sky.

Chapter 30

Although the moon was still bright at 24,000 feet, making the clouds below look like an endless plain of pack ice, red streaks were beginning to show on the eastern horizon. Soon the sixteen Mosquitoes were able to close ranks like two troops of horsemen, their streamlined bodies rising and falling against the brightening sky. In A-Apple, leading the two formations, Harvey's face was showing satisfaction beneath his oxygen mask. So far so good. Either weather conditions were better than expected or the glycol they had rubbed on the Mosquitoes' airfoils at Sumburgh was working better than he had hoped.

In T-Tommy, leading the second flight of Mosquitoes, Millburn was showing equal satisfaction. "It's looking good, boyo. I thought we'd be slithering all over the goddammed sky by this time."

Gabby, in one of his Celtic moods after being dragged out of bed at 02.30 hours, gave him a scowl. "We aren't there yet. There's still time for it to slap us into the drink."

Millburn grinned. "I don't know how you do it, boyo. I really don't."

"Do what?" Gabby muttered.

"Keep so cheerful. It must take a hell of an effort. I admire you, kid. I really do."

The sixteen aircraft droned on, the sound of their engines reduced to a neutral murmur. To the most imaginative of the crews, particularly to young Donovan not long out of art school, the mission began to seem unreal. The world in which they floated was too beautiful, too tranquil, too full of moonlight and auroral promise to be part of a world at war. Somehow their wings had carried them above it all and they were on their way to the stars.

But in A-Apple Harvey had no such illusions. He was only too aware how treacherous wartime beauty could be, how it could suddenly explode in a welter of blood and fire. For at least the sixth time since leaving Sumburgh he asked his navigator their ETA.

Martin, a young man who had shown up well during Harvey's illicit part in Operation Crisis, sounded reassuring. "It's still the same, skipper. We're in luck with the wind tonight."

"Good, but watch it when we go down," Harvey told him. "We can't afford to spend time searching for the valley once we've gone past the Lancs."

Martin did not need to ask why. Like the rest of the crews he knew that the German Freya radar scanner would have picked them up almost as soon as they took off for Sumburgh and would have kept tracking them to the moment when the Lancasters with their Mandrels spoilers began patrolling the Norwegian coast. From then on the enemy controllers would not know their destination but as soon as the Mosquitoes flew past the Lancasters' line of flight the hunt would be on.

The minutes slipped past. The sky was growing lighter, reducing the waning moon to a pale, white bubble. Aware the squadron must be down at sea level before they passed the Mandrel screen, Martin gave Harvey a signal. Still under radio silence , Harvey waggled his wings, switched on his recognition lights, and began diving down to the ice plain below. Behind him, obeying their earlier orders, pilots opened out the formation, switched on their own lights, and followed Harvey down.

The sunlight disappeared as clouds closed around the cupolas of every plane, forcing pilots to fly blind. Tension rose as navigators searched for tell-tale lights that might herald a collision. As the clouds suddenly became blacker and Gabby felt T-Tommy yaw slightly, he turned triumphantly to Millburn. "Who's cheerful now? You've only to get into one of these storm clouds and you're smothered in ice."

With Millburn busy keeping T-Tommy on course, his reply was a growl. "Stop bellyaching and keep your eyes open."

To the crews' relief, ice began shredding off airfoils as their descent took them under 9,000 feet and had disappeared when their altimeters read 4,000. In A-Apple Harvey's eyes were sore as he searched for a break in the dense clouds. The last weather report had said the cloud base was three thousand feet over their target but the Yorkshireman was all too aware that no climate in the world was more fickle than a Norwegian winter and conditions could have changed drastically in the time it had taken them to cross the North Sea.

To his great relief A-Apple broke into the clear at 2,800 feet, exposing a waste of grey sea below. He turned to Martin again. "How do you think we stand with the Lancs now?"

"We should be past them in four to five minutes, skipper."

And then the fun might start, Harvey thought. "Are you going to find this valley OK when we fly at low level?"

"I hope so, skipper. Squadron Leader Millburn said our sighting point is Lillestad and a plateau to its right."

Acutely aware that the enemy controllers would be searching every inch of air space once the Mandrel interference had ceased, Harvey put A-Apple's nose down again and made for the sea. Behind him, like a ball of string unwinding, the other superbly-piloted Mosquitoes went into line astern and followed him. In less than a minute all sixteen aircraft were skimming like cormorants over the tossing sea.

Land was sighted in eleven minutes, which brought a grunt of praise from Harvey. "Good work, lad. Now let's find that valley before any bandits find us."

Seeing no plateau on the approaching coastline, Harvey was forced to fly north for three minutes before Martin gave a cry of relief and pointed a finger. "That must be Lillestad, skipper. At 2 o'clock. You can see the plateau as well."

Skerries and occasional inshore fishing boats were now flashing beneath them. Raising his string of Mosquitoes up to seven hundred feet, Harvey glanced at the ceiling of cloud above. It looked dark and threatening but at least it was still high enough to provide the visibility he needed. Knowing the Mosquitoes could now be seen by German observers on the coast, he decided there was no longer any point in keeping radio silence. "Dragonfly Leader to squadron! Drop your tanks and test your guns. Then go into orbit."

Seconds later drop tanks toppled into the sea and Mosquitoes swung briefly out of line as their short-barrelled cannon spat fire. Then they followed Harvey into an orbit over the sea, less than a mile from the mouth of the valley.

Harvey addressed Martin again. "You are listening for Squadron Leader Adams?"

Martin nodded. "Yes, skipper. But I can't hear anything yet."

Although London had ordered Adams to transmit from 10.00 hours onwards, this had always seemed a weak link in the operation to Harvey. So many factors could conspire against the reception. Adams might not be in fit shape to reach the valley; the mountain might not allow signals to reach the low flying Mosquitoes; worse, a lengthy transmission might give away Adams' position and result in his capture again. With so many things that could go wrong, Harvey had made a private decision that if no transmission was heard on his arrival at Lillestad, he would waste no more than a couple of minutes before launching his attack. Hopefully all the partisans would be in position to light the flares, whereas, with the squadron now visible from the coast, they would be in danger from enemy fighters if kept waiting too long.

As it happened Harvey had not to make the decision. Martin gave a sudden start, then glanced at the Yorkshireman. "I think it's him, sir, although it's very faint." Then: "Yes, it is. It's Guy Fawkes."

A grin crossed Harvey's rugged face as he waggled his wings to the crews orbiting behind him. "I hope he does a better job than that poor bugger did. All right, lad. I'll talk to him and find out if it's OK to start."

He heard Adams' faint, crackly voice a few seconds later. "Hello, Dragonfly. This is Guy Fawkes. Do you read me?"

"Hello, Guy Fawkes. This is Dragonfly leader. Have you got the gunpowder stacked under the bastards yet?"

Even with its static interference, relief at the squadron's arrival could be heard in Adams' reply. Harvey exchanged a few more words with him, then waggled his wings again. "Dragonfly leader to squadron. I'm going in now. Red Two follow in fifty seconds!" Lowering his face mask, the Yorkshireman turned and winked at the pale-faced Martin. "O.K. lad. Let's go and get the bloody job over."

The words had hardly left his mouth before half a dozen white flakes flashed past A-Apple's windshield. Giving a start, Martin turned to the Yorkshireman. "Did you see that, skipper? They were snowflakes, weren't they?"

Harvey gave a violent curse. As another flurry of snow swept past the Mosquito's cupola, he addressed the alarmed navigator. "Get a message to Troubleshooter. Tell 'em what's happening and that I must have a decision right away. Hurry it up, for Christ's sake."

Adams, heavily clothed in woollen hat, anorak and snow smock, glanced at Arne who, along with Helga, was lying in the nest of frozen rocks alongside him. "Don't you hear anything yet?"

Arne, with earphones clamped over his balaclava helmet, shook his head. As the anxious Adams muttered something, Helga laid a comforting hand on his arm. "Perhaps they won't transmit until they're in the valley. Perhaps they want to keep radio silence all the way."

"There wouldn't be much point in that," Adams pointed out. "Not once the German observer corps see them approaching the coast. They couldn't have decided to cancel at the last minute, could they?"

"Why should they do that? Arne says they sounded thrilled when they learned you'd escaped. They're probably just a few minutes late on their ETA."

Adams was gazing at the sky. It had been getting steadily darker during the last half hour and his fears for the operation were growing. If it had to be postponed, he felt a subsequent mission would be a disaster. The enemy were anything but fools and must have guessed or at least considered the possibility that Adams' appearance in the valley was related to the mine. Simple prudence would demand heightened security, which among other things would mean an inflow of guns. A single day might not give time for heavy

271

guns to reach the valley but two days should be ample for an army as efficient as the Germans.

He gazed down into the valley. With the nest of rocks perched on the north-eastern edge of Trollhorn he could see down into the narrow pass through which the Mosquitoes would have to fly and, by turning his head, the distant wood in which lay their target. Between the two extremes lay Rosvik, its tiny houses clinging like flies to the sides of the deep, intimidating valley. Once again I'm an onlooker, Adams thought in his self-deprecating way. I have a ringside seat to what might be a disaster if the weather closes in much more and Davies still orders the Mosquitoes to attack.

The icy wind, cutting across the valley, blew up a flurry of snow from the surrounding rocks. Hiding a shiver, Adams shifted his position to ease the pain in his back. Since receiving his beating he had been passing blood in his urine and needed to urinate more frequently. With little or no cover around him, the shy Adams began wondering what he would do if the need became too urgent.

Helga's question broke into his thoughts. "Do you think the Germans will use smoke this side of town?"

Adams shook his head. "I honestly don't know. No one appears to have seen any smoke generators beneath the two bluffs but that doesn't mean there aren't any."

"But wouldn't this wind blow any smoke away?"

"It might," Adams admitted. "But it might not be blowing so hard down below. In any case smoke would rise and these passes are so narrow it wouldn't take much to throw aircraft out of line. Even in bright sunlight a pilot would have to be crazy or desperate to fly through them. That's why I had to come."

"Will you still light the flares if the Germans don't use smoke?"

"Yes. Particularly now the visibility is so bad." Adams motioned at the wood at the foot of Helsberg. "If only we'd had some way of marking the position of the mine with flares. We don't know if Jerry has guns there or not but as he's using camouflage and the mine is so important to him, I can't believe he hasn't provided some protection. If it's smoke, I'm just hoping this wind doesn't drift it over Rosvik and hide our reference light."

272

As he was forced to shift his position again, Helga showed concern. "Are you in much pain?"

"Just a little stiff," Adams lied. Remembering the precaution he was taking in case Larson's radio on the other bluff did not pick up his orders, he handed the girl a torch. "Don't forget the signal, will you? Dash — dot — dash repeated."

As she pressed his hand, Arne made a sudden exclamation and motioned them both to keep quiet. For a long moment the only sound was the bluster of the wind. Then Arne swung round to Adams. In his excitement he spoke in Norwegian. "He says they're here," Helga said. "What orders have you got for them?"

Adams' heart was suddenly pounding like a triphammer. Snatching the earphones from Arne, he moistened his dry mouth. "Hello, Dragonfly leader. This is Guy Fawkes. Do you read me?"

Watching him, Helga saw a tense smile cross his swollen face as he listened to Harvey's answer through the crackle of static. After a moment he clicked his switch over. "Yes, Dragonfly leader. We've got the gunpowder stacked and we're all ready with the matches. Are you coming now?"

"Aye, we're on our way. Keep your channel open. We won't be long."

If you start right away you'll he here in two and a half minutes, Adams was thinking. That is if my calculations are correct and you keep to the airspeed I sent to London. Unless, of course, there are distractions like smoke, heavy flak, enemy fighters or some other obstacle I haven't catered for ...

Working against time now, he checked with his radio that Larson on the other bluff had heard the exchange. "Fire your first flare in sixty seconds," he told him. "No later. Acknowledge."

Receiving Larson's confirmation, Adams checked again that the wire of his first flare was securely attached to the electric generator. Then he glanced at his watch again.

Forty seconds to go. If Larson slammed down his generator plunger on his signal and all went well, the two flares should illuminate both bluffs at the same time. And Mrs Helgenstrom should switch on her reference light. Adams was thinking how critical that light would be when Helga touched his arm. "You were right, Frank. They are flooding the wood with smoke."

Startled, Adams spun round and saw she was right. Columns of grey smoke were rising from at least a dozen places around the wood and drifting across it. As Adams listened, he could hear the far off wail of an air raid siren. Seeing his expression, Helga moved closer to him. "You foresaw all this so don't be distressed. You have done everything in your power to overcome it."

Adams tried to speak but shook his head instead. Discovering he was trembling with nervousness, she reached out a gloved hand and gripped his own. "Remember something else," she whispered. "If anything goes wrong you must not punish yourself. Everyone admires and respects you for all you have done."

Grateful, Adams was about to reply when he felt something cold touch his face. As he glanced up he heard Arne give an exclamation of dismay. A moment later a sprinkling of white flakes swept over the circle of rocks. Adams heard his own voice, desperate with alarm. "Helga! It's starting to snow!"

Chapter 31

Back in the Operations Room at Sutton Craddock the tension was almost palpable as the minute hand of the huge clock on the wall jerked round. Only five men were present, Davies, Simms, Henderson, the Navigation Officer and a radio operator. During the hours it had taken the squadron to reach Norway, when radio silence had been imposed, Davies had been working off his nervous tension by wandering around the station and inspecting every branch of the squadron's infrastructure, much to the annoyance of Henderson. But as the squadron's ETA had drawn nearer, his visits to the Operations Room had become more frequent and when Simms had arrived thirty minutes ago, he had remained there with the Brigadier.

Not that it had improved matters, Henderson reflected. With nothing to take his mind off the operation now, Davies had spent the long minutes either by pacing up and down beneath the large map of Europe or sitting on the bench beside the radio operator and drumming his fingers on the table. For a brief moment relief had come when Harvey's message had announced the squadron were safely in position at the mouth of the valley. Davies had jerked upright like an excited puppet and swung round on Henderson. "It's looking good, Jock. They've arrived without any problems."

Although relieved, the canny Scot had felt obliged to offer a word of caution. "They haven't made their attack yet, sir."

Davies had glared at him. "I know they haven't. Give them time, for Christ's sake."

That had been two minutes ago. Since then Davies's drumming on the table had reached a new intensity as he watched the second hand of the clock moving round. All five men were acutely aware that the Mosquitoes were now entering a valley that might turn out to be a death trap, and the silence that followed hurt the ears of the waiting men.

It made the sudden buzz of Morse sound like machine gun fire when it came thirty seconds later. Leaping to his feet, Davies bent over the radio operator. "What is it? What does he say?"

With a plea for silence, the radio operator began writing on a pad. A few seconds later he tore off a sheet, which was immediately snatched away by Davies. As the other three men crowded round him, Davies stared at the sheet, then gave a groan.

Henderson's voice was sharp with alarm. "What is it, sir?"

Looking like a puppet whose strings had gone slack, Davies handed the scrap of paper to Simms. Seeing the soldier's face turn pale, Henderson put his anxious question again. "What's happened, sir?"

Ignoring him, Simms glanced back at Davies. "You know the answer, Davies. I'm sorry but we have no choice."

For a long moment Davies hesitated. Then he turned back to the waiting radio operator, his voice hoarse and unsteady. "Tell Dragonfly to continue with the mission. Good luck. Troubleshooter."

As the radio operator began tapping out the message, Davies dropped heavily on the bench. Seeing Henderson about to question him again, Simms handed the Scot the piece of paper. Henderson read it, then gave a gasp of dismay. "Sir, you can't permit this. It's monstrous."

It was then Davies made an admission no one had heard from him before. "War is monstrous, Jock. Haven't you learned that yet?"

With radio silence already broken, Harvey addressed his two orbiting sections. "Dragonfly leader to Red and Blue sections. Don't worry about the snow. It's only light as yet. I'm going in now and the rest of Red section follow me at fifty second intervals. If we run into any flak posts, we'll transmit their positions. That's all. Good luck."

With that Harvey swung A-Apple towards Lillestad. With the sixteen Mosquitoes already spotted by enemy ground observers, flak crews had already been alerted and their guns were ready. As

Lillestad's oil tanks, Falun red warehouses, and coastal ships grew in definition, puffs of black smoke began to appear around A-Apple. As Harvey swept over the small docks, a row of neat holes in his starboard wing reminded him that at near zero height he was well within the range of light machine gun fire. He lifted his face mask. "Dragonfly Leader to Red section. Watch the docks when you come in. They've got 37s and LMGs."

To Harvey's relief the snow flurries eased as Lillestad fell behind the speeding Mosquito and the wooded slopes of the valley began to close in. A waterfall flashed past, its drifting spray white against a background of trees. A fan shaped patch of scree appeared with clumps of snow trapped on its ledges. Tiny cottages set in narrow, snow-covered pastures came and went. For a few seconds the valley narrowed as the road and stream were flanked by reticulated walls of wet rocks. An enemy transport appeared, its soldier occupants pointing and then ducking down under its canvas cover as the Mosquito roared over them. Seeing how tense the young navigator was beside him, Harvey gave him a grin. "That gave the bastards a fright, lad. Pity we haven't time to give 'em a squirt."

As Martin managed a smile, Harvey addressed his R/T again. "Hello, Guy Fawkes. Do you read me?"

Only a crackle of static answered him this time. As the Yorkshireman had feared, the narrow confines of the pass and the twin bluffs at its far end were now interfering with R/T reception. He glanced at Martin again. "Let's go through the drill again, lad, in case we can't contact Adams when we reach the end of the valley. You know the course we take once we're past the last bluff?" As Martin nodded, Harvey went on. "It's your job to see I keep on it until we see the reference light at the far end of town. As soon as we pass over it, I take a ten degree turn to starboard. What happens then?"

"We keep an airspeed of two hundred and seventy for sixteen seconds," the young navigator told him. "Then we release our incendiary spray."

"Good lad. Remember it's your job to watch our compass bearings and the timing. I might be too busy flying the old kite if Jerry uses smoke over the wood."

"Do you think he will, skipper?"

As always Harvey's reply was right to the point. "I would if I were in his shoes, lad. So we'd better expect it.

The Heath Robinson plan had come from Adams. Although he had been unable to ascertain the exact location of the mine and its compound, the map in the doctor's surgery and his own map reading skills had helped him estimate its direction and its distance from the reference light he had planted in the bakery. The task then had been to set a compass course for the aircraft after they rounded Trollhorn, give them a second compass course to turn at the precise moment they passed over the light, and then to decide on a fixed airspeed for each aircraft that would enable him to plot a time of arrival over the target.

Thus by choosing two hundred and seventy miles per hour Adams had known the Mosquitoes would be covering four and a half miles per minute. As he estimated the compound was approximately a mile and a quarter from his reference point, it was a simple calculation to work out that the Mosquitoes should reach it in approximately sixteen and a half seconds.

With no other reference to guide Adams, these had been the instructions he had given Arne to radio over to London and the vectors the crews had been given by Davies at their final briefing. With Adams fully aware the doctor's map might have misled him, it was yet another cause for his apprehension when the operation had been finally launched.

In A-Apple Martin was beginning to relax. "It's looking as if the Air Commodore was right, skipper, and Jerry hasn't got any flak posts in the valley."

Harvey's eyes were fixed on the first of the two bluffs that was beginning to appear ahead. In the overcast light and the light snow that had started falling again its finer details were unclear but it was growing larger and more formidable by the second. His reply had a mordant humour that was typical of the man. "Don't say things like that, lad. Otherwise life has a way of kicking you in the backside."

Rocky walls closed in again, reverberating back the roar of the Mosquito's Merlins. A waterfall flashed past, followed by an isolated building, and a large truck loaded up with timber. Then dense woods appeared on either side, rising up steeply to the snow-filled sky above.

The huge bluff of Kaldhorn was now thrusting across the valley like a malignant, heavily-bearded face. The white flakes were falling faster now, giving the impression the bluff was lying behind a massive lace curtain. Estimating the flares wouldn't be ignited for another forty seconds, Harvey lifted his face mask. "Dragonfly Leader to Guy Fawkes. Visibility getting poorer. Light your flares now!"

With only another crackle of static answering him, Harvey cursed and gave all his attention to the oncoming bluff. As it swept towards him, the Yorkshireman was beginning to believe something untoward had happened to Adams but then a dazzling light blazed out from its crest. A couple of seconds later a similar light ignited among the trees opposite.

Blessing Adams beneath his breath, Harvey headed for the gap between the two lights. A few seconds later the roar of A-Apple's engines was massive as their sound reverberated across the narrow passage. As Harvey kept his eyes on the flanking walls, a sudden fork of tracer came stabbing up from the road below. Taken by surprise, the Yorkshireman instinctively swung the Mosquito to port, only to swing violently back as he narrowly missed contact with the trees that climbed the northern flank of the pass.

Sweating with the nearness of their escape, Harvey heard Martin's shaken voice. "So they have brought guns in, skipper!"

"Aye, it looks that way, lad. And put that one in just the right place. Try to get a message back to our section."

There was no time for further talk. Trollhorn was looming ahead next, its rocks and trees starkly delineated by Adams' flare. Aware that in all likelihood there would be another gun or guns sited at its base and that he would be unable to manoeuvre A-Apple once he committed her to a straight and level path, Harvey gritted his teeth and deliberately flew straight at Trollhorn. With Martin frozen in his seat, the Yorkshireman waited until the trees and black rocks filled his windshield. Only then did he swing A-Apple over, heave back on the control column, and flip her over into a starboard half roll as Trollhorn fell away. As Harvey expected, two whips of tracer came slashing up from the road but they curled over A-Apple's cupola as she swept through the pass almost on her side. A few seconds later she was clear and heading for the small town that was appearing below.

To Adams, perched on the crest of Trollhorn, it had seemed for long seconds that Harvey had crashed on its western face and A-Apple's re-appearance as it darted between the two flares was an immense relief. At the same time, with his position preventing him from seeing the earlier gunfire, Adams was shocked by the forks of tracer that had tried to impale the Mosquito. "They must have guessed why I'd been sent here," he told Helga. "And brought guns in."

"Not necessarily," she pointed out. "The defences might have been there all the time."

Doubting it, Adams could only hope there had been too little time to bring in enough flak guns to make the attack impossible. His eyes were fixed on A-Apple that had now swung on to its correct compass course and was heading over Rosvik towards the single light shining up from the huddled town. Mrs Helgenstrom had kept her word to the letter and Adams could only hope that no German outpost was high enough above the town to notice it.

Aided by the wind, the smoke was now covering the wood and drifting towards the town. Praying it would not conceal the light, the fascinated Adams watched the diminishing A-Apple sweep over the reference point and then turn sharply to starboard. Holding his breath, Adams started to count.

Flying towards the town, Harvey was eyeing the smoke ahead with mixed feelings. To the veteran Yorkshireman it meant the Germans had not had time to swamp the target area with guns or they would have left their crews a clear view of the raiding aircraft. At the same time it was going to make it much more difficult to identify and destroy the target. Weighing up the pros and cons, Harvey decided he preferred the smoke and his tone was lighter as he spoke to his intent navigator. "There's our light, lad! Open the bomb doors!"

Despite the poor light and the falling snow, details of the small town could be seen clearly as A-Apple swept over it at only four hundred feet. Although the air raid siren and yelling German soldiers had driven the townsfolk into their houses, here and there flags and scraps of white linen fluttered from windows as Norwegians welcomed the unexpected arrival of their allies. But although Harvey waggled A-Apple's wings, his eyes were fixed on the light shining up from the bakery. As he flashed over it and banked to starboard, he began counting. "One, two, three ... " As he reached sixteen he gave a yell: "Now!"

Half a second later a yellow spray plumed out from one of the two cylinders loaded in A-Apple's bomb bay. Given the *nom de guerre* of Smoke Curtain Installations, they had been originally designed to contain mustard gas should that poisonous substance be used during the war. As it was they proved ideal receptacles for the incendiary spray first used in Operation Crisis.

With A-Apple sweeping over the wood now and encountering the thickening smoke, all Harvey's attention was needed to avoid collision with the trees or the towering mass of Helsberg so perilously close ahead. As the last of the spray sank down and Harvey swung A-Apple steeply to port, neither he nor Martin were conscious of the panic the spray was causing below. With Adams' calculations proving accurate, part of the spray had sunk down on the camouflage nets and its colour had convinced the German occupants that mustard gas was being dropped. As a consequence men were rushing hither and thither to collect their masks while a duty officer was frantically ringing a gas warning.

With his initial task completed, Harvey was now fighting to avoid collision with the sinister Helsberg. As A-Apple swept to port with murderous rocks no more than fifty feet away, the Yorkshireman realised everyone's predictions had been correct and the cutting was the only way out of the tight bowl of mountains.

Although by this time he had left the smoke behind, he discovered the snow was falling more heavily and now becoming a threat in its own right. Through it he caught a glimpse of a large stone quarry. As he swept over it, the mountains ahead dipped and gave way to the pass that led to the fjord. As A-Apple thundered into it, Harvey caught a glimpse of abandoned machines lying at the base of a wooded neck that linked the two mountain ranges. For a split second he glimpsed a dark hole at the base of the neck, then A-Apple was past and sweeping towards the far end of the pass. Relaxing for a moment, Harvey addressed the tense Martin. "You see the tunnel back there?"

There was no time for Martin to answer. The *Königsberg* lay directly ahead and she had been informed of the raid the moment Harvey had entered the valley. Frantic sirens had hooted and helmeted men had raced to their battle stations. Gun turrets had swivelled round and shells had been loaded into breeches. Now, as A-Apple came sweeping out of the pass, a deadly screen of shells burst before it.

Expecting the murderous barrage, Harvey took the action given to all his crews at their final briefing. Pushing A-Apple's nose down, he dropped to zero height until the rocks and dwarf trees that flanked the fjord were almost brushing the Mosquito's engine nacelles. Although one or two of the LMG gunners were quick enough to follow her and she shuddered for a moment under the impact of bullets, the heavier guns were caught by surprise. As Harvey swept a quarter of a mile along the fjord before attempting to climb, he heard static crackling in his earphones and knew someone, Adams or a member of his crew, was trying to contact him. Anxious to know what was happening, he began making altitude.

Immediately a cage of shell bracketed him: the *Königsberg* gunners were seeking revenge. For a moment he was driven to take shelter in the heavy clouds where he addressed Martin. "Give those valley gun positions again. The lads should hear them from this height."

As Martin obeyed, Harvey glanced at the time. Incredibly the entire action since the release of the spray had taken less than two minutes. Even so Harvey knew at least two aircraft of his section should have made their attack. As he dropped beneath the clouds in the hope of gaining a view, an unmistakable voice suddenly rattled his earphones. "Hello, Dragonfly Leader. Oi thought that bastard cruiser had sunk yer."

Gazing round, Harvey saw pods of smoke bursting a few hundred yards on his port side. "Hello, Paddy. What happened to your incendiaries?"

"Oi couldn't see for the smoke, skipper. If they landed on the nets, there wasn't time for it to show."

Harvey was straining his eyes but the falling snow hid all details of the valley from him. He lifted his face mask again. "Dragonfly leader to Blue leader. Come down and harass the cruiser. Right away. Acknowledge."

To his relief Millburn's reply came back immediately. "Blue leader to Dragonfly. We're on our way."

Harvey then tried Adams. "Dragonfly leader to Guy Fawkes. Can you hear me?"

There was a long pause, a crackle of static, then Adams' voice sounding as if it were a thousand miles away. "Hello, Dragonfly leader. Hello. Dragon ..." A louder crackle of static came, then Adams' voice faded away altogether.

Harvey cursed. "Damn these bloody mountains." He lifted his face mask again. "Follow me, Red Two. I'm going back to the valley to see what's happening."

Chapter 32

To Adams, whose view of the cruiser was impeded by the configuration of the cutting and the falling snow, only the distant thunder of gunfire had told him that Harvey was facing the cruiser's guns. He had wanted to confirm the Yorkshireman had escaped them but his attention had been riveted on Machin's Mosquito whose cargo of incendiaries might confirm or refute his theories and calculations.

To his immense relief the experienced Irishman had avoided the guns of both bluffs and had headed towards the wood. The snow had made visibility difficult but by using his binoculars Adams had caught glimpses of M-Mother as it had swept on towards the bakery light. As it swung to starboard he had lost sight of it for a moment, then it re-appeared, skimming like a bird over the smoke that was drifting towards Rosvik.

Counting as he knew Machin would be counting, Adams had hoped to see the Irishman's incendiaries fall, then discovered the distance and conditions made that impossible. Instead he had watched the aircraft bank steeply to port to avoid the murderous Helsberg and head for the cutting. Swinging his binoculars back on the wood, he had watched and waited in an agony of suspense while another heavy roll of gunfire told him Machin was now facing the wrath of the *Königsberg*.

At first he could see nothing but the pall of smoke. Then suddenly a darker plume had risen above the grey blanket, followed by a glow and then a glimmer of flame.

A moment later, like a whirlpool in the centre of a grey lake, a circle of smoke had dissolved and a hundred small fires appeared.

In his excitement Adams had swung round on his two companions. "That's it! The netting's burning!"

Arne shook his head. "It could just be trees on fire."

His euphoria dampened, Adams focused his binoculars again. "Would they burn so quickly? They'll all be damp, won't they?"

"The smaller branches will burn," Arne told him.

Deflated, Adams had no time to speculate further. Red Three of Harvey's section, flown by young Donovan, had rounded Kaldhorn safely and was heading for the pass below. As the trio gazed anxiously down, they saw a vicious fork of tracer stab into the nose of the Mosquito and rip along its entire length. The aircraft shuddered, then turned over like a gaffed fish. It reeled into the mountainside opposite and broke into pieces like a child's toy. As the pieces fell or fluttered down, Adams gave a groan. "Oh, my God."

Helga gripped his arm tightly. Adams eyes, wide with dismay, gazed at her for a moment. Then, as he was about to turn to the radio, two huge explosions sent shudders through Trollhorn and brought down cascades of snow. Donovan and his navigator had fused their bombs early and they had exploded on the valley floor.

Shaking his head, Adams grabbed up his binoculars and gazed at the wood again. The fires were subsiding and the smoke drifting back over them. Adams hardly recognised his voice as he glanced at Helga. "If they don't get a bomb on it soon, it'll be lost again."

Red Four appeared half a minute later. In passing Kaldhorn its starboard engine was hit and a thin stream of glycol was showing white against the dark trees. Expecting the worst as it headed toward Trollhorn, Adams could hardly look as it came within range of the guns below but although tracer came lancing up, the bomb explosions must have temporarily unnerved the gun crews because the Mosquito cleared the pass without further damage.

Brushing snow from his spectacles and binoculars, Adams followed it as far as the bakery light and saw it swing to starboard. Losing it then and so unable to see where its bombs fell, he kept catching glimpses of the Mosquito in the seconds that followed as it rose above the smoke and struggled to evade the towering mass of Helsberg. Like a moth drawn against its wishes to a flame, it fluttered vainly in and out of Adam's vision. Then a bright flash appeared and was gone. With one engine giving insufficient power to escape Helsberg, Arthur Pearson would play the piano in the Mess no more.

To hide his expression, Adams began connecting a new cable to his electric generator. As he fumbled with the connections, he saw two bright flashes from the corner of his eye and heard two heavy rolls of thunder that reverberated round the bowl of mountains. Grabbing up his binoculars he stared at the wood again. In spite of the poor visibility he could see tiny objects still falling from the twin explosions and fierce fires burning holes in the smoke. Although aware the uprooted objects might only be trees, he was about to make a comment to Helga when he heard a crackle in his earphones. A moment later a familiar voice sounded. "Do you think we hit the bastards, Guy Fawkes?"

Feeling Arne nudge him, Adams glanced up and saw two Mosquitoes circling above the valley. "I don't know, Dragonfly leader. But it's possible."

"Then shall I tell the rest of the lads to bomb the fires?"

Knowing how momentous the decision was, Adams hesitated, then took a deep breath. "Yes. But ask the first crew to check the site. With the fires burning away the smoke, they should be able to see if it's the mine and compound that's hit."

"OK. I'll tell 'em."

With Harvey now high enough to reach his crews on R/T, Red Five received his message as it was approaching Kaldhorn. It survived the first gauntlet of fire but as it approached Trollhorn a vicious burst of cannon fire tore through the cockpit floor and ripped open Liston's body like a butcher's saw. For a couple of seconds G-George flew straight and level, then its nose dipped and it flew under full power straight into the road below where it exploded. No bomb explosions followed: Liston's bombs had not yet been fused. Only a furnace of burning petrol was visible, running across the road and igniting a clump of trees alongside it.

Adams' torture at the loss of his young colleagues was matched by Harvey's fury. His harsh voice made Adams' earphones rattle. "Machin, I'm taking out those sodding guns. Stay up and keep a watch out for bandits."

The words had barely left the Yorkshireman's mouth before A-Apple dipped a wing and went down like a bird of prey. Entering the valley half a mile east of Kaldhorn, Harvey went raging along it towards the deadly flak guns. To his disgust he missed the first gun crew: his late entry into the valley added to the difficulty of avoiding Kaldhorn. But his attack unnerved the gunners enough for him to make the passage unscathed and when Trollhorn loomed before him, Harvey was ready for the gunners who had wrought such carnage on his crews. Sighting the first 20 mm post among trees on the northern mountainside he went for it like a mongoose attacking a snake, his cannon shells cutting down trees and men in a welter of destruction. Banking steeply away, he went searching for the second post.

Seconds later it betrayed its position by opening fire. With the animal fury that possessed him, Harvey flew straight at the murderous tracer, pressing his attack with such purpose that Martin alongside him could see discarded shell cases leaping out of the enemy guns and loaders being hurled aside like carcasses of meat by A-Apple's cannon fire. As the Mosquito swung violently away and mountains and sky reeled before her windshield, the unfortunate Martin believed his last moment had come.

It took Harvey's harsh voice to convince Martin he was still alive. "Did we get the bastards?"

Martin never knew how he got the words out. "Yes, skipper. I'm sure we did."

Clear of Trollhorn, Harvey was now making height and heading towards the distant wood. He lifted his face mask. "Are you there, Guy Fawkes? I'm going to check on the target."

Before Adams could reply, another voice broke in. "You don't need to worry about the first flak post, skipper. Oi've been down and seen 'em off meself."

Harvey's sweating face managed a grin. "Well done, Paddy. The boys should be OK now."

Adams, who had witnessed and marvelled at Harvey's attack, knew the Yorkshireman was right. By this time Red Six had reached the bluffs and in spite of the falling snow had negotiated them both successfully. He listened to Harvey giving instructions to Millburn's Blue section, then turned to Helga. "It all depends now whether we're hitting the right target. Hopefully that's something Harvey should be able to tell us in a moment or two."

Like himself, she had been showing distress at the squadron losses. "But will they have enough bombs left?"

Trying to keep an eye on A-Apple as it approached the wood, Adams nodded. "Yes. He's just instructed Millburn to send three of his section down the valley."

The next few seconds were the longest of Adams' life. When his earphones crackled again his heart contracted and then gave a heavy thump. "Dragonfly Leader to Guy Fawkes! You've done great job, Guy Fawkes. The Houses of Parliament are going up in smoke. Now we just have to finish 'em off."

Lowering his binoculars, Adams turned to Helga. "It's all right. It is the mine and the compound."

With a cry, she threw her arms round Adams and hugged him. "You've done it, my love. In spite of everything. I think it's wonderful."

For the moment Adams was feeling euphoric. "Thank God it hasn't all been for nothing."

Two more explosions reverberated around the bowl of mountains. The fire in the wood was now like a furnace, burning away the smoke and reflecting on the heavy clouds above. Harvey, circling high above, allowed his remaining crews to saturate the site, then turned to Martin. "Send this to Troubleshooter. Target and compound totally destroyed. Tunnel next. Three aircraft lost so far. End of message."

Back at Sutton Craddock Davies's hand was shaking as he took the message the radio operator handed him. For a moment he seemed unable to believe what he was reading. Then he swung round on Simms, his high-pitched voice exultant. "They've done it, sir! They've destroyed that bloody mine and everything around it!"

Simms looked as if a great load had fallen from his frail shoulders. "Are you sure, Davies? There isn't any chance of a mistake?"

"No, of course there isn't." Almost rude in his euphoria, Davies thrust the scrap of paper at the Brigadier. "Read it yourself.

You can tell Churchill my boys have pulled it off." Grinning like a triumphant hobgoblin, Davies turned to Henderson. "You hear that, Jock? I was right not to abort, wasn't I? I thought snow wouldn't stop the lads."

Although his relief matched the Air Commodore's, Henderson had no intention to let him take all the credit. "I'd say it's been a terrific job by Harvey, wouldn't you, sir?"

Just for a moment Davies was checked in his tracks. "Yes, that's true. He's done a fine job." Then his eyes twinkled maliciously. "But who picked him as squadron commander?" Before the Scot could recover, Davies's euphoria swept him on. "That Heath Robinson scheme of Adams must have worked like a charm. Isn't it marvellous?"

Henderson's thoughts were elsewhere. "How many aircraft are down, sir?"

"Only three, Jock." At the Scot's expression, Davies's tone moderated. "Well, it's fewer than we expected, isn't it?"

Henderson took the slip of paper from the Brigadier and scanned it. "I see the job isn't finished yet, sir. There's still the tunnel."

"What's the matter with you, Jock? The mine and stocks were the main job and they've been wiped out. That ought to make Churchill reach out for his brandy and cigars before he gives your boys a commendation." Laughing at his own joke, Davies bent over the radio operator. "Send this to Dragonfly leader, corporal. 'Congratulations! Close the tunnel and then come home. Troubleshooter.' "

Harvey received the message as he saw the first of the Blue section Mosquitoes rounding Trollhorn. He lifted his face mask. "Dragonfly Leader to Blue Two, Three, and Four. Target totally destroyed. Your new target is the tunnel. I want it closed. Over."

Hearing the faint voice in Adams' earphones, Helga glanced at him. "What does Harvey say?"

As he gazed at the glowing furnace within the wood, Adams suddenly remembered Vogel and the Camp Commandant and his euphoria died. To Adams there was no triumph in orchestrating the

289

deaths of brave and decent men. He took off his spectacles and wiped them. "He says the compound's totally destroyed. All they have to do now is close the tunnel and the job's over."

"That's wonderful." She hugged his arm again, then her tone changed as she noticed his expression. "You're doing what I feared, aren't you?"

Adams, sustained until now by the excitement and suspense of the raid, was suddenly feeling deflated and chilled to the bone. His expression was almost defiant as he replaced his glasses. "I wasn't surprised. We knew there'd be losses."

"But you take the losses of your friends so much to heart, don't you, my love."

To avoid her gaze, Adams connected a third cable to the generator. When he spoke, the wind almost carried his low words away. "Perhaps it wouldn't be so bad if we knew it would end the war sooner. But we've no way of knowing that, have we?"

"How can you say that? Churchill must have known or he would never have demanded this sacrifice."

Adams shook his head. "No. Churchill was only playing safe. It's quite possible those stocks wouldn't have lengthened the war by a single day."

"But isn't that war, my love? Isn't war all guesswork and speculation?"

Adams, who knew six young friends and many Germans would be alive today without his dream and his interference, would not have believed his voice could contain such bitterness. "War is obscene, Helga, and so are we. No animal would be so vicious and vile to slaughter its own kind in this way. God, how I hate the whole filthy business."

In the mood he was in at that moment, it was as well Adams could not see the slaughter being dealt out in the upper reaches of the fjord. Ordered to divert some of the *Königsberg's* awesome firepower from the Mosquitoes as they swept from the cutting, Millburn's Blue section was engaged in a life and death struggle with the giant cruiser. As the Mosquitoes came in at different heights, some so low their slipstreams ruffled the sullen waters of the fjord, the cruiser's pom-poms were spewing out deadly streams of shells to destroy her tormentors. In less than a minute the snow-filled sky resembled a huge black and white net in which it appeared no aircraft could survive.

To avoid as much flak as possible, Millburn had led the first attack on the cruiser's stern with the intention of knocking out the gunners with rocket or cannon fire. Coming in at slight angle, he had first released a rocket, then opened fire with his cannon. As T-Tommy shuddered under the recoil, the American had a blurred glimpse of tracer zipping past his windshield like electric sparks ... his rocket striking a lifeboat and swinging it crazily away ... two ratings collapsing on the armoured deck ... a pom-pom's gun barrels swinging round to engage him. Then he was past the huge armoured hulk and hugging the water in an effort to escape her vengeful guns. For a moment T-Tommy shuddered under half a dozen hammer blows, then the fire lessened as the *Königsberg* gave her attention to her next attacker.

Millburn's voice was breathless. "You all right?"

Gabby was clearly shaken. "No thanks to you. Christ, the bastard's the size of a battleship."

Ignoring him, Millburn made height and watched the rest of his section in action. One of Van Breedenkamp's rockets blew a huge hole in the cruiser's gun deck, another struck its armoured hull. Rockets from Larkin smashed into its navigating bridge and made a tangled wreck of a gun turret. Flames could be seen on both fore and aft decks, with fire crews fighting to contain them.

But the belligerent *Königsberg* was handing out punishment too. Barely a Mosquito escaped without some damage and Millburn was only too aware of the long journey that had to be made home. Ordering the rest of his section to withdraw out of range, he gave an order to McDonald. "Beam attack, Blue Five. I'll take port, you take starboard. Get her beneath the waterline."

With two aircraft diving from opposite sides of a target, it was a well tried ploy of the squadron to share out and reduce its firepower. As he dived down to sea level, Millburn glanced at Gabby. "You OK, kid?"

"No, I'm not," Gabby grumbled. "What are we doing attacking the bloody thing anyway? She wasn't on our brief."

Knowing his man, Millburn grinned. "She is now. Let's finish her off."

Flying at zero height, Millburn watched the cruiser growing like a metal castle in his windshield. As a blizzard of fire swept towards him, he released his last two rockets. Then, almost blinded by tracer and flak bursts, he swung violently to port, missing the bows of the cruiser by only a few feet. As the *Königsberg* fell behind and T-Tommy began to make height, Gabby was about to unload his tension in criticism when a loud explosion froze the words in his mouth. T-Tommy lurched violently and almost turned over before Millburn could correct her. As the startled Gabby turned to Millburn, he saw the American's face was contorted with pain. "What is it, Millburn? Are you hit?"

Millburn jerked his head. Anxiously Gabby leaned towards him. "Where?"

Millburn was fighting to overcome the shock of his wound. "In the arm I think."

"Can you get her any higher?"

"Yeah, I'll try."

Below McDonald was even less fortunate. When one of his rockets had struck the *Königsberg* below the waterline, he had let out a jubilant yell, only for it to choke in his throat as his port engine suffered a direct hit from the hell of fire reaching out to him. The huge explosion blew away the propeller and welded hammering pistons and valves into a mass of fused metal. As McDonald swung away to port to avoid T-Tommy, a long tongue of flame leapt out from the shattered engine. As C-Charlie skimmed over the water like a fiery meteor, fragments of burning wood flew from her shattered wing. Fighting to control her, McDonald was defeated when the wing tore off and she went into a violent cartwheel. Seconds later the sullen waters of the fjord closed over her. McDonald would borrow no more Hank Jansen novels from his colleagues.

While this was happening Harvey was watching the third and last of his valley aircraft complete the blocking of the tunnel. Initially the Yorkshireman had expected airborne interception before the operation was completed but was now realising the snowfall had turned out to be a blessing in disguise by grounding or at least delaying fighter attack. As he followed the Blue section Mosquito

292

from the cutting he was in time to see the blazing C-Charlie crash into the fjord. His urgent voice was heard by all the crews. "Dragonfly leader to Blue leader. Call off your attack. The job's finished.

A dismayed voice with a Welsh accent followed his order. "Millburn's wounded, skipper."

Harvey sounded startled. "How badly?"

This time Millburn answered himself. "I'm OK, skipper. The gremlin's just having one of his turns."

"How bad is it, Millburn?"

"In the arm. It's OK. I'll get a tourniquet on it."

"Can you stay with us?"

There was no suppressing Millburn's humour. "I'll have to, won't I? I don't want to be left alone with this moaning Welshman."

As both laughs and anxious questions flooded the channel, Harvey's brusque voice drowned them. "Belt up and listen. We're going home now. Formate behind me when we're in clear air above the clouds. Blue Two stay close to your leader. Out."

One by one the battle-scarred Mosquitoes followed Harvey into the clouds, leaving behind them a smoking and listing cruiser, a mine whose minerals would never again be used in weapons against their country, and a man whose integrity would allow him no share in the youthful crews' paeans of victory.

Chapter 33

Above the dense clouds it was a different world to the storm swept gloom of Norwegian valleys but to some it was proving no safer. The twelve surviving Mosquitoes were less than halfway back to Sumburgh when Harvey's R/T crackled and Gabby's voice was heard. "Dragonfly leader. Millburn's having trouble breathing in his oxygen mask. Have we permission to fly lower so he can take it off?"

Harvey glanced at his own fuel gauges before replying. "You'll use more fuel down there, Gabby."

"I know that, skipper. But as I see it we haven't much choice."

Fully aware that if Millburn were to lose consciousness it would in all likelihood be certain death for both men, Harvey had little option but to agree. "All right, Blue leader. You can go down." As Gabby thanked him, Harvey's brusque voice changed in tone. "Blue Two! Come and take my place. I'll fly with Millburn."

Half a dozen protests immediately filled the radio channel. Larkin's New Zealand drawl was prominent among them. "That's crazy, skipper. You could end up in the drink. You've used more fuel than any of us. Let me stay with Tommy. We'll be OK."

The Yorkshireman's bark rattled the crews' earphones. "Do as you're bloody well told, Larkin. At the double!"

Reluctantly Larkin swung away from T-Tommy and took Harvey's position in the forefront of the formation while the Yorkshireman dropped back to take his place alongside Millburn. "You hear me, Tommy?"

A weak, breathless voice answered him. "Yeah. I'm OK, skipper. Get back up there or you could be in trouble. It's just the gremlin that's panicking."

Harvey replied before the indignant Gabby could respond. "Get her down, Millburn. We'll first try 8,000 and see how you feel. Let's go."

A moment later the two Mosquitoes dipped and disappeared into the heavy clouds. As he reached 8,000 feet and found the clouds still dense around him, Harvey realised there was no way he could keep in contact with T-Tommy until the cloud base was reached. "Dragonfly to Blue leader. Keep going down until we have visual contact. Over."

Millburn's unsteady voice answered him. "It'll be too heavy on fuel for you, skipper. We'll be OK on our own."

"Stop arguing, Millburn, and do as you're told. Do it now!"

Both Millburn and Gabby knew Harvey's reason for being in attendance. Should T-Tommy crash, the Yorkshireman would be able to radio its co-ordinates to Air/Sea rescue. But at sea level fuel consumption was at its peak and because of his actions over Rosvik Harvey had bitten deeper into his fuel reserves than any of the other crews.

To the relief of all four men visibility returned at 2,500 feet, revealing a grey and threatening sea. In T-Tommy Gabby was eyeing Millburn anxiously. With his oxygen mask removed, the American's face could be seen more clearly, drawn with pain and alarmingly pale. "How're you feeling, Millburn? Do you want me to release that tourniquet again?"

Millburn shook his head. "Do you see Harvey?"

"Yes. He's spotted us and closing in."

"He's a bloody fool. He could be in more danger than we are."

With the American's voice weak and shaky, Gabby doubted that but said nothing. As he saw Millburn's eyes close for a moment he leaned across again in alarm. "You're not going to sleep, are you?"

Millburn's eyes shot open. "What the hell do you mean?"

"You closed your eyes just then."

"No, I didn't."

Knowing his man well, Gabby decided his best chance of keeping the American awake was by dispute and confrontation. "You bloody well did. Keep your mind on your job, Millburn. Remember I'm in this bloody kite as well as you."

Millburn's pale lips attempted a grin. "I'm not likely to forget it, am I, you moaning little fart."

Gabby decided that was better but kept an anxious eye on the wounded pilot as the long minutes passed. To add to his fears for the American, the shell that had exploded and wounded him had blown a hole in the side of the cockpit and the blast of icy air was chilling both men. With Millburn having only one effective arm to hold the control column, Gabby was driven to lean over and help him. When he saw Millburn's heavy eyes drooping again, he decided on different tactics. "When are you seeing that ferry pilot bird, Millburn?"

For a moment Millburn's gaze was blank. "What did you say?"

"I asked when you're seeing that ferry pilot again. The one you fell for back at the station."

"I'm seeing her on my leave. Why?"

"If you don't get your finger out and fly this bloody kite, she's going to wait a long time for that date, boyo."

A grin crossed the American's drawn face. "You didn't want me tied up with her, did you? You like me around to get you out of trouble."

Gabby decided he had struck a rich vein here. "I've never needed you, Millburn. All you've ever done is get me in the shit. Like now. If you hadn't made that second run on the cruiser, we'd be laughing all the way home."

In A-Apple Harvey's concern for the two men had been growing as he noticed their Mosquito occasionally veering off course. He was only too aware that if T-Tommy crashed into the sea and the two men were immersed, its pitiless cold might render Air/Sea rescue useless.

Realising Gabby would be needed to assist Millburn, he had flown ahead to take the responsibility of navigation off the Welshman. Now, hearing the two men's banter, he gave Martin a relieved glance. "If the two of 'em can keep that up, they've got a chance."

Although he nodded, the young navigator's eyes were on the fuel gauges. "Do you think we're going to make it, skipper?"

Harvey's impatience was tempered by the thought he was putting the young man's life in danger as well as his own. "Of course we will, lad. We're flying at our most efficient cruising speed. And we've only another thirty or forty minutes to go."

In T-Tommy Gabby was doing his best to keep the banter going. "You know your trouble, Millburn? It's because you're American."

At that moment T-Tommy rocked and side-slipped a full twenty feet. Correcting the slide with a huge effort, Millburn lifted a heavy eyelid. "It is?"

Gulping down his panic, Gabby nodded. "Yes. You've never had to rule the bloody world like we have. So Americans have no sense of responsibility."

Instead of the derisory reply Gabby expected, Millburn's eyelids drooped again. As Gabby shook the American, Harvey's sharp voice sounded. "Gabby! What's happening?"

Gabby's reply betrayed his distress. "He's getting weaker, skipper."

"Have you given him a benzedrine tablet?"

"Yes, he's had two, skipper."

"Give him another."

"But isn't two the limit?"

"Give him another," Harvey ordered. "If you go down in the drink it won't matter either way. So do it."

By this time T-Tommy was slithering about the sky like a man who had lost his reflexes. Struggling to hold on to the control column with one hand, Gabby fished into his emergency pack, then shook the pilot again. "Millburn! Wake up, for Christ's sake."

The rough treatment brought consciousness back to Millburn. As his blank eyes stared up at the Welshman, Gabby pushed the benzedrine tablet between his lips and forced him to swallow it.

For a long moment Millburn showed no response. Then, as Gabby shook him again, he pushed himself wearily up in his seat and took a firmer grip of the control column. As T-Tommy steadied, Harvey's anxious voice came again. "How is he, Gabby?"

"I think he's coming round, skipper. But I don't know how long for."

"Keep him awake, for Christ's sake. If you must, punch his wounded arm. But keep him awake at all costs."

With their fuel gauges perilously low, the two Mosquitoes droned on, their crews desperately trying to equate their distance to Sumburgh with the most economical air speed. As the grim vectors shrank and shrank, a vicious squall came sweeping in from the west, increasing their fuel consumption and whipping up the sea below. As its swell increased and white tops appeared, it seemed to young Martin that the sea was baring its fangs to receive them.

Davies's voice was sharp with frustration. "Is the phone line still u.s.?"

The Signals corporal nodded. "Yes, sir. I think they've had gales up in Sumburgh. But they said they'd keep in touch by radio."

"Then why haven't they?" Davies growled. "It's fifteen minutes since they said the squadron was back." He turned to Henderson who was sharing the Operations Room with him. "It's getting dicey, Jock. They must be running short by this time."

Henderson, sitting on the long bench near the radio corporal, had the appearance of a man prepared for bad news. "I'd say the two of them were already overdue, sir."

Knowing the Scot was right, Davies scowled. "Why the hell did he do it, Jock? He knew the rules better than anyone."

Henderson sighed. "Rules can't change a man's nature, sir. Millburn and Gabby are his friends."

"For Christ's sake, Jock, he's in the Services. You don't throw away serviceable crews and aircraft for crippled ones. If everyone did that we'd he on the bones of our arses in no time."

Henderson sighed again. "I don't think Harvey's ever accepted that directive, sir."

"There's a lot of directives the hugger hasn't accepted, Jock. Only it's starting to look as if this is the last one he'll ..." The sudden buzz of Morse made Davies jump round like a startled rabbit. "Is it Sumburgh?"

Giving Davies a nod, the corporal scribbled down the message and handed it to him. A keen observer would have noticed a muscle contract in the Air Commodore's cheek before he handed the message to Henderson. "I'm afraid that's it, Jock. They say there's no hope now. They're far too long overdue."

Henderson sat staring at the paper for a long moment. Then he glanced up at Davies. "You do realise Anna will have to be told, sir?"

For a moment Davies's expression was full of dislike. "Of course I know."

"Then shall I tell her? Or will you?"

For a moment Davies hesitated. Then his features set. "I'll do it. It's the least she deserves."

Henderson showed relief. Then, moving as if his body had suddenly become arthritic, he rose to his feet. "In that case I'd better get back to my office. With nearly half my squadron gone I've some reorganising to do."

Davies's eyes followed him to the door. "You're not blaming me, are you, Jock?"

Surprised by the question, the Scot paused before turning. "I'm past blaming anybody these days, sir. All I want is this bloody war to end so I can go home and get pissed for a fortnight. On second thoughts maybe I'll make it a month." Before Davies could find an answer to that, he disappeared through the door.

Davies turned to the radio operator. "All right, corporal. You can close down now." As the corporal nodded, Davies picked up his overcoat and shrugged it on. Then, leaving the NCO to attend to the Operations Room he made for the station gates.

A drizzle was falling as he crossed the road to The Black Swan. A single bird was picking at the berries on the crabapple trees and gave him a baleful look as he walked up the private path to the front porch. Reaching it, he paused for a long moment. Davies, the man who without hesitation had sent off hundreds of men on perilous and sometimes suicidal missions, knew he was dreading the ordeal ahead. Taking a deep breath, he swung down the heavy iron knocker.

Maisie, the inn's buxom barmaid, answered the door. In the months and years since the squadron had first come to Sutton Craddock, Maisie had never failed to run out and wave to the Mosquitoes on their return. It was a ritual that assured the surviving crews they were home and safe. But today, with no returning aircraft for her to welcome, her smile was both hesitant and apprehensive. "Hello, sir. Do you want to see Mrs Harvey?"

Davies nodded. "Please. Is she in?"

"Oh, yes, sir. She's never left her room all day."

"Will you ask her if she'll see me?"

"Yes, sir. If you'll just wait in the hall for a moment." Moving towards the staircase, Maisie found her apprehension too much and glanced back at Davies. "Is there any news of the squadron yet, sir? You know how fond we are of the boys."

Davis fought against his security training and won. "They're back. They'll be returning to base either tonight or tomorrow."

"All of them, sir?"

Davies frowned. "I can't discuss that here. I'm sure you understand."

Maisie's face had turned pale. "But you want to see Mrs Harvey?"

"Yes, please. If you'll kindly tell her I'm here."

Looking distressed, Maisie ran up the stairs. Davies heard voices, then the girl appeared again. "If you'll go up, sir, she'll see you in her room."

Watched by Maisie, Davies climbed the stairs and found the bedroom door ajar. To his dismay he found his heart pounding. "Anna! Can I come in?"

A quiet voice answered him. As Davies pushed the door further open and entered, he saw the tall elegant figure of the German girl standing in front of the latticed window. With the fading afternoon light behind her, he could not see her expression. Davies, who had tried to rehearse the right words on his way over, suddenly found they had all abandoned him. "Hello, Anna. I was hoping you would be here."

"Where else would I be today?" she asked quietly.

"That's true. It was a stupid question." Groping for words, Davies fell back on the old standby and fumbled in his overcoat pocket. "Will you have a cigarette?"

"No, thank you. But if it will help you, please have one."

Davies paused with a lighter in his hand. "Help me?"

"Yes. You've come to tell me that Frank is missing. Did you think I hadn't guessed that when I saw you coming over?"

Lacking the sensitive tuning to pick out the emotion beneath the girl's self control, Davies was feeling relief that he was spared the need to break the news himself and that she was taking it so calmly. "I'm sorry to say he is, Anna. It happened on the way back. He went down to escort Millburn who'd been wounded and we think they both ran out of fuel."

She nodded. "How like Harvey. To die as he lived."

Davies cleared his throat. "Yes. It was a brave act. Particularly as he had no cause to do it."

Her tone changed. "No cause? He had every cause. Millburn was his friend."

Davies shifted uncomfortably. "I meant he had no military commitment to stay with the crippled aircraft."

Her laugh had a brittle sound. "So Frank broke your rules once more. You never understood him, did you, Arthur?"

Davies wondered how and why he was suddenly discussing the character of a man to his newly widowed wife. "I wouldn't say that. I knew he was a fine pilot and a first class leader."

"But you never understood the real man, did you?"

Davies moved cautiously. "I'm not sure I know what you mean."

"It's simple enough. You never understood that Frank disliked the system you all live under."

Davies was struggling to follow her. "Many men find service life difficult. But in the end they usually find it's the only way things can be done."

Suddenly her controlled bitterness was deluged with contempt. "I'm not talking about the Services. I'm talking about civilian life now and before the war. The system of privilege, the domination of money and possessions. The system that elevates avaricious men to power and bludgeons the poor into despair. The system that makes it easy for tyrants like Hitler and Stalin to gain power. Frank hated the materialistic and uncaring side of capitalism. He wanted a different world where children are taught ethics, not self-interest; to value men for their morals and their talent, not for their pocket books or their status. Frank was the kind of idealist you could never understand. Ian Moore and Frank Adams finally learned his true value and worth. But you only saw him as an undisciplined rebel."

The bewildered Davies had never imagined he would be under such an attack at such a moment. "Yet he fought for this country well enough. So he can't have disliked our values that much."

"Of course he fought for his country. He once admitted to me he loved England, even although his background made him want a different life within it. I suppose you never knew that his mother was driven into suicide?"

Davies gave a start. "Suicide?"

"Yes. Because of the power of money, his parents were forced into bankruptcy and lost everything. Frank saw his mother put out into the streets homeless. Because she was an honest home-loving woman who saw bankruptcy as a disgrace, she killed herself. Can you wonder what Frank thought of a system that could allow a thing like that to happen?"

Davies frowned. "I was never told about this."

"Of course you weren't. Who would tell you? And what would you have said if they had?"

Davies felt a sudden need to defend himself. "You have to admit this wasn't the image he gave to the world."

"Of course it wasn't. His background had taught him never to show weakness. But as his wife I can tell you there never was a more gentle or caring man."

"And yet he fought the Nazis as if he hated them?"

"He did hate them. Caring men aren't all pacifists, Arthur. Some men hate injustice and cruelty so much they fight them all their lives. Frank saw the Nazis as I see them, as bullies and murderers. And because he hated bullies whether they wear bowler hats or uniforms, he had to join up and fight. But after it was over, he wanted a better system and a better world." Suddenly and frighteningly the girl's control broke. "And now he's dead and all that idealism is dead with him. Damn you for breaking your promise to us, Arthur. I'll never forgive you. Damn you to hell."

As she swung back to the window and caught the light, the grief that disfigured her lovely face shocked Davies. "I'm sorry, but I had my duty to do. He was the finest squadron commander I had left. I couldn't put my boys under anyone else."

"So that's your excuse? The well being of your crews?"

For the first time since entering the room, Davies felt on safer ground. "Yes. Could I have had a better reason?"

In the sudden silence that fell Davies heard Sam whimper. Turning, he saw the dog move across the room and sink down at the girl's feet. As she glanced down, Davies saw a spasm of despair cross her face. He had to strain to catch her words. "Please go now, Arthur. You've done what you came to do. Please leave me now."

He made a last try to comfort her but the reproach in her eyes silenced him. Picking up his cap he went to the door and glanced back. She was gazing out of the window again, a motionless figure that seemed to embody all the loss, tragedy and despair of war. A shudder ran through Davies as he turned and ran down the stairs. Ignoring the anxious Maisie, who came out of the bar and called after him, he hurried outside. As he reached the crab apple trees a gust of wind tore off the last of their dead leaves and blew them across his path. Shuddering again, Davies turned up his greatcoat collar and hurried to the security of the airfield.

Chapter 34

Adams felt he was being squeezed by a playful grizzly. "You've done a great job, Frank. Why don't you stay and help us finish the bastards off?"

Catching his breath as the giant's arms released him, Adams glanced at the smiling Helga who was standing alongside Steen. "Don't tempt me. I only need one more excuse to dodge another sea trip."

The giant's laugh bellowed out. He glanced round at the group of men who had escorted Adams to the rocky beach. "You hear him? He takes on the Gestapo single-handed but he's scared of bringing up his supper. What do you make of a guy like that?"

As the men laughed with him, a fisherman in oilskins standing on a berthed fishing boat shouted something to him in Norwegian. Nodding, Steen turned back to Adams. "He says you have to leave now or you might run into a Jerry patrol boat when daylight comes. So you'd better get your goodbyes said."

Nodding, Adams approached the group of partisans and shook hands with each in turn. "Thanks for everything you've done. I'd have wasted my time over here without you."

Steen grinned. "You're all bullshit, Frank." He extended his hand again. "Come over after the war and teach us how to play cricket."

Adams glanced at Helga. "I don't think you'll be able to stop me."

Grinning again, Steen took the hint. "OK, you guys, let the man have a moment with his girl." As the partisans shouted their last farewells and began climbing up the ridge, Steen turned to Helga.

"Don't be long, *kjaere*. We must be back on the plateau before dawn."

With the girl's face framed by a furlined hat, Adams had never seen her look more appealing. Left alone with her, he made the plea he had made a dozen times during their journey to the beach. "It's hellish leaving you here in danger. Come back with me. One way or the other I'm going to divorce Valerie."

She put a finger on his lips. "I want to come, my love, and yet I know I wouldn't be happy if I left my friends at this time. Be patient. The war will soon be over and then we can have a lifetime together."

As another impatient cry reached them, Adams knew it was hopeless and kissed her for the last time. Then, not allowing himself a glance back, he scrambled on to the slippery wreck and climbed aboard the fishing boat.

Helga was standing watching him when Steen appeared from nowhere. "You're a fool, *kjaere*. You should have gone with him."

Before she could reply, the boat's diesel engine coughed and fired. At the same moment Steen made a sudden exclamation, cursed, and started towards the intervening wreck. She caught his arm. "What are you doing?"

Fumbling beneath his snow smock, the giant pulled out a small pill box. "I forgot to give him these. Arne asked for them to be sent in the air-drop."

"What are they?"

"Seasick pills. I kept them as a surprise for Frank." As he spoke Steen made an attempt to climb on to the wreck, only for his booted feet to slip and drop him heavily on the stony beach. She snatched the box from him impatiently. "I'll take them."

Hiding his grin, Steen watched her climb nimbly over the wreck and jump on the deck of the fishing boat. As she ran up to Adams, who was standing by the cabin door, the diesel suddenly burst into full power and swung the boat away from its moorings. Steen watched her grab the arm of the skipper, who shook his head, then turn towards him. Her urgent cry sounded over the wash of the waves. "Steen! Tell him to come back! Steen!"

305

The giant's great laugh boomed back. "Too late, *kjaere*. You're on your way to Blighty. You'll be there just in time for Christmas. Tell Frank to throw a big party for you."

"Steen, you can't do this! Call him back! Steen!"

Her cries died away as the boat began nosing its way through the wave-washed skerries. Steen stood watching it until it reached the sea beyond and only its bow wave could be seen in the darkness. Then, wiping a wet sleeve across his face, he turned and began climbing up the ridge of rocks. Half a minute later his huge voice sounded over the sob of the night wind. "All right, you guys. Put your cigarettes out and let's get going. The war isn't over yet."

The staff car, taking Davies back to Group Headquarters, was approaching the station gates when a corporal ran out from the guardroom and halted it. Davies wound down a window and thrust his head out. "What's the problem, corporal?"

The breathless young NCO, looking flushed by his confrontation with an Air Commodore, indicated the guardroom where a sergeant was standing by an open door. "The CO's on the phone, sir. He told us to stop your car."

Davies stared testily at the flustered youngster. "Stop my car? What for?"

"He says he has an urgent message for you, sir. That's all he said."

Watched by his attractive WAAF driver, the puzzled Davies threw open the door and climbed out. As he disappeared into the guardroom, the girl leaned across to address the young MP. "Haven't you any idea what this is about, corporal?"

"No, Miss, I haven't. The CO just said stop the car. But he did sound excited."

Davies appeared twenty seconds later. To the girl's surprise he began running towards the station gates. His shout drifted back to her. "Wait there, Hilary. I'll be back in a few minutes."

"What is it, sir? What's happened?"

If he heard her, Davies showed no signs of it. To the astonishment of the two sentries on the gate, who had never seen a high-ranking officer on the run before, he ignored their salutes and scampered across the road to The Black Swan. There, breathing hard from his exertions, he hammered on the oaken door.

Maisie looked astonished by his appearance. "What is it, sir? What's happened?"

"Is Mrs Harvey in her room?" Davies panted.

"Yes, poor dear. But what is it, sir?"

Ignoring her, Davies ran down the hall and up the stairs. "Anna! I must see you. Can I come in?"

Unsure whether he heard a reply or not, he pushed open the door. The room was in darkness and in his impatience he fumbled for the light switch and turned it on.

The dog, who was lying alongside the girl's bed, jumped up and gave a warning growl. Anna, who had been lying fully dressed under a coverlet, sat bolt upright, her grief-stricken face staring at the breathless Davies. As she tried to speak and the words caught in her throat, Davies ignored the dog and hurried to her bedside. "Anna, I've wonderful news for you. Frank's alive! In fact all four of 'em are alive."

As if sensing the import of Davies's words, the dog suddenly wagged his tail and gave an excited bark. Anna, however, showed no sign of understanding. Her lovely face gazed at Davies as if he were talking about a change in the weather. In his excitement, Davies caught her arm. "You're not taking it in, are you? Frank's alive! It seems when he realised they probably wouldn't reach the mainland, he made for a small island off the Shetlands' coast. They crash-landed there and because of the condition they were in and their distance from any habitation, it's taken all this time for the news to come through."

She tried again to speak but failed. Recognising shock when he saw it, Davies gazed round and saw a bottle of whisky standing beneath a wash basin cabinet. Half-filling a glass, he took it to her. "Drink this. As much as you can."

Like a child obeying its guardian, she swallowed, then began coughing. Putting an arm round her, Davies held her until the paroxysm eased. "Drink some more. Sip by sip. That's better."

A little colour was returning to her cheeks now. Yet her expression betrayed that her mind was still in a wasteland of despair. As her pale lips moved, he had to bend down to catch her question.

"How can I believe you? You were so sure they were dead. How do I know this isn't just a rumour?"

Davies's arm tightened around her shoulders. "It's no rumour, Anna. Henderson's had it checked. They're alive and as soon as Frank's cuts and bruises are attended to, he'll be coming home."

She looked frightened rather than relieved and he could feel deep tremors running through her body. "I'm afraid to believe you, Arthur. I can't take any more shocks if you are wrong. I'd rather die than take any more."

Davies gave a nod of contrition. "I know and I'm sorry. I shouldn't have said anything to you today. But I knew what you'd be thinking when you heard the rest of the squadron were back. And Sumburgh was certain they were lost."

He could feel her struggling to believe him in the silence that followed. She broke it with a dismayed cry. "I should be delirious with happiness, shouldn't I? I should be leaping into the air with joy. But I can't feel anything. Nothing at all." Like a child seeking comfort, she fumbled for his hand and gripped it tightly. *"Lieber Gott,* what has happened to me, Arthur?"

Davies cleared his throat. "You're in shock. It's my fault. I'm desperately sorry."

She said nothing for a moment. Then she shook her head. "No. You did what you thought was best. It's just that I cannot seem to ... *Mein Gott* why don't I laugh or cry? Why do I feel so dead inside?

With her slender hand trembling and as cold as ice, Davies was wondering if she had taken too much punishment during the last few weeks. As he searched for words, Sam put his front paws on the bed and tried to lick her. When Anna reached out to stroke him, the dog wagged his tail and began barking.

The sound, with all its associations with Harvey, shivered and then shattered the prison cell that was withholding the girl's thanksgiving. As the truth escaped and ran like a joyous messenger down every artery and vein, she gave a sudden convulsive sob. A moment later, to Davies's immense relief, tears began pouring down her cheeks.

Recognising the change in her, Sam leapt on to the bed. Throwing her arms around the delighted dog, Anna hugged him as if he were part of the miracle that was bringing her back to life. Her unsteady voice, broken with sobs, made Davies turn to the window to hide his expression. "You believe it, don't you, Sam? You know your master's alive and is coming home soon. He might even be home for Christmas. Isn't it wonderful news, Sam? Aren't we lucky, you and I?"

As Davies gained control of himself, the girl's words made him remember what the war had made him forget. In three days' time it would indeed be Christmas. For the briefest of moments, before his hard shell closed protectively around him, Davies found himself wondering for the first and perhaps the last time in his life if now and then miracles really did happen.

THE END

If you enjoyed this book, look for others like it at Thunderchild Publishing: https://ourworlds.net/thunderchild_cms/

CPSIA information can be obtained
at www.ICGtesting.com
Printed in the USA
FSHW04n1107190418
47190FS